BETRAYER
OF
BLOOD

E-Book ISBN: 978-0-6453899-1-3

Paperback ISBN: 978-0-6453899-0-6

Cover design by: Maria Spada
Published by: Drucci Publishing

CONTENT WARNING

THIS BOOK CONTAINS THE FOLLOWING,
BUT IS NOT LIMITED TO:

EXPLICIT DEPICTIONS OF VIOLENCE
BLOOD & MURDER
EXPLICIT SEXUAL CONTENT
DEPICTIONS OF PHYSICAL ABUSE & OTHER ABUSIVE
BEHAVIOUR
MENTIONS OF SELF HARM
MENTIONS OF CHILD ABUSE

PLEASE READ THIS NOVEL WITH CAUTION

Werewolf Hierarchy

FIRST BLOODS — THE BITTEN

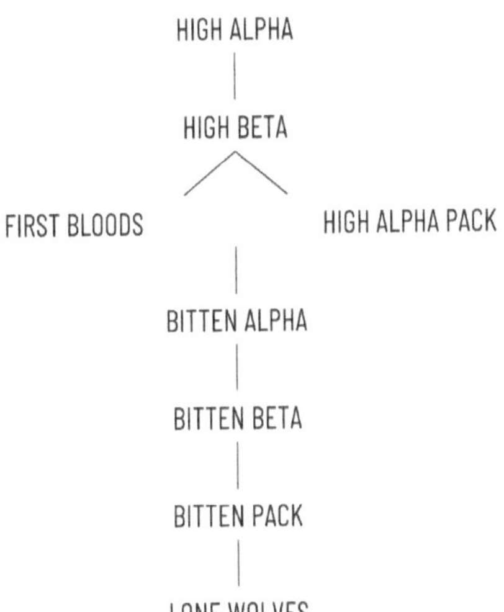

Vampire Hierarchy

PURE BLOODS — LILIM-MADE — ADAM-MADE

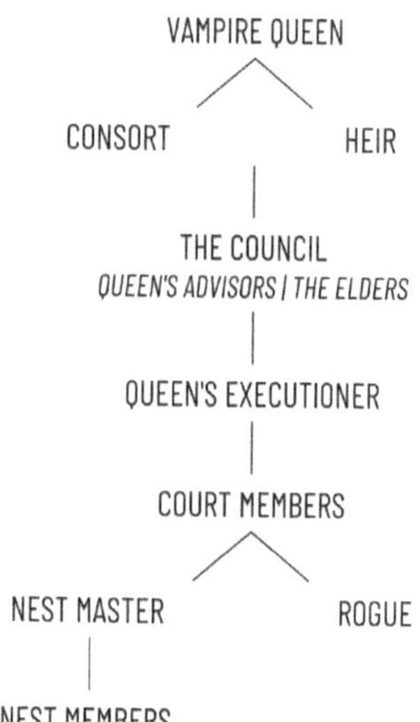

Fae Hierarchy

SUMMER — WINTER — CELESTIAL — UNDERWORLD

LIVE YOUR DREAMS

1

Nova

Harlem, New York City

I'M IN DESPERATE NEED of a nap.

My eyes burn with exhaustion as I turn the beaten up pick-up truck through the black iron gates and onto the small, curved driveway of Sanctuary Hotel. A tall, ornate lamppost emits a soft glow over the garden nestled against the gates and the aging white stairs.

The scents of the city abuse my senses; New York has a unique aroma of steel, car fumes, and decay mixed in with fresh pretzels and sweetness, like cotton candy.

I ascend the steps, fatigue screaming in my bones.

Screw the nap, I'll take a light coma.

Pushing through the frosted glass doors, warm air rushes out of the foyer carrying a vetiver scent which loosens some of the tension in my shoulders. The space is simple with its soft cream walls and dark wood floor. I approach the large, black desk against the back wall, passing double doors with a switched off, neon sign above that reads 'Bar'.

The door behind the desk opens and an aging, human woman walks out. Her silver hair is braided into two thick strands that reach her waist and her caramel brown eyes shine with knowing as her thin lips curve into a small smile.

I set my bag down by my feet as I reach the desk. "Are you Sidelle?"

She nods, coming up to stand in front of me. Sidelle is one of the rare humans in the world who know of the creatures that roam the shadows.

"I'm—"

Sidelle holds up a hand. "I suggest picking another name."

I clear my throat. "You can call me Aster."

"Aster, welcome to Sanctuary. Please, call me Sid." She opens the large green book in front of her, flipping through pages and pages of signatures. "How was the drive?"

"Long, but fine."

It only took four days to get here, when it was supposed to take me a week from Texas through the contacts that my sister-in-law Patricia gave me. I needed more space between me and the nightmare I just left, so after my night in North Carolina, I drove directly here with minimal stops.

Sid flicks back and forth between a few pages, settles on one with a nod, then scribbles something at the bottom of the page. She lifts the book onto the raised part of the desk, turning it toward me, placing a pen on the book.

"Sign here," she instructs as she points to the blank signature box next to my newly appointed fake name, 'Aster Wilford', then turns to the wall of mailing pigeonholes, pulling a set of keys from one.

I pick up the pen, noticing the date on the top of the page. "This is dated a month ago."

"Mhmm," Sid murmurs as she slips into the back office.

Too tired to question the woman, I sign, ensuring I use my new name, and set the pen down. Sid returns with a few other pieces of paper, placing those in front of me along with the keys.

"I need you to sign these too," she states.

"What am I signing, exactly?"

Sid perches on a stool I didn't realize was there and leans her elbows onto the desk. "Sanctuary has rules if you are to stay here."

I nod, waiting for her to continue.

"Sanctuary is neutral territory for all supernatural species, from any walk of life. You walk through those doors and any vendettas or politics cease to have power here. *Everyone* is off-limits. If you disturb the peace, or piss me off, you're banished with no exceptions and no redemption. Is that understood?"

I nod again.

"One paper in front of you is an agreement and acknowledgment of the rules, and consequences, that everyone signs the first time they stay here. The second one is just an incidental form for the room and payment information."

My heart stammers. "I... I don't have much money."

Sid sighs. "I'm trying to run a business here. I can suggest somewhere—"

I thrust my hands in my parka's pockets, fisting the few bills I have left and put them on the desk along with my keys. "You can have the pick-up truck. And I'll work for you. Any job, even grunt work. Just, please, don't send me out there alone."

Her tan, weathered face softens as her eyes scan me, snagging on my neck. My hand flies up to the scarf, readjusting it to cover up the bruises that haven't healed yet.

"What happened to you?" she asks softly.

"I... I can't say. Please, any work you have, I will do for my keep."

Sid plucks the room key out of my hand before unhooking a carabiner from her belt loop, taking off a set of three silver keys. She slides them across the desk in front of me and gives me a slow once over.

"Have you ever worked at a bar before?"

I shake my head. "No, but I'm a quick study."

"Good. You'll meet me here at noon tomorrow." She takes the payment sheet back and the car keys, pushing the cash toward me. "Just sign the one about the rules, then follow me."

I do as instructed, shove the scarce funds I have left back into my pocket and pick up my bag. Sid walks around the desk, her slight frame moving with a surprising amount of grace as she leads me up the steps.

"You'll stay in room 113. There's not much to it, just a private bathroom and a bed," Sid calls over her shoulder. We walk down a long hallway bare of any color, passing a few doors, most of them with signs that say 'private' or 'staff only'.

We stop in front of the second-to-last door on the left, and Sid turns to me. "I'm sure whatever exact circumstances landed you here were not the best, but you're safe here. No one will bother you here, and if they do, let me know."

I nod. "Thank you, Sid. See you at noon."

Sid steps to the side. "Don't be late," she calls as she retreats down the hall.

I unlock the door to a moderately sized room with a bed against the far right wall and a nightstand on either side. Dumping my bag and keys on the dresser by the door, I shrug off my parka, drop it on the edge of the bed, and move to the armchair across the room. I pull the curtains back, revealing a window overlooking the front of Sanctuary.

Sid descends the front steps below, climbs into the truck and a few seconds later pulls out of the driveway, turning right into the street.

I sink into the armchair and hug my knees to my chest, my thumb brushing over the white stone on the bracelet wrapped around my wrist.

How did I end up here?

Almost a year ago, I was about to complete my mate bond, and now I'm a murderer.

What am I supposed to do now?

I close my eyes as exhaustion tugs at my consciousness, sending the world into silence.

White light blinds me, and pain explodes across my face. The force of the slap throws me off my vanity stool and onto the plush carpet. I try to curl up into a ball to cushion the next blow, but a stiff boot lands a hard strike into my ribcage.

Tears roll down my face freely as my father pulls me up by my jaw, crushing our foreheads together.

His eyes are no longer their usual turquoise blue, but his wolf's deep gold, and he growls. "Listen to me carefully, you little shit. You will mate with Viggo tonight, and like the good little bitch you are, you will breed. Do you understand me?"

"I would rather be dead than let that vile creature *look* at me, let alone touch me," my voice comes out coarse.

My father forces me back into the floor, his hand squeezing my neck, cutting off my ability to breathe. My eyes burn, feeling like they'll pop out of my head, and my tongue is thick in my mouth.

I claw hard at his hand; despite the skin being broken, he won't let go. Black spots crawl across my vision as unconsciousness looms.

I hear a commotion through the fuzziness in my brain, and suddenly I have air in my lungs. I roll over, coughing and wheezing, struggling to suck in air through my damaged throat.

I stay on my side on the floor, blinking away the spots and tears in my vision to see my older brothers Junior and Stefan both struggling to hold back our father. He's blind with rage as his wolf growls and crawls under his skin.

The residual energy from the full moon of last night morphs his face slightly and changing his fingers into claws.

They manage to drag his thrashing body out of the room.

Patricia rushes in as they clear the doorway and slams it behind her. I pull myself off the floor and sit back onto my stool, ignoring the screaming pain in my ribs as she reaches me. She cradles my face gently, trying to assess the damage, tears slipping down her face. I wrap my arms around her, pressing my face to her swollen belly, choking on the tears that soak the material of her dress.

She strokes my hair with her small hands, her indecipherable words a comforting hum. I focus on my nephew's heartbeat just under her skin. His fast, steady rhythm calms my breathing and stops my crying.

A sharp knocking on the door makes me jump, my heart pounding hard.

"Nova, it's me," my twin, Kristjan, calls from the door.

Patricia pulls away, opening the door. The first thing I see is the busted lip and blotchy red skin around his left eye.

"What happened?" I ask, my voice barely audible, as he rushes towards me, sinking to his knees.

His featherlight hands and familiar jade green eyes skim the side of my face, my neck and prods my side, making me hiss as pain shoots across my ribcage.

"Fucking *bastard*," Kristjan mutters.

"What happened to your face, Kris?" I force out through my damaged vocal cords, clutching the sides of his head, keeping his focus on my face.

Kris shrugs. "I told Dad you're not going to do it. And we got into it."

"How many times have I told you not to—"

"He's trying to mate you with that fucking psycho, Nova," Kris growls.

My hands drop as Patricia gasps behind Kris. "He really agreed to offer you to Viggo, even after last year?"

Kris jumps up and starts pacing. "I knew something was happening when Dad sent me to those Bitten Pack meetings instead of Stefan. The bastards knew I'd fight them on this."

"And Junior agreed to this?" Patricia asks.

"It was unanimous, Pat," I croak.

My father and my brothers offered me to Viggo of the Daygrsson Pack, a vile man with no respect for Pack law, as his mate.

"I'll talk to him, make him change his mind," Pat insists.

"There's no point," Kris states, continuing to pace, "your husband is a stickler for the rules, and won't go against the High Alpha's decision."

"But he's your brother," she counters, talking to me. "He wouldn't want his sister to be hurt."

Anger runs hot in my veins. "I'm just a commodity to trade for Pack alliances, Pat, you know that."

Kris stops pacing, facing me. "We're getting you out."

I scoff. "Sure."

He steps forward, sinking to his knees again. "I'm serious. You're done here."

I blink at him a few times. "I... I know nothing else."

He grabs my hands in my lap, squeezing. "So you'll *learn*. You survive this hellhole every day. You can do anything."

"Come with me," I whisper, eyes stinging with unshed tears.

"I can't. People know who I am, but only the other High Alphas and a few of their sons know who you are, and they're easily avoidable."

"You need to go, baby," Pat adds, coming forward. "I would rather you not be here than have you follow your mother's path."

I swallow back the bile threatening to choke me. I pull my hands out of Kris' grip, turning back to my vanity mirror. The red hand marks on my neck will eventually bruise, even with my fast wolf healing, but the slap mark has already faded from my face.

"How are we going to do this?" I ask Kris, catching his gaze in the mirror.

A determined glint sparkles in his eyes. "I have a plan."

I startle awake, pain lancing down my back as I straighten from my curled position on the armchair.

Lowering my stiff legs to the floor, I squint at the brightness streaming in from the window as I fish out the burner cell from my pocket and check the time; it's already mid-morning.

I stand, stretching out my muscles, and return to my backpack, pulling out my last remaining fresh clothes and scarce toiletries as I cross the room into the bathroom.

The space is small but functional. I have a quick shower, change, and twist my waist-length hair into a high bun. I check the knot in the leather cord around my wrist, making sure the amulet is secure, and the high collar of my top covers my neck before lacing up my worn combat boots, scooping up my keys and phone and leaving the room, locking it behind me.

Sid is at the front desk, handing over the guest book to a man before turning to the wall behind her. The scent of burning sage stirs around me and my heart freezes. He's a werewolf.

I tremble, frozen halfway down the staircase. Is he hunting me? Does he know who I am?

Sid pulls the guest book toward her and passes the keys to the wolf. "You know the rules. Enjoy your stay."

He nods, taking the keys and heads for the elevator left of the front desk. I wait until he steps in and the doors close behind him, before making the rest of the way down the stairs.

"Good morning, Aster," Sid murmurs as she writes in a small red book.

"Mornin'," I return. Being called by another name will take some getting used to.

"Have you eaten?" Sid asks, continuing to write.

"Um, no, but I'm fine."

She lifts her head, eyes narrowed. "I can't have you passing out on me, I have a business to run. Go eat something."

I drop my gaze to the floor. "Sorry, Sidelle."

"It's Sid. Speak to Chef in the dining hall on the second floor. Don't take too long."

I take the elevator to the second floor and find the human man, Chef, chopping vegetables in the open kitchen at the back of the large space, behind a long serving counter. His ochre brown face beams as he instructs me to sit at one of the long communal tables while he gathers up some food.

After scarfing down an overflowing plate of eggs, sausage, toast, and having two cups of coffee, I return to the reception in record time where I spend the rest of the day shadowing Sid, learning how to check guests in and out, and taking a quick tour of the hotel.

The hotel's sixteen-story, red brick building holds around ninety rooms over twelve floors; the first four floors housing the reception, bar, Sidelle's private floor, the kitchen and dining hall, and hotel amenities.

"There's also a basement," Sid says as we step into the elevator, taking it back down to reception. "I mainly use it for storage. The kegs for the bar are down there too."

"I assume your bar is quite a busy one?" I ask, stepping out of the elevator.

The fear-spiked scent of honeysuckle distracts me as a small, human woman stumbles across the foyer. Her eyes search around wildly as she clutches a duffel bag close to her side, her breathing heavy. Her dark eyes find Sid and she sobs.

Sid rushes forward to meet her, catching the trembling woman before she hits the floor. She steers the woman towards the desk as the front door swings open again.

A tall man heaves in gulps of air as he takes a step into the foyer. His scent of pungent eucalyptus stings my nose. Werewolf.

"Baby," the Bitten wolf pants, stepping further across the foyer, "come back home. I'm sorry."

The woman sobs harder, sliding along the front desk, and backing up behind it. I step into the wolf's line of sight, blocking his way to her. "I don't think she wants you here."

Rage sours his features. "You know nothing, *breeder.*"

Breeder? I take a step toward the wolf. "You've stepped on Sanctuary property. You know what that means, right?"

"I don't give a fuck. I'm here for my woman."

"You should leave," I warn.

The wolf barks out a laugh. "What's a pathetic Bitten bitch going to do to a Beta? Go back to your master before you hurt yourself."

I smirk. Werewolves are male-dominated supernaturals. If I *were* a Bitten wolf, he could make me submit, but unfortunately for him, I'm a First Blood. If I wasn't wearing the amulet suppressing my true nature, then he'd be on his knees by now.

But knowing my father, he'd be hunting me already, so I need to stay under the radar or risk being captured.

The wolf tries to step around me, but I move with him. "There are rules here, wolf. Don't make me break them."

He growls, his hand swinging down toward my face, but I catch his wrist. I deliver a swift punch to his gut, winding the wolf and sending him bowing forward. I drive my knee into his face, connecting with his nose, hearing bones crunch. He grunts as he lands on his ass, clutching his now bleeding nose.

"You broke my nose!" he bellows.

"And I'll break more of your bones if you don't leave this woman alone."

"You can't keep me away from my mate."

"Are you mate-bound? Have you completed a mate bond?" I ask. He responds by spitting blood on the wood floor. I cross my arms over my chest. "That's what I thought. You have no claim on her. Now, leave, and never come back."

His brown eyes burn with fury as he gets off the floor and stalks out of the foyer.

I turn to the woman and Sid, both watching me with wide eyes. "I'm sorry," I breathe, "I'll pack my things."

Sid's mouth twists into a sly grin. "Don't bother. You're going to fit right in around here."

2

Vladislav

MY BROTHER IS AN idiot.

I sit back in my office chair, watching Renard throw a chair across the room, the wood splintering apart as it hits the wall.

"Ren, you need to stop destroying my furniture," I say in a lazy tone.

His usual cobalt blue eyes shine a bright emerald green as he faces me. "She *dumped* me, Xander."

I roll my eyes. "You were chatting up the new girl in front of her."

"I was being *friendly.*"

"You were being 'friendly' when you started flirting with her too, remember?"

He opens his mouth, closes it, and then storms out of my office. Maddox appears around the corner, chuckling at the mess. "Did she dump him?"

"Yeah," I sigh, standing from my seat, buttoning my black suit jacket.

"Did she quit?" Maddox asks, as he picks up pieces of the ruined chair.

"As they usually do," I mutter, pulling out my phone and messaging Dominic, the only werewolf who works for me, to set up auditions for dancers.

Electric-blue hair and translucent wings in the doorway catch my attention. Marin smiles, holding out a glass of what smells like whiskey. "Did Ren get his heart broken again?"

I step around my desk toward the faerie, accepting the glass. "He did."

She sighs. "He's a sucker for a pair of good tits."

I smirk. "And we have an abundance of those around here."

"One of the *perks* of a strip club."

I shake my head, following her down the hall toward the bar.

"It's admirable that you're around so many beautiful people and you haven't succumbed to love," Marin muses as we stop in front of the dressing room door.

"I swore off the feeling many, many years ago."

Marin's bright, honey-brown eyes narrow. "Why?"

A tugging sensation stirs in my chest, and I suppress the feeling immediately. "It can lead people down a road they don't wish to travel."

I leave Marin puzzled as I continue down the hall, past the stage door and through the 'Staff Only' door into the club. Viktoria shakes up a drink behind the white marble bar as I cross to her, drinking my whiskey in one mouthful.

"Have you seen Allura?" I ask, watching her pour the cocktail into a martini glass and add a twist of lemon rind into the clear liquid.

"I'm not her handler," the vampire states, taking a sip of her drink.

The entrance opens, unleashing afternoon sun rays down into the club. I hurdle myself over the bar to take cover with Viktoria. The familiar scent of jasmine floats down the entrance stairs as the heavy metal door closes with a thump.

"Damn it, Allura," I growl as I rise from behind the bar.

The small faerie stands at the foot of the stairs, confused. "What?"

"Sunlight and vampires don't do each other, remember?"

Her translucent wings flutter nervously, and her bottom lip quivers. Tears trail down her face as she disappears behind the staff door.

"Faeries are so dramatic," Viktoria comments, still holding her martini. How she didn't spill a drop is impressive.

"But they're excellent dancers," I surmise, pulling out one of the top shelf whiskeys, and pouring myself another drink before heading back towards my office.

Faeries and humans in various stages of undress block the hall. Sobbing from a dressing room catches my attention, and I sigh.

The crowd parts for me as I come up to the closed door, where Marin knocks softly. "Let me in, sugar."

Allura's sobs get louder.

I knock. "Allura, let us in."

Shuffling steps come closer, and the door opens. I look into the stricken face of the faerie; her large, ocean blue eyes are red from crying and mascara smudges her dark bronze skin. I can feel the anxiety and fear oozing from her like murky water. She ushers me and Marin in, then closes the door.

"Lu, baby, what's wrong?" Marin asks, brushing the mess of bouncy, caramel brown curls away from her face.

"I'm in trouble," she whispers, her body trembling as Marin guides her to sit on a chair.

"What's going on?" I ask softly, crouching down next to her.

"I..." her heartbeat thunders as fear pours off her, hitting me like a heatwave, turning my stomach. I touch her arm, and the cool caress of calm blooms at my touch, instantly easing the fear storm surrounding Allura; she breathes easier.

"What happened, Allura?" I ask again.

She swallows a few times. "I'm pregnant."

I raise a brow. "And?"

Marin's eyes go wide and her mouth pops open. "Impossible," she whispers.

Allura nods once at the other faerie.

"Impossible," Marin repeats, shaking her head softly.

"Anyone going to tell me what's going on?"

Allura clears her throat. "It's Loch's."

"My cousin," Marin adds as she collapses into another chair.

Marin and Loch are Winter Fae, and high-ranking fae in the Winter Court. Allura isn't just a Summer Fae, but she's Heir to the Summer Court.

And she has broken the only law in Faery: no interbreeding between Fae Courts.

Fuck.

Horror fills her eyes as new tears stream down her face. "They're going to find out. I can't go back to Faery. They'll do horrible things. They—"

I place my hand on her knee, sending soothing energy into her again. "It's okay, Lu, just breathe."

"Does Loch know?" Marin asks as she stands.

"No, I haven't told him," Allura whispers, her emotions calm again.

"That's good," Marin states. "He's been summoned back to the Winter Court. I'm escorting him to the Crossing in three weeks. He won't know a thing."

"But they'll *know*," Allura sobs.

Marin places a hand on Allura's shoulder. "They won't sense it until you're much further along. And you're Earth-side, it'll take them longer to notice. We'll work it out later. For now, it's our secret."

Allura stands, wrapping Marin in a tight hug. Relations between Winter and Summer Fae are rumored to be tense in Faery, the realm that the majority of faeries reside in, but from what I've seen, the lines are often blurred for the faeries that are on Earth.

I step out of the dressing room, leaving the two faeries and returning to my office.

The atmosphere cools as I take a seat behind my desk. The sun is finally setting, like a hot weight lifting off the Earth. My phone buzzes with a message from Dominic, confirming the auditions for tomorrow. My dancers are either fae or human, so Dom will conduct the auditions during the day.

Immortal is a vampire-only gentleman's club, catering to a select clientele via my invitation only. I provide them with almost everything they desire, given they agree to three rules: always ask permission before you touch, no tasting the entertainment and respect my employees at all times.

After finishing a few tedious reports, I make my way back to the main bar. Dancers in lingerie, leather, lace, and corsets shuffle back and forth between dressing rooms.

Allura appears by the stage door barefoot in a light blue lingerie set, assisting one of the male dancers with tightening his waist corset. Marin exits a dressing room in a leather number, sending me a wink as I push through to the main floor.

The club is primarily dark now, except for blue and purple lights that glow softly. A slight sheen comes off the black velvet sofas and armchairs, which are placed in clusters by the main stage and two platforms to each side: the steel poles on the main stage glint from the faintest of spotlights above.

Carlos—the other muscle in Immortal apart from Ren—is on his phone, standing by the drawn indigo curtains to the left of the bar, which leads to the private alcoves. Viktoria and Maddox stand behind the bar chatting amongst themselves, Viktoria nursing a fresh martini. As I cross the floor, the door to the right of the bar opens and Ren sulks in from the storage room.

Anger and sadness pulse off him as he leans up against the bar, crossing his arms over his chest.

I walk up to him, clapping him on the shoulder. "All I ask is that the next one isn't a dancer."

I get a smile out of him before he shrugs off my touch and goes towards the main door. Our clients filter in slowly, and I greet them one by one, as they take their usual seats and order their usual drinks.

The soft thrum of music builds in volume and beat. The pulsating rhythm is almost in sync with the dancers' heartbeats as they saunter onto the stage.

Two male dancers step into the cage on the small platform to the left, one human and one faerie. Marin claims the pole at the end of the short runway. The emotions of the vampires around the main stage filter over to me in soft waves, excitement and predatory satisfaction being the most prominent ones.

Another faerie glides onto the stage, hips swaying and hands running slowly down her body. She walks over to the platform to the right where a large, steel square frame looms.

Her iridescent wings are still on her back, but the lights of the club dance on them, making them mesmerizing. Allura, who has materialized from the staff door, meets her on the platform with bundles of silk rope in her hands for their performance.

"Vladislav," the familiar smooth drawl distracts me from the show.

I turn to my old friend at the bar. "Mydas, back already from Court?"

His hickory-brown eyes roll as he smirks. "You know I can't stand Court frivolities."

"Liar, I know you love a good party," I comment, coming up to his side.

"Okay, the party was excellent as always," he admits with a laugh, but quickly sobers. "I have news from my visit that you might find interesting."

"What are the whispers these days?"

Mydas takes a mouthful of the dark liquid in his glass. "A position on the Advisory Council for the Queen has become available. As of ten days ago, Advisor Eleanora is no longer." The ruler of our species always has three Advisors by her side, giving their recommendations on affairs to do with governing vampires. Being immortal, a position becoming available is a rare occurrence.

"Well, that is unexpected. I thought that crone was going to outlive the entire species. How did Eleanora meet her end?"

Mydas clears his throat, a trickle of fear souring his aura. "By the Queen's hand."

"I see she hasn't changed her ways." My voice is clipped as anger spears through my chest.

"She's getting worse," Mydas comments, eyes focused on his drink.

"Carlos," I call, the vampire appearing next to me, "take over for Renard at the door."

Carlos disappears, and Ren soon emerges at the base of the stairs. He steps over to Mydas and I; the anger bubbling in his aura, telling me he heard the conversation.

"I already contacted Advisor Savino," Ren announces, "he confirms the vacancy."

What else did he tell you? I ask Ren telepathically as I pick up the drink that Maddox slides over to me.

Renard can hear the thoughts of anyone in the same vicinity as him, and can project his own thoughts to a select few people. My head is easiest for him to access, most likely because we're blood-related. My dark gift is the ability to sense emotions of any species and manipulate them with my touch.

Ren's eyes flash green. *He said she's coming for you.*

I take a controlled breath, suppressing the fury begging to be unleashed. I told Medea I would never return, and I warned her not to hunt me, or there would be dire consequences. But our Queen, my ex-wife, has always been too much of an overconfident bitch to heed warnings.

Scents of jasmine and fresh snow swirl around us as Allura and Marin approach us dressed in sheer dressing gowns. Marin sidles up to Mydas, who wraps an arm around the faerie.

"Mydas, welcome back to New York," she croons, planting a soft kiss on his cheek.

Mydas' eyes darken. "Marin, you look ravishing, as usual."

She lets out a breathy laugh, pressing a hand into his chest. "Shall we take this party somewhere more private?"

Mydas smirks, pulling Marin toward the private alcoves. She always knows when to diffuse a situation. A warm hand lands on my bicep and I turn to Allura's concerned eyes.

"Medea doesn't control you anymore, remember that."

"That's difficult to believe when she's the Queen of my entire species." I turn back to the bar, motioning to Maddox for another drink.

"I'll listen out for reports of her movements," Ren says behind me, his footsteps retreating toward the entrance. *We won't be her puppets ever again, Xander, I promise you that.*

The doors close at three, we all make a ton of money, and patrons leave satisfied. Most of the dancers go home shortly after, and I call Ren, Viktoria, Maddox, and Carlos into my office.

"Maddox? Carlos? Anything to report?" I ask, taking my seat behind my desk.

They both shake their heads as Carlos claims the chair in front of me, and Maddox perches on the arm. Viktoria's blank face behind them says enough to know her following words won't be good.

"News from Dom. Shit has gone down in the High Alpha Packs." Werewolf news from Dom is never good. I nod for Viktoria to continue. "A female wolf from the Jónasson Pack murdered the sole heir to the Daygrsson Pack at their mating ceremony six days ago, and she's in the wind."

"Fuck." Ren breathes from his position against the wall.

I frown. "Did he have any other details?"

"She stabbed Viggo Daygrsson with a poisoned hunting knife in front of both Packs and then disappeared. No one knows what she looks like, and she supposedly escaped with no help, but the rumor is one of the younger Jónasson sons assisted the escape. Now the High Alpha Packs are on the hunt, and other Packs are on alert."

"If other wolves don't know what she looks like, how do they know if it's her?"

Viktoria shrugs at my question as she takes a seat on my desk.

A soft knock sounds at the door. "Come in."

Allura and Marin step into the room, leaning against the closed door. Tense energy comes from both of them.

"News from Faery," Marin announces, "there's been a disturbance in this realm."

"A disturbance?" Ren asks.

Marin's eyes flick to Allura's cool expression, then turns to Ren. "A magical disturbance. It was a small tear in the barrier between this realm and the Other Side, but it was patched in a matter of seconds."

"Not that I understand most of what you said," I say, "but I assume that a tear is concerning?"

"Not at the moment," Allura says, her voice a little rough, "but they'll be monitoring this realm a little closer than usual for any changes in the balance of magic."

I nod, knowing that we will have to keep Allura's pregnancy a secret for as long as possible. "Any other news?"

"My mother has sent a summons," Allura announces.

"When?" Ren asks.

Tears fill Allura's eyes. "It came through about an hour ago. She wants me back in Faery by the Summer Solstice."

"For good?" I ask.

Sorrow pierces through her emotions as she nods, tears spilling down her face. Ren wraps his arms around her and she sobs against him.

"We'll find a way around it," I promise. Even before the pregnancy, Allura didn't want to go back to Faery.

"A summons from a Queen is almost impossible to petition," Marin says, rubbing Allura's arm softly. "Particularly hard since Lu's the heir to the throne."

"We'll find a way," I repeat.

Marin nods, curling her arm around Allura, replacing Ren, and they leave the office.

I sit back and run my hands through my hair. "If there is nothing else, I'll see everyone tomorrow."

They all leave with brief goodbyes. The same tugging in my chest from earlier tingles under my sternum. Memories of Medea flash in my head, spiking my anger once again. I don't need the reminder of what that monster did to me and to the people I care about.

The tugging sensation in my chest, the residual mate bond I have with Medea, worsens, not wanting to be ignored. I lash out, flipping my desk over and scattering everything on it over the floor.

I push hard at the bond, blocking it out once more, the tugging disappearing. Maddox appears in the doorway, hesitating with a drink in hand.

I sigh, rubbing a hand over my face. "Clean this up for me, Maddox—I'm going home."

He nods, holding out the drink. I take it as I head down the hall towards the elevator.

3

Nova

Sanctuary Hotel, Harlem

THE GLOW OF FIRE dances off the garage at the end of the driveway of the Den House. Pat's hand stops me by the oak tree, and we step into its shadows. She reaches into her small bag and pulls out a navy jewelry pouch.

"Your mother gave me this before she left us. Freyja told me to give this to you if you ever needed the strength to keep going. She may not have had that strength, but you do. Don't put it on until you're running towards your future and never take it off."

I wrap my hand around hers, clutching the velvet pouch. "Thank you for everything, Pat."

Her lip trembles slightly as she nods once and clears her throat before pushing the pouch into my palm and continuing down the driveway. My stomach twists in tighter and tighter knots as I shove the jewelry pouch into my bra and head towards the backyard.

Light bulbs lined the porch and a giant bonfire burns in the center of the yard. Wolves from my Pack chat and laugh in small clusters like this whole thing isn't my worst nightmare.

My body trembles and my lungs still as sorrow and fury ravage my soul. Memories bubble up from the abyss as I breathe slowly through my nose, weaving my way through the crowd towards the porch.

"Happy birthday, Nova," Pack members call to me as I walk past.

I give them a small smile. "Happy Ostara."

Kris and I were born on the Spring Equinox, because apparently the universe couldn't have given us a mundane birthday. Our Pack believes we're a blessing from the Gods, that we're some sort of sign of our Pack's power, and fated for 'great things', or some bullshit like that.

None of it makes sense since we're the youngest of the High Alpha's children, so unless our four older brothers meet their end, neither of us will become High Alpha. Not to mention I'm female, and Kris is the bane of father's existence.

My father and brothers sit or stand on the porch, talking and eating. My father takes in my black turtleneck dress, black waist belt, black cardigan, and black combat boots with a deep frown.

I give him a saccharine grin as I walk up the stairs and take the seat next to him, looking straight ahead at the bonfire.

He leans toward me in my peripheral vision. "What on Earth are you wearing?"

I turn to him. "Since this is the death of my freedom and self-worth, I thought it'd be appropriate to wear my mourning attire."

His hand lift to strike me, but Junior forces it back down to the arm of his chair. I notice the red welts on it from my fingernails, and my smile deepens. He deserves it.

"You'll regret those words, Nova."

I lean forward, staring into his cold, turquoise blue eyes. "Will I, Dad? What will be my punishment? Will you mate me with the one person I hate most in the world? Or maybe this time you'll finish the job you started earlier today and end my life. Either way, *High Alpha*, I'll be away from you and won't have to listen to your shit ever again."

His eyes turn gold, and a growl rumbles in his chest. As he's about to beat me again, he stills, and a blinding smile consumes his fury, his eyes returning to their usual color. He stands and walks down the steps towards Daygr Serafiem. They exchange a brief handshake and embrace.

I swallow the violent growl threatening to pierce the night sky as I stand and walk towards Daygr. I hate that my father is getting so much satisfaction out of this.

I give him a polite yet empty smile and bow my head. "Hello, High Alpha Daygr."

He returns a polite smile. "Nova, my dear, you look lovely. I'm pleased to know you are joining our family."

I continue to smile as I swallow the bile rising in my throat. The hairs on the back of my neck stand straight up, and goosebumps cover my entire body as a towering presence looms behind me.

I already know it's Viggo before I feel his hand glide down my back. I resist the urge to punch him in the face.

"Nova," he breathes into my ear.

I turn and step away from him. "Viggo."

I look into his dirty hazel eyes, and my stomach lurches. I want to throw up, scream, and rip his throat out with my bare hands all at the same time.

My heart beats faster at those thoughts and also crumbles into a thousand heartbroken pieces, leaving me breathless for a moment.

Viggo's eyes darken, his foul scent deepening betrays his lust, turning my agony back into disgust and rage.

I stalk off to the other side of the porch where Kris is pouring himself a drink. I snatch the cup from his hand and down the whole thing. The scotch sears down my throat, turning my stomach into a burning furnace.

"Hey," Kris complains as he pulls the cup from my hands and fills it again. "Get your own." His eyes flicker gold as they snag on someone behind me.

"Kristjan. It's been some time." Viggo, standing way too close to me, holds out his hand to my brother, his arm brushing mine.

Kris laughs. "I don't shake the hands of murderers."

Viggo steps forward, his body against mine. "I had—"

Kris clicks his tongue in dismissal. "I don't speak to them either."

Viggo's arm wraps around my waist, pulling me against his chest. "That's no way to speak to your future brother-in-law."

I throw a hard elbow into Viggo, connecting with his sternum. He stifles a groan as I turn to him, fury blazing through me. "The only reason they didn't let me kill you is because you're the only heir to the Daygrsson line."

Viggo's shit-eating grin deepens as he tucks a strand of my hair behind my ear. "That will change the next full moon."

"In your fucking dreams."

"You can't say no to me, my pet. You are mine now to do with as I please."

I jerk up in the bed; the sheets tangle around me and my body is damp with sweat. I look out of the open window, the glow of the lamppost settling my mind.

New York. I'm in New York. No one knows who I am, and no one knows where I am.

I let out a shaky breath, repeating the words in my head, my eyes dropping to my wrist.

The amulet is a small, polished stone shaped into an oval, with a small carving of an eight-point star inside a circle in the center. It has the most interesting color—it's almost like glittery white shadows swirl under the polished surface. The stone is encased in gold, and leather cord is threaded through the ornate swirls on each side.

I untangle myself from the sheets and head for a shower. After a brief rinse off, I dress, pick up my phone, and leave the room. It's early in the morning, the sun is only just lighting the sky, but like every day this past week, Chef is in the kitchen already cooking for the day.

"Do you ever sleep?" I ask as I approach the awaiting plate of food under the heat lamps.

"I could ask you the same," Chef chuckles, "you work in the bar until the early hours, and then you're here for breakfast by dawn."

"I've always been a terrible sleeper," I lie, taking the plate to my usual spot at the end of the communal table closest to the coffee station.

I fill a tall mug with coffee and creamer as my phone buzzes in my jacket pocket. The only person with this number is Sid, and I know she won't be up for another couple of hours. I return to my seat, hands trembling as I pull out the phone.

UNKNOWN

Hey, it's Kris. I don't want to know where you are, but please just let me know you're alive. Pat and I miss you. This number will be deactivated by dawn tomorrow. I hope you get this message.

Tears sting my eyes as my thumbs race over the keyboard.

Kris, I'm alive. Are you okay? Give my love to Pat. I miss you too.

A new message arrives almost immediately.

UNKNOWN

Thank the gods. I'm alright, but things are tense here. Dad has hunting parties throughout our territory looking for you, so if you're still within the Jónasson lines, get going. I'll contact you again when I can. Be careful.

I read the messages again, my hand absently tracing the tattoo above my elbow. Kris and I got into Junior's tequila two years ago and got tattoos for our twenty-first birthday. I'm sure it was torture for the wolf tattoo artist to succumb to our ironic choice to get a set of moon phases, but that night is one of the few good memories I've had with my twin.

I delete the messages and set the phone down, picking up my fork. New York is well within High Alpha Lárusson's territory, so I'm good for now, and I've managed to avoid any high-ranking Lárusson wolves on the few occasions I've been out of Sanctuary.

After breaking the wolf's nose my first day here, Sid told me about that Sanctuary isn't just a neutral zone, but the place people end up when they're trying to get out of dangerous situations. She told me it wasn't just supes, but humans who have fallen into this world and don't know how to get out.

Supernaturals are hidden to the mass human population, but it's not uncommon for some to slip through the cracks and get in over their head. Sid has a network of trusted people all over the world who help these people out, and I immediately offered my help.

Apart from working the Bar here at Sanctuary, Sid has sent me to get those who require a little more muscle to get out their situations. I must admit, breaking the limbs of smug vampires and wolves has been a *little* satisfying.

The door to the Dining Hall opens as I'm halfway through my meal, and a man walks in. His honeycomb and teakwood scents drifts toward me as he strolls over to the counter separating the kitchen from the room. He's a Bitten wolf.

"Chef, it's been a while," he says as he extends his arm toward the cook.

"Big D," Chef bellows, clasping the wolf's hand, "you're back so soon. What trouble are you in this time?"

"Same shit, different day, Chef. Can I get my usual?"

"Of course! I'll bring it right out."

I turn back to my plate before he turns my direction. Not that I can hide in an empty room. I listen to his steps crossing the room, and his tall frame darkens my periphery. I continue to eat, praying he doesn't want company, but suddenly he's sliding onto the bench opposite me with his steaming cup of coffee.

"I've never seen you here before," he announces.

I look up from my plate into his dark brown eyes. "It's a little sad that the staff here know you so well."

His thick, plump lips curve into a beaming smile, showcasing perfect teeth. "What can I say? My job requires a safe haven now and then."

"Surely a Bitten Alpha like yourself would leave the grunt work to his Beta," I challenge, picking up my coffee.

He raises a thick brow. "So you *scented* me?"

"It's hard not to when you're sitting opposite me."

"Please, continue to sniff me, and tell me more about myself," he says, leaning forward, tilting his head slightly to the side, exposing a little more of the smooth brown skin of his neck. Bold move for a wolf.

I roll my eyes, bringing my cup to my lips. "Your arrogance is blocking my nose."

The strength of his scent tells me he's somewhere in his late forties, though he looks like he's in his early thirties, the benefits of our extended aging.

He sits straighter, his handsome face bright with amusement. "Fine, I'll *tell* you that I'm a Lone Wolf, so I do all the dirty work myself."

Lone Wolves are almost always wolves that have been exiled from their original pack. Most don't stay alone for long, picking up strays and starting new Beta Packs in other territories, but this guy seems to enjoy the solitude.

Chef's heavy footsteps distract both of us as he sets a plate of food down in front of the wolf, along with some cutlery.

"My famous *Huevos Rancheros* as requested, Big D, enjoy," Chef announces, retreating toward the kitchen.

"*Big D?*" I ask, my curiosity getting the better of me. "Were you given that name at birth?"

"The name was earned for *other* things," he croons, picking up the fork.

"Please don't make me lose my appetite by explaining it to me."

He flashes that beaming smile again. "I'm Dominic Herrera. Most people call me Herrera, or Dom. The most privileged call me Big D."

I shove the last few forkfuls of food into my mouth and polish off my coffee before standing, collecting my dishes. "Nice to meet you, Herrera."

His hand reaches out to grab me, but I step out of his reach. His eyes narrow slightly at my aversion to his touch. "And who might you be?"

"Enjoy your stay," I say dismissively as I walk away.

The Sanctuary Bar, as usual, is packed to the brim with supernaturals tonight. The first couple of nights I felt like my heart was going to stop with the amount of wolves in this place, but the amulet is doing its job.

Not one of them thinks of me as anything other than a Bitten wolf. I caught on to bartending pretty quickly after getting over my initial hesitation, and now it's like second nature.

It's still odd to see all types of supernaturals in one place. Back home, I was rarely permitted to leave the High Alpha Pack's boundaries, which were my family's farmlands. When I was let out with one or more of my brothers, we came across other supernaturals, but they didn't intermingle like this.

None of these Bitten wolves know that the only female First Blood born in the last six decades serves them their beer. I fight a shudder at the thought of what would happen if anyone were to find out.

I check the knot in the leather cord of the amulet for possibly the hundredth time today before picking up a tray of glassware and shoving it into the dishwasher.

I turn, walking to the other side of the bar as a group of wolves shoulder through the crowd to the bar. Just like every other wolf, they shout out their orders and then proceed to shamelessly flirt with me as I prepare the beverages. I turn them down politely, take their cash, and proceed to the next patron.

I approach the order screen at the end of the bar, adding drinks to a regular's tab as someone tall appears in my periphery.

"*Aster*," Dom announces, drawing out the name.

I look up. "Herrera. Can I get you something?"

"There's so many things you could give me," he sighs, his eyes roaming away from my face and down my body.

"Hey," I click my fingers in front of his face, "my eyes are up here. Do you want a drink, or do I need to kick you out?"

He scoffs. "You can't kick me out. I have platinum membership to Sanctuary."

Sid appears next to Herrera, reaches up, and smacks him on the back of the head. "That doesn't exist, Dominic. You're just a troublemaker. And Aster has every right to kick you out, so stop flirting with her."

He holds his hands up, taking half a step back from Sid. "Apologies, Sidelle, and to you, Aster."

Sid nods once, stepping to behind the bar, squeezing my forearm gently as she walks past me.

Dom orders a beer and takes up residence on one of the bar stools at the end of the bar, pulling out his phone. I forget he's there, getting distracted by other patrons, until two boisterous wolves push up next to him.

"Dominic Herrera. Should you be in this part of the city?" the brunette closest to Dom asks.

"This is Sanctuary, wolf, not part of the Lárusson territory," Dom responds, not once taking his eyes off his phone.

The brunette's companion, the blonde, leans over the bar. "I heard you turned down the hunting bounty."

A short, stocky wolf next to the blonde whips his head around. "There's a hunting bounty?"

The blonde nods. "Yeah, for the female that murdered Viggo."

I will my body not to freeze as my heart stammers, my breath lodging in my throat.

"Who's funding it?" the stocky wolf asks.

"High Beta Espen. He has a hefty price on her head," the blonde confirms. Espen, one of High Alpha Lárusson's sons. I've never met him, but he was one of my father's potential matches for me.

"He's just trying to get into High Alpha Jónasson's and his father's good graces," the brunette adds, then turns his attention back to Dom. "Why *did* you turn down the hunt?"

Dom finally looks up from his phone and directly at the brunette. The wolf leans away from Dom's stare, an Alpha's stare.

"Don't you remember," the blonde says, elbowing the brunette, "Espen was the one to hand down the exile orders from the High Alpha." So he *is* exiled. I'm surprised he's on Lárusson territory and not getting attacked, even if we are at Sanctuary.

"High Beta Espen is probably pissed," the stocky wolf comments, picking up his drink, "that the best tracker in the entire Lárusson territory turned him down."

The best tracker in Lárusson territory? Fuck. My chest burns with the lack of oxygen, and my stomach twists in painful knots. I need to get out of here. I turn to Sid, who is polishing a glass and watching me, and give her a weak smile.

"I'm going to take a break," I say, my voice weak.

I walk out from behind the bar at a steady pace, not drawing any attention to the fact that I'm about to fall apart. Making it through the mass of bodies and into the foyer, I take the stairs two at a time as the first tear slips down my face. I running down the hall to my room, trying to fish out the keys from the back pocket of my jeans.

"Aster, are you okay?" Sid calls from the end of the hallway.

"Y-yeah, I'm fine," I croak. My hands are trembling so badly, my vision blurred from the tears, that I keep missing the lock with the key.

"Aster," Sid murmurs softly, her hand covering mine with the keys, "babygirl, talk to me. You look like you're about to run."

I give Sid the keys, letting her open the door and usher me into the room. I pace the length of the room as Sid closes the door behind her, crossing her thin arms over her chest.

"Aster."

I stop, turning to Sid. "*Nova*. My name is Nova Jónasdóttir, and I..."

"Jónasdóttir?" Sid asks, "as in High Alpha Jónas' *kid?*"

I nod.

Sid unfolds her arms, her caramel brown eyes widening slightly. "You're the female I've heard talk about who murdered Viggo Daygrsson."

"Yes."

I don't know what I'm expecting, but I don't expect Sid to take my hands and lead both of us to sit on the edge of the bed. She keeps a firm hold of my hands, her caramel brown eyes piercing through me. "Tell me everything."

4

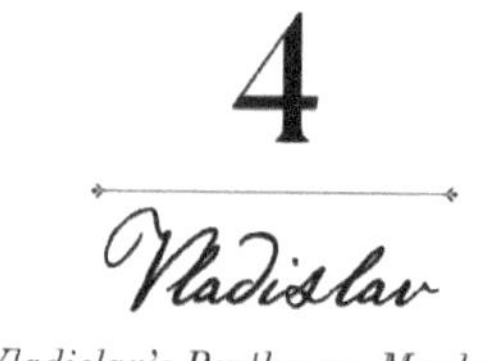

Vladislav

Vladislav's Penthouse, Manhattan

I HEAR THE FRONT door open from my study and heavy heels clip across the floor, heading toward the kitchen. I shut down my laptop, making my way through the apartment to find Delia setting grocery bags down on the island counter.

"Good afternoon, Delia," I say, opening the fridge.

"Oh, Mr. Vladislav, shouldn't you be asleep? It's the middle of the day."

I sigh, pulling out a bag of blood and a pear. "I had to sit through another round of auditions this morning, the third one in the last three weeks."

Delia chuckles. "Renard needs to stop breaking so many hearts."

"Tell me about it," I grumble as I take a seat at the breakfast table with my lunch. As I am Lilim-made vampire, I am fortunate to still have a limited capability of eating and digesting food. I don't need it to survive, but food was a pleasure for me as a human, so I'm grateful for the ability to still enjoy my favorite delicacies.

"Do you have any requests for dinner this week?" Delia asks behind me.

"Delia, you know you don't need to feed me, or do any of the other things you do for me."

"You might be this powerful vampire, Mr. Vladislav, but you don't even know where the vacuum is in this apartment."

I chuckle, turning in my seat to face the aging human. "I can learn, but I'm serious Delia. You don't need to keep coming around here. Go home and enjoy your time with your grandchildren."

She stops sorting out the groceries, eyes hard on me. "You've done so much for me and my sister. This is the least I can do."

"You owe me nothing."

She rolls her eyes, resuming her grocery sorting. "We're going to have to agree to disagree, like we always do. Now, any requests?"

I shake my head, turning back to my meal. "Anything you make I enjoy."

I eat the crisp, sweet pear and drink the awful bagged blood before retreating to my bedroom for a quick shower. After a careful suit selection, I make my way out of the apartment, down the hall to the elevator, and hit the basement level button for Immortal.

As I walk through the long back hallway and into the main bar, Ren and Dominic are seated with one of the expensive bottles of whiskey.

"Some people frown upon drinking this early in daylight hours," I comment as I pull a glass from a rack behind the bar.

Dominic chuckles. "I run on a night-dweller's schedule. This is technically a nightcap."

"Dom was just about to tell me about his last assignment," Ren says, passing me the bottle of liquor.

"How did your hunting go?" I ask the wolf.

Dom sighs, taking a healthy swig of his drink. "I didn't get much information on Medea. So far, she hasn't left Court." Agitation swirls around him.

"How many vampires did you piss off this time?" I ask.

The wolf smiles. "A few."

Ren scoffs, sitting back in the armchair he's sprawled across. "So that's why you were lurking around Sanctuary."

Dom shrugs. "Thought I should lie low for a few days." Amusement bleeds through his agitation, along with an emotion I haven't felt from Dom in a long time: interest. He hasn't been this *lively* since before he lost his mate.

"Seems like there was another reason you were lying low for two weeks," I challenge, sipping on my whiskey.

His dark brown eyes flash silver as he smiles. "There may have been other reasons."

"You've been holding out on me, Herrera," Ren says, leaning forward, "tell me about this new woman."

Before Dom can answer, we hear the back door of the club open and voices echoing in the back hall.

"Did you want me to call back any of the dancers from today?" Dom asks, standing from the sofa.

"Deflection," Ren murmurs as he stands as well. "It must be serious."

I roll my eyes, finishing off my drink. "Call the male fae and the female human with the short hair. Tell them they start tomorrow night."

Dom nods, pulling out his phone and typing away.

"Dom," I say, drawing his gaze. "I hope she can keep up with you."

Being two nights away from the full moon, the energy tonight is different.

You'd think the full moon would only affect wolves, but it seems to put all species on edge. Both Carlos and Ren had their hands full, refusing entry to three of the city's newer Lilim-made vampires and kicking out one of our regulars for trying to feed on a dancer, and we're only halfway through the night.

Heads up, Bartese is here, Ren informs me.

I take a deep breath, making my way to the foot of the entrance staircase. New York City has five Nest Masters, powerful vampires who oversee the lesser vampires in their territory. Each of the Nest Masters in the city oversees a borough, Bartese being the Nest Master of Brooklyn, and just like most of the others, he's a pain in my ass.

A thin, shorter man in a pristine three-piece suit descends the stairs along with Mydas.

"Mr. Bartese, it's been some time," I greet with the slightest bow of my head.

His thin lips lift into a smile, his arrogance pulsing off him, making me fight to keep my annoyance in check. He might be older than me, but I could easily take his seat as Nest Master if I wanted it.

"Vladislav, I'm surprised to see you here," Bartese comments, motioning towards the bar, probably at Viktoria like he usually does, for a drink.

"Why wouldn't I be in my own building?" I ask, leading Bartese to the cage platform, where two human females are performing a sensual striptease.

"I heard through my contacts at Court that you have been summoned to the Queen's side to resume your duties as her Consort."

I force my face to show none of the irritation and surprise bubbling. "Your contacts are mistaken."

The insult sizzles in Bartese's aura as his dark eyes narrow. "My contacts are never wrong."

"I just returned from Court four days ago," Mydas interjects as he takes a seat in an armchair, amusement swirling around him, "and I wasn't made aware of any summons."

"I got this information last night," Bartese argues, taking a seat on the sofa.

"We shall see in the coming days," I say, turning on my heel and leaving before I berate the Master and cause a scene. Bartese always has to be right, and perhaps he is, but I would rather not start a conflict with him.

I exit the main floor, leaving Carlos to monitor the patrons as I head to my office. I slip off my gray suit jacket, hang it in the closet behind my desk, and take a seat. If Medea has truly issued a summons, then she's going to get a rude shock when I ignore it.

A soft knock distracts my thoughts. "Come in," I call.

The scent of jasmine drifts toward me as Allura slips into my office, wrapped in a white silk robe, looking a little flushed. Concern curls around Allura as she takes a seat.

"What's wrong, Lu?" I ask.

"Has Marin come in yet?" she asks, a little breathless.

I blink. "I thought she was in one of the private rooms."

Allura shakes her head, wringing her hands together. "She left early this morning to escort Loch to the Crossing, telling me she would meet me at work, but she's not here."

I pull out my phone from my pants pocket. "I'll get Dom to check it out."

She nods, standing from her seat. "I hope she didn't get herself into trouble."

"We'll work—"

You need to come to the floor now, Ren urges into my head. He sounds angry, and that's never a good sign.

Clear the club if you need to, I respond as I text Dom to contact Allura about Marin.

"I have to go to the floor," I say, sliding my suit jacket back on. "Dom will call you shortly. Stay in the dressing room."

The faerie nods, following me down the hall where dancers are filing into the dressing rooms, tendrils of confusion weaving its way through them all.

As I re-enter the club, the only patrons remaining are Bartese and Mydas. The rest have left, but a newcomer leans up against the marble bar. Someone I thought I wouldn't see for the rest of my existence.

"Hugo," I seethe, as I come up to Renard's side by the entrance stairs. "Shouldn't you be dead?"

The too-sharp features of his pale face morph into sinister amusement, and arrogance wraps around him like velvet. "Ah, Vlad, for someone in hiding, you were quite easy to find."

"I was never hiding," I state, my body buzzing from the exertion of staying in place and not destroying the bastard in front of me. "Why are you here?"

Hugo straightens to his full height, a hand sliding into the inner pocket of his tailored suit. "Our Queen sent me, a trusted member of her Court, to give you this." He pulls out a black envelope with the Queen's crest in red on the front, extending it towards me.

I can feel the satisfaction rolling off Bartese to my left as I take the envelope from Hugo. I break the red wax seal on the back and pull out thick, cream paper, reading the summons to return to Court. Stupid bastard was right.

"You can tell the Queen that her *request* is denied," I state, as I place the summons back into the envelope and hand it to Ren.

Hugo's black eyes with mirth. "It's amusing that you think you have a choice, Vlad. You're obligated by vampire law to return as Consort."

I smirk. "I renounced the title and duties of Consort to both Medea and the Council almost a century ago."

Hugo's brow crease slightly in confused irritation. "You reject the call of your mate?"

I swallow down the fury burning on my tongue. "Please, remind your Queen of my proclamation, and not to bother me again."

His eyes flash red and anger rumbles through his aura before a smile returns to his face as he slides his hand over his perfectly styled back white hair. "I will deliver your message. I'm sure we will meet again."

"I doubt it," I say, stepping away from the stairs to the exit.

A mix of knowing and that thick layer of arrogance coats Hugo as he chuckles, striding past Ren and I, leaving Immortal.

"Mr. Bartese," I call, turning to the cocky prick. "I do apologize for cutting your visit short, but it's time for you to leave."

Anger bleeds through his aura as he says nothing and stalks up the stairs, Ren trailing behind to lock the front doors.

I turn my attention to Mydas, my anger lashing out. "Tell me why you withheld information about a summons coming my way, and that Hugo is a courtier now, when he should be rotting somewhere in Siberia."

Mydas holds up his hands, bowing his head slightly, his pale olive skin a little more pale than usual. "I was coming here tonight to update you about my trip, but I swear I didn't know about Hugo."

"But you knew about the summons?" I ask, striding over to the bar, pulling out a bottle of whiskey and pouring myself a drink. Viktoria and Maddox both dart into the back room, knowing it's time to collect their things and go, Carlos following behind them.

Mydas approaches the bar tentatively, keeping a healthy distance away from me. "Well, it's a little redundant now, but I was coming to tell you that the Court knew where you were, and Medea was insistent on coming straight for you, but I convinced her to send a summons instead. I offered myself as the messenger, but she said she had someone else in mind, obviously that person being Hugo."

"She actually had an audience with you?" I ask incredulously.

Medea may be Mydas' Sire, but once she had used him for her own agenda, she threw him away like trash. Like so many before and after him.

He nods once. "I told her you may consider an official summons, especially coming from a brother, rather than her trying to force your hand in person."

"She clearly chooses to ignore the fact that I don't have the title of Consort."

As if I summoned the goddamn bond, it twists hard, the threadbare tether sending jolts of pain thundering in my chest. I struggle to keep upright and stone-faced as I war with the bond, shoving it back into its cage, the pain subsiding into a dull ache.

Mydas clears his throat. "That was the other bit of news." Nervousness and a trickle of fear whispering around him. "She's ordered the Council to reinstate your Consort title."

Hot rage sears in my consciousness and my fangs drop, the muscles in my body bulking, almost tearing through my suit. Mydas cringes, taking a few steps back. I'm going to do what I should have done so long ago and destroy the miserable bitch.

"Don't even think about it," Ren snaps, reading my thoughts, as he stalks towards the bar, eyes emerald green. "You know if you even attempt to harm her, you will be convicted of treason." *You wouldn't let me do it the first time*, Ren adds into my mind, *so there's no fucking chance I'm letting you do it now.*

I take a few moments to breathe through the rage, and allow my body to return to its usual size. I run my hand through my hair and down my suit, then pick up my drink.

"Next time you find out anything regarding Court, Mydas." I pin him with a hard stare. "Fucking call me, instead of waiting to tell me in person."

More fear laces through his aura as he nods, apologizes, and follows Ren to the front door.

The staff door opens and Allura walks out, now clothed in an oversized sweater and skinny jeans, her emotions still tainted with worry.

"I spoke to Dom," she says approaching the bar, sitting on one of the stools. "He went to the Crossing and said there's nothing amiss in the area. He said she definitely came back through because he followed Marin's scent to the street nearby, but it stops there, like she caught a cab or a car."

"Did he try your apartment?" I ask. The distraction from the other shit going on is a blessing, but Marin's disappearance is worrying.

She nods, loose curls bouncing around her face. "He said there's no fresh scent at our apartment, so she hasn't been home." Her bottom lip trembles and tears fill her eyes. "He can't find her anywhere."

Ren appears next to her, placing an arm around her. "Maybe she went on one of her benders. She's always edgy when she returns from Faery."

She nods again, sniffling and blinking. "Dom's coming now to take me home."

I refill my glass with whiskey. "We'll wait until after the full moon, and if she doesn't show up, we won't rest until we find her."

5

Nova

Sanctuary Hotel

MY SKIN FEELS LIKE ants are crawling all over me, and if anyone else tries to flirt with me tonight, I may murder them.

The days leading up to the full moon are always a roller coaster of emotions and urges, and it's not fun at all.

Only First Bloods can fully transition into a wolf; the Bitten have a diluted form of wolf energy, which makes them bulk up in muscle mass and a lot more aggressive on the full moon.

Changing to your complete wolf form uses an explosive amount of magic, levels which build up between moon cycles, and can be a vicious experience, sometimes even resulting in death.

In a Pack, the days leading up to a change are used to expend some of that pent up energy, and then at the time of the change, the magic disperses through a Pack's connection, making the change a little more bearable. It still hurts like hell, but you don't run the risk of dying like you would if you did it alone.

I've never turned alone before, so needless to say, I'm terrified.

Not only am panicking about the physical effect it will have on me, but I'm also concerned about doing it here at Sanctuary. The only time a Bitten wolf can turn into their complete wolf form is when they are in the presence or vicinity of a First Blood, sharing their raw wolf energy.

If I turn with all the wolves here, it won't take long for them to work out who I am.

"Maybe I should go?" I say to Sid next to me at the reception desk. We closed up the bar half an hour ago, and being so close to dawn, we're waiting for Chef to come in so we can eat before going to bed.

"Nova," she breathes.

"It's two days until the full moon. I have time to get to a remote place in a state park away from other wolves, and then I'll come back after the turn."

She turns her to me, brows pinched together. "What happens if your mind breaks under the stress and you can't bring yourself back to your human form?"

I open my mouth to reply, but close it. She has a point. There's a possibility of my wolf's energy being too much for my mind, and it could fracture the human side of me to the point of no return. I could get stuck in my wolf form, or die.

I blow out a breath. "How am I supposed to do this on my own, Sid?"

She scoffs. "You're doing this on your *own*?"

I roll my eyes. "What I meant is, how am I supposed to do this without another wolf? Or doing it here without getting found out?"

Sid's phone on the desk in front of us with a message, and she smiles. "Well, one of our questions is answered." She picks up the phone and types furiously. "I'm sending you an address. You need to speak to the faerie there."

"That's incredibly vague," I mutter, pulling out the buzzing phone from my back pocket. I groan, reading the address. "This is all the way in Lenox Hill."

"The run will be good for you."

When I was back home, my brothers and I would go on runs through the Pack territory to expend some built up energy before the full moon, and since I don't have a Pack to run with, Sid has been sending all over the city on jobs to try to do the same.

My heart pangs thinking about Kris and Pat. I wonder if Pat has given birth yet? Is Kris okay? No, I can't think about that now. Sid thinks if I keep a clear head, it should also help reduce the risks of the turn fracturing my mind.

I leave Sid at the desk, twisting my long ponytail into a tight bun as I bound up the stairs to my room. I change into a crop top and bike shorts, throw a loose t-shirt over the top and pull on a thick, zip-up hooded sweatshirt.

Swapping my beloved combat boots for running shoes, I take my phone and keys from the dresser, and slide two switchblades in the pockets of my jacket before locking up as I leave the room, making my way back to reception.

After I told Sid everything about my past, she showed me her armory filled with all types of weapons, magical and otherwise, and gave me a comprehensive education on every single one of them. She also made me promise that I'd always have a weapon on me when I leave Sanctuary.

"You'll need this too," Sid says, waving a wad of cash in the air.

"Who is this fae?" I ask, snatching the cash from her and stuffing it into my bra.

"A friend, now get going before the world wakes."

I salute her, and even though I haven't taken it off since I put it on, I check the amulet is secure around my wrist, before taking off through the foyer and out into the crisp morning. I set a comfortable pace, knowing it's about an hour to Lenox Hill on foot, enjoying the quiet, still dark city around me.

I'm warm and breathing a little harder as I near Central Park. I can feel the dense presence of wolves in the park, so I slow my pace, alert, scanning for wolves in the area. Luckily I'm downwind, so any Packs lurking this early won't catch my scent.

The fresh scent of jasmine and sweet oranges distracts me about halfway down the park. Another scent, a familiar one, blends with the jasmine: honeycomb and teakwood.

My head turns toward Dom's scent. He's across the street with a female faerie chatting as they walk out of a building further down the block.

The Fae are tricky creatures. They catch your eye and draw you in, enchanting you with their words and dazzling you with their magic. Faeries come into Sanctuary all the time, and their lure doesn't stun me as much anymore, but none of them have been as exquisite as the faerie with Dom.

Even from this distance, I'm almost entranced. She's small, much shorter than Dom, and looks slender under her oversized sweater, but she exudes the energy of the sun.

Her butterfly-shaped wings are iridescent and not quite visible, but look as if they're made from fragments of splintered glass.

They reflect light in a kaleidoscope of colors even in the artificial glow of the street lamps.

Apparently, faery wings look solid to other faeries, supernaturals see them like this, as translucent shapes, and humans don't see them at all.

I can't see the specific color of her eyes from here, but they're light, and they contrast off flawless, deep bronze skin. Her hair of curled, radiant caramel brown is up in a messy bun on top of her head, and her small, heart-shaped face is pinched with worry.

Dom looks a little distressed too, his broad shoulders hunched in slightly and his silky brown hair a little disheveled as he leads the faerie toward the familiar black sports car parked four cars away from them.

The hairs on the back of my neck stand up suddenly, and the feeling of being watched washes over me. Did wolves in the park spot me? I start to turn toward the park to check when the pungent aroma of papaya curls under my nose.

Movement in the corner of my eye sends my head whipping to my left, looking down the street.

Two vampires stalk toward Dom and the faerie, hunger clouding their faces. I scan the street on my right and see three more vampires at the corner of the next block, waiting and watching the other two. I turn back to the other two vampires, who are moving quicker now.

I'm racing forward before I know it, toward the two vampires advancing on Dom and the faerie. My eyesight focuses, and all the muscles in my body tighten. My canines thicken, and adrenaline pumps through my veins as I see Dom's face register what's happening before I slam the vampire closest to the faerie into the brick wall.

I hear shrieks, snarls, and fighting behind me as I slam my forearm into the vampire's throat, holding the thrashing male against the crumbling wall.

There's only a ring of glowing orange around his blown pupils, and they're focused on something behind me as he flings his arm out, like he's trying to reach for whatever he has his eyes on. I avoid his sharp nails as I pull out a switchblade and sink the blade into his heart between two ribs, straight into his heart.

The blade is coated in silver, which is poisonous to vampires as wolfsbane is to wolves, so the vampire stops struggling immediately, and a white film glazing over his eyes and his skin starts to gray and decay.

I pull out my blade and jump back, dropping him, then turn around to see the faerie's back plastered against a car. Her eyes, a brilliant, deep ocean blue, are wide as she gapes at Dom, who has the other male vampire by the throat.

This vampire is acting the same as the other one, not interested in Dom, but the faerie. I stalk up behind the feral vampire and sink my blade into his heart with a powerful thrust, this time slicing through ribs.

Dom drops the limp vampire as he decays. We both pant, Dom pinning me with a shocked gaze.

"Aster," he pants.

My neck hairs stand up again, and I turn to the other group of vampires that were down the street, but they're now blurs as they advance towards us.

"Fuck," I bark as I pull out the other blade, tossing it to Dom who catches it. "More coming."

"Fuck," he echoes, moving to stand in front of the faerie, facing the new threat.

I take a position next to him, my arm brushing his, creating a wolf barrier around this faerie. I almost laugh at the absurdity of two wolves protecting a faerie from vampires. This would not happen in Texas. The trio, two females and a male, are almost upon us when two more vampires appear from the building. Fuck, I don't think we can take on five at once.

The two new vampires turn toward the approaching trio.

"Are they friendly?" I ask Dom, keeping my eyes focused ahead.

"Yes," he responds.

The vampire in a white shirt grabs one female by the throat and punches through her chest, ripping out her heart. The other one, the bulkier one, slams into the approaching male, sinking his fangs into his jugular and tearing out his throat, dark blood spraying everywhere. I race toward the remaining female, tackling her to the ground, and striking my blade through her chest, piercing her heart.

I pull the blade out, rising to my feet, honing in on the other vampires. The male from the trio now has his head rolling next to his decaying body. The two supposedly friendly vampires turn toward me, snarling.

I lower myself closer to the ground, ready with my switchblade. I could probably take both of them, or at least take one of them out with me.

"Who are you?" White Shirt spits through a double pair of fangs.

I found out one of my first few days at Sanctuary that when vampires drop fang, it's not just their canines but also the incisors next to them that lengthen into lethal points.

"No one of concern," I say. From their overpowering scents of dark chocolate, smoke, and peaches turning my stomach, they're both pretty powerful. This might be a bit of a challenge.

"She's good," Dom calls behind me, drawing the bulkier one's attention. White Shirt continues to size me up.

"Correction, I'm amazing," I say, not daring to move from my defensive position.

The bulkier one chuckles. His eyes, which were green a moment ago, are now a dazzling cobalt blue, giving me a once over. "You seem like fun."

White Shirt is still wary, but he relaxes slightly, his swirling bourbon-brown eyes taking in the carnage behind me. "You put a hole in the side of my building."

I straighten slightly. "You can afford to fix it."

I retreat slowly; both vampires track my movements, making my adrenaline and heartbeat spike. It's time for me to go.

A warm body slams into my right side, unbalancing me, as two slim arms wrap around me. I pry them loose and turn; the faerie has giant streaks of tears down her cheeks and a dazzling smile on her face.

"You saved me!" she beams as she throws herself into me again, her beautiful wings flutter wildly in my vision.

"Uh, you're welcome," I mumble, trying to pull her off me again, but her grip is tight.

"Allura, let go of the stranger," the blue-eyed vampire says at our side.

The faerie, Allura, steps back, tears still streaming down her face. Blue Eyes leads the faerie to Dom's car, shutting her into the back seat.

Dom steps up to me, holding out my switchblade. "Thanks for the assist, Aster."

"Keep it, I have plenty."

He pockets the blade, stepping backwards toward the car. "See you at Sanctuary." He hops in the car and pulls away from the curb, escaping into the New York morning.

Blue Eyes chuckles. "So *you're* the reason Dom was away for so long."

I cross my arms over my chest. "I don't know what that means."

He laughs again, stepping toward me. I skirt to the side, backing up a few steps, my hand going for the blade again. He's not heading for me, but for the dead vampire by the hole, which he picks up like he weighs nothing, and carries him over to the trio.

"You seem to have done this a few times," I state as White Shirt taps away at his phone next to the growing pile of dead vampires.

I grab the legs of the other vampire by the car and start to drag his body toward the pile.

"This isn't a typical nightly activity we concern ourselves with," Blue Eyes announces as he appears next to me, shooing me away as he hoists up the body.

"It's Vladislav," White Shirt announces as I turn around to see him with his phone to his ear, staring at the pile of decay in front of him. "I need a cleanup in front of my building as soon as possible. Five dead, plus wall and car damage." He hangs up and pockets the phone.

"So, *you're* Vladislav," I drawl. "I've heard things about you."

Serving drunk people at Sanctuary has its perks when it comes to freely given information. Vampires coming through Sanctuary talk about Vladislav with a mix of fear and adoration. Apparently, he's one of the most powerful vampires in the city, with a reputation for being ruthless.

When he looks up, I'm a little awestruck. His eyes are no longer bourbon brown, but a brilliant, crystal-bright amber. Those stunning eyes narrow slightly, roving over my face, before wandering further down.

"It's not polite to ogle."

His lift in the slightest smirks. "You are very...shiny."

I look down and groan. "Gods damned faerie dust."

Faeries apparently shed the glittery substance when they're happy, and it does *not* like to come off. It looks like a healthy glow or a slight shimmer to a human, but in the supernatural world, it's like a fucking beacon.

I don't even bother attempting to remove it and unzip the jacket. The faerie dust is also on my t-shirt. I groan, pulling off the glitter smeared fabric, and use clean parts of it to wipe off most of the dust from my shorts and arms.

I hear Vladislav clear his throat in front of me. He's staring at my chest now. "Don't make me rip out your eyes."

He smiles, and damn, it's a *good* smile. "I apologize. The dust is very distracting."

His intense amber eyes don't seem to know how to stay on my face. I turn to the windows next to me, seeing the dust glittering on my chest and neck. I sigh loudly. How the fuck did it even get there?

I use the t-shirt to clean my skin and toss Vladislav the shirt and jacket, which he catches effortlessly. "I gotta run."

6

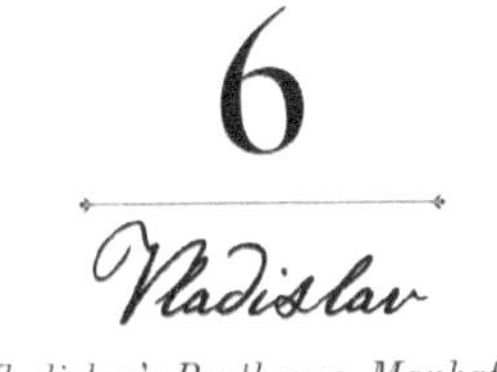

Vladislav

ROLLING OVER IN BED for the umpteenth time, I can feel that the sun is now glaring down from the middle of the sky. I shut my eyes, intending to sleep for another few hours, but my mind drifts to thoughts about the wolf that saved Allura three nights ago.

This wolf, Aster, as Dom called her, seemed to be a Lone Wolf, which is extremely uncommon for female wolves. I'm told they're rarely born, and most human females don't survive a wolf bite, so females don't generally live a solitary life.

So who is she? She was strong, stronger than some vampires that I've met, and adept at fighting.

I give up on sleep and throw on some clothes before making my way through the sunlit apartment. I'm convinced a vampire invented ceramic window film, which every window has in my eighty story building, as it allows us to see the sun once again without turning into a charred corpse.

Hushed voices filter through the apartment as I turn into the kitchen to find Allura and Dom sitting at the glass breakfast table, both with somber auras.

"Marin hasn't surfaced?" I ask, already knowing the answer as I pull out a bag of blood from the fridge and a glass from a nearby cupboard.

"There's not a trace of her at any of her usual haunts," Dom grumbles, his emotions a mix of concern, frustration, and confusion.

I take a seat next to Allura who's on the brink of full panic mode. "I don't know if she's dead or captured. And after the other night with those vampires trying to attack me; I don't know what to think."

I place my hand over hers on the table and send calming energy through to her. She takes a shuddering breath and sits back, her emotions more controlled as I remove my touch. I pour the blood into the glass, focusing on Dom.

"What's our next move?" I ask, having a mouthful of blood and cringing. I don't enjoy hunting and taking blood from humans, but at least it doesn't taste like a stale kill and chemicals.

Dom runs his hand through his hair, the frustration melting into anger. "I have no idea. I've tried everything to track her, and there's no sign of her at all. The few werewolves I've contacted have nothing on faeries disappearing into thin air, and most fae and vampires avoid werewolves."

"I can send Ren to talk to some vampire contacts," I offer.

Dom shakes his head. "They know who's in the Immortal crew, they'll never open up."

"I can't go near the Fae," Allura says, "they'll find out about the other thing."

The pregnancy, shit. If everyone in the city knows who's in my circle, then we'll never get answers. I take another sip of the blood, perhaps I can send Mydas through the Nests, see if he can rustle up some information.

Dom sits up, realization pulsing around him. "How about someone no one knows?"

"Who did you have in mind?"

Dom smiles. "Our new friend."

"We're going out," I announce to Viktoria, Maddox and Carlos in the storage room as they're collecting their belongings.

"I'll pass," Viktoria announces, zipping up her leather jacket.

"It's mandatory," I state as I exit the room and meet Dom and Ren by the staff door.

The three vampires file out shortly after me and we collect Allura from her dressing room before exiting out the back door into the alley behind the building. We all hop into one of the Range Rovers and head toward Sanctuary Hotel.

"Why is this mandatory?" Viktoria asks from the back.

"Because we're going to interview a potential new member of the crew," I say as I flick through emails in the front passenger seat.

"I'll probably hate them anyway," she grumbles.

"Come on, Vik," Maddox encourages next to her, "we need some fresh meat in this troupe. I hope he's cute."

Dom chuckles from the driver's seat. "*She's* not your type, Maddox."

"We'll see about that," Maddox challenges, enticing a smile from me.

"She is so beautiful," Allura sighs in the far back of the car. "You're all going to fight over her."

"I only have eyes for you, *mon petit papillon*," Ren drawls next to Allura. I can hear Carlos grumbling about the lack of personal space next to them.

I bark out a laugh, not taking my eyes off my phone. "Who wants to wager that Renard is the first person to attempt to seduce her?"

A slew of bets are placed, all the cash given to me to hold onto. I add a hundred dollar bill, betting it'll happen by the end of the week.

The place is already overflowing with supernaturals as we roll into the short driveway of Sanctuary. This is one of the few places that all supernaturals can go where they don't need to hide their true selves. It can be a wild place on the best of nights, so tonight being two nights after the full moon, there's bound to be trouble.

We all climb out of the car, except for Dom, who will park the car in Sanctuary's parking lot next door, and ascend the stairs to the foyer of the hotel.

The crowd is mostly werewolves or fae, but there's a few low level Adam-made vampires dispersed throughout. Clusters mill around with drinks in the foyer, spilling out from the bar which is attached on the left.

We weave in and out of the crowd, making it through the double doors into the dark bar. Booths occupy the far wall, all full of boisterous supernaturals, except for the one directly next to the bar. The long, worn timber is littered with beer bottles, tumblers, and the edge is crammed with people fighting for a bartender's attention.

A rotund human man serves people at the far end of the bar, his gray t-shirt darker in patches from sweat. Sid taps away at an order screen at the other end, closest to us. She lifts her head to the customer in front of her and takes his cash, her warm eyes noticing us by the door.

"Chef, you're on your own for a bit," she calls, pulling change from the cash register and giving it to her customer, before walking around the bar towards me.

"Vlad, so good to see you again. It's been a while." Sidelle kisses both of my cheeks.

"I wish it were under better circumstances, Sid," I reply.

She nods, leading us toward the empty booth to the left of the bar, and we all take a seat, Sid included. She searches the crowd for a few moments and then waves someone over.

Through the throng of people, Aster pushes her way toward us with Dom following close behind.

As Allura said in the car, she's beautiful. She's taller than most women, her body is a dangerous combination of deliciously soft curves and taut, feline muscles, all of it shown off by skinny jeans and a long sleeve t-shirt. Her oak brown hair hangs down to her waist in thick, wild waves and sways slightly as she comes to a stop in front of our table.

"I found your pet," she quips, peering up at Dom.

"Rude," he says, bumping shoulders with Aster before turning towards the bar.

She shakes her head, smirking, returning her attention to the table. "Can I get anyone a drink?"

Her large, jade green eyes meet mine, and I'm struck with the fact that I can't feel anything from her. I push my gift toward her, trying to sense her emotions, but I get static. Odd. Her light, sun-kissed skin pinks slightly over her cheeks as she breaks our staring contest, listening to the table rattle off drinks orders, and then she heads toward the bar.

"How long has she worked for you?" I ask Sid, eyes still following Aster as she steps behind the bar and starts pulling out glassware.

"A few months," Sid replies vaguely, the feel of her amusement turning my attention back to her. Knowing shines in her caramel brown eyes, and her smile is soft.

"Don't you usually have a limit to how long people can stay at Sanctuary?" I ask.

"Tell that to Dominic who is here every other week," she says, leaning back into the cushioned back, and crosses her arms. "He said you're having some trouble locating one of your dancers."

"Her name is Marin," Allura interjects, "she's a Winter faerie."

Sid arches a manicured, silver brow. "Aren't you Heir of the Summer Court?"

Allura nods in answer. Sid narrows her gaze at the non-verbal answer.

"What we were hoping," I add before either of them start going on a tangent. "Is if you knew of anyone trustworthy to try to locate Marin, as we have exhausted all our resources."

Sid's attention returns to me, wariness swirling around her. "You already know who you want to help you."

"Is she part of your *other* business?" I ask, eluding to Sid's underground rescue missions.

Protectiveness laces through the wariness as Sid slides out of the booth. "You'll have to ask her yourself."

The crowd instinctively parts for Sid as she heads back behind the bar, leaning into Aster, talking into her ear. Aster's eyes drift over us, and then back to Sid, chatting for a few more moments before lifting a tray full of drinks and heading toward our table.

"Your drinks," Aster announces as she places the tray in the center of the table. Dom appears suddenly, sliding into Sid's empty spot with a beer in his hand.

"You took my seat," Aster says, hands on her small waist.

"Your seat is right here," Dom offers, patting his thigh.

She smirks, then wedges herself between Dom's lap and the table, placing her crossed arms on the table. Shock and then that interest a felt back in Immortal flares in Dom. No, not interest, *desire.*

"Sid said you have a proposition for me," Aster says, drawing my attention back to her.

"We do," Allura answers before I can say anything. "My best friend, Marin, is missing."

"I've been told you're very *persuasive* in these kinds of hunts," I comment.

Aster narrows her eyes, laying her hands flat on the table, and leaning closer to me. Her eyes burn jade green. "Let's get one thing straight," she almost whispers, her scent of amber rum and fresh milk wraps around me, "I don't hunt people, I help them."

"I apologize for my poor choice of words. Marin needs help, and I've been told you're good at what you do."

"You mean *amazing*," Dom corrects with a smirk.

"Damn straight," she says, smirking, sinking further into Dom's lap. "When was the last time you saw Marin?"

"Four nights ago," Allura answers.

Aster frowns. "You waited this long before you started looking for her?"

"I've been trying to find her since we realized she was missing," Dom grumbles into her shoulder.

"When did her scent fade?" Aster asks, angling the question at Dom.

"Yesterday."

Aster cranes her neck to scan the crowd, then slides off Dom's lap. "I'll see what I can find out." She walks into the thick of the crowd.

"I don't trust her," Viktoria announces. I turn back toward her glaring after Aster.

Carlos chuckles. "You're just annoyed she's making moves on Dom."

Vik shoots him a murderous as she sips her martini.

"She smells different than other wolves," Dom comments, continuing to watch Aster, ignoring Carlos' comment.

"A lot better than most wolves," Ren pipes in.

"I agree," Maddox sighs next to me, "she smells *delicious*."

I agree, but I frown at Maddox. "The last time you were with a wolf, you almost got eaten," I chastise, "let's not go down that road again."

He pouts, scooping up his cocktail. We all chat and drink, waiting for Aster to return from whatever she's doing.

Her rum and milk scent swirling around me announces her arrival. She sighs. "It's not good news."

"Tell me," I demand.

"Sid told me that over the last decade or so, fae have vanished and then found weeks or months after their disappearance dead, completely drained of blood."

"Fuck," Ren says at the end of the table.

"Vampires killing fae?" Maddox asks next to me. "Why would they do that?"

"Lux," Aster and I say together. Lux is the street term for fae blood, which is sold unlawfully for many reasons, mainly as a partying drug. It's incredibly addictive, particularly to vampires. It was long ago agreed upon by all species that it is punishable by death for anyone found to be trafficking or selling the stuff.

"The Nest Masters of New York City eradicated the Lux Pits decades ago," Carlos, sitting next to Vik, adds.

"The Lux problem has never really been resolved," I counter, "the sale and distribution has just gone further underground."

"Sid said it's ramped up again in the last year," Aster adds, "in the short time I've been here, we've had three calls for aid, but gotten to them too late."

"You're not so *amazing* at what you do, then?" Viktoria challenges, her anger rolling off her in waves.

"Lux-crazed vampires will do anything for a fix," Aster explains, glaring at Viktoria. "Any threat to discovery, they kill their prisoners and hunt for new prey."

"Those vampires the other night," Allura murmurs, "they were going after me for my blood, weren't they?"

Aster nods. "They must have been out hunting and caught your scent, and thought the five to one odds against Dom would be a breeze."

"I could have taken them," Dom says.

She places a hand on his shoulder. "It's okay to admit your shortcomings."

Ren and Carlos snicker as Dom brushes her hand off and downs the rest of his beer.

"How did they get to Marin?" I ask.

"There's reports of vamps snatching faeries from somewhere called the Crossing," Aster says.

Allura gasps, ocean blue eyes widening.

"Not many vampires know about the Crossing," I say, stroking a thumb across my jaw. "And not many people knew Marin was going to the Crossing that day."

Caution flutters through Aster's eyes. "There are also rumors that Earth-bound fae sell out other fae to vampires to protect themselves from getting taken to a pit themselves."

"So you think..."

"Someone in your club sold out Marin to someone running a Pit."

7

Nova

Sanctuary Bar

AN INTENSE CONVERSATION IN what I'm assuming is Russian erupts around the table, so I slip away, heading back to the bar.

"What did they say?" Sid asks. I give her a rundown on the conversation and my conclusion on what has more than likely happened to Marin.

Sid sighs, defeated. "This fucking Lux problem is getting worse. I'm going to have to speak to the Nest Masters again."

"I'll do it," Vladislav announces from the entrance of the bar behind me.

I turn to the tall vampire. I'm five-foot-ten, but I still have to tilt my head to meet his gaze. "Did you need another drink, Mr. Vladislav?"

His wide, full lips curve up on one side. "No, but I would still like to offer you a job."

Sid melts away from my side. "I already have a job."

"I'd like you to uncover the traitor in my club."

"There's plenty of other—"

"But I want *you*." Tingles spread over my skin at his declaration, heating my cheeks.

"You don't know me." The statement comes out a little breathless.

His glittering amber eyes are very distracting. So is his face, and his presence. He's so handsome that it's almost impossible, and he has a predatory focus about him, a dangerous edge; it's a lethal combination. He could ruin someone without much effort.

"Dom vouches for you, and I saw what you did for Allura, who was a stranger to you."

"How does that make me trustworthy?" I challenge. He doesn't even know my real name, or what I've done.

He sighs, straightening the cufflinks in his white shirt. "No one else will actually give a shit about finding Marin alive."

"What's she to you?" I blurt out, my curiosity escaping its cage.

A smirk flashes on his face before he's serious again. "She's one of the few people in my circle. Someone I care for."

I lean up against the preparation bench. "What exactly do you want me to do?"

"Come work at Immortal, see if you can flush out the traitor."

I raise a brow. "I know what kind of club Immortal is; I'm not stripping for you."

A smile spreads across his face. "I know some people would love to see you on my stage, but I was thinking working behind the bar would make you feel a little more comfortable."

"It's a solid plan. Assimilate into the club, get to know the staff and clients, investigate from the inside." Thinking about being away from the safety of Sanctuary sends my heart into a free-fall. "I don't think I'm the person for the job."

Vladislav loosens a breath. "All I ask is for you to think it over." His hand snakes into his suit jacket and he extends a black card. "This has my cell on it. Let me know your final answer tomorrow."

I nod, taking the card, my fingers brushing over his—a sharp zap tingles up my arm, my breath hitching as I look up to Vladislav. His brows are furrowed, his irises swirl between amber and bourbon brown. I pull the card from his hand looking down at his name embossed in gold, avoiding intense stare.

"What are you going to do with the person responsible?" I ask suddenly, my voice a little hoarse.

His bourbon eyes harden. "You don't fuck with people I care about and get to live."

His response warms my chest in wicked satisfaction. I should probably feel conflicted about the idea, but I'd be a hypocrite if I did. I did the exact thing he's promising to do.

"I'll let you know," is all I say as I slide his card into my jeans back pocket.

He gives me a curt nod and heads for the foyer door. I turn to the booth; the entire group is gone.

Chef, Sid and I work to get everyone out at around three, Chef heading home shortly after, announcing he is taking the day off.

"Do you cook?" Sid asks, flipping the last of the chairs onto the tables scattered throughout the dark space.

"I love cooking," I answer as I put cleaning supplies away, "especially baking."

Sid approaches the bar, passing me her cleaning supplies, grinning. "If you ever get the urge to bake, please don't hesitate to use the kitchen. Chef would love the company, plus he's an awful baker, so he may learn a thing or two."

I smile. "I'll keep it in mind. Should we go up and make breakfast before we call it a night?"

An hour later, Sid and I are in the Dining Hall with a spread of food in front of us and two mugs of piping hot tea. I wait for Sid to serve herself and take her first bite before I serve myself.

"What are your thoughts on Vladislav's job offer?" Sid asks as she stirs brown sugar into her oatmeal. She had overheard most of the offer, and I filled her in on the rest.

I sigh, peeling a banana and cutting slices into my own oatmeal. "I honestly don't know. I don't know Vladislav, or his crew, and they don't know me."

"I've known Vlad for many years," Sid's eyes dim a little, "he helped me set up Sanctuary."

"He did?" I didn't expect that. This place has safety and *love* imbued in everything, and Vladislav's sharp, business-like aura doesn't correlate with that in my mind.

Sid eats a few spoonfuls of oatmeal before sighing, resting her elbows on the table, her eyes fixating on the bowl in front of her. "I met my wife when I was twenty-two. She was the daughter of extremely religious parents, and I'm from a Native American family who have strong values that run deep, so you can probably guess how difficult our coupling was to them."

Was. Her wife is...

Sid's caramel eyes harden, lost in memory. "I had just finished nursing school when she came into emergency having left her fiancé, a wolf. He'd broken so many bones and done enough nerve damage in her right arm that she never regained full function of the limb. That was the day I was thrown into the supernatural world and the day I found the other half of me that I never knew was missing. We married three years later, and decided to dedicate our lives to helping and protecting the vulnerable from the harshness and horror that laces this world."

"So, you created Sanctuary together?" I ask in almost a whisper.

Sid shakes her head. "We didn't get that far. We moved around a lot, helping people anywhere we went, until we both decided to make New York City our permanent residence. About five months into settling into the city, her ex-fiancé found us. We didn't know he had changed Packs. He was...unstoppable. He took her from me, and then tried to take me from this world, but I got him first."

"Gods." Sometimes I'm ashamed to be a wolf. I'm beginning to understand that every species has veins of violence, but wolves don't seem to be ability, or care enough, to keep it in check.

Sid swirls the spoon in her bowl, her gaze far away.

"Does the hollowness ever go away?" I ask. I know what it's like for someone you love to be stolen from you.

"No," Sid breathes, "but it got manageable when I had Sanctuary to focus on."

"How did Vladislav get involved?"

Light comes back into her eyes as she sips her tea, and I resume eating. "I had just opened Sanctuary, and it was still very underground. Vlad came in one night, and I knew immediately what he was. Before he opened his mouth, I shot at him."

I almost choke on a laugh and the mouthful of oatmeal.

Sid smiles. "He talked me out of killing him, obviously. He heard whispers of a safe haven from one of his dancers, and by the end of that night, we had worked out how to turn this place into what it is today. A neutral zone, a place of peace in a world of turmoil."

"How you got Lárusson wolves to agree into giving you this building out of their territory is beyond impressive," I say as I start adding banana into my second bowl of cooled oatmeal. "They are known for being possessive, territorial bastards."

Sid chuckles. "It was a process, that's for sure, but High Alpha Izar was a lot more amenable those days."

His present reputation says otherwise, but time and circumstances can change a person. That I can confirm. We both finish off our food, collecting our dishes and heading to the kitchen.

"What's your biggest reservation?" Sid asks as she passes me a bowl to dry.

"Leaving Sanctuary," I say as I set the dry bowl down and accept another. "I go out now, with a clear task, and I get it done quickly. Then I'm back behind these walls, knowing that no one can touch me here."

"Do you think they'll work out who you are?" Sid asks, handing me another clean dish.

"The amulet hides who I am, but not what I am. To the world I'm an unmated Bitten female wolf with no pack, that alone is a dangerous thing to be outside of these walls."

"The entire city knows who Vlad is, no supernatural in their right mind would try something with someone in his circle."

I put down the dry dish. "But someone did do something to Marin."

"And they'll regret it," Sid states.

"I still don't know," I sigh, picking up the clean dishes and putting them away as Sid wipes down the basin.

"Immortal, in a way, is a safe haven as well," Sid leans against the bench, "a few of the women we helped now work for Vlad. He doesn't allow any bullshit to happen in his club."

I know it's a vampire-only club from what I've heard, so at least there aren't any other wolves to cause more trouble, apart from Dom. And Sid finds Vladislav trustworthy enough to refer women to him, which speaks volumes in itself.

I fish out the card from my back pocket, and my phone, typing in Vladislav's number, then sending him a text.

> I'm not wearing lingerie.

He responds almost immediately.

VLADISLAV

> I won't go lower than scantily clad.

> I hope you like combat boots.

VLADISLAV

> I can make arrangements for clothes. Are you in?

I take a deep breath.

> I'll find her. When do you want me to start?

VLADISLAV

> Today. I'll send Dom in the afternoon to pick you up.

Viggo and I stand chest to chest on the platform, I try not to gag on his vile moss and driftwood scent stinging my nostrils. My father has finished reciting the Old Norse marriage blessings, and we've exchanged wedding bands. At this point we're meant to split our palms open and clasp the wounds together, marrying our blood.

In the eyes of the Pack, after the blood bonding, we're officially mated for life, the human aspect of a marriage license gets signed later.

Viggo looks into my eyes and quietly chuckles. "I get to own you like no one ever has done before, my pretty pet."

I pull out the hunting knife hidden in my clothes and thrust it into the side of his chest, between two ribs before he takes his next breath. His arrogant expression slips into one of confusion as he looks down at my left hand clenched around the knife hilt. I twist it, enticing a choke from him as I lean forward, catching those dirty hazel eyes.

"I will *never* be yours," I hiss in his ear as I wrench the knife from his body.

The blood that gushes out of the wound is already black, the wolfsbane doing its job, as I drop the weapon on the platform, rip off the bloodied wedding band and launch into the cornfield behind us.

Terrified shrieks and angry growls chase me as I bolt towards the truck Kris parked on the other side of the field. Hunting howls call out from the Den House and the rustling of corn follow me as

I push myself faster through the field, dodging corn attempting to whack me in the face. I fumble in my bra for the jewelry pouch Pat gave me earlier.

The rustling is closer as I manage to pull out a small white stone on a long leather cord. With no time to contemplate what exactly this thing is, I rip off the gold chain around my neck, tossing the sapphire necklace on the ground and loop the new accessory over my head, the stone warming my skin as I duck around a particularly large corn stalk.

The rustling stops and frustrated shouts from the hunting party gets further away. I exit the field, finding the black pick-up truck parked on the side of the dirt track. Kris said the keys would be in the ignition and a burner cell on the passenger seat, along with the bag I packed earlier. I find exactly that as I wrench open the door and climb in, fire up the engine and punch the gas.

Winding through the back streets towards the highway, I stay alert, checking the mirrors for any of the Pack cars. I know they won't give up that easily, I just killed the only heir to the Daygrsson Pack.

My head is pounding as I pull myself out of bed and into the shower. I look forward to the day the events of that night stop stealing my sleep.

I dress in black jeans, a gray tank top and faded blue, loose denim jacket before I pull on my combat boots and exit my room with nothing but my phone, keys and a switchblade tucked into my boot.

As I descend the stairs, the familiar scent of honeycomb and teakwood drifts up to me. Dom leans against the wall by the door with dark sunglasses on, dressed in a fitted black suit.

"Who thought you could scrub up so nicely," I comment.

He lowers his glasses, his dark brown eyes meeting mine with a smirk. "Does the corporate look do it for you, Aster?"

I scoff, walking over to the reception desk. "You look like a funeral director."

Dom chuckles. "Not the worst thing I've been compared to. Are you ready to go?"

I drop my keys into a drawer under the cash register and turn toward Dom. "Let's go."

Dom pushes off the wall, returning his glasses to their place and holding the door open for me. We climb into his sleek, black sports car parked at the foot of the entrance steps, and the engine softly purrs to life.

"How many funerals did you coordinate today?" I ask as we slip onto the busy Manhattan streets.

Dom laughs. "I'm not a funeral director."

"Then you're attending a wedding?" I offer.

Dom's head shakes in amusement, his eyes on the road. "No, smartass, I'm the head of security for Vlad's building. I was in meetings this morning."

"How fancy," I muse, fiddling with the radio functions of the car. I find a station with classical music and sit back in the soft leather seat, needing to calm my frazzled thoughts.

The sunset is a beautiful sight in New York. The last of the rays bounce off the walls of glass on high-rises and glitter through the trees lining parks and streets. As the breeze changes from warm to cool and the streetlamps glow to life, you can almost feel the supernatural world shift.

Werewolves rule over the sunlight hours, but vampires own the night sky. The Fae have a whole different realm they dominate.

"Which High Alpha do you serve?" Dom suddenly asks, pulling me out of my thoughts.

My heart gallops, panic seizing the muscle, my breath frozen in my lungs. I push the feeling down, locking up the images of my father threatening to break through, as I turn to Dom. "None of them."

"What?" Dom frowns, his eyes flicking to mine then returning to the road.

"I'm a Lone wolf."

"You're kidding."

I understand his confusion. Now that I'm enveloped in his honeycomb and teak scent, I can pick up the slightest notes of copper, indicating that he once served under the High Alpha Lárus Izar of the Lárusson pack. If I didn't have my amulet, he'd be able to smell the gold in my scent; if I went through with my mating ceremony, he'd smell silver for the Daygrsson pack.

I swallow. "The night I was turned, I was abandoned and never claimed."

"Who would abandon someone through their change?" he asks listlessly, eyes still on the road.

"He thought I died." The lies roll off my tongue so easily that the guilt twists in my gut.

We are both silent for the rest of the car ride. As the sun is about to dip out of view, we stop in front of a townhouse in Brooklyn. Climbing out of the car, I stretch and follow Dom to a gorgeous chocolate brown townhouse with two doors. He knocks on the one to the left.

Allura opens the door. Her bronze skin glows, and her wings vibrate as she ushers us in.

We step into a large apartment. The entire first floor is open with the living room at the front, the kitchen at the end, and a dining area sitting to the kitchen's right. A narrow staircase with a black railing is opposite the front door.

Allura leads us all the way into the black and white kitchen. The entire back wall is glass, which shows a small patio and a lovely small green garden beyond.

Dom and I take a seat at the breakfast bar as Allura floats around the kitchen, placing a kettle on the stove and pulling out mugs.

She turns to Dom. "Coffee?" He nods. She turns her attention to me, and her smile almost splits her face. "Coffee or tea?"

"Tea, please."

She claps her hands together once and swivels on a heel, getting to work on our beverages. Within a few minutes, a steaming cup of tea is in front of me. Allura also puts a small pourer of creamer, sugar cubes, and a plate of cookies on the island bench. They smell freshly baked.

I take in the other scents around me: wild jasmine and sweet orange blankets the whole place. Dom's teakwood and honeycomb swirls around as he's sitting next to me, but there's another scent lurking in the background.

"Fresh snow," I murmur, stirring creamer into my mug, "Marin, I'm presuming?"

Allura's eyes widen slightly. "Your nose is pretty powerful."

I shrug, adding a sugar cube into my tea, continuing to stir. "Did she live here?"

Allura nods. "Did you want to see her room?"

"If you don't mind. I just want to get a better read on her scent."

"While you're snooping," Dom pipes in, "Vlad wants you to give something to Aster to wear tonight."

I eat two cookies and drink half my tea before Allura drags me up the stairs. We come to a landing that runs parallel to the stairs with three doors, one on each end and one halfway down the short landing.

"This is my room," Allura points to the door in front of the stairs. "Marin's was the one at the front of the house."

Allura hesitates to open Marin's door, taking a deep breath and then twists the knob. Marin's scent washes over me as the door swings silently open.

Her scent reminds me of fresh, crisp winter snow on a clear, sunny morning. Her room is neat apart from the large, unmade bed in the middle of the room. The desk to the right of the door has books scattered across it, and the door to her wardrobe is open.

"As a Winter Fae," I muse, walking towards the bay window at the opposite end of the room. "I didn't expect her to like indoor plants so much."

Varieties of vines, flowers and succulents fill the windowsill, and the small table sitting between the window and the armchair facing it.

Allura giggles. "That's my influence. This room gets the best light."

I smile as I commit Marin's scent to memory, and then follow Allura out of the room and into hers. A large white bed sits in the middle of her room; the large window on the far wall overseeing the garden below also has indoor plants filling the windowsill. Allura shuffles over to the walk-in closet to the left of the room.

I take a slow breath, feeling relaxed for the first time in a long time as I drift over to the window. Exhaustion washes over me. I'd only just gotten out of bed yesterday afternoon after my brutal full moon turn.

My whole body ached for days after all my bones broke and realigned, organs were rearranged, and snow-white fur pierced through my burning hot skin. But my mind didn't fracture, I didn't die, and I wasn't discovered by other wolves.

Sidelle's shady fae friend gave me a barrier spell which Sid and I set up in her basement that blocked my wolf energy from everyone else. However, it didn't save the basement floor as the force of my turn cracked the cement and broke a few glass jars on the shelves.

Being on the run is also ridiculously tiring. All I want to do is curl up in a bed and sleep for an eternity.

A soft touch on my shoulder makes me turn. Allura's eyes narrow slightly in concern. "Are you okay, honey?"

I nod. "Just extremely tired."

She pulls me towards the bed. A blush-colored dress and white pumps are laid out with a few necklace and earring choices. "This color will look amazing with your skin. What underwear are you wearing?" Allura asks.

"A sports bra."

Allura snickers. "That is *not* going to work for this dress." She goes to a bedside dresser and pulls out a white bra and pantie set. "I hope these fit you," she says as she hands them to me.

I stand there for a moment, running my fingers over the delicate fabric.

I look up at Allura's amused face. "They're clean, I promise."

I smirk. Allura passes me the dress and heels and ushers me out of the room. "Bathroom is the door in the middle of the hall."

"Do you have a spare razor?" I ask. I should have expected to wear a dress and shaved my legs last night; it's been a while since I've had to bother.

Allura smiles. "There's some under the sink in the bathroom."

I take the items to the all white bathroom. I find what I need and make quick work of shaving my legs before slipping on the lingerie. The soft fabric clings to my hips and butt, riding up so far that it's basically a thong. Trying to secure my breasts is laughable, but after a few adjustments, I manage to contain them before pulling on the dress.

"Damn," I mumble as I peer into the mirror. I collect my clothes, slip on the heels and leave the bathroom. I knock on Allura's door before opening it slowly. She is wearing a simple pair of faded jeans and a hooded zip jacket.

"This dress is going to get me into trouble," I murmur.

Allura turns, and her mouth falls open. Her wings are very still.

"Does it look okay?" I whisper.

"You look *incredible*."

I look down at the low-neckline and heaving boobs. "You don't think this neckline is too low?"

Allura almost doubles over in laughter. "We're going to a *strip* club, remember? You'll be wearing more clothes than most people." She checks her watch. "We better go."

I pull on my denim jacket, Allura hands me a bag to carry my other clothes before reaching up to pull my hair from its bun and comb her hands through my curls gently, making a satisfied sound in the back of her throat.

As she pulls me out of the room, her eyes roll back, and she staggers.

I steady her before she falls. "Are you okay?"

She takes a water bottle out of her bag and takes a few sips. "Yeah, I'm fine. I just have to remember not to move so fast."

"Do you have fae diabetes or something? Do you need a cookie before we go?"

Allura laughs. "No, honey, I'm excellent."

She pulls me upstairs, where Dom is leaning against the front door looking down at his phone.

Dom lifts his head as he hears us and straightens, eyes wide, and speechless as he takes in my outfit.

I smirk, leaning closer to Allura. "I told you. Trouble."

Allura scoffs. "I can't wait. Let's go. I'll do your makeup in the car."

8

Vladislav

Vladislav's Penthouse

A MESSAGE FROM DOM flashes on my phone.

We're on our way back.

I get up from the armchair in my home office and head for my bedroom. The scent of onions caramelizing in butter distracts me, so I divert to the kitchen to find Delia pouring a small mountain of vibrant red paprika into her hand. I lean up against a nearby cupboard, peering into the pot, curious.

"Is that chicken paprikash?" I ask. She insists I eat a full meal at least once a day, even though she knows I don't need food to actually survive.

Her lips curve up. "A recipe my mother taught me."

"I thought you were Greek?" I ask, crossing my arms.

Her eyes flick to me before returning to the caramelizing onions. "My father was Greek, but my mother was Hungarian."

I stand there for a few moments before Delia asks, "Did I hear correctly from Dominic that we have a new addition to the family?"

Aster.

Her jade green eyes haunt my dreams, and she stirs up feelings of desire that I shouldn't have. I *want* her. She has this magnetism that I find enthralling.

"We have a new employee, yes," I answer, turning to the fridge and taking out a blood bag, distracting myself. "Her name is Aster."

"Aster, what a lovely name," Delia muses as she adds pieces of chicken into the pot and starts stirring them with her wooden spoon.

"She's going to help us find Marin."

Delia's emotions dim into worry. "I hope she's okay."

"We have to hope that she is." I pour the blood into a tumbler and take a swig. I'm still furious that there's someone who thinks they can take *my* people from under my nose, and get away with it. They have no idea what kind of suffering coming for them.

"I'm going home for a few hours, after this is finished, then I'll be back after you finish work," Delia says as she adds more ingredients into her pot, and puts a lid on it.

"I don't expect you back."

She pins me a stern look. "Well, I will be."

I shake my head, downing the rest of my drink and then head for my wardrobe. I walk into the large room and pick out a crimson red shirt and dark gray suit, place black cufflinks on, fasten on a watch, and slip into black leather shoes. I run my hands through my hair a few times and before leaving the apartment.

My phone buzzes in my pocket, *'Renard'* flashes on the screen. "Yes?"

Ren sounds out of breath. "Where are you?"

"Heading down to Immortal. Why?"

"I'll be in your office," Ren says and then hangs up.

I frown, pocketing the phone and enter the elevator, descending the eighty floors to Immortal. I find Ren lounging in one of the seats in front of my desk.

"Tell me," I demand as I sit in my chair.

Ren's eyes flicker green as he runs a hand through his hair. "She's holding Trials."

He's talking about Medea. "In person?"

Ren nods.

"Where?" I ask.

"She just left Chicago."

"What was the damage?"

He sighs, his emotions roiling in annoyance. "She took out about a dozen members of the Chicago Nest."

"For what crimes?"

His eyes simmer emerald green. "From what I've heard, absolute nonsense. Four Lilim-made were executed for treason, but no justification. Three Adam-made executed for looking at her in the eye. The list is ridiculous."

I'm speechless for a moment. Trials are usually held at Court by the Council, which is made up of the Queen's three Advisors, the three Elders and a rotation of three random Court members. It's our species' democratic way of dealing out punishment to avoid tyranny. Trials are never held by the Queen herself.

"Where is she now?" I ask.

"No one knows," Ren bites out.

"You're telling me that no one knows where the fucking *Queen* is right now?"

Ren stands and starts to pace. "She's completely off the radar. Her sister doesn't even know. Apparently they returned to Court after Chicago, and now Medea is in the wind."

Irena, Medea's sister, never leaves her side. If she doesn't know the whereabouts of Medea then the whole species is fucked.

"Is Mydas at Court now?" I ask.

Ren stops pacing, frustration pulsing off him as he grasps the back of a chair. "He's off the fucking grid too. All I know is that he's still in New York. I'll keep trying to contact him."

The sound of laughter drifts down the hall as dancers enter from the back door. I stand from my desk, buttoning up my jacket. "Send Dom to track him if you have to, but we need Mydas in Court to work out what the fuck is going on."

Ren nods, pulling out his phone.

"Ren," I say, my brother lifting his gaze to mine, "find out where she's gone."

I nod greetings to the dancers as I walk down the hall and head straight for the bar.

Maddox refills the bar fridge as he asks Viktoria, "What do you *really* think of Aster?"

Viktoria crosses her arms over her chest. "Why would I have any opinions about that mutt at all?"

"She must be allergic to dogs." Aster's smoky voice makes me turn and I still.

She stands in the doorway next to Dom. The dress she is wearing is like a second skin, gliding over her hips, the short length accentuating her long legs. Her hair is down, flowing over her denim covered shoulders, the lights of the club glinting off the shiny curls.

Her scent of amber rum and milk wraps around me and I fight the urge to roll my eyes closed.

Sweet mercy, she's going to be the ruin of me.

9

Nova

Immortal

MY WHOLE BODY FEELS like it's on fire.

Vladislav's eyes are darkening to bourbon, his eyes *devouring* me from head to toe as I walk over to him. He suddenly remembers how to breathe and composes himself, his eyes return to their usual dazzling amber and his face back to its confident businessman facade.

I take a seat next to him at the bar and turn to the two staff behind it who I recognize from Sanctuary last night. Scents of watermelon and caramel mix in with peaches and smoke, overwhelming my nose. It's going to take some getting used to being around so many vampire scents.

"I'm Aster," I say with a small wave.

The female vampire is stunning. Her eyes are a striking blue-gray, surrounded by long black lashes, and her black brows are arched to perfection. Her face is smooth, porcelain white, but the scowl she has across her face seems to be permanent. Her glossy black hair is braided into a long, thick rope resting over one shoulder.

She's about the same height as me, but a lot more curvaceous. She knows exactly what she's doing by wearing a tight black top that dips scandalously low and accentuates her ample chest. The top disappears into high-waisted, skin-tight leather pants that hug her round hips and thick thighs, the cut of the pants creating a sensuous curve to her soft middle.

The male vampire next to her is equally beautiful. He's lithe and much taller than the female, with honey blonde hair fashioned into a smooth, high bun, and his multiple ear piercings sparkle in the club's lights. The long, black silk slip dress he's rocking is cinched at the waist by a thick belt with an ornate buckle, the thin straps showing off his golden, well-defined tattooed arms and shoulders.

His warm, espresso-brown eyes glint as he smiles. "I'm Maddox, and this grumpy bitch is Vik."

"Nice to meet you," I say as Vik rolls her eyes and struts away, disappearing into a door at the end of the bar.

Vladislav shakes his head, his gaze turning to me. "Apologies. She's like this with new people."

Maddox snorts. "She's like that with *me* most of the time, and I've known her for sixty years."

I smile. "It's fine, I don't expect us to be friends, just hopefully civil."

Maddox chuckles. "Good luck, girl, you'll need it."

I like him. I turn my head back to Vladislav. "What am I doing tonight?"

"You will work the bar with Viktoria and Maddox."

"Hell fucking no," Vik barks, reappearing in front of us with a box of bottled beers.

They stare at each other for a few moments, then Vladislav closes his eyes and sighs. "Fine. You can serve drinks. Can I convince you into lingerie today?"

I scoff. "I'm basically naked already." I stand up and take off my denim jacket. I feel every pair of eyes on me. My attention flicks to Vladislav. His eyes are darkening again, and I'm pretty sure I saw his fingers twitch on his thigh.

He stands; I suddenly feel short, even in heels, as he towers over me.

Without taking his eyes off me, he instructs Vik to show me what to do and then glides off towards the 'Staff Only' door with Dom following behind him.

I turn to Vik, staring at me with her arms crossed over her chest. "Follow me," she instructs as she struts down the bar.

I hurry after her and through the door she escaped into earlier, which turns out to be a storage area. The small gray room has rows of shelves against two walls and lockers on the far wall. Cases of beer and wine are piled in the middle of the room near a small table with four chairs around it.

"Put your shit in the locker at the end," Vik instructs as she picks up a case of wine and storms out.

I approach the last locker on the left, finding it empty, and place my jacket in it, glancing at myself in the mirror on the inside of the locker door.

Soft music starts on the main floor, and I can hear two males laughing and heading towards me. As I close the locker door, two vampires I also recognize from last night walk in. They both stop talking momentarily as they spot me, then appear on either side of me. Fast bastards.

Blue Eyes, who was with Vladislav the night I saved Allura, grabs my hand and kisses the top of it. "I'm Renard Vladislav. We met last night."

I pull my hand away. "A relative of the other Vladislav, I presume?"

"His better-looking brother." Renard smiles and places a hand against the lockers, trapping me between him and his buddy. Renard's scent reminds me of a bonfire and s'mores, overly roasted marshmallows and rich dark chocolate with a hint of smoke. His friend's scent is sugared almonds.

"Nice to meet you. I'm Aster," I say with a smile. I try to step around him, but Renard leans in closer.

He inhales and his head tilts slightly. "Why don't you smell like other werewolves?"

I shrug. "Perfume?"

His buddy chuckles, but Renard isn't amused as his eyes roam my body and then back up to my face. Renard looks almost exactly like Vlad, maybe ten years older and a little taller.

"I have to go," I say as I stand straighter.

"Tell me more about you," Renard croons, "like why I can't read your mind?"

I step closer to the towering vampire and whisper against his lips, "I guess that's a secret you'll never know." I wink as I use my werewolf agility to dip under Renard's arm quickly and saunter away.

I walk out of the storeroom into a sensual oasis. Soft blue and purple lights reflect off the black velvet sofas and armchairs, the main stage and platforms are the floor's focus, and music drifts through the space, adding to the erotic ambiance.

I stand by the bar entrance; if I go any further, Vik will probably maim me.

She walks over with a martini in her hand and sighs. "All our patrons are old, powerful, and bitter. They don't come to the bar; you go to them. We will tell you who is who. What drink goes where. If you fuck up, I'll inflict permanent damage." She takes a mouthful of her martini without looking away.

I just nod in response. She turns from me, places a drinks tray on the bar, and then makes an assortment of beverages.

Vladislav enters from the staff door and glides toward me. He has the grace of a predator, and interestingly, I don't find it as unnerving as I should.

He leans against the bar beside me, a tumbler with dark amber liquid being offered to him by Maddox. He takes the drink as his eyes look past me. I feel Renard and his friend behind me, so I turn and smile.

Renard looks down at me. "You should really have her on the stage, Xander."

A laugh rumbles out of Vladislav's chest behind me, but he says nothing.

"I have stage fright," I state, narrowing my eyes at Renard.

Renard's smile deepens. "Lap dances, then?"

I step into him, placing my hand on his chest, looking up throw my lashes with a coy smile. "In your dreams."

Renard's buddy chuckles, clapping him on the shoulder. "If you're not careful, Aster, you'll end up the next Mrs. Vladislav."

I step back with a smirk. "I think I'm suddenly exclusively into women."

Renard's buddy chuckles as he walks over to the purple curtains near the other end of the bar. Renard says nothing else as he disappears up the stairs to the front entrance.

I turn back to Vladislav. How is it possible in the dim light that his amber eyes are so vibrant? He takes a step closer to me, and I suck in a tight breath. "My patrons are some of vampire's elite. They think they're entitled to whatever they want. Immortal has rules, but I can tell you now that some of them will want you and may get a little, let's say, over-indulgent."

I clear my throat. "Don't throw punches. Got it."

Vlad nods curtly as he turns and walks over to the base of the stairs. I could watch this man all day and never tire of the view. I wonder what he looks like naked?

I force my focus back to the bar, my cheeks burning. Maddox places drinks on the tray next to me as Vik is on the other side of the bar, poking away at a cashier screen. As patrons filter in, Maddox points out every vampire by name and instructs me on which drinks to give to them.

I pick up the loaded tray. "What do I say when I give them their drinks?"

"Introduce yourself, place their drinks down and tell them to enjoy the show. Don't worry, you'll be fine."

I blow out a breath and walk over to the seated males. Let's hope I don't make a fool of myself in these heels. I plant a smile on my face and stand by the small table in front of them. Eyes roam my body as I say, "Good evening, gentlemen, I'm Aster, your server for tonight."

I place their drinks down quickly without spilling any. "I hope you enjoy your evening."

Before I can leave, one of the vampires, whose name I've already forgotten, catches my wrist, stopping me in my tracks. I look down at his pale face.

"You are not human or fae," he states in a thick Russian accent.

I swallow. The power radiating off him hits me like a tsunami. "No, I'm not, sir."

His pungent aroma of candied ginger turns my stomach as his grip on my wrist tightens, and ice penetrates my bones under his grasp.

His eyes don't leave mine as he calls for Vladislav. I can't look away from his intense gaze, but I feel Vladislav materialize next to me. "Yes?"

The vampire's eyes flick to Vladislav, and the pressure of his power completely disperses around me, even though he is still holding onto my wrist.

They exchange words in Russian, the vampire next to them chiming in as well. Vladislav places his hand around my forearm, his grip surprisingly warm, and tugs slightly, making the vampire finally release my wrist.

Vladislav says something in a tone that sounds like he shouldn't be questioned, and then the patron turns and collects his drink. Vladislav places a hand on the small of my back; the contact tingles on my skin as he guides me back to the bar.

"Sorry about that," Vladislav whispers into my ear.

I tuck the tray under my arm as I rub my wrist, trying to eliminate the icy feeling embedded in my skin. "He didn't like that I was a wolf, I'm guessing?"

His sigh is answer enough. "I'll keep them in check."

I nod as we reach the bar. When he removes his hand, my skin is still on fire from his touch.

I place the tray back down on the bar as Maddox approaches me with curious amusement on his face. "What was that about?"

"They don't approve of my species."

Maddox rolls his eyes, then fills up my tray again and directs me to where they need to go. I walk over and introduce myself, place their drinks down, and walk away, but not before another patron places a hand on my bare thigh, trying to get under my dress. I stop his exploration quickly and walk away as fast as I can.

I make a few more rounds of delivering drinks. Every time, someone places their hands on me, and every time I fight the urge to shove my heels into their crotch. I return to the bar, breathing heavily and ready to throw the tray at someone.

Maddox walks over with one drink in his hand and places it down on my tray. "Not going so well, huh?"

I shake my head, knowing if I say something, I might lose it.

The air shifts as blueberries and frankincense rolls around me. A vampire slides up next to me at the bar in a simple gray suit and white shirt. "And *who* are you?"

I give him a small smile. "Good evening, I'm Aster."

His hickory-brown eyes roam over me as he flashes me a wide grin. "You're perfect," he sighs.

"Mydas," Vladislav's low, curt tone pulls our attention to him as he steps up to the bar. "Where have you been?"

The new arrival, Mydas, directs his grin to Vladislav next to him. "Good evening to you too, Vlad."

Vladislav's eyes narrow slightly, before sweeping his hand towards the purple curtains at the other end of the bar. "Shall we take this to somewhere more private?"

Mydas nods, turning back to me. "Only if you join us, Aster." He says my name like it's a new ice cream flavor he's tasting. I try not to cringe; this guy is too *much.*

I turn to Vladislav, his gaze hard on Mydas. His intense gaze flicks to mine and he nods once before walking towards Renard's friend from before, Carlos, at the curtains.

"I'll bring drinks," I announce to Mydas, hoping he takes that as a clue to leave. His attention is unsettling. I don't like him.

"Bring one for yourself too," he croons with a wink as he follows Vladislav.

10

Vladislav

Immortal

I WALK MYDAS DOWN the short hallway into the last of the three alcoves of the private area. We step through the black curtains into an intimate space with three burgundy sofas against each wall and a small stage in the center with a silver pole gleaming in the soft light above.

"Where were you hiding that glorious ass?" Mydas asks as he sinks into the furthest sofa, his wanton lust almost chokes me.

Possession creeps up out of nowhere and then goes in the next breath. "The Sanctuary," I answer, clearing my throat slightly, "I owed Sid a favor, so I gave Aster a job."

"I've never seen such a perfect specimen," Mydas sighs.

"The rules of this establishment still apply to you, Mydas," I warn, my tone a little harsh, even to my ears.

Mydas lifts a brow speculatively, and he chuckles. "You're no fun, Vlad."

Aster's clicking heels sound in the hall and she pushes through the curtains with a tray with three drinks. Her hips sway in a slow, sensual way as she approaches. I don't think she realizes how her presence captures a room.

Aster's smile doesn't reach her eyes as she passes Mydas a tumbler filled with what smells like whiskey. Mydas takes the glass, making sure to cover her hand with his, and I watch her stiffen a fraction, sliding her hand away just a touch too quickly.

She turns to me and her eyes soften slightly as she passes me another tumbler of whiskey. I avoid touching her as I accept the drink and murmur my thanks.

"Please," Mydas purrs, patting the sofa next to him, "join me."

She picks up her own drink, which smells of just soda and lime and perches on the small stage in front of us. Mydas sinks back, sipping on his drink, watching Aster.

His attention on her is pissing me off. The need to step between both of them makes my muscles stiffen. I clear my throat, trying to focus on the current discussion we need to have.

"Where have you been, Mydas?" I ask, drawing his attention.

He shrugs. "I was doing Nest business for the boss man, why?"

His emotions are too sedate for that to be the truth, but I drop it for now. "Do you know anything about the Queen's location right now?"

Mydas sips on his drink, his attention waning back to Aster. "Where are you from?"

Aster's shoulders rise in a shrug. "Here and there."

Mydas' lips curve slightly. "No Pack?"

"Nope."

"Mydas," I chastise.

He sighs, his eyes returning me. "No word of the Queen, she's in the wind."

"You need to go to Court, see what you can find."

He rolls his eyes, finishing his drink in one mouthful. "Yeah, yeah. I've already been told to go. I'm leaving tomorrow night."

I loosen my shoulders, if anyone is going to get answers, it'll be him. I flick my eyes over to Aster. Her gaze is curious, flicking between Mydas and I, swirling the straw in her drink between two fingers.

"How do you two know each other?" she asks Mydas.

Mydas leans toward her slightly. "Well, we're brothers."

Aster raises a brow at me. "*Another* brother?"

"Mydas is a brother in vampire terms, not by human terms."

"But Renard is your human brother?"

I nod.

Aster closes her soft pink lips around the straw, drawing some of her drink into her mouth. I watch her throat work as she shallows and heat curls down my spine. I pull my attention away from her, trying to ignore the desire pulsing off of Mydas as I stand.

"Are you staying for the evening?" I ask Mydas.

He nods, eyes fixated on Aster. "I think I might. Send Marin."

Aster blinks, brows creasing slightly. "Marin's gone."

Mydas' head whips to mine, shock fizzling out his desire. "What?"

"She went missing five days ago," I inform him. His shock swirls into confusion and anger.

"What do you mean *missing*?" he asks.

"We're looking into it," I say, holding my hand out for Aster, "could you please get Mydas another drink?"

Aster takes my offered hand, stands, and places her half finished drink on her tray before picking it up. She turns and accepts Mydas' empty glass. "Nice to meet you, Mydas."

As she walks out I turn back to Mydas. "When did you see her last?"

"Here, a week ago," Mydas says, pulling out his phone. "How is she missing?"

"She never came back after her trip to Faery. Hopefully, she'll show up soon."

Mydas nods absentmindedly at his phone. "I'll see if any of my contacts have heard whispers about her."

"I appreciate it."

Mydas taps away at his phone for a few more seconds and then pockets his phone. His emotions turn dramatically as mischief and desire pour from him.

"Are you sure Aster is off-limits?" Mydas asks.

"Yes," I state, pulling out my phone. "If you'll excuse me, I have some business to attend to. I'll send someone to you."

I turn and walk out of the alcove before I start a brawl. I stop to briefly speak to one of the faeries before making my way directly to my office. I have the overwhelming desire to take my anger out on my desk again, but I resist and take a seat.

I close my eyes and concentrate on calming myself. Ren has always been the hot-headed Vladislav, but it seems like my fuse is almost nonexistent these days.

Aster is my trigger lately. She seems to bring out many long-buried emotions, and I don't like it.

A soft knock comes from the door; I lift my gaze to find Aster leaning against the door frame with a drink in her hand. She walks in and places the glass in front of me. Her rum and milk scent wraps around me, stirring up a growl deep in my chest. I swallow it down as she turns on her heels, heading back for the door.

"You're not much of a talker, are you?" I ask, stopping her in the doorway.

She turns with an amused expression. "I actually talk too much. It gets me in trouble most of the time, and I don't want to be fired my first day."

I smile and gesture for her to sit down. As she sinks into the armchair in front of the desk, I can't help but watch her body move languidly. She's a work of art, and I'm sure she doesn't realize it.

Aster looks neutral as she sits in a chair in front of my desk, but her heartbeat has hitched and she's breathing a little too shallowly. Reading someone's emotions the old-fashioned way is quite tedious.

I study her, and once again I'm mesmerized. Those bright, deep-set eyes pick up every detail, always assessing, even as she has a soft smile on her face. Those lips, full but small and pouty with a deep cupid's bow; I'd love to know what they taste like.

I pull myself from those thoughts. She's a wolf, she'd have no interest in a vampire. And she's an employee, here to do an important task.

"Where are you really from?" The question escapes my lips.

Her smile deepens, tucking her hands under her thighs. "The East coast."

"With that accent you're trying to hide, I'd say more south," I challenge.

She sits further back into her seat, lifting one shoulder. "Do you *need* to know where I'm from?"

"I do a background check on all my employees, and the name 'Aster Wilford' doesn't exist."

Her heart starts to race as her spine goes straight, ready to spring out of her chair and run.

I hold my hands out. "No one else knows. Sid told me not to ask too many questions, but I would appreciate a little background information on someone who's going to be around people import to me."

She takes a shaky breath, pushing her hair off her shoulders, relaxing slightly into her seat. "Fine, I'm from the South. I ran from Pack. All I want to do is start over in peace where no one knows me."

I brush my bottom lip with the tip of my finger, brows slightly furrowed. "Why did you run?"

"I ran from an abusive mate."

Anger springs to life in my chest. Who would even think about harming her? Before I demand more information in order to find this wolf and skin him alive, I open up my laptop to a new personnel file.

"So, Aster Wilford. Age?" I ask.

"Twenty-three."

"So young," I muse.

"For someone over three-hundred years old, maybe."

I smirk. "That's a pretty accurate guess."

She crosses her arms under her breasts, pushing them higher, and the image of my teeth marking her pretty skin floods my brain.

"Social security number?" I ask, my voice hoarse.

"I don't have one of those."

"How do you *not* have one?"

"I probably do, but I can't give it to you."

My eyes narrow in confusion. "Why not?"

"I was never given access to that information." A sardonic laugh escapes past her white teeth. "I've never seen my birth certificate either. I don't have a driver's license or a passport, either."

Absolutely no form of identification. Probably a way for her Pack to keep her from leaving. Those pricks have it coming for them.

I blow out a breath. "I'll keep your employment off my books and pay you through my personal accounts, so there's no trail linked to the company accounts."

"It probably comes to no surprise when I tell you that I don't have a bank account, either."

"I thought as much." I tap away for a few more seconds, then close the laptop and stand, fish my wallet out of the inner breast pocket of my jacket. I pull out a black bank card and walk around the desk, offering it to her. "I'll deposit your pay into this account. The code is temporarily your birth year. You'll need to go to the bank and change it tomorrow."

She stands, taking the card. "Thank you."

I look down into her pointed face; we're standing only a foot away. This close, I can see that there's a halo of the palest green around her pupils, and the smallest fleck of golden brown at the edge of her right iris. These are eyes I could fall into, and never want to leave.

"You're welcome," I say. "There's a deposit in there for you to go with Lu tomorrow to purchase clothing. Think of it as a uniform." Our eye contact doesn't break as she nods once.

The world dims around her. Something deep inside of me begs me to step closer, to touch her. It's an unsettled feeling deep in my gut, a burning ember of unease. It's nothing I've ever felt before, but it feels oddly comforting. I involuntarily take a step forward, closing the distance. The embers flare, spreading warmth into my chest as the unsettled feeling stirs again.

Aster's eyes darken and flash gold, before she gasps and blinks a few times. I loosen a breath as the world returns to my vision.

"What the fuck was that?" Aster breathes as she takes a step back.

I blink, my breathing uneasy. "You felt that too?"

"Was that you doing some weird vampire hypnotism?"

"No, I can't compel people. That was something completely different." I feel my fangs have lengthened in my mouth, and my body is straining in my suit.

"Wait, vampires can actually compel people?"

I smile, Aster's comment releasing the tension in my body and my fangs retract. "Some vampires are gifted. Some with compulsion, some with other gifts."

"Do you have a gift?"

"I do."

She's about to ask more questions as one of my male dancers taps on the door and announces that I'm needed in the club. We walk together down the hallway, Aster's focus on the card in her hand.

"Mr. L. A. Vladislav. What do the initials stand for?" she asks.

I smirk. "That's something you're going to have to work out for yourself."

The last couple of hours go by without another incident, the patrons too busy ogling the dancers to bother Aster again. She splits her healthy amount of tips with Vik and Maddox, shocking the both of them.

As the dancers go home, I invite everyone up to the Penthouse for after-work drinks, Dom and Vik are the only ones to refuse.

Carlos chuckles as they turn to leave. "Come back in one piece, you two."

Vik flips him off as Dom smirks, slapping her on the ass and then both escape up the entrance stairs. Ren locks up then takes a full bottle of bourbon from the bar as Aster appears from the storage room, sporting her denim jacket and carrying a backpack.

We make our way to the elevator and Allura pops out of her dressing room, linking arms with Aster, looking tired and paler than usual. She told me last week that her pregnancy symptoms were starting to take their toll on her.

We all load into the elevator; Maddox, Carlos, and Ren argue in Russian about some sports game, while I try not to breathe. Aster's scent is everywhere, and I'm salivating. I need to pull myself together.

Employee, she's an employee, think of the legal repercussions. Think of anything but burying my hands into her thick hair and devouring her lips against the elevator walls.

Her eyes widen suddenly, and she breathes, "Oh."

Her eyes flick to Allura's stomach and then return to Allura's face. The faerie smiles and nods slightly, squeezing Aster's arm a little tighter. She's worked out the pregnancy.

The elevator opens and as we file out, I lean closer to Aster. "How did you know?"

She taps her nose twice. She can smell it?

"I can't detect a change," I murmur.

Her eyes swim with humor. "Vampires got the ears in the divorce; wolves got the nose."

11

Nova

ALLURA LAUGHS AT MY response as we walk toward the French doors in the hall. Vladislav keys in a code to the lock and opens the doors into heaven, or at least what I think it would look like.

The floors are rich timber, and the walls are a light tan. Allura leads me around a large glass table in the foyer and into a beautiful living area. I wander over to the wall of windows on my left, stopping in front of the low bench seat that runs almost the entire length of the glass.

The view from this high is incredible. The jungle of steel, windows, and lights of the city embrace the calm slumber of Central Park below.

I turn on my heel; everything in this space is warm, from the timber flooring to the large beige sofas and dim lighting. The place would look spectacular in the daylight.

I turn to the wall covered entirely in books; the only interruption in the shelves is a flat screen mounted to the wall and an opening by the windows leading to another part of the apartment. I brush my fingers over the spines of the books as I follow them to the other side of the vast room, past a partition wall separating two spaces.

Books cover the partition wall on the living room side, and the other side has an extensive buffet and a large, exquisite painting. A long concrete dining table dominates the room's center, with twelve emerald-colored velvet seats around it. Another wall of windows completes the space.

Walking around the table, I pass through an open sliding door into a large breakfast area and kitchen.

An oak bar lies flush against the window to my left, showcasing the sprawling city beyond, with two barstools tucked underneath that match the velvet of the dining chairs. Renard, Carlos, and Maddox are sprawled around the glass table occupying the room's center.

Vladislav, Allura, and a dark-haired woman converse in the kitchen. It's a white and timber dream with white marble bench tops and stainless-steel appliances. There was a ridiculous amount of money spent on this kitchen for a vampire's lair. I cross over to the island and take a seat on a barstool.

The woman turns to me, gray-hazel eyes bright. Her heartbeat is steady, and her soft vanilla scent tells me she's human. "You must be Aster. I'm Delia, or *yia-yia*, whichever you prefer."

I smile. "It's lovely to meet you, Delia."

"Are you hungry?" she asks.

"I'm starving, actually."

She gives Vladislav a stern look. "These vampires forget that some people have to eat regularly. I'll gather you a plate."

I make eye contact with Vladislav. He rolls his eyes as he walks over to the boys at the table. The tang of blood mixes with the smoky scent of bourbon as my eyes land on the tumblers they've been drinking from.

It feels like I shouldn't be here watching this. I turn back to Allura and Delia, who are both busy making something that smells so incredible it masks all the other scents in the room instantly.

I'm going to have to train my nose to be around this many vampires—I thought I was getting used to it at Sanctuary, but all the vampires that work or frequent Immortal are *much* older than the ones passing through Sanctuary.

This is still better than what my life should have been by now. A shudder runs down my spine at the thought.

A cold arm draping over my shoulders interrupts my reverie. My breath hitches. Not Viggo. Not my father. I ease a breath out of my tight lungs as Renard presses his body to my side. "Are you cold, babe?"

I angle my head toward him. "If I was, you'd be making it a lot worse."

He tips his head back and laughs. It vibrates through his body and I fight the urge to recoil as he pulls me closer. I'm not trapped. I could get out of this place if I needed to.

When his gaze locks back onto mine, I notice his eyes are glassy. Is he drunk?

"Why can't I read your mind?" he asks.

"Your gifts obviously don't work as well as you think."

"Bullshit," Renard slurs slightly, "I can hear everyone's minds in this room right now *except* yours. So I want to know how you're blocking me."

"I don't have an answer for you."

Vladislav appears behind Renard and places a hand on his shoulder. "Give it a rest, Ren."

"No, Xander, I want to know how this little minx is keeping her secrets from me." Ren glares at me for a few more seconds and stumbles off with a frustrated growl.

Vladislav slides onto the stool beside me. "Please excuse my brother. He can't handle his liquor."

"How do you get drunk if liquor doesn't affect you? It's takes me a lethal amount to even get tipsy."

Vladislav lifts his tumbler towards my nose and swirls the dark liquid. At first, the metallic tang of blood filters up to me, then a sharp burn abuses the back of my throat. "This is frat boy blood. Our procurers compel drunk college kids to donate blood."

Delia slides a massive plate of food in front of me as I'm ask a slew of questions.

"It's chicken paprikash," she announces with a satisfied grin as she places a much, *much* smaller version of my plate in front of Vladislav. Allura comes around and takes a seat next to me with a small bowl of cereal and cut up apples.

I wait until Vladislav and Allura take a bite of their food before I dig in. "Gods, this is the best thing I've ever eaten in my life."

Delia's eyes sparkle as she places the pot full of extra greens and rice in front of me before disappearing into the hallway.

"I didn't know vampires could eat food," I comment between bites, trying not to inhale all of it at once.

"It's luck of the draw if you retain the ability after the change," Vladislav answers after a swig of his drink. "I like to eat human food more for enjoyment than necessity. It tastes a lot better than blood bags."

"You never go for a fresh kill?" I ask. Allura chuckles next to me.

"You ask a lot of personal questions," he chides.

"I told you my mouth gets me into trouble."

His eyes lower to the treacherous body part.

I see something like lust flicker before he averts his gaze back to his plate. We sit in a comfortable silence as we finish our meals. The men behind us are in the midst of a lively conversation in a language I don't understand. Actually, it sounds like *three* languages. As I rise to collect the plates, Delia reappears, shooing me away as she cleans up with Allura.

"What's the time?" Allura asks as she stacks the dishwasher.

"It's about forty minutes to dawn," Vladislav announces.

"Are you cool if Aster and I stay here?" she asks Vladislav. "Dom is preoccupied."

"I can walk back to Sanctuary," I announce.

"No need." Vladislav stands. "There's three guest rooms here."

My heart stammers. I haven't spent a night away from Sanctuary since I arrived in New York. I'm about to protest, but Allura claps her hands and floats over to us.

"Let me show you the rooms." She wraps her arm around mine and pulls me out of the kitchen, into a long hall. Allura shows me the three gorgeous guest rooms, one already has my bag from Dom's car in it. She points out the room she's sleeping in and announces she's going to pass out.

I pull out my phone, messaging Sid and letting her know I won't be back tonight as I manage to make my way back towards the living area. The windows overlooking Central Park beckon me as I end up in front of the low bench admiring the slumbering city below.

Footsteps echo behind me, and Vladislav's towering presence appears in the window's reflection.

"This is one of my favorite spots in the apartment," he murmurs, his breath tickling my shoulder, sending tingles down my spine.

I catch his eye in the reflection. The same uneasy sensation from his office earlier bubbles in my gut. The feeling is... insatiable, like hunger, and it draws me to him in ways I don't understand. I turn, and my arm brushes Vladislav's chest. An uneasy sensation burns through my veins, tearing at my chest, demanding me to touch him again.

I raise a hand slowly over his heart, my gaze focused on Vladislav's eyes. This close, I notice the bottom third of his left iris is cobalt blue, and the edges blend seamlessly into the amber; his other eye is perfect, clear amber.

He steps forward, making contact, and my eyes almost roll back at the sensations it creates in my body. Heat hums through me as Vladislav wraps a strong arm around my waist, molding our bodies together. His eyes darken to bourbon brown as I run my hands over his chest and his wide shoulders, relishing in the zaps of electricity pulsing through my fingertips.

A rumble slips from my chest, as I continue my exploration down his biceps. His body seems larger than usual. Are his arms straining against his shirt?

A returning deep, rumbling growl vibrates through Vladislav's chest, making my stomach clench. I look up and notice that his double-set fangs poke out of his wide, perfect mouth. What would it feel like to have his fangs in my neck?

That thought is like cold water on my heated body as I clear my throat and step out of his arms, the unease returning with a vengeance as I put distance between us.

"I don't understand what's happening," I say, a little hoarse.

"Neither do I," Vladislav rumbles, as he inhales deeply. Tension seems to loosen in his shoulders and his shirt isn't straining anymore. "Shall we join the others in the kitchen?" Vladislav asks, extending his hand in that direction.

"I think I'm going to go to bed." I take a step back toward the foyer.

Vladislav nods. "I'll walk you to your room."

We take a few steps toward the foyer, the gnawing in my stomach making me very uncomfortable. I turn on my heel abruptly. "Sorry, can I just try something?"

Vladislav nods, and I press my palm into his chest, stepping closer to him again. The gnawing eases. I take in his scent more deeply. At first, it's cedarwood and smoky, but there's a punch of dry tobacco and sweet, ripe peach. He's mouthwatering. I could be surrounded by this scent all day, and it wouldn't matter.

"Your scent doesn't bother me like everyone else," I murmur more to myself than to him.

My hand slips away and the unease lurches in my stomach, begging me to touch him again. I push the feeling down and continue toward my guest room.

"You know the sun is rising, right?" I comment as we reach the door. "Shouldn't you be retreating into a coffin or something?"

Vladislav laughs as he leans against the door jam. "Even if this building didn't have a UV coating on all windows, vampires don't sleep in coffins. They're really uncomfortable."

I raise a brow. "But you *have* slept in one before?"

"We had little choices in the eighteenth century. But now I can lounge in the sunlight anywhere in this building without dying." The thought of Vladislav's naked body bathing in sunlight flashes in my mind, and heat stirs deep in me.

"Thank you for letting me stay, Mr. Vladislav."

"Please, call me Vlad, and you're welcome any time." He pushes off the door jam, and turns to retreat down the hall.

I slip into the room, leaving him to his brooding. I find an oversized white t-shirt waiting for me on the bed. The scent of peaches and smoke swirls under my nose as I pick it up.

My wolf stirs in my chest. She's usually dormant, in the recesses of my mind unless it's close to a full moon. But she's curious about Vlad's scent; she wants to explore the different notes more, wants to taste it. *Mine.*

I shake the ridiculous notion as I peel out of my clothes, pull the shirt over my head and climb into bed, curling up on my side. I try to relax, but I'm restless, my mind reeling.

I roll over onto my back, a new wave of peaches and smoke strokes over me. I tremble, my skin tight against my bones. That insatiable feeling is back, pulling towards the vampire that has caught the attention of my wolf. She wants to hunt the source down and cover herself in his scent. I don't want to admit that I might want the same thing.

Would he taste like peaches? Or something darker?

What would Vlad's hands feel like against my skin? Caressing and tracking every inch of my skin with those large hands? Could he hold both wrists with just one?

My own hand slides down my body, slipping between my legs to find myself wet. Gods. I circle over my clit, holding back a whimper as I imagine Vlad's tempting lips all over me, and strokes of that wicked tongue driving me to insanity.

I increase my rhythm, grinding against my hand desperately, feeding the ember of need in me for a man I just met. Would he fuck with the restraint I see searing in his eyes when I touch him, or would he give me everything?

I want to see him undone under me, completely at my mercy.

A sheen of sweat covers my skin as I chase the impending orgasm, the embers turning into a fiery spark as my legs shake and my hand moves faster.

Peaches and smoke caress my senses, making me dizzy, thinking about how exquisite it would be for the taste of Vlad to be on my tongue. My teeth ache at the thought. Would Vlad mark me?

My breath hitches. Would he torture me by delaying the pleasure, biting but not breaking skin? Would he feed on me, taking his time to savor the taste of my blood?

I clamp a hand over my mouth, smothering the groan, as I come, my whole body shuddering. I ride the wave of pleasure, my body sated, but that gods damn tug in my chest simmers with the demand for more.

As my breathing levels out, I sit up and slide out of bed on shaky legs. I wash my hands in the adjoining bathroom and then decide

Vlad won't mind me snooping through his house and picking out a book from his vast collection.

The shirt is long enough to not bother with pants as I pad down the hall into the living room, listening for anyone awake in the apartment. The whole place is dark, the sun hasn't quite risen yet.

Living in Sanctuary as a wolf, there aren't many times that the place is completely quiet; there's always movement and murmuring of voices on the higher floors. And there's so many scents at the hotel that it can make me nauseous.

Vlad's place has tendrils of scents, but most of the place smells like peaches, so the combination of silence and familiar scents is a balm on my frazzled mind.

I get engrossed in scanning the shelves, almost missing the sound of footsteps. I turn to see Vlad appear by the windows. My wolf pushes forward with ferocity as his peach and cedar smoke scent wraps around me, and my own treacherous body clenches as it takes in his gloriously bare chest and dangerously low-slung sweatpants.

Vlad's body is carved out of stone, each muscle defined. His usually neat black hair is deliciously rumpled, a couple stray curls brushing his brow. His eyes still seem to glow, even in the low light.

"You're still awake," I murmur. My wolf brushes against my nerves, insistent that I step closer so she can investigate her new interest.

"I couldn't sleep." Vlad's voice rumbles lower than usual.

"Do you have any book recommendations?" I ask, fighting to keep my breathing level. My mind feels hazy, like it's blending with my wolf's consciousness, like before a turn on a full moon.

Vlad steps forward. "I could—"

He stops, his nose flaring. His broad chest rises and falls deeply. He's scenting me.

Odin, help me.

I step back, and Vlad tracks the movement, his face hardened. He looks harsher, the angles of his beautiful face more defined. I move back, and Vlad mirrors my movement. I turn to leave, but he appears in front of me. I bump into the bookshelf as I try back away from Vlad's hulking frame.

He leans forward, one hand lifting and resting on the books beside my head. He radiates heat, his eyes a bourbon fire. "What have you been up to, little wolf?"

"Nothing." My voice cracks, barely a whisper. My heart thunders in my chest.

Vlad angles his head down, inhaling at my neck. "*Nothing?*"

Peaches. Sweet, decadent peaches. Cedarwood. Smoke. Burning tobacco.

My eyes roll closed as I drown in his scent. I want his decadent flavor on my tongue. I wonder where it'll be the strongest? His neck? His cock? My wolf keens a pathetic sound in the recesses of my mind. She also wants a taste. Just one. *Mine*.

"Were you thinking about me?" Vlad asks. "When you were fucking yourself."

His words, in that deep tone sends a bolt of lust straight through my body.

"Yes," I croak.

The air shifts around me, my nipples hardening as Vlad leans closer, his heat consumes me, his breath on my neck. "Did you want me to touch you?"

I clear my throat, every inhale making me want to sink my teeth into his skin. "Yes."

Is he going to touch me now? My wolf definitely hopes so as she rumbles approvingly.

"Where?"

My eyes open to hungry bourbon flames. My body floods with lust, and I tremble against the shelves. "Vlad, I—"

"Show me," he rumbles.

My shaking hands brush over my nipples. Vlad's eyes watch my hands, his body bulking in size. My hand trails down the center of my body, slipping to my left thigh.

"With hands or with teeth?" Vlad pants, his eyes flicking up to mine.

"Both," I barely push out.

"Where else do you want my teeth?"

My hand slips between my legs, Vlad's eyes dropping to them. He sways forward, a growl rumbling through his chest as his fingers wrap around my wrist, his hold firm.

"Vlad," I breathe, begging for something, *anything*.

"Next time, little wolf," Vlad whispers, and then he disappears.

Movement on my bed makes my eyes open and my body alert, pulling me from a blissfully dreamless sleep, only to discover Allura sliding into the bed next to me. "Mornin' Lu."

"You mean afternoon. It's just after two o'clock."

I groan as I stretch in the exquisitely soft sheets and pull myself upright. Lu wraps an arm around mine and lays her head on my shoulder. "Xander said I can take you shopping today. How exciting."

My cheeks heat, remembering our encounter last night. It's probably a good idea to get out of here for a while. "Can we grab a bite to eat before we go?"

Allura scoffs. "As if Delia would let us leave without having breakfast. She's already making us pancakes."

My stomach growls on cue, and we both get out of bed. As we enter the kitchen, Delia is humming a light tune as she flips pancakes at the grill. Two places are set at the breakfast bar by the window, along with steaming pots of coffee and tea. It's definitely a coffee type of day. Delia places the pancakes from the griddle on the growing mountain of them next to her.

She turns with the platter and smiles. "Good morning, my darlings. I hope you're hungry."

"I definitely am," I say as I take in the sheer abundance of food laid out on the island bench.

Cut up fruit, cereals, bacon, multiple condiments, and the pancakes flitter to my nose, and my stomach clenches. I wait for Allura to pick up a plate first, picking her way through the food before collecting my own and piling on anything I can fit. "It seems like you've fed a werewolf before."

Delia chuckles. "Dominic is here often, so I am aware of the amount wolves eat."

"You're a smart lady." I abandon decorum and take the entire bottle of maple syrup with me to the bar.

Allura's selection is significantly smaller than mine as she takes her seat. We eat in silence for a few minutes before Delia clears her throat behind us. "Did either of you need anything from the grocery store?"

"Some more of those crackers, please?" Allura asks as she turns in her stool, fruit bowl in hand.

"Done. And for you, Aster, dear?"

I blink, turning in my seat. "Oh, I'm fine, thank you."

Her black brows pinch slightly. "Are you sure? There's no snack or drink preferences you would like stocked here?"

I smile and shake my head. Delia sighs softly, then turns her attention to a list in front of her.

"What exactly is your position here, Delia?" I ask.

"She's the glue that holds all of us together," Allura comments beside me. "I don't know what we would do without her."

Delia smirks, pulling on her thick cardigan. "Thank you, darling. I technically don't work for Mr. Vladislav, but he saved my life so I owe him."

"You know there's no debt, Delia," Allura says softly.

Delia smiles. "He saved me from my own stupidity; I wouldn't be here if he didn't." She crosses over to us and kisses Allura on the cheek, squeezes my shoulder softly, then wanders off with her handbag.

I turn my attention back to Allura. "So, she does all this for free?"

She scoffs. "Definitely not. Vladislav pays her a wage, even with the many, many protests for the last twenty-five years."

Twenty-five *years*? "What happened?"

A haunted expression darkens Allura's face. "It's not a story for me to tell."

I nod. "How are you feeling today?"

She smiles. "Less queasy than usual. Who knew growing a babe would be so exhausting?"

I return her smile. "I haven't had the experience myself, but it makes sense with all the changes happening in your body. How far along are you?"

Allura lifts her steaming cup of tea to her lips, focusing her gaze out the window. "I think about eight or nine weeks? I'm not sure. I haven't gone to a doctor yet to confirm."

"As a faerie, would you go to a human doctor or a fae doctor, or something else?"

Her smile falters as she places the cup down. "I would have normally gone to a fae healer, but under the circumstances, I suppose I'll be going to a human doctor."

I furrow my brow. "What circumstances? The father? Did he hurt you?" If he did, I will hurt *him*.

Allura laughs, the sound musical. "Goddess, no. Loch is a sweetheart, a little spoiled as he's a Royal, but he wouldn't hurt anyone."

"Is he still around?"

Allura shakes her head, spreading some butter on a piece of toast. "He doesn't know. I didn't tell him before he was summoned back to Faery, our homeland."

"Do faeries frown upon children out of mating or marriage, or something? Are you afraid to tell them?"

Her big eyes meet mine, watery with unshed tears. "In the eyes of my kind, the child growing in me is an abomination. A destroyer of worlds. Loch is Winter Fae, and I'm Summer Fae."

"An abomination?"

Allura's bottom lip quivers. "It's the law in all of Faery that fae can't breed with fae from another court. It's pretty much our *only* law."

"How is a *child* the 'destroyer of worlds'?"

Allura shrugs and picks up her cutlery. "I'm not exactly sure. A child of two courts has never been conceived, let alone born since the beginning of time. That's the assumption anyway. I've heard stories about it drastically disturbing the balance of magic in the world."

"This just sounds like a story to scare kids at bedtime. I'm sure you have nothing to worry about."

Allura nods once, and then we continue to eat. We clear away our dishes and put the rest of the food away then both retreat to our rooms to change.

The ensuite's shower pressure and the heat of the water are a dream on my tense body. I slip into my clothes from yesterday, check my amulet is secure, put all the borrowed clothes into Allura's bag and make my way into the foyer.

Allura meets me wearing an oversized, cream sweater with jeans and ankle boots. Her eyes catch the amulet. "What a gorgeous bracelet."

I look down. "Thank you. It was a gift from my mother." Fuck, I shouldn't have said that.

Allura steps closer and reaches out for the stone. "You know in Faery, this symbol–" As her fingers brush the amulet, she retracts her hand as if she's been zapped, eyes growing wide.

She tugs me back towards the guest rooms. Once the door closed behind us, she places both palms on the door and chants in language I've never heard. Her hands glow with golden light and a shimmery golden film creeps over the guest room's doors, walls, floor, and windows.

Allura drops her hands once the whole place is covered and turns to me. "No one will hear us. Who are you?"

I swallow a few times, fiddling with the amulet. "I don't know what you're asking."

Allura face softens, she must sense my panic. "The stone in your bracelet is a powerful Fae amulet. Are you in danger?"

"I... I am."

"Are you hiding from someone?" she asks.

"How did you know that?"

Allura gestures at the amulet. "The spell on that stone is a strong protection spell, one that manipulates your identifying markers like scent. I've only seen a similar spell one other time in my life, and it was for the same reason."

Do I trust her with my past? She did tell me about her secret pregnancy, so maybe? It's either tell her or kill her, and the thought turns my stomach. With a shaky breath, I unwind the amulet from my wrist and place it on the bed.

Allura's eyes open a little wider, those ocean blue irises being swallowed by her pupils. "You're a First Blood?"

Feeling completely naked, I tell Allura everything. My real name, about my family, and the night I escaped. Tears trail down her face by the time I'm finished.

I step forward, rubbing my hand on her upper arm. "Why are you crying?"

"Because you have lived such a hard life and I feel so helpless, not being able to stop the things that have already happened."

"If those things didn't happen, then I wouldn't be here."

Allura nods, hugs me briefly and then approaches the gold film by the door as I secure the amulet back onto my wrist.

"The amulet will protect you in any way that allows people to identify you. It'll protect you from most vampire abilities as well." She locks eyes with me over her shoulder. "Don't take it off in the presence of anyone else. You never know what they might be able to do."

I nod, gathering both our bags. Allura chants again, and the gold barrier disintegrates.

"What language are you speaking when you do that?" I ask as we exit the room.

"It's the Fae Tongue."

"That would be why I can't understand any of it."

Allura laughs, links arms with me, and we leave the Penthouse.

12

Immortal

"**T**HE SITUATION IN TEXAS is tense, to say the least," Dom reports. "High Alpha Jónasson is pissed with his trackers not being able to find this murderous female."

"Why is a lowly female wolf such a personal priority for a High Alpha?" I ask from my seat at my desk as Dom paces back and forth.

Dom sighs, running a hand through his hair. "High Alpha Daygrsson's heir situation was critical before his only son was murdered. And for High Alpha Jónasson to present a mate to extend the Daygrsson line, only for the bitch to murder Viggo, is a grave insult. If he doesn't find her, and soon, there will be a war between the two First Blood Packs."

"And Lárusson's opinion about it all?"

Annoyance laces his emotions as he shrugs. "I have no idea. His Alpha Pack has closed rank, so no information is leaking out."

The door from the bar opens in the distance and chatter comes closer to my office door. Allura and Aster stop at the open door.

"Oh, Dom," Allura muses, "I didn't expect you to be here."

Dom, now leaning up against the wall, smirks. "Why wouldn't I be here?"

Allura giggles. "I thought you'd still be tied to Vik's bed."

Dom chuckles, pushing off the wall. "You have a filthy mind, Lu." He turns to me. "I organized another round of auditions for tomorrow at noon. I'll see you then."

He stops in the doorway to kiss Allura and Aster's cheeks before disappearing down the hall. A pang of annoyance sears my nerve endings at his attention towards Aster.

I shake it off and rise out of my chair, smoothing down the lapels of my jacket. "Did you ladies enjoy your day?"

"You know I always enjoy a day of spending your money, Xander," Allura sighs.

I meet Aster's amused gaze. "And you?"

She shrugs.

Allura elbows her in the side. "You better get used to it, because we'll be doing a lot more of it."

Aster groans. "Odin, help me."

Ren and Carlos come up to the Penthouse before shift with a bottle of frat blood, and mischief coating the both of them.

"What are you two up to?" I ask, leading them to the lounge area.

Carlos shrugs. "I stole this from Nest Master Housden's stores, thought we could have a pre-work party."

"And why did you steal it?" I ask. Housden runs the Queens Nest, one of the largest in the city, and is Carlos' Nest Master. I'm pretty sure Housden is very close to throwing him out of his Nest since Carlos is always making trouble.

Carlos shrugs. "Because I could."

Ren is gone and back with three tumblers in a matter of seconds. "Let's not waste your efforts, then."

I roll my eyes as Carlos pops the top off the bottle and pours out the stolen goods as we wait for Aster and Allura to appear from the guest rooms. The frat blood is quite potent, and after one glass all three of us are feeling the effects.

"What the fuck is in this?" Ren asks, examining the bottle. "I'll pass out if I have any more."

Carlos shrugs, his emotions a little too fuzzy to decipher. "I don't know, but it's fucking *good*."

"Shouldn't you boys be downstairs already?" Allura announces from the entrance to the dining room. She stands there with her hands on her hips in a matching, blue sweatsuit and her wild curls a halo around her face.

Aster rounds the corner and I almost keel over. That dress is downright sinful. Slinky golden fabric clings to her in all the right places and creates wicked curves. The pathetically thin straps look so easy to snap and the neckline drapes dangerously low over her chest. The length, sweet *fuck*, the length would make a pious woman faint.

I feel my muscles straining as possessiveness washes over me again. If anyone *looks* at her wrong, I might kill them. I drag my eyes to hers, the jade green even more prominent from the brown shimmer on her eyelids, and they're glued to me. Her glossy lips are short-circuiting my brain.

Ren stands next to me, pulling my attention back to the present as he scoffs. "You aren't the boss, woman."

Allura crosses her arms. "Don't take that tone with me, *Renard*."

Ren appears at Allura's side in a flash and flings her over his shoulder, inciting a yelp from the faerie. She slaps his ass.

Ren growls. "Hands to yourself, Lu."

She laughs, wings fluttering. "You love it."

Renard laughs, too, walking towards the elevators. Allura waves her goodbyes as he disappears into the foyer, Carlos chuckling after them.

"Are they dating?" Aster asks, still in the entrance.

I stand, buttoning my suit jacket. "They might act like it, but no."

Aster takes a step toward the foyer, and I can't help but track the movement. Amber rum and milk drifts over to me, piquing the interest of the predator lurking in me. She almost broke my resolve last night when her arousal wrapped around me like an invitation.

I wanted to taste her, mark her, claim her as *mine*.

Her breath hitches as she takes a few more steps, those sky-high stilettos clicking on the hardwood floors, echoing in my brain. I take slow, measured steps after her, trying to wrestle the hunting instincts pushing forward.

As we approach the door, I skirt around Aster, startling her as I open the front door. Her eyes flash gold before she looks at the ground, a flush heating her cheeks softly.

"I'm trying incredibly hard to keep my hands to myself, little wolf."

A devious smile crosses her face as she looks up at me through her long lashes. "Maybe you shouldn't."

Fuck.

I hold myself back as she walks out the door, not missing her shaky exhale as she walks out.

This night is about to go to shit. Housden walks in with one of his Nest members, Mr. Noble, and he's bound to start some fucking trouble.

And I knew the scrap of gold Aster is wearing was going to be very popular. The number of offers she's had to warm people's beds have been many; I'm surprised she hasn't gotten into an altercation yet. I'm finding it hard not to throw every one of these assholes out.

I'm taking a few moments in my office to calm my short fuse when one of my human dancers appear at my door.

"I think you might want to come to the floor," he says, his eyes a little panicked.

I nod, following him down the hall and into the bar.

Fucking Noble. He has his arm around Aster's waist, trapping her against the bar, and his mouth to her ear. "Come home with me," he croons.

"Apologies, Mr. Noble, but I'm not able to do that," Aster murmurs as she tries to push against the heavy vampire. I walk across the room at a leisurely pace, reining in the anger pounding in my head.

Aster changes tactics by relaxing in Noble's hold and turns in his arms with a soft smile on her face. "Mr. Noble, you know the rules of this establishment," she purrs.

"Indeed, he does." I lean against the bar next to them, straightening my cufflinks, taking measured breaths.

A low growl rumbles in Noble's chest. "This one isn't a dancer, Vladislav, and she's too lovely not to taste." His fangs lengthen, his thin mouth dangerously close to her neck.

A menacing, deep, chuckle slips from me and halts Noble in his descent to Aster's neck. Does he really think he can pull this shit at *my* club, with *my* girl?

Aster's panicked eyes are on Noble's mouth as I grasp Noble's shoulder softly. I think of terror and fear, and push the emotions into him. His lust-drunk aura shatters, replaced with dread. He lets go of Aster and scrambles back, falling to the floor. His nose starts to bleed and he claws at his scalp, drawing blood.

I smile, placing a hand in my pants pocket. "Run along now, unless you'd like to lose your hands."

Noble disappears in the next breath.

I turn to Aster who isn't breathing. I reach out on instinct, to ease the fear in her eyes, but she steps away from my touch, picks up a tray of drinks and walks away with a watery smile.

She actually *recoiled* from me. Anger burns a torrid path through my veins.

I feel a tug deep in my gut; I should make it right, ease her worries, but I can't when she's *running* from me. I run a hand through my hair and down the bourbon in front of me in one mouthful.

"Vladislav," Housden summons me to the cluster of sofas by the cage where a faerie in nothing but panties is enticing patrons nearby.

"Yes, Mr. Housden?" I ask as I reach him.

His eyes narrow, his annoyance coating him. "Was that necessary?"

"Yes."

"Since when did you care so much for those beasts?"

"I would think twice before insulting my employees," I warn, "unless you would like a reminder similar to Noble's."

His usual bright moss eyes darken to a deep forest green as he rises from his seat, the offense bubbling around him. "You may be the Queen's pet, but threatening a Nest Master is punishable by death."

I laugh, sliding my hands into my pockets. "You're putting yourself in a precarious position, Housden, Nest Master or not." I'm just fueling his rage.

"If you expect to stay in this city—"

"Your empty threats are futile." This prick thinks he can banish me from *my* city? Idiot.

He laughs, the sound raking against my ears. "You don't have power or authority since you relinquished your Consort position."

I smirk. Technically, I do, since Medea forced the Council to reinstate it, but clearly Housden doesn't know that.

"Do you want to test your theory?" I challenge.

A shadow of doubt whispers in his eyes and his aura, but he covers it with more insult as he walks out of the club without another word, his other companions following him. Why must all New York City Nest Masters be pretentious assholes? I could challenge any of them for their position and annihilate them.

Well, except for Beau.

A message on my phone buzzes in my jacket pocket.

As if the thought summoned the Nest Master of Manhattan.

BEAU

I'm stopping by before closing. It seems like you're being quite the nuisance.

Fucking Housden.

Ten minutes before we close the doors, the air seems to cool, the pressure intensifying in the club as Beau strolls in. I see Aster bristle next to me as she wipes down the bar; her hands still and her nostrils flare slightly. She cringes, turning to face the potential threat.

Beau stands in the doorway, his attention solely on his phone.

He's tall, not as tall as Ren or me, and well built—a fighter's body. As he lifts his eyes, his power and age pulse out of him. His eyes are like a big cat—wide, slightly uptilted, and a dazzling sand color, a stark contrast to his rich, dark skin.

One of the oldest vampires still around, Beau is someone you wouldn't want to piss off.

His eyes flick from mine to Aster, his lips lifting into a seductive smile.

"Well, I see what all this fuss is about." His voice is silken, designed to lure in his prey.

He slides his phone into his jeans pocket as he glides toward us, his movements liquid, predatory. The gold bands and rings in his black, tightly dreaded hair glitter in the club lights, his hair sweeping to the side, just brushing his broad shoulders. As he approaches, I feel Aster shift ever so slightly toward me as she stops breathing.

Beau's amusement and inquisitiveness flows as he tracks Aster's movement. "I'm one of the better demons, love."

Aster manages a small smile as she lets out a shaky breath. Beau stops a respectful distance away from us, holding out a hand towards Aster, bending at the waist in a half bow. Aster's eyes turn to mine, confusion swirling in their jade green depths.

I give her an encouraging smile. "Beau's abilities require touch."

"What abilities?"

Beau laughs; the sound a sensual promise to those who dare. "Just a little trick to determine if you're trustworthy."

She steps forward and reaches out, the tremor faint in her hand, and places her palm into his. His long fingers curl around her small hand, and his eyes turn sunset orange.

Shock shoots through his emotions as his gaze flicks to mine. "She can block my gift."

Beau's gift is psychometric; he can see one's past and sense their future by touch. His eyes return to Aster's, narrowing slightly as they lock gazes. His power swirls around me, making my stomach roll.

He blinks, eyes wide. "Nothing at all... how *interesting*."

Aster says nothing as she steps back, returning to my side. Beau's eyes return to their usual bright hue, his hands returning to the pockets of his denim jacket. "What shall I call you, beautiful wolf?"

"Aster."

Beau inclines his head. "Beau, Nest Master of Manhattan."

Aster's eyes flick to mine. "Nest Master?"

Beau chuckles. "I'm the one in charge of the miscreants who reside in this borough."

"So, Vlad's boss?"

I scoff. "Definitely not."

Amusement sparkles in Beau's gaze. "No, Aster love, Vladislav is a Rogue who I allow to live in my territory."

I roll my eyes. "You're here because of Housden, I assume?"

Beau sighs, meandering over to the nearest armchair, and drapes over it. "Apparently, you attacked his second."

"A false accusation." Technically.

Beau's smirk deepens. "What *did* you do to our dear Mr. Noble?"

I can feel Aster's eyes on me as I shrug. "I may have instilled a little fear and terror."

Beau drops his head back and laughs, the sound warm. "Oh, Vlad, I love that little trick."

"What does that mean?" Aster blurts out like she couldn't hold in the question. Her cheeks pink.

I smile. "I... encourage him to feel those emotions. The combination tends to plague you with images and sensations of your worst fears."

"There are levels of severity," Beau adds, "and it seems like Vlad went for the extreme."

"He broke the rules of this establishment."

Beau pulls out his phone and starts typing at an astonishing speed with a mischievious grin across his face. He probably sent Housden some smartass response to his complaint.

Housden really doesn't comprehend that I could destroy him quite easily, and if I didn't, Beau would probably do it for fun.

Beau returns his phone to his pocket, lacing his fingers behind his head, eyes turning severe. "We have one more matter to discuss."

13

Nova

Immortal

VLAD FROWNS AT HIS guest, crossing his arms over his chest.

Beau is the most powerful vampire I have met so far. His presence is overwhelming, terrifying, and disturbingly alluring. His scent is an intense marriage of a field of bergamots, juicy blackcurrants, and a heady, seductive musk. It promises eye-rolling, panting gasps in wicked positions. He's the personification of sex and violence.

My stomach twists, my head hazy. I'm trying my hardest not to gag or crawl to him on my knees, begging to be touched. Everyone else dissolved away when Beau arrived, I didn't even see them leave, so it's just the three of us. I'm assuming, hoping, Lu is somewhere in the building with Ren.

Vlad sighs, finally breaking the silence, and walks over to the armchair opposite Beau. "Do you know where she is?"

Beau lifts a shoulder. "No."

Anger rolls in Vlad's eyes, but he says nothing.

"Who is this *she*?"

Both males' heads turn to me. Why can't I keep my damn mouth shut? I don't need to know anything about this business.

Beau's full, soft lips curl into a smirk. "I'm surprised you don't know about our precious Queen."

I shrug. "I've been here for two days."

Beau chuckles, the sound doing funny things to my breathing. "Only two days, and you're already causing havoc? Delicious."

A flush burns across my cheeks. Beau stands slowly, purposely, like he knows he terrifies me. He moves towards me, hands behind his back, stopping a breath away. His stunning eyes search my face, his head slightly to the side.

His scent wraps around me like a lover's caress, a devastatingly sensual challenge, and a lethal noose. I swallow, my breath shaky; the urge to find out what those muscles under his white t-shirt feel like, and to fight my way out of here wage war on my senses.

I clear my throat. "Would you like a drink?"

His eyes swirl the same sunset orange as before, his eyes flicking to my neck, his mouth a hard line. Fuck, no, not *me*.

Fangs flash as he smiles and inches forward.

My heart pounds in my ears as I step away, my back hitting the cold bar. I'm stuck. Shit.

I'm ready myself to fight like hell as he comes closer, then his arm stretches out and around me. I hear the clinking of bottles and the scraping of glass as he pulls one from behind me, his orange swirling eyes never leaving mine. His other arm stretches out, more glass clinking, as he pulls out tumblers from the rack on the other side of me.

And then he straightens, eyes back to their dazzling sand, and a smirk returning to his sensuous mouth. "I like this one, Vladislav. She's ready to fight me."

I let out my breath as Beau returns to his seat opposite Vlad. His power, and even his scent, seems to have dissipated slightly. Vlad's expression is passive, but something tells me there's something else boiling beneath the surface. The foreign unease, which has been hiding all night, stirs. I push the feeling down; I don't need to deal with that right now.

Beau pulled out three tumblers and bourbon. He pours the amber liquid into the glasses. "Please indulge me in a drink, Aster. You definitely earned one."

I walk around the two men, leaning against the platform in front of them, Beau passing me a glass, and then one to Vlad. He raises his own. "I look forward to getting to know our newest Manhattan resident." We all clink glasses. I sip the bourbon, the fiery burn a welcome sensation.

"Have you heard from our elusive Queen, Vlad?"

"Not directly, no. Ren contacted her sister."

Beau's smile deepens. "Irena," he purrs, "I haven't seen her in centuries. What did she have to say?"

Vlad rolls his tumbler in his hands. "She doesn't know where she is either."

Beau shakes his head incredulously, then tips back his entire drink. "Another Queen going off the rails. How fun. I wonder how long this one will last." Beau stands and turns to me, offering out his hand again, a sensual challenge in his eyes. I place my hand in his. No tremor this time. He kisses my knuckles, my gut clenching. "I will see you again soon, love."

I smile. "I'll be around."

He releases my hand, turning to Vlad, head tilting down. "Vladislav."

Vlad returns the nod. "Beau."

One second, he's standing in front of us, and the next, he's gone. The air in the club seems to heat, the lights are a little brighter. I take another sip of my bourbon, willing my fluttering heart to calm.

"I just want you to know," Vlad says quietly, making me turn to him, "that I'd never do what I did to Mr. Noble to you. Or anyone who doesn't deserve it." His eyes search mine.

I nod. "I know."

He lets out a breath, finishing his drink. He gathers Beau's empty glass and the bottle of bourbon as he walks over to the bar. He places the items down, fishes his phone out of his pocket, and taps a few times on the screen, then lifts it to his ear.

"He's gone," he states into the phone and then pockets the device again. I finish my drink, the bourbon warming my stomach as I walk over to deposit my glass with the others.

"Well, she's not dead," Viktoria's disappointed voice announces from behind me.

She saunters over from the back area, followed by Maddox, Ren, Carlos, and Allura, whose face is full of relief as she rushes over to me, wings fluttering frantically. She grasps my upper arms, holding me at arm's length, eyes assessing my body for injuries.

I laugh at her concern. "I'm fine, Lu."

She laughs nervously, releasing me. "I had to be sure. Beau is an unpredictable specimen."

I shrug. "He seemed fine." He's a scary bastard, a threat for sure, but he didn't seem *that* bad.

Allura smirks, then gives Vlad the same inspection.

Ren bellows with his head tilted back. "*Fine?* Are we talking about the same vamp?" He points to Carlos next to me, who is pouring a very large glass of tequila, eyes haunted. "This poor bastard was Beau's plaything for half a century." Ren bursts into laughter again. "He's never been the same."

Carlos shudders, taking a long drink. He turns his chestnut brown eyes to me, hazy with memories. "It was the best and the worst time in my existence. Be wary of Beau."

"I'm so jealous," Maddox muses, sipping on red wine behind the bar. "The things I want to do to that beautiful bastard."

"Trust me," Carlos takes another swig. "Be glad you aren't in his service. It was wild, but—" he shudders again.

My curiosity is blazing to know what happened to Carlos to make him look like he's about to throw up and cry with joy.

Maddox sighs and finishes cleaning the dirty glassware, not commenting, but his face is alight with amusement. Vik polishes off a martini, pulling out the olive, popping it into her mouth. Her gaze runs over me as she chews. Her impeccably arched brow lifts as those icy blue eyes meet mine.

"Hm," is all she says as she walks out from behind the bar into the back room. Was that approval? Surely not.

"Aster?" Allura snags my attention. "Can you stay at my place tonight? It feels weird being alone in my apartment."

I smile. "Sure. I just need to stop by Sanctuary on the way."

Ren stops his swanky red sedan in the Sanctuary driveway, and I jump out.

"I won't be long," I tell Ren through the window and then shuffle up the entry steps with my bag of clothes and Allura at my side.

The foyer is warm but empty, the rabble from the bar already kicked out. Sid is behind the desk, chatting to none other than Dom. Her eyes widen as she takes in my dress; her shock turns into approval as she nods appreciatively.

Dom turns and gapes. "*Dios*, Aster, that dress is unholy."

I smirk, sidling up to him at the desk. "That's exactly what Allura was going for."

The faerie giggles, going up to her toes to plant a soft kiss on Dom's cheek. "You're welcome."

I turn back to Sid, who has my keys already in her hands. "I'm crashing at Allura's tonight."

Sid sighs. "You get a new job and you've already abandoned me."

I chuckle. "Talk to the faerie about it. She suckered me in with those pretty blue eyes."

I leave the three at the desk and climb the stairs, heading to my room.

As I enter my room, a small mountain of boxes are stacked at the foot of the bed with a white envelope on top. I close the door and kick off my heels as I head for the note, opening it and smiling.

Aster,
I arranged some of the clothes you purchased
today to be sent directly to Sanctuary. The rest
is at the Penthouse.
Vlad.

I open the top box—this must all be my new casual clothes; the Immortal-appropriate stuff is probably at Vlad's place. I rummage through other boxes and pick out underwear, sleep shorts, jeans and a couple t-shirts, shoving it all into a black backpack from under my bed.

After washing my face and putting my hair into a high ponytail, I change into athletic leggings, a long sleeve t-shirt, a hooded jacket and ditch the heels for running shoes before collecting my bag and phone and leaving the room.

Allura and Dom are still chatting with Sid when I descend the stairs, the only person noticing my arrival is Dom.

"How do you still look hot in workout gear?" he asks as I pass my keys back to Sid.

"Good genetics," I answer, hooking Allura's arm in my free one. "Let's go, Princess."

Sid gives Allura an ominous nod as we walk out of the foyer, calling our goodbyes over our shoulders.

"What was that about?" I ask her as we descend the stairs to Renard's car.

"She's sending me information for a doctor she trusts," Allura says in a hushed tone.

I nod. "You'll be in good hands."

Allura brightens at that and slides into the backseat of Ren's car. We drive through Manhattan and into Brooklyn at a dizzying speed, Ren racing the sunrise. He drops us off safely and bids us goodnight, saying he'll pick us up tomorrow.

Allura pulls out a spare blanket and pillows and points out the small powder room under the stairs before grumbling her goodnight and retreating upstairs. I change into sleep shorts and a t-shirt, then curl up on the huge, soft gray sofa with the blanket and pass out.

I wake up to the sizzle and smell of bacon. I surprisingly feel rested after another night without dreams. Pulling myself out of the soft cocoon of blankets, I stretch, noticing a stiffness in my body. I really need to work out more before I lose muscle mass or stamina.

I pick up my phone from the coffee table and trudge my way toward the kitchen.

I find Allura in a soft, white robe at the stove, pulling bacon from a pan and onto a plate. Toasted bread, a pile of scrambled eggs, and fruit sit waiting to be consumed on the island bench. Two plates and cutlery are set up in front of the barstools.

"You guys are spoiling me with all this food," I comment, drifting over to the fresh pot of coffee next to her. "You know I can feed myself."

Allura giggles. "Delia and I are kindred spirits; we like to look after our people."

"You're going to be an amazing mom," I muse as I pull two mugs from an overhead cabinet.

I fill mine with coffee and go in search of a tea bag for Allura. She shoos me away, pulling out tea from another overhead cabinet. I pick up the plate of bacon, as well as my coffee, taking both to the island.

I wait while Allura finishes making her tea. She turns, eyes confused. "Why are you not eating?"

I flush. "Sorry, it's a wolf thing. The head of the pack, or household, serves themselves first. The rest of us get what's left."

Allura's mouth pops open. "I'm not—" she grips my wrist surprisingly hard across the island. "Nova, I'm not... There's no hierarchy here. Please, eat," she gestures to the food, "you'll never need my permission, or *anyone* else's ever again."

Tears sting my eyes. I blink them away, clearing my throat, serving the both of us.

Allura and I eat and sip on our hot beverages for a few silent moments. My phone buzzes next to my plate with a message notification.

UNKNOWN

It's Kris. I hope you're not in jail. Dad is still pretty pissed, but what's new? Keep your eyes and ears open. More hunting parties are being dispatched to the other territories.

Also thought you should know that Pat had the baby last week. She named him Theodore, like you suggested. Refused to name him anything else. Teddy obviously loves his uncle Kris more than everyone else. We send our love. Here's a photo of your nephew.

I'm deactivating this number tomorrow.

Teddy's perfect, sleeping face almost sends me into a puddle of tears. He has Pat's heart-shaped face, Junior's scowl, and the Jónasson signature curly, oak brown hair. He's an absolute angel.

Gods, look at that precious face. Give him a secret kiss from me and one to Pat. I'm obviously not in jail, jerk. I'll look after myself. I miss you more than words can describe. Stay safe, loser.

"What's on the agenda today?" Allura asks, startling me out of distracted thoughts.

"For me?"

"Well, yeah," Allura smirks.

"I was thinking we could go to some of Marin's haunts, see if I can find anything."

Allura nods, her eyes flashing with worry. "We'll go after breakfast."

We make our way through the food, Allura only eating a couple pieces of toast and fruit, and I demolish the rest. She starts gathering the empty dishes, but I stop her. "Please, let me clean up."

She frowns, but she nods. "I'll get in the shower. You can have the water after me."

As I finish stacking the dishes in the dishwasher and wiping down the bench, movement outside catches my eye. Two men walk into the small garden area, one with a foiled covered dish and the other in track pants and a t-shirt. What the fuck?

Their scents float through the open windows. Raspberries, a human. And rosemary and cypress. A wolf. My heart hammers as I move over to the back door and open it.

"You have five seconds to tell me who you are."

Both heads whip over to me. The guy with the dish is startled, the human, his wolf friend steps in front of him. "Who are *you*?"

"I'm not the one trespassing, buddy." I step out onto her small deck and shut the door.

The human laughs nervously. "W-we're Allura's neighbors. I'm Jasper, this is Art. We share the doorstep. And the garden."

"Right," I drawl, crossing my arms over my chest.

The door opens behind me and Allura steps around me. "Hi, honey!"

Jasper's face beams as he lurches forward the same time Allura does. Both Art and I step in front of them, facing off.

"Which High Alpha do you serve?" Art demands.

His rosemary and cypress scent is pretty strong, he's a Bitten Beta, and he has the slight undertone of copper. "You're one of Lárusson's chums?"

Art's hazel eyes narrow, a growl rumbling out of him.

"Aster," Allura whispers, "It's okay. I've known Art and Jas for years."

"He's let a human know of our existence," I argue. That's a big no-no in every species' laws.

Jasper chuckles behind Art, pushing his wire frame glasses higher on his nose. "I knew of supes before I met Art, my parents are wolves."

I blink. "What?"

Jasper tries to step around Art, but he mirrors his movement. "Art, it's fine," Jasper grumbles and steps to the side again, Art allowing it this time.

"I was adopted by wolves as a baby," Jasper beams, stepping closer to us slowly.

"You grew up in a Pack?" I ask, my curiosity taking over.

He smiles, stopping a few paces from me and Allura, and nods. "In a large Lárusson Pack in Japan."

Allura skirts around me before I can stop her, and leans into a hug with Jasper. "Sorry for Aster, she's protective."

"I know the feeling," Jasper chuckles, pulling out of Allura's hold. His attention is back on me. "Are you coming to dinner later?"

"She'll be there," Allura answers for me.

"I guess," I grumble. Allura doesn't let me say no to anything. I realize I'm still in my pajamas and curse myself.

"I have to go shower. Are you good, Lu?"

The faerie shoos me away without stopping her conversation with Jasper about the pie he has in his hand, and I retreat into the apartment, throwing one last sneer at Art.

Allura takes me to a few places through the city that Marin liked to frequent, but I don't get any leads.

It's like this woman just vanished into thin air, and I'm frustrated with the lack of information. We stopped by a grocery store before heading back to Allura's apartment.

I convince her to allow me to bake dessert while she has a nap before dinner. Music plays softly as I stir the ingredients together for the pineapple cake, so I don't hear movement on the deck, but movement snags my attention. I'm at the back door and tackling a solid, warm body to the ground before I take my next breath.

A growl rumbles underneath and then I'm spun, pinned to the floor, bright copper eyes blazing in the dark and a hand is around my throat. A rosemary and cypress scent registers in my brain.

"Art," I croak under his tightening grip.

His weight is off me my next moment, and he lifts me by the elbows. "Gods, woman, what the fuck?"

I step back from Art's massive frame, brushing off my jeans. "Do you not know how to use the front door?"

Art's eyes are back to hazel as he rolls them, picks up a cooler bag he must have dropped when I tackled him, and walks into Allura's apartment like he owns it. Cocky asshole.

I follow him, return to my bowl of cake batter, watching the wolf in my periphery, as he pulls out beer bottles from the bag and puts them into the fridge. The fridge door shuts suddenly, and Art turns quickly, and I drop my spatula and skirt to the other side of the island, my heart stammering wildly.

His face softens, and he holds his hands out in front of him. "I think we got off on the wrong foot." He walks slowly around the island toward me. "I'm Carter, Bitten Beta from the Lárusson Pack. Most people call me Art."

I take a steadying breath, holding out my hand. "Aster, Lone Wolf."

Art takes my proffered hand in his and shakes once. "I'm sorry if I startled you."

"I'm sorry for tackling you."

Art retracts his hand, his handsome face relaxing into a smirk. "I'll try to remember to use the front door."

I return to my cake and Art claims a barstool as Jasper comes through the back door with a huge bowl in his arms and a messenger bag over one shoulder. Art chuckles and stands to take the bowl from Jasper.

"Something funny?" he asks, dumping his messenger bag on a dining chair.

"*You* didn't get tackled," Art points out.

I roll my eyes as I line the pie dish with brown sugar, melted butter and pineapple slices, then spoon in the cake batter and place the dish into the heated oven. We all hear Allura climb down the stairs humming as Jasper pulls his pie dish from the fridge.

"Good evening, loves," Allura sighs as she plants a kiss on Art's cheek and walks over to Jasper, then to me, doing the same, before sliding onto a barstool.

"So, Aster," Jasper calls over his shoulder as he slides his dish into the oven on the rack above my cake. "How do you know Allura?"

"I work at Immortal with her."

Art raises a dark brow and smirks. Allura giggles. "She's a bartender, Art, keep your mind out of the gutter."

"How do you two know each other?" I ask Jasper as I turn to the sink and wash my cake bowls.

"We met in college," Jasper answers, moving to the island behind me.

"We lived across from each other for two years before I saved his crazy ass from a pack of wolves," Art adds.

Jasper laughs. "I tried to talk my way out of it when I should have run like hell."

Art's tall frame approaches my side with a dish towel in hand. "There was a rogue pack on our campus haphazardly turning students," he murmurs, taking the wet dish from me and drying it.

"Is that how you got the scar?" A faint, pink scar runs from behind his right ear and across his neck, stopping just before his clavicle.

Art halts in his drying, drawing my attention to his face. Sorrow shadows his hazel eyes as he shakes his head. His eyes remind me of a forest canopy. Rich green wraps around the pupil, bleeding into warm brown on the edges, with a few specks of a lighter brown dispersed throughout. Art resumes his drying, shaking his head a little. "I caught up to them before they could get to Jas, but it was close."

"It didn't deter me from my research," Jas continues behind us.

"Research?" I ask.

"I was a history major in college, specializing in the history of the occult."

"He's a walking supernatural textbook," Art teases, accepting the last bowl from me.

"I am not," Jas argues as I turn from the sink. "I know very little about the Fae, and I'm still digging up things for vampires, not to mention the other wolf histories—"

"Okay, okay," Art laughs, knowing where to put all the dishes away. These two are obviously always here.

"Did you want to continue with our conversation from the other day?" Allura asks Jas as I sidle up next to him and Art reclaims his barstool.

Jas beams. "Oh, yes!"

I smile. "I'll finish this salad, and you do your thing."

I replace Jas in front of his giant bowl of salad as he rushes over to his messenger bag and pulls out a thick brown leather-bound book and a few pens.

"Did he do this to you?" I ask Art, amusement plastered across his face.

"Oh yeah, for the last six years. You're probably his next target."

My face remains calm as I will my heart to keep a steady beat as I put together a salad dressing.

Jasper drags a stool over to my side of the island, planting himself directly across from Allura, opening his notebook to a fresh page, pen at the ready. I've never seen someone so happy and so serious at the same time.

Allura's wings flutter, excitement shining in her eyes. "There are four courts in Faery—Celestial, Summer, Winter, and Underworld. You'll almost never see Underworld or Celestial Fae in this realm—they like to stay in their own Courts. Almost all the fae you meet on Earth will be from the Summer or Winter courts."

"And the difference between the two?" I ask as Jas scribes wildly.

Allura smiles. "Summer, like myself, are descendants of land nymphs, so our magic originates from earth and fire. Winter fae are descendants of sea nymphs; their magic derives from water and air. Celestials use light magic, and Underworld use dark."

Allura and Jas go back and forth with names of previous Queens of each court, and I take a moment to take in Art. His high cheekbones, soft eyes and chestnut brown hair brushing over his forehead work in all the best ways, but something tells me life handed him some shit already that set his square jaw a little too sharp, and his brows always in a slight frown.

"I still can't believe that you're Queen Rhoswen's daughter," Jas sighs next to me as I stir the dressing and pour it on the salad. "She must be so pissed you're Earthside."

"She sent a summons," Allura announces, sorrow dimming her eyes.

"When are you expected back?" Art asks.

"Summer Solstice," she murmurs.

The oven dings, distracting all of us. Allura stands, aiming for the oven as Jas continues to scrawl in his book. I finish the salad, sliding it to Art, who takes it to the table. He's tall, his muscles sinewy; he would come off intimidating to most, but he surprisingly isn't to me anymore. I turn to the drawers behind me, bending down to collect plates.

"You're a Beta?" I ask Art as he pulls out bottled water and beer from the fridge.

"What is a Beta?" Allura asks, moving the pie from the counter and placing it on a marble plate, which Jas takes to the table. She returns to the oven to check my cake which still has a little more to go.

"Betas are Alpha's second in command," Art explains, depositing the drinks on the table. "We do whatever an Alpha requires, but mostly, we train everyone in the Pack, keeping them strong, making sure they know how to defend themselves and keep the pups in line."

"They don't include females in that training," I say as I approach the table with plates and cutlery.

"With most wolf mentalities, females *especially* should be trained," Art grumbles, handing out the plates and cutlery then sits down opposite me, next to Jas, handing him a beer and offering me one.

I didn't expect that opinion from him. "I agree." I refuse the beer.

"Art taught me a few things," Jas beams. "He said I should know how to throw a punch if I'm going to go poking around other supes."

Allura laughs, approaching with four glasses, a serving spoon, and tongs for the food, taking a seat beside me. "It's a handy skill, for sure."

I nod and start serving. "The only fighting skills I have are from growing up with brothers."

"That's not the same as proper training," Art counters, holding out his plate.

"Why don't you train her, Art?" Jasper offers, now holding his plate forward.

"I don't—"

"I'm happy to," Art says, "but I am a hard-ass."

"She can handle it," Allura comments as I serve her food.

Art nods, taking a swig of his beer.

I finish serving myself, Allura pouring herself and me some water. She raises her glass. "To new friends."

"New friends," we echo clinking glasses and dig in.

Art wasn't lying, He *is* a hard-ass.

We're in Allura and Art's yard, the sky gray, a storm on the horizon. I'm severely out of breath, elbows leaning on my thighs; my legs are on fire and about to give out. Escaped tendrils of hair stick to my forehead and neck as sweat drenches my entire body.

Art chuckles in front of me, barely out of breath. "How is your stamina *this* bad?"

We've been doing hand-to-hand combat drills every day for the past five days, and I feel like I'm worse off than day one. "I think... I think I need to lie down."

"Definitely not," he rolls his shoulders, swinging his arms, "your goal is to knock me down."

I groan, straightening up. Inhaling deeply, I launch at Art, trying to tackle him. He steps out of the way, kicking the back of my knees, sending me rolling onto the grass. "I can predict your every move; it's written all over your face before you strike."

I spring up to my feet, facing Art, a growl in my throat. He strikes this time, a right hook towards my face. I block it with my left arm, striking him in his abdomen. He's winded but recovers quickly, landing a strike into my hip.

Pain throbs in the joint, sending me stumbling back. He launches, arms stretched out. I sidestep, sweeping under his arms, landing a foot on the back of his left knee. The knee drops into the grass, but Art somersaults forward, out of my reach, and straight back onto his feet.

I don't wait for him to turn as I strike him in the kidney with a hard punch, grabbing his wrist, wrenching his arm behind his back.

He grunts, twisting out of the hold, pulling me into his iron grip, trapping my arms. Trapped.

My body goes stiff. I feel my wolf grip my mind, determined to get us out of capture.

I force all my energy into throwing my elbows hard into Art's chest, and at the same time, I lean forward, biting down on his arm. Art yelps, releasing his hold around me.

I swivel on my heel, gripping Art's arm again, wrenching him forward, connecting a knee into his diaphragm. The wind is knocked out of his lungs as I step around him, twisting his arm harder behind him, shoving him towards the earth, both knees in his back.

He coughs, his face crushed into the grass. "Yield," he groans.

I release him immediately, rolling off to sit on the grass. I pull my knees to my chest as hard shudders rake my body. Trapped. I was trapped again.

Art sits upright in front of me, keeping a comfortable distance between us as he rubs the spot on his sternum I hit.

"What happened?" he asks, concern in his eyes.

I can't speak, my breath coming in too fast, my teeth chattering from the shudders. His eyes don't leave me as I let the panic subside, my breathing calming, the shakes easing.

I blow out a breath. "Sorry, I just, I don't like being trapped."

Art's eyes darken slightly, but he says nothing, nodding once. I let go of my legs, crossing them, spreading my fingers in the soft grass, closing my eyes, feeling the earth beneath me. I'm free, trapped no longer. A tear slides down my cheek as I continue to run my hands through the grass. Not trapped. Free. Not trapped.

"Her name was Genevieve," Art says softly.

My eyes flutter open. His eyes are on the grass, his fingers fiddling with a blade. "My family weren't high ranking wolves, so my brother and I went to human high school. I met her in freshman year," he looks up, a small smile lifting his lips, "she was this small punk kid that always had her nose in her textbooks, rolling her eyes at jocks like me."

"Of course, you were a jock."

Art chuckles. "It was the best way to expend every ounce of energy ripping up our bodies. Our high school won a lot of championships while we were there."

"I can imagine."

His smile falters a fraction. Art leans back on his hands, staring at the gray sky. "We were mate-bound from our first kiss, and like the true angel she was, Eve embraced my true nature like she always knew." His eyes return to mine, a bittersweet look on his face. "I turned her on her nineteenth birthday, despite my reservations. We were going to complete the bond after her body had time to adjust."

I remain still, allowing him the time to collect his thoughts. He resumes fiddling with a blade of grass, his eyes fixated on it. "Eve insisted she attend the First Blood Pack's Summer Solstice party when we were twenty. I didn't want to, something felt off about it, but I was a sucker for those sparkling blue eyes."

"First Blood festivities are a bunch of peacocks showing off."

Art's eyes lift to mine. "I know, but Eve was so fucking excited for all the extravagance."

"What happened?" I ask softly.

He clears his throat, running his hands through his hair. "One of the High Alpha Lárusson's sons, Brandt, was hosting."

Good gods, Brandt was a prick. Self-entitled and cruel. But he's—oh shit.

Anger boils a copper inferno in his slightly down-turned eyes. "He took one look at Eve and wanted her, so he challenged me."

The parallels of our stories constrict around my heart. "Was it a sanctioned challenge?"

He shakes his head stiffly. "Eve pissed him off by laughing so we fought right there. I broke his spine in the end."

Memories of Eros flash past. His warm blood slick between my fingers. The tender touch on my hand as I screamed and sobbed. The soft smile he gave me, just for me, as he faded away. A sob lodges in my throat.

"High Alpha Izar was livid. I thought he was just going to execute me, and I was okay with that, but he—" Art's voice breaks. He blows out a shaky breath, his watery eyes meeting mine.

"He thought there was a possibility of me becoming a Bitten Alpha someday and he didn't want to waste an asset. So, he... he took Genevieve. Slit her throat in front of me, my family, our whole Bitten Pack." A tear escapes down his face as his eyes hit the grass again.

"They took the people I loved away from me too." I hug my knees to my chest again; maybe if I squeeze hard enough, my heart won't shatter further. "But I'm a female wolf, a possession to be traded again, so I ran."

"I train female wolves when I can," Art confesses, "so they can at least bite back. Helped some escape too. I couldn't save Eve, but I'll save them."

I place my hand on his forearm. "You're a good man, Art. Far too good for our world."

14

Vladislav

Vladislav's Penthouse

THE SUN FINALLY DIPS out of the day, the sky darkening by the minute. I push away from my home office desk, leaving the office for my room.

I change into a crisp white shirt, black slacks, and leather shoes. I pull out the cufflink drawer, contemplating which to choose. I select the sapphire blue set, setting them in my cuffs, and slip on a black suit jacket as I head for the kitchen.

Delia is in her usual spot, cooking something at the stove as I head straight for the fridge. I pull out a blood bag, noticing the stock is low. My appetite has increased, which means I'll have to go for a vein soon.

After filling a glass with the blood and eyeing Delia's pot, I take my beverage to the spot in front of the window overlooking Central Park, Aster's spot. I've seen her every night of this week, and yet I still feel like I'm not seeing her enough. She's quickly become a person I *need* to see.

I take a deep breath, pushing down the obsession growing for a particular wolf and focus on the swaying trees below. The street lamps glow to life throughout the park and the city, the stars covered by heavy clouds. The front door opens and closes, the clicking of heels sounding throughout the foyer. Allura strikes up a conversation with Delia in the kitchen.

Aster appears in the window's reflection next to me, looking out at the city below.

Air freezes in my lungs. She's dressed in sapphire blue; the entire outfit fits her like a glove. The cropped top sits off her shoulders, accentuating her collarbones and chest dusted with shimmer, catching the lights. The matching calf-length skirt is high-waisted, leaving a sliver of torso exposed, hugging her muscular thighs. Her pointed heels are high and an eye-catching silver.

My eyes follow the curves of Aster's hips, her waist, her neck. Her neck is exposed, her hair piled up in a high, thick bun. The leather corded bracelet she usually wears is now wrapped around that slim neck, the white stone sitting in the hollow groove. My eyes flick to her plump lips, the need to claim them grating on my resolve.

I notice Aster is no longer looking out the window but at my reflection, eyes assessing, hungry, taking in the entire length of me. Her gaze reaches mine in the reflection, lips curving up.

"Hi," she breathes.

Heat bubbles in my chest at the word. A simple fucking word, and I'm ready to fall to my knees and give her the world. "Hi."

She turns her body to me, but her eyes drop to the floor, and her hands clutch each other. That unease in my chest burns as I turn towards her, reach out slowly and tilt her chin up towards me. Her jade green eyes meet me, and the world fades.

I can hear her heartbeat; strong, rhythmic, hypnotic, and her breathing; deep and controlled. I move my hand from her chin, tracing her jaw, to cup her cheek, savoring the heat of her soft skin. Aster shivers, her lips part slightly, pupils dilating, gold flashing in her eyes.

She drifts closer, and the unease twists hard, my breath constricting again. Her rum and milk scent whirls around me; I will never be able to rid her scent from memory. I trace the skin behind her ear, down her neck, following the curve into her shoulder, trailing my fingers down her arm, and falling back to my side.

"How are you?" I ask, my voice hoarse, deeper than usual.

Her throat bobs, a small smile returning to those perfect lips. "Peachy."

"Good."

Allura appears from the dining area. She's got a bounce in her step, wearing her usual oversized clothes. She floats over to us, rising onto her toes to plant a kiss on my cheek. "Dinner's ready."

Allura, Aster, and I eat dinner before heading down to Immortal. It felt as if we have done it for years.

The night goes by with no incidents. Maddox has gone from trying to seduce Aster to being her best friend, so much so they've already exchanged clothes. Aster and Carlos have found common ground in giving Ren a ribbing, and even Vik seems a fraction less annoyed by her presence. The fact that Aster feels comfortable with this rabble of vamps gives me a feeling of contentment.

"Meeting is at the apartment once Dom gets here," I announce to the crew as I send a message to Dom.

Vik and Maddox finish packing up the bar, collecting their personal items, and making their way up. Aster is perched on a stool at the bar on her phone, waiting for Allura to dress. Ren comes down the entrance stairs after locking up the front door and takes a seat with Carlos on the edge of the main stage.

Allura enters the bar through the stage door, skipping down the small catwalk towards the two vampires. She squeezes herself in between the two, Ren wrapping an arm around her waist, planting a kiss into her hair. How those two haven't ended up tangled in sheets together is a mystery to me.

As they talk nonsense between the three of them, my eyes end up on Aster again. She's still staring at her phone, her brows pinched together slightly. Her eyes dart across the screen, reading something, eyes clouded with worry or sadness, maybe both. Not being able to read her emotions is the bane of my existence. I drift closer to her side.

"Are you okay?" I ask softly.

I startle her as she looks up, tucking her phone away. She gives me a small smile. "Oh, yes, perfect."

"I may not be able to read your emotions, but I am perceptive."

Her lips tilt up on one side. "So that's your gift, reading emotions?"

"Yes."

"And you can't read mine?" she inquires.

"Unfortunately, no, but if you need an ear for your troubles, I have two."

Her smile deepens. "I'm glad to know you don't have three." She takes a solid breath in. "Beltane is in two days."

Beltane is a dusk until dawn festival that supernaturals celebrate every year. For wolves—according to Dom—it's a fertility festival instead of its origins to bless cows and crops. Huge bonfires are lit with bushes of fertility herbs and resins as offers for good fortunes in the year's breeding seasons. For the rest of the supernaturals, it's just another excuse to party.

"Beltane is a wild ride in New York City."

"I can imagine."

"But that's not what's upsetting you."

Anguish bleeds into her expression. "I lost someone last Beltane."

My hand reaches out on its own accord, but I force it back into my pocket. "I hope they are resting peacefully."

"Me too," Aster murmurs as she slides off the stool, running her hands down her skirt. She turns to me, her smile masking the hurt she's probably feeling. "I need to get out of these heels. See you up there."

She saunters over to the group at the stage, holding her hand out to Allura. "Let's go get naked."

Carlos stands. "Please, allow me to assist you."

Aster laughs. "Boy, you can't handle all of this."

He leans closer. "Let me prove you wrong."

She cups his cheek sweetly, stepping closer. "I don't want to play with Beau's discarded toys."

Ren tips his head back, his booming laugh fills the room.

Carlos laughs too, draping his arm over Aster's shoulders. "You're a little shit."

"You love it," she counters as they head toward the elevator, with Ren and Allura close behind them.

These four are going to give me hell for the rest of eternity.

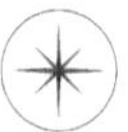

Carlos tries to offer his assistance again to the girls in undressing before they escape into the guest rooms, and I herd him and Ren to the kitchen. Vik and Maddox have already cracked open a bottle of expensive red wine, and Delia is dumping a huge amount of pasta into boiling water on the stove.

Ren disappears momentarily and comes back with a bottle of vodka from the dining room, while Carlos fishes out glasses from the cupboards. I take out some blood packets from the fridge and claim a seat by Maddox, accepting a drink from Ren.

Allura floats into the room in comfortable clothes and crawls into Ren's lap, much to his delight, with a bottle of sparkling water. As Maddox is talking to me about his latest bed conquest, the scent of amber rum and milk drifts over to me. I don't turn to Aster, but I can see her in my periphery hovering at the entrance to the kitchen.

"What are you making?" Aster asks Delia. I turn to see Aster, now dressed in bike shorts and a loose t-shirt, sitting on the counter next to the stove, peering into Delia's pan.

"It's creamy pesto sauce for the spaghetti," she informs Aster, adding cream and thick pesto paste into the pan.

"I've never had it," Aster murmurs, "but it smells heavenly."

Delia hands her the wooden spoon. "Keep stirring this; make sure it doesn't burn. It needs to thicken up."

Aster hops off the counter, putting all her focus into her new task, stirring it carefully with the spoon. I stand from the table, taking my drink with me, as I drift over to Aster, needing to be closer, wanting more of her scent coating my senses. I stand behind her, tilting my mouth close to her ear.

"Smells delicious," I breathe. Her body heat blazes in front of me as I brush my nose softly on her neck.

"Are you referring to me or the food?" she murmurs.

"Both," I answer.

She steps back, her whole body flush with mine, and I inhale sharply, holding back a groan. She turns off the heat, the sauce now a light mint color, and rests the spoon on the edge of the pan.

"Hey Delia, I think the sauce is ready," she calls as she turns, sliding her body along mine and meeting my eyes with a heated gaze.

Aster pulls my drink from my hand before stepping from me and sauntering away, past Delia's amused face, and taking my seat at the table. I follow after her, watching her take a sip of the vodka and then immediately pulling the glass away from her lips. I lean down from behind her, sliding my hand down her arm, plucking my drink from her hand, enjoying this game we're playing.

"Not only do you take my drink, little wolf," I whisper so softly that if my lips weren't brushing her ear, she wouldn't hear me, "but you take my seat too?"

I feel the soft tremor in her body that she's probably trying to suppress and it fills my chest with heat. She turns in the seat but stills as Dom walks in with that cocky smile. She leans forward, away from me. I swallow the growl. Does she want him? I hope not, because I don't particularly want to murder one of my closest friends for touching what's mine.

"Food is ready, my darlings," Delia announces behind us.

Ren, Allura, and Aster stand from the table and approach the set island bench followed by myself and Dom. A large serving tray of spaghetti with the pesto sauce lays in front of us with a heaping tray of garlic bread and a bowl of salad.

Allura snags a piece of bread. "Thank you, Delia, you magic woman," she sighs as she takes a big bite out of it.

Dom, Ren and I serve ourselves before Allura picks out a little pasta. Aster doesn't touch the food until she sees Dom take his first bite, and then dives in and fills her plate. Dom's emotions swirl with approval at the move as Ren begins a tale about his last time in Italy.

Ren turns to Dom. "What about you Dom?"

He looks up from his second serving of food. "Italy is fine."

"*Fine?* Just fine?" Ren comments.

Dom shrugs. "I'm only ever there on a hunt."

Ren whacks a hand hard against the island marble. "We're all going to Italy in the spring."

I chuckle. "We are not having another spontaneous trip to the mother continent. Do you remember what happened to you last time?"

Ren winces, and Allura bursts into laughter.

"Have you been?" Dom directs at Aster.

Aster shakes her head, swallowing the food currently in her mouth, bringing her napkin to her lips. "Nope, but I'm down to go on a bender with Ren."

Ren chuckles next to me. "You have no idea what you're in for," he warns.

She shrugs, picking up a piece of bread. "It's a challenge I'm willing to accept."

"Where have you traveled?" Dom asks Aster.

"I haven't left the continent," she says with a flat smile.

"Where are you from exactly?" Dom asks.

She shrugs. "Here and there. I spent most of my time in Tennessee."

"And you were human?"

She nods. "Yep. I was turned just shy of eighteen."

Dom leans forward on his stool. "Who turned you?"

Pain shadows her eyes, her eyes drifting to her food as she twirls her fork in the remaining spaghetti on her plate. "Someone convinced that we were mates."

Allura's hand covers Aster's next to her. "You don't have to tell us."

Aster turns her hand, squeezing Allura's. "It's okay," her attention turns to Dom. "He watched me for a long time, and then one night, he dragged me into an abandoned house and turned me."

Dom sits back slowly in his seat. Rage burns around him as well as sympathy. "And he left you there on your own?"

"He thought he killed me, and he almost did."

"And what of your parents?" Allura asks. Allura's emotions are of concern but a sliver of relief passes through her. Odd.

"They didn't bother to report me missing." Her eyes flick to mine before returning to Dom.

"So, you've never been part of a Pack?" Dom asks, his emotions tinged with a little sadness.

"I ran with some Lone Wolves here and there over the years. One wolf always decided they wanted to own me, so I split." Her eyes connect with Allura briefly before returning to Dom. "Then I ended up at Sanctuary. Sid took me in, gave me a job, and the rest you know."

Dom nods, picking up his glass, acceptance swirling around him. I concentrate on Allura, her emotions pulse with relief.

The conversation in my office with Aster comes back to me. Lies. All of it.

Aster's lying through her teeth, and she's making a convincing show of it. And Allura knows it's all lies. Aster told me she was running from an abusive mate, which I confirmed with Sidelle. So why is she lying to Dom?

Maddox appears at Aster's side. "Enough questions," he shoots daggers at Dom, grasping Aster's arm, pulling her off the stool. "Come and drink Xander's *super* expensive wine with me."

She allows Maddox to pull her out of the kitchen and we all soon follow suit, leaving Delia and Allura clearing up the dishes.

Dom strolls over to one of the large sofas, sinking into the seat, and Vik drapes herself over his lap. To my complete shock, he hesitates, his eyes flicking to Aster. But she's sitting on the bench in front of the window, shoulder leaning on the glass, and her arms resting on her bent knees as she watches the park below.

Vik growls low, pulling Dom's attention back to her; he gives his signature smile, wrapping an arm around her waist, and the other hand cups her ass.

Ren cringes at the exchange, scooting to the other side of the sofa. Allura tucks herself into Ren's side. He swings an arm over her shoulder, taking a long sip of his drink. Maddox and Carlos argue in a mix of Russian, English, and French on the other sofa as I approach Aster and take a seat next to her, itching to touch her. Her face is blank, further agitating me that I can't read her emotions. I lean against the cool glass and face the rest of the group.

"Any updates?" I ask the room.

Maddox runs his hands through his hair, sighing. "Beau has been making a lot of Nest visits."

"Why?"

"Sidelle called him." Maddox smirks. "Told him about the Lux problem spiking in the area."

"She called Housden as well," Carlos adds, "but he isn't doing anything about it."

"Sid's not someone to sit back and watch destruction in her city," Aster murmurs next to me, eyes on her phone.

"Has Beau flushed out any users or distributors so far?" I ask Maddox.

He shakes his head. "Not yet."

I nod, bringing my attention to Ren. "Anything?"

His eyes narrow slightly; he knows what I'm asking about. "Nothing on the Queen yet."

I move on before I think about *her* too much. My eyes land on Dom, who's now got his tongue down Vik's throat. "I don't mean to disturb you two, but can we focus on this meeting for another five minutes?"

Viktoria flips me off as she pulls away from Dom, her annoyance blasting me. "Get laid already, Vlad."

I shake my head. "Do you have any updates?"

She rolls her eyes. "Maddox just informed you on what our Nest Master is up to."

"And you, Dom?"

"The wolf side is the same. Jónasson is still trying to find the murderer. Daygrsson is still pissed." Aster shifts next to me, but I don't look in her direction.

"He is, however," Dom continues, "looking for a new bride."

"Ew. Isn't High Alpha Daygrsson like a hundred?" Vik asks.

Dom chuckles. "He's almost hit his eighties, but physically, his late-forties. He can still sire another heir."

"Any contact with Lárusson?" I ask.

Dom's eyes narrow slightly, frustration whipping around him. "Not yet."

I nod. "The only thing left to discuss is Beltane."

Everyone's eyes light up with anticipation, and Aster sighs softly next to me.

"What are we doing this year?" Maddox asks.

"Please say rooftop party," Allura pleads.

Ren snorts. "Most of the supernatural bars have banned indoor fires because of Carlos."

"Who has alcohol and rage-fueled vampires inside a bar filled with *more* alcohol and a giant bonfire?" Carlos retorts.

"Gerrie's Bar was the coolest place, and you burned it to the ground," Ren chastises.

Carlos sits back, arms crossed over his chest. "I paid Gerrie for all the repairs," he pouts.

"How about Midnight?" Vik suggests.

Allura gasps, her head whipping towards me. "Can you get us in? I heard their Beltane party is incredible."

Midnight is a multilevel club in the Theater District. "Let me call."

I dial the owner. He picks up on the third ring. "Vladislav," he answers.

"Beau."

"What do I owe for the pleasure?"

"A particular faerie would like to know if you could allow us to enjoy your Beltane celebrations."

A deep chuckle filters through the phone. "Is that so? Put Aster on the phone."

I turn to Aster, holding out the phone.

She blinks a few times, gingerly plucking the phone from me, putting it up to her ear. "Beau."

"Aster, love," Beau purrs.

"That's me," she responds dryly.

Beau chuckles. "Your enthusiasm is infectious."

"What can I do you for Beau?"

"Well, now that you've offered to *do* me—"

"In your dreams, Beaufort."

Laughter erupts from the phone. "Beaufort?" he echoes.

Aster smirks. "I'm assuming Beau is short for Beaufort."

Laughter continues. "You honestly think my parents called me Beaufort?"

"No, but I'm certain they called you a pain in the ass."

"Ah, Aster, my love, you are a delight. What are you doing for Beltane?"

"Taking a long nap."

"Can I join you?" Beau croons.

Aster scoffs. "Definitely not."

"Then you'll be attending my party."

"Thank you, but I decline."

"Well, from what I've seen, you go where your beautiful faerie friend goes, yes?"

Aster's face screws up. "Don't do it."

Beau chuckles. "Allura and the Immortal crew are on the VIP list. I shall see you soon, love."

Allura squeals, clapping her hands, her body lit up with a golden glow. "Put eight on your list, Beau," she shouts across the room.

"Done, my winged temptress," Beau rumbles.

"Damn you, Beaufort," Aster growls into the phone, hanging up.

15

Nova

Sanctuary Hotel

A LARGE ARM WRAPS around my waist, pulling me into a warm chest. "I love you, but if you touch my coffee, I will punch you in the face," I muse as I take my first sip of coffee for the day.

A laugh rumbles through his chest, vibrating at my back. "Feel better?"

"Much," I croon into the cup, taking another mouthful.

Eros' hand glides from my waist to my hip, pulling me around to face him. I tip my head back, catching his soft brown eyes, my heart swelling.

"Hi, baby," I whisper, bringing my free hand up to caress the soft stubble on his jaw.

His plush mouth curls up on one side. "Miss me?"

"I did." He's been gone for two days with my father at a High Alpha meeting.

Eros leans forward, planting each hand on the counter either side of me, pushing me into the marble top, his eyes flashing gold. "How much did you miss me?"

I take another sip of my coffee, my eyes not leaving his. "Do you want me to show you?"

"Gods, take that shit elsewhere," Kris grumbles as he stalks towards the coffee pot next to us.

Eros chuckles, taking my coffee from my hand. Before I can follow through with my face punching promise, he scoops me up, flinging me over his shoulder, a shriek falling out of me.

"You guys are disgusting," Kris calls as Eros carries me out of the kitchen, and up two flights of stairs to our bedroom on the third floor.

He places me on our bed, passing me my mug then scoops up his duffel bag from beside the door.

I crawl back under the covers, cradling my drink, watching Eros unpack. "How did the meeting go?"

"Tense as usual."

"Are they still bickering over territory lines?"

Eros turns to me, sighing, running his hand through his unruly brown hair. "Of course they are."

"I don't understand why they can't just–" my words are stopped by Eros' huge body pressing me into the bed, and warm lips capturing mine. For such a large person, he moves so quietly.

My coffee is somehow on the nightstand as my hands find Eros' curls, pulling him closer to me. Our mate bond burns bright and hot as I buck Eros, turning us and straddling his hips without breaking our kiss.

"I was thinking," Eros murmurs between light kisses down my neck, "maybe we should do it tonight, instead of waiting for the Summer Solstice."

I open my eyes, looking into his face. "We could."

"Are you ready, though?" he asks, searching my face.

Was I ready? After seeing all the destruction of my parents' mate bond, Eros had been patient from the moment our bond surfaced. He knew I would need time. And five years later, he's still here, willing to wait longer for me to decide when we complete it. What did I do to deserve such a beautiful person by my side?

"I think I am," I whisper.

His face softens. "You're sure?"

I nod. "You're my forever, let's make it official."

"Thank you."

I blink. "Why are you thanking me?"

Eros runs his nose over mine. "For choosing me."

I cup his strong jaw with my hands. "I knew the first day you saved me that you were the one. You forget all the things you've done for me and this Pack."

He tucks a strand of my hair behind my ear. "You saved me too."

I brush a soft kiss on his lips before I swing off Eros' lap. "I'm going to have to tell Pat our plans, or she will kill us for not giving her adequate time to get *more* food."

Eros laughs, rolling off the bed. "Your father should probably be warned too."

"Meet you here later for a nap?" I ask, picking up my coffee.

"See you later, my love," Eros says, swatting my ass as he walks out of our room.

Pat burst into happy tears when I told her about the surprise wedding. The word didn't take long to travel through my brothers, all of them grumbling that they didn't get a chance to give Eros a bachelor party. My father was pleased at the news, giving us his blessing to hijack his Beltane party.

After spending the next hour getting ready with Pat, my family, Eros and I walk over to the Den House three fields down from home. Light bulbs lined the porch and a giant bonfire burns in the center of the yard. The sky is pitch black tonight apart from the half illuminated moon.

Eros weaves us through the crowd of our Pack members towards refreshments, almost everyone stopping us to share congratulations for the mating ceremony later in the night. We eventually get our refreshments before Eros is pulled away by a few older wolves and I'm steered toward the small group of females in the Pack.

The air stirs with new scents as a group of wolves from the Daygrsson Pack appear by the house, led by High Alpha Daygr. My father greets the wolf, chatting for a few moments and then gestures toward the festivities. The Daygrsson wolves disperse into the crowd, finding familiar faces.

I try to listen to the conversation between the gossiping females, but my eyes drift over the crowd, in search of Eros. I spot him on the other side of the yard, laughing with a group of wolves consisting of both Daygrsson and Jónasson wolves. Eros' birth Pack was a Daygrsson Beta Pack before he moved here in search of something new.

As if he can sense my gaze, his eyes find mine immediately, a smile curving one side of his lips. We step away from our groups, both of us drawn by a pull too potent to resist.

We're two halves of a whole, always able to find each other, always coming back.

We meet in front of the fire, the heat warming my side as Eros pulls me to his body, resting his forehead on mine, the fire dancing in his eyes.

"Eros," a rumbling voice calls from near us, disturbing our blissful bubble.

Eros lifts his head, frowning slightly. I recognize the voice and the face as we turn to him.

"Viggo," Eros acknowledges Daygr's only son and heir.

"We haven't finished our conversation from the High Alpha meeting."

Eros scoffs, his arm tightening around me. "There's nothing left to discuss."

Viggo's whole posture is off. He's too wound up, his eyes flicking between Eros and I constantly, his hands are tight fists at his sides. What happened at this meeting to put Viggo so on edge?

"You forget who you're speaking to," Viggo warns, taking a step toward us.

Eros growls, his arm still around me but he angles his body so he's between Viggo and I. "You will *never* get what you want."

Viggo starts taking in massive gulps of air, rage screws up his face as his eyes burn are a silver fire.

"Eros Leon, I challenge you," Viggo spits.

"You don't want to do that, Viggo," Eros warns.

Viggo's silver orbs land on me and a sinister smile darkens his face. "I challenge you for the bitch who clings to you."

I feel Eros tremble, holding himself from launching at Viggo. Eros turns to me, his eyes a rich gold. He kisses me hard. "Don't worry, I'll knock his spoiled ass to the ground in no time," he whispers before stepping away from me.

"This isn't–" my protests get cut off as Viggo barrels toward Eros.

I take a few steps sideways, out of the way as Viggo tries to tackle Eros, but fails, giving Eros the opening to land a hard blow into Viggo's ribcage. Cracking of bone sounds and Viggo grunts in pain as they jump back, circling each other as a group of onlookers gathers around them.

Jostles are common at most celebrations, so there's nothing but a wild excitement buzzing through the air. But Viggo, he *challenged* Eros, he...

The two wolves start to launch at each other, kicking, punching, scratching, and growling. Blood blesses the dirt floor, bruises bloom, and bones break. Eros doesn't seem at all fatigued despite the bruises and swelling getting worse on his face. I'm going to punch him myself when this is all over.

They circle each other again. Viggo is limping already and his nose is bleeding pretty badly, he should just concede now before Eros has to actually put him on his ass. As Viggo passes near me, his hand lands on his jacket pocket, and a flash of silver catches my eye. Is that...

"Eros–" I warn, but Viggo charges.

The world falls silent. Eros' eyes widen on Viggo's, flicks to mine, then looks down at the hunting knife in his ribcage. Viggo turns the blade, causing Eros to groan, then rips it out. Eros falls to his knees, clutching the wound as blood pours through his fingers. I run to him as he falls, gasping, eyes fixed on the wound. Everything erupts around me.

Shouts, growls, blood, the scent of iron, and sweat, and... and the acidic scent of wolfsbane. Poison. The blade...

I press down on the wound and Eros winces, his bloodied hand coming over mine.

"Nova," he breathes.

"No," I gasp. The blood seeps through our hands, the wolfsbane potent, the scent coating my tongue. *No.*

"Nova," Eros whispers again, snagging my attention away from the blood.

His beautiful eyes. So soft and rich brown, reminding me of a warm cup of cocoa. They're half closed, gazing up at me, burning with love as he smiles that half smile.

"Eros," I sob, tears slip down my cheeks. Splinters of my being are being ripped from me as the bond tethers fray. "No."

"I know, baby," he whispers.

"*Why?*"

"I don't know, love," Eros croaks, his body trembles, the blood too dark, almost black. "Before I..."

"Please, please don't leave. I need you," I beg, leaning forward, brushing my lips on his. Pain slices through my heart as more of the tether unbinds.

Eros inhales, pressing his lips further into mine, before dropping his back onto the earth. "Remember to live, my love. Live long and live well. Don't give into grief, please, baby. Live."

"I love you."

"You have my heart," he breathes, "so I will always be with you, in this world and the next."

"I'll meet you on the Other Side."

The bond snaps, sending scorching pain through my veins, twisting my shattered soul.

The sparkle in his eyes dim, and my favorite half smile fades from his face as his heart stops beating.

I wake up sobbing, my heart shattering into more pieces. A year since the love of my existence was stolen from me. I want to kill Viggo all over again. I turn to my side, hugging my knees, tears still streaming down my cheeks, my eyes closed to the midday sun streaming into my window.

I desperately want to visit Eros' gravestone. I always felt a little more put together after a visit, and knowing that I can't, makes my already destroyed soul ache more. I breathe through the shudders of pain and the rest of the tears before dragging myself out of bed and heading for the shower.

I take the time to dry my mountain of hair, and dress in soft leggings and a plain t-shirt; my outfit for tonight is at Allura's house. As I'm lacing up my combat boots, my phone chimes from my nightstand with a message.

UNKNOWN

Hey, it's the more attractive twin. Nothing new here, just party prep. I visited him for you today. Poured out a tequila shot, as our tradition of Beltane dictates. Patty and Teddy say hi. Stay safe, sis. I will cut this number off tomorrow.

I wipe my tear-stained cheeks with my fingers, shaking as I type back.

You spelled "narcissistic twin" wrong. Thank you for seeing him. It means so much. I'll be thinking of you both when I have my shot later. Kisses to all of you. Don't flirt too hard tonight, weirdo xo.

Sid drops me off at Allura's apartment, thankfully not mentioning anything about Beltane today. Allura answers the door before I have a chance to knock with a blinding smile.

"Are you excited?" she asks. Her smile falters as she takes in my face. "What's wrong, honey?"

I clear my throat. "It's just the anniversary of the worst day of my life," I confess, "so my heart hurts a little."

Allura's face falls into realization, pulling me into a tight hug. "I forgot. I'm so sorry, I shouldn't have encouraged this outing."

I pull away, looking into her big, beautiful eyes. "It's okay, it'll be good for me. I did enough wallowing earlier today. Have you decided between those two dresses yet?"

She cups my cheek for a moment, eyes sad, before returning to giddy excitement. "I did. Come see," she says over her shoulder as she skips further into the apartment.

The doorbell rings. As Allura, Dom, and I are the only day-dwelling members of the Immortal crew, we're arriving first, and the others will join us when the sun goes down. Allura descends the stairs ahead of me, dressed in a bouncy lilac dress and sparkling silver pumps, opening the door for Dom. As I stop at the bottom of the stairs, Dom's eyes widen slightly.

"Happy Beltane," I offer softly. He's in a sharp black suit, with a black shirt underneath and black leather shoes.

Dom is too busy taking in my outfit to answer. Allura picked out a cropped corset in crimson red velvet with a swooping neckline and thick straps. The steel boning gives my vital organs a little more protection if shit goes down. We paired it with high-waisted leather shorts and thigh-high boots, the heel thicker than usual, also for tactical reasons.

Allura has kept most of my hair out and in its natural curl but pinned the top half of my hair in two buns and made my make-up smoky and shimmery, whereas her hair is in a messy updo and her make-up matches her outfit; shimmery and lilac. Her entire ensemble makes her look like a storybook faerie.

Allura elbows Dom in the ribs. He clears his throat, his head bowing slightly. "Happy Beltane. May your year be prosperous."

I fight the urge to cringe and cry. Eros and I should have been celebrating our first anniversary as a mated pair today. My heart constricts, and I push the thought down.

Dom descends the front steps, waiting on the last one. I slip on a black leather jacket and zip it up as Allura wraps a white faux fur shawl around her shoulders. Dom holds out his hand to Allura, assisting her down the steps and then doing the same for me. His sleek black sports car waits at the curb, and he opens the back door for us. Despite the heartache threatening to consume me, I am a little eager to see what New York has to offer.

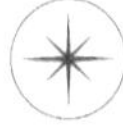

Past the blinding kaleidoscope of Times Square's lights, we arrive at a tall tower of glass. It looks like black obsidian shooting into the sky, reflecting the city around it. Dense lines of people buzz with anticipation behind velvet ropes on either side of the building's enormous double door entrance.

A valet attendant wearing a black suit with gold accents and a top hat holds his gold gloved hand out at the curb, indicating Dom to stop the car. Another attendant opens Allura's door, holding out his hand for her. She takes it, sliding out of the car, and I follow right behind her.

Dom steps out, giving the attendant his car key. "You don't want to know what will happen if you scratch her."

The attendant rolls his eyes, probably used to the threats, as he slips into the car and pulls away from the curb. Dom holds out both of his elbows. "Ladies."

Allura giggles, looping her arm in his, and I follow suit. It's very odd seeing Dom this... relaxed. His dark brown eyes have an amused sparkle in them, and he's not sporting his usual pinched expression.

We stroll right up to a burly human in a tight polo shirt at the front door. His eyes narrow on Dom's face. "Name, please."

"Vladislav, three of the party of eight."

The security guy scans his clipboard, scribbling something on it, and then nods at his buddy next to him with the velvet rope in his hand.

We breeze past the grumbling queue of supernaturals and humans alike and enter a vast foyer. Black marble covers the entire place. Long, low black sofas cluster in the center of the space underneath the largest crystal chandelier I think I will ever see in my existence. The lights reflect off the teardrop pieces, creating a starry night feeling throughout the room.

A long reception desk made of more black marble sits at the end with four attractive females dispersed across, all wearing black.

"Beau sure loves his black," I comment.

Dom snorts. "Wait until you get into the elevator."

The blonde receptionist at the farthest right end looks up and smiles at us, standing from her seat as we approach her. "Good evening," she takes our jackets and belongings, gives us a ticket and shows us to the bank of elevators. "Please, enjoy Midnight. And Happy Beltane."

We approach the elevators, and one slides open on its own. Fancy. As the doors glide silently closed behind us, lights cut out, the whole elevator going pitch black. My heart stammers wildly, the air around me going still. Trapped again. My hand lashes out, connecting with a warm, solid body, and I step closer.

"Just wait for it," Dom murmurs into my ear, brushing a hand over mine gripping his bicep. He steps around me, bringing his body flush against my back, his heat a comfort to my scattered thoughts.

The elevator ascends, and the whole space glows. Tiny white lights twinkle and wink, covering all the walls and roof.

They cluster and swirl together in a symphony of, "constellations?"

Allura's breathy laughs fill the space. "How magical."

I tilt my head up, taking in the replica of the night sky, my head brushing Dom's chest. I think I hear a faint rumble from him before the lights go out and the doors slide open to, surprise, a black hallway. The polished floors reflect the crystal lighting above as we walk towards the heavy black curtains ahead. Allura practically skips down the hall, leaving Dom lingering next to me.

"You don't like the dark?" he asks softly.

I turn my head toward him. "I don't like feeling trapped."

Dom nods, looping my arm back in his as the curtains pull back as we approach. I'm temporarily blinded, not by a bonfire as I expected, but by the sunset. This high above New York, the unobstructed view is mesmerizing. Puffs of tangerine and blush clouds drift lazily in the sky, the last of the vibrant gold sunlight lining their edges against the darkening lilac and periwinkle sky.

I drag my eyes away, taking in the rooftop. Across from the entrance, a bar of black marble runs along the entire length of the vast space. Bar height tables and stools are dispersed about, leaving a vast dance floor in the center, lights swirling a kaleidoscope of colors onto the concrete floor from large steel contraptions that also hold huge speakers pumping music.

We step away from the hallway to find clusters of comfortable sofas lining the other side of the rooftop, each group wrapping around a low marble table with a fire burning in the center.

"Modern take on a huge bonfire, I guess?"

Dom chuckles. "They learned from Carlos' disaster at Gerrie's."

I smile as Dom leads me to the bar. There are already quite a few people milling about, drinking and laughing. A group of faeries hovers around the bar, their wings glittering with the last sun rays of the day.

I halt our approach, scanning the length of the bar, panic rising in my chest. "Where's Lu?"

Dom presses closer to me, his heat warming my bare arm. "Drinks first, then we'll go find her. No magic is being thrown, so she's fine." He leads me the rest of the way to the bar where a human bartender approaches, polishing a glass.

Dom leans an elbow on the bar, twisting to me. "Pick your poison."

I give him a demure smile. "A shot of tequila, with a lime wedge, and then, something fruity."

He raises an eyebrow.

My smile deepens.

His eyes flash copper so fast, I would have missed it if I blinked. "Make it two shots of tequila each, something fruity for the lady, and a bourbon on the rocks," he orders, never taking his eyes off me.

The bartender nods once, placing the polished glass away, and starts on our drinks.

I lean both elbows on the bar, surveying the space. The fires' scent drifts over in the light breeze; cinnamon, oak, musk, and applewood. "How long have you been working with Vlad?"

"A while."

My eyes dart to Dom. "That's not an answer."

Those deep brown irises sparkle. "Nosy as always."

"Indulge me, *Big D*. You know you want to."

He chuckles, a hand running over his shiny brown hair. "It's been around twenty-five years, give or take."

I keep the surprise off my face. Twenty-five years, and he's still a Lone Wolf? "And you've never thought about leaving?"

Dom laughs. "I think about it all the time. Vlad is a pain in the ass."

I smile. "You've never wanted to start a Pack?"

"Never."

"And you wouldn't join another?"

He frowns at me. "Not one ounce of me wants to join a Pack."

"I can relate."

Dom raises a brow, leaning toward me slightly. "Why are you alone?"

"I don't trust very easily," I turn back towards the bar, "especially wolves."

"I can relate," Dom mutters as they line our drinks up in front of us. "Put these on the Vladislav tab."

The bartender nods, drifting over to another patron. We both pick up a shot glass and a wedge of lime from a small dish, facing each other.

Dom's eyes have their sparkle back. "Happy Beltane."

"Cheers," I respond, before tipping back the shot. *I miss you, Eros.*

The intense peppery burn distracts me from my grief as Dom and I pick up the next shot and tip them back swiftly before shoving the lime wedge in our mouths, the fresh citrus juice easing the bitter taste assaulting my mouth. I take the green cocktail, taking a tentative sip. As promised, the drink is wonderfully fruity.

Dom picks up his drink too and places his other hand in the curve of my back, his fingers lightly brushing against my bare skin. "Let's find this faerie of ours."

We circle the dance floor's outskirts, scanning the massive space for Allura in the last of the sun's light.

My eyes catch her iridescent wings in the far corner. Black velvet ropes separate the section from the rest of the space. A large table sits in the area, a more significant fire crackling in the center. The two large sofas that wrap around it are a deep gold velvet instead of black like the rest, and a huge gold armchair looms in the corner, facing the entire floor.

I laugh as we approach. "Tell me that isn't a throne?"

Allura turns from the security guard she was talking to in front of the velvet ropes. "It's Beau's."

I narrow my eyes. "Why are you in Beau's space? Did you bewitch security?"

She rolls her eyes. "He approached *me;* thank you very much."

"She's right, Ms. Aster," the hulking human adds, opening the velvet rope.

"Don't ever call me that again. Just Aster is fine," I say as I walk past him. "Also, tell your boss he's a dick."

The human coughs, covering the laugh as he closes the rope behind Dom, who is chuckling. The sky is shifting into deeper blues and purples; the stars are a breath away from making their appearance. I sip on my drink, soaking up some of the warmth from the fire.

The chill in the air is surprising for this time of year, but I guess the South gets the heat a lot different from the East coast. Kris would love this party; he's going to be pissed when I tell him about it. That is, if I get to see him ever again.

The sun dips out of the day, and the sky goes a soft blue-black, and stars twinkle; a roar of shouts and howls come from the still-growing crowd across the whole rooftop.

Allura crushes her arms around me, startling me out of my reverie. "Happy Beltane, honey!"

"Happy Beltane." I return her hug, making sure I don't spill my drink.

She releases me, turning and pouncing on Dom. They murmur their greetings as Allura floats back over to the human guard.

Dom turns to me, leans down, and plants a soft kiss on my cheek, his hand on my waist. "I hope New York treats you right," he murmurs into my ear before pulling back.

"May your year be prosperous," I mutter. His eyes flash copper again, and the hand still on my waist flexes softly, his body moving a fraction closer to mine.

The music ramps up in volume and tempo, but an excited murmur goes over the crowd. I step out of Dom's reach, clearing my throat and downing my drink. I'll need quite a few more if Dom is going to look at me like *that* all night.

My eyes scan the rooftop; vampires have appeared, gliding between the crowds and over to the bar. A tall, wraith-thin vampire approaches the human security guard, shaking his hand and stationing himself on the other side of the entrance to our space.

I turn on my heel, waltzing over to Beau's 'throne.' The armchair has a high back, high rolled arms, and is big enough to sit two quite snugly. It's even on a slightly raised platform. I snort, climbing the step, and drape myself over the soft velvet with both knees over one arm, letting my legs dangle off the edge, and I prop myself up with my elbow on the other.

Dom smirks, shaking his head, sinking into the sofa closest to him, pulling his phone out of his jacket. He swipes a few times on the screen, then looks up at me. "They have just arrived."

My stomach does a little flip. Why am I so nervous?

A stunning black-haired server saunters over, the security letting her through. "Good evening, welcome to Midnight. I'll be your server for the evening." Her smile is soft at Dom but falters on me. "D-do you know where you're sitting?"

Dom laughs. "She does. She'll have a tequila shot and some sort of sweet cocktail. Another bourbon on the rocks for me, make it a double."

Allura skips over, propping herself on the sofa next to Dom, beaming ear to ear. "I'll have an orange juice, please."

"Also, bring two bottles of your finest champagne and about a dozen glasses," I add. The server dips her head once and saunters off.

I tip my head back, staring up at the stars above; this high above the city's lights, they're clearer and brighter. The thin crescent moon is sharp, hanging low. I take a deep breath, closing my eyes.

A hush rolls through the rooftop, even the music lowers slightly. My eyes open, peering over to the entourage assembled at the entrance.

Viktoria looks like the devil's mistress. Her long black hair looks like liquid in its soft waves, spilling over her shoulders. Her midnight blue dress fits like a second skin, accentuating every single curve, the neckline wrapping around her shoulders and dipping into a sharp V between her breasts. And damn, those large breasts catch every eye in the place.

She saunters with feline grace across the floor, colossal teardrop diamonds in her ears sparkle in the lights, and the high splits in the floor-length dress expose her shapely legs with every step. She's going to have an entire congregation worshipping her by the end of tonight.

Ren and Carlos are the next to take off into the crowd, both in sharp suits and sporting predatory smiles. Maddox saunters after them in a stunning crimson satin floor-length dress, cinched in by a matching corset over the top, and sporting black glittery combat boots, his long, silky honey blonde hair down almost to his elbows and dead straight, his exposed tattooed arms shimmering with some sort of body glitter.

My eyes return to the last remaining members of the party. Beau holds most of the attention in the club. He looks so... regal in his perfectly cut dark suit. It's black but looks like it has a gold shimmer woven in the fabric that catches the lights. The shirt underneath is deep gold silk, and his long dreads are pulled back and tied at the nape of his neck. He meanders over to the bar with his hands in his pockets and a trail of panting humans after him.

My skin tingles in awareness of someone watching me. My eyes flick to Vlad, and my mouth goes dry.

His eyes bore into me as he stalks through the crowd towards us. His silky black hair is perfectly ruffled, just brushing the collar of his crimson suit jacket. The white shirt is pristine, unbuttoned at the collar, making the smooth skin of his corded neck look more tan than usual.

He's stopped by Ren halfway across the dance floor who introduces him to two female humans. Possession sours my stomach; I'm going to throttle those bitches if they touch him.

I blink. Before I can process that reaction further, a deep chuckle drags my attention away from Vlad.

"Aster, my love."

I tilt my head up, giving Beau a saccharine smile. "Beaufort."

His smirk deepens. "Comfortable?"

"Extremely," I respond, letting a little purr season my statement.

Suddenly, I'm being hoisted into the air, and a shriek escapes me.

16

Vladislav

Midnight, Theater District, Manhattan

ASTER'S SHRIEK PIERCES THROUGH the rooftop, sending my head whipping towards her. Her shriek turns into laughter as Beau scoops her off his seat and sits, draping her over his lap. She punches him in the arm as he bares his fangs teasingly.

Fuck, no.

I abandon the two humans Ren is trying to push toward me and glide over to Beau's private space.

Allura jumps up from her seat at my arrival, flinging her arms around my neck. "Happy Beltane!"

I wrap an arm around her swiftly before releasing her. "Happy Beltane, Lu."

My attention drifts to Dominic on the sofa behind her. His usual dark irises are flashing copper as he eyes Beau's arms around Aster. His jealousy sours his aura. A server arrives in the corner of my eye. I smile at the human.

She blushes. "Mr. Vladislav. Welcome back to Midnight."

I follow her past the rope barrier, skirting around the large marble fire table straight to Beau and Aster.

Aster's eyes roves over my suit, which matches that devilish corset. I hold out a hand, bowing slightly. "Aster. Happy Beltane."

She places her blazing hand in mine, sliding her legs off Beau's lap, and stands. "Happy Beltane."

I keep the smug satisfaction off my face as Beau watches Aster with predatory precision, sunset orange flashing in his eyes. I lead Aster to the table with a hand on her waist, where Dom hands her a red cocktail and a tequila shot. She clinks his glass of bourbon with her tequila and then tips it back, washing it down with a sip of her cocktail.

I order a few other drinks from the black-haired server as Ren and Carlos arrive. Ren hoists Aster into a bear hug, wishing her festival greetings, and Carlos pecks her on the cheek.

"What's the plan tonight?" Aster asks the group.

"To enjoy ourselves," Ren drawls, eyes scanning the dance floor.

"Are you looking for a lay or a snack?"

Carlos and Ren laugh at Aster's comment.

"Can it not be both?" Ren asks.

As Maddox and Vik arrive, Aster empties her whole drink in one mouthful, wipes her mouth with the back of her hand, and starts pouring out the champagne. She hands it out to everyone, summoning Beau from his sulking.

"To our host, Beaufort," she says with a beaming smile.

Beau rolls his eyes. "You know, I have every right to hurt you for disrespecting me."

She raises a brow. "You can try."

"Tempting," he purrs as he raises his glass. "To me."

"To Beau," everyone clinks their glasses, taking a sip of their champagne.

Aster puts her glass down, grabbing my hand and Beau's, tugging. "Let's go."

"Where?" Beau questions.

She laughs. "To the dance floor."

"I don't dance," I muse.

Ren laughs. "He does if you get him inebriated."

Aster rolls her eyes, tugging on our arms again. "Doesn't matter if you dance or not; we aren't going to find you guys someone to play with if we're all here brooding in the corner."

Beau pulls her towards him, catching her around the waist as she stumbles forward. "What if I just want to play with you?"

Aster clicks her tongue. "I'm not on the menu."

Beau releases her with a chuckle.

She wraps her arm around Dom, peering out to the crowds. "Pick the most unattainable woman in the place, and I'll make it happen."

His eyes immediately go to Aster.

Vik catches the exchange and steps forward. "Challenge accepted."

Aster's eyes light up. "At least one of you knows how to have fun."

"This I've gotta see," Ren comments as he follows the two females, with Carlos, Maddox, and Allura tagging along.

Dom, Beau, and I watch as Vik points out an attractive female wolf standing at one table by the bar. Werewolves and vampires rarely mix, so she's definitely setting out a challenge.

Aster smiles, meandering to the woman, striking up a conversation, pointing at the woman's necklace. They talk for a few moments before a tall wolf stalks up to them, putting his arm around the female possessively. Aster doesn't even falter as she holds out her hand to the newcomer for a handshake.

Within a few minutes, she has them both at ease and laughing. Aster snakes her hand behind her without stalling, sticking two fingers up in the peace sign, and then drops her hand to her side.

Vik approaches the group, tapping Aster on the shoulder, and they hug like old friends running into each other. She introduces Vik to the other two, both taking in the new addition to their group. I can tell the male appreciates the view, and it seems like the female is also curious.

After a few moments of chatting, laughing, and gesturing, Aster steps back from the group, going towards the bar where Ren, Allura, and Carlos are watching like hawks.

The two wolves exchange a look, the female nodding softly, and then the male wraps an arm around Vik, all three exiting the rooftop together. I hear the roars from the remaining group, all high-fiving, chatting animatedly, and laughing.

"Impressive," I drawl to the two men beside me.

"What a little minx," Beau chimes as he glides away towards the group.

"I wonder what she said to them?" Dom muses.

"How about we find out?"

Dom shakes his head once, bringing his glass to his lips. "I'm good."

He wants her, it pulses off him, and for some reason it ignites fury in my veins. The predatory part of me demands the wolf's head. I've never wished ill will on Dominic, but tonight?

Tonight, I want to rip his eyes out for even looking at Aster.

Did he touch her before I got here?

A growl burns in my chest, but I swallow it down, willing my body to relax.

I reach the bar, barely restrained as I summon a vampire bartender. "Give me the top shelf elixir and keep it coming."

He nods curtly, and within seconds, a tumbler with frat blood slides toward me. I down the whole thing and another appears.

Aster sidles up to me, her nose wrinkling, but those jade eyes burn in wicked delight. "You're finally ready to play, I see?"

A wolfish smile creeps across my face as I clink my glass with hers.

It's deep into the night, the fires are still blazing, a lot of alcohol has been consumed, and the entire space is packed. Aster used her determination and charm to pair off all the boys, apart from Dom and me. Even Beau has two stunning humans sprawled over him on his throne.

"Give me something blue, no, purple this time," she orders with our server, swaying slightly on her feet.

"Bourbon, Mr. Vladislav?" the human asks.

"Stronger," I command. She turns on her heel and wanders away.

I turn to Aster, who's scanning the rooftop and bopping softly to the music. "Are you having fun?"

She gives me a broad smile. "Definitely. And you?"

"Yes."

"Liar."

"Oh really?"

"You look like you're... hungry or something."

My eyes narrow. "And why exactly do you think that, little wolf?"

She folds her arms across her chest, the move pushing her breasts higher. "It's in your eyes. And your general broodiness."

I chuckle, scanning the rooftop. "Perhaps you should use your exceptional lure to pick me out a companion." I look at her. "I prefer brunettes."

Her eyes are a molten pool of liquid gold, and a low grumble vibrates her throat. "No."

I lean closer. "*No?*"

"You can find yourself a blood sack tonight."

I smile. "You'll do it for everyone else, but not for me?"

Before she can answer, the waiter is back with our drinks. Aster snatches her cocktail and stumbles over to where Dom is sitting on a sofa, looking at his phone. He looks up in time to lash out an arm to steady Aster as she sits in his lap; shockingly, she didn't spill one sip of her cocktail.

She snuggles, *snuggles*, into him, running her free hand down the lapel of his jacket. Dom, who is more than halfway to a blackout, wraps one arm around her waist, his hand resting on her hip and the other on her bare thigh, his fingers flexing into the muscle possessively.

I take a controlled breath. I want to tear Dom's arms off his body.

I don't care if it makes sense for Aster and Dom to be together, but something deep down thinks Dom would look better as a corpse.

17

Nova

Midnight

I 'VE HAD WAY TOO much to drink, but I'm still sipping on this tangy purple drink. I can feel Vlad's scorching gaze on me as Dom wraps himself around me. Dom's chest rumbles in pleasure at my bold move to sprawl over his lap.

He probably thinks I'm considering what I know he's been trying to convey all night; he wants to court me, see if we could be a good mate match.

In his drunken haze, he doesn't even realize that I'm allowing him to paw over me because the thought of picking someone else for Vlad sends me into a downward spiral of nonsensical jealousy.

Vlad turns curtly towards the main dance floor and storms off. My eyes track his movement as he heads towards Ren and Carlos, surrounded by attractive humans.

"How have you not been claimed yet?" Dom muses, his nose at my throat.

"Some have tried, but none have succeeded."

"What did they do wrong?"

"Their narrow views wouldn't allow me to have a life."

"And what *do* you want from life, Aster?"

I blink, pulling my head back and twisting to face Dom. His eyes are hazy but earnest. "I don't think anyone has ever asked me that before."

His full lips curl into a smile, his eyes on my lips, then my neck. His hand brushes curls over my shoulder. "Well?"

"There are so many things. I guess I want to have the freedom to do it all."

"Do you see a companion in that future?"

"Um, maybe? I guess we'll see."

"I want to... ask if you would consider me."

"I thought you were content being a Lone Wolf?"

His lips quirk up on one side, his hand strokes my thigh. "I am, but I've never met a female who interested me."

I scoff. "What's so interesting about me?"

"You're beautiful." He traces my jaw with a warm finger. "And you're strong but courteous, qualities worthy of an Alpha's mate."

"*Worthy?*" I push out of his lap, staggering up. "So, females are supposed to be meek little sunflowers, which are good for nothing but what? Breeding and looking pretty?"

His eyes shutter between brown and copper. "I didn't mean it like that."

"Yes, you did."

I abandon my drink and stalk into the throng of partiers. It's better to dance off this fury than beat the shit out of Dom in the middle of this club. I put myself in the center of the hot, swaying mass.

Earth and sweat and a plethora of sweet scents coat my senses as I let the thumping of the music settle in my bones. I move and sway with the beat and the crowd, closing my eyes.

Anger and frustration, heartbreak and sorrow, wash through me, and I allow myself to acknowledge them, feel them. I choke on the sob threatening to consume me. I breathe in deep and broken, in and out, until my lungs ease. The music changes, and the lights pulse with the new beat.

Through all the music and noise, my ears pick up a random conversation nearby. "Do you have it?"

"Of course, I do," another voice answers.

"Is it the good shit?" the voice is female, a little... desperate. I open my eyes, continuing to dance, as I try to find who's speaking.

"Baby, I wouldn't give you anything but the best." A male voice, cocky.

"Can I have a taste now?" the female asks.

"Not in the middle of the floor," the male chastises. I roll my hips, turning on the spot, scanning the crowd.

"*Please*," she begs, "just a sniff then."

"Fine," he grumbles.

A faint fresh snow scent drifts past me. *Marin.*

I turn again, tracking the scent, continuing to dance, and spot them. Two young vampires are swaying to the beat near the edge of the dance floor. The black-haired woman has her eyes rolled back as she smells the small vial in a blonde man's hand, before he corks it.

They slip from the crowd and weave their way through the rooftop, towards the bathrooms, and I follow. As the couple enters the dark hallway, they walk past the lines for the bathrooms, heading toward a black door, and slip into what looks like a stairwell.

As I open the door, I find the male pinning the female vampire against the wall with his hips, the vial between them. I let the door slam shut as I dart over and snatch the vial and press his whole body against the female, pinning them both.

"What the fuck?" he hisses, showing his fangs.

"Where did you get the Lux from?" I demand, the female frozen in shock. I stash the vial in my back pocket.

"Fuck *you*," the guy splutters as he struggles against my hold. I push him further into the female, the pressure making her whimper.

"Give me the information I want," I warn in a low voice, "or I will rip your girl's throat out."

Horror coats her face. "Just tell her," she begs her partner.

"No, fuck this bitch," the male grunts.

"Your fangs look like they'd make a lovely necklace," I suggest, running a finger along his jaw, toward his mouth.

"*Fine*," he spits, relaxing against his partner. "It was a vampire dealer in Queens, in Astoria."

"Where did he get the Lux from?" I ask.

"How would I know? All I know is that he gets the best quality."

I pull out my phone. "I need his contact information."

The male rattles off a phone number and then I pocket my phone. "Have you had this Lux before?"

"No," he murmurs, "it's a new supply he said. I've never scented something this potent."

I press further into the couple, bringing my lips to the male's ear. "Don't do anything stupid like warn the dealer I'm after him. I have your scents now, I will hunt you both down."

I release the vampires and slip back into the hallway heading toward the main bar.

Laughter cuts through the cacophony of sound. That laugh: a deep rumble, a sinful caress to my senses. I scan the crowd, finding Vlad on the dance floor's outskirts, leaning up against a bar table, with Ren and Carlos and a pack of female humans. The four of them dance and drink in front of the vampires, all three assessing the group with sharp, predatory stares.

I move towards them, weaving through the crowd, eyes trained on Vlad. Hot, sharp possession overwhelms me as I sidle up between him and Carlos.

Vlad turns to me. "Little wolf."

The rumble in his voice when he calls me that makes goosebumps cover my skin. I narrow my eyes. "I don't like that name."

He arches a brow, his finger trailing up my arm. "Are you sure?"

I turn my body towards Carlos, pressing my chest into his arm. "You're in Housden's Nest, right?"

"What do you need, *chica*?" Carlos asks with a smirk.

Carlos' usual chocolate brown eyes turn molten as I take his hand and slide it onto my hip, guiding it into the back pocket of my shorts. His eyes register the moment he feels the vial. "It's Marin's blood. He said he got it from a dealer in Astoria. I'll send you his contact information."

Carlos leans down until our noses are almost touching, his molten eyes boring into mine. I grab the lapel of my jacket, licking my lips, drawing his eyes to my tongue. Maybe, I should...

A deep growl rumbles behind me and a hot body presses closer to me.

Carlos slides his hand out of my pocket as he chuckles. His eyes flicking up, shaking his head slightly. "I'll let you know what I find out."

A warm arm snakes around my waist, pulling me closer as Carlos disappears into the crowd.

"Do you enjoy torturing me, little wolf?" Vlad grumbles into my ear.

I turn in his arms to find bourbon brown eyes. "You don't like the teasing, Mr. Vladislav?" I run my hands down the lapels of his jacket, enjoying the slight tremor in his chest.

"What do you want?" he asks, his face searching mine.

"I want..." *you*. I don't want to admit it to him, so I give him a sly smile. "I want to know if you think about me."

Vlad returns my sly grin. "I think about you every time I come."

My body clenches hard, my wolf suddenly pushing up against my senses. Fuck.

"Do you like that, little wolf? Your eyes are gold."

I clear my throat, wrangling my wolf as I push softly out of Vlad's arms and turn to face the crowd. I can't give in to the overwhelming urge to fill my need for Vlad. He doesn't even know who I really am, doesn't know what I've done.

"See anything you like?" I ask Vlad, gesturing at the humans dancing with Ren, my voice clipped.

Vlad frowns, angry confusion crossing his face before he flicks his gaze back to the females. "I do."

A growl rumbles out of my chest before I can stop it. "Have any of them touched you?"

"Perhaps."

My head whips to his face. "Did you touch *them?*"

He leans down, his breath tickling my cheek. "What will you do if I say yes?"

My wolf pushes forward again, suggesting I mark Vlad as mine so everyone knows exactly who he belongs to. *Odin, help me.*

"Do whoever you want, Vlad," I growl as I push off the table, angling towards Allura at the other end of the rooftop.

As dawn approaches, most vampires have slipped out of Midnight, along with many of the human patrons. The atmosphere, even the music, has morphed into something quieter and mellow.

Beau left about an hour ago with the two humans he's had with him all night. I didn't see when Ren and Vlad left or who they took with them. Dom drank himself almost to a stupor, his brooding palpable as he left us not long ago, leaving Allura and me alone.

A human security guard who's been standing vigil all night, brings over a thick blanket informing us that dawn is minutes away. Allura kicks off her shoes, bringing her knees to her chest, and pulls the blanket around us.

The crowd consists of wolves, faeries, and humans still milling about, claiming lounges and blankets. The fires have turned into glowing coal pits. Huge, plush cushions have materialized on the dance floor where clusters of patrons settle into them, awaiting the first rays of the new day.

Allura leans her head on my shoulder. "This has been the best Beltane to date, and I'm not even going to be hungover."

I chuckle, resting my cheek on the top of her soft hair. "Admittedly, this has been a lot more enjoyable than what I had planned."

"Are you... are you okay?"

"I'm faring better than I should be."

Allura lifts her head, ocean blue eyes crinkling in understanding. "Nova, you deserve to be happy. Eros wouldn't want you to be miserable forever."

"He was supposed to be my forever, Lu. He was the only male I'd ever trusted with my heart, my body. And here I am, only a year after his death, lusting over someone else."

Her eyes go wide. "Who?"

Shit, I shouldn't have admitted that.

"I..." Excited murmurs from the crowd divert Allura's attention towards the sky.

The sky lightens, going from a deep navy to cobalt blue. On the horizon, blue blends into gray, deep orange, and magenta.

"Wow," Allura muses, leaning over to scoop up a glass of champagne on the table and sparkling water in a champagne flute. She passes me the champagne, and we clink glasses.

I sip on the fizzy liquid, watching the grays morph into sand, chasing the last remnants of the night sky. Orange turns into amber and honey; lilac ripples from the magenta horizon before blending into the new periwinkle sky.

Allura yawns, stretching her arms. "Let's get out of here."

I nod, pulling the blanket off of our laps and folding it while Allura slips back into her shoes. After we retrieve our belongings from reception, Allura and I crash out of the building, laughing, breathless, as the sun warms the new day.

Allura wraps her arm around mine. "Let's walk to Xander's, crash there."

I laugh. "Good plan. I need to get my bearings around the city, anyway."

Allura points out significant landmarks and food vendors as we make our way back. Unfamiliar sights and scents filter to me, a complete contrast to Texas farmland's clean, warm scent; New York has a specific blend of steel, car fumes, and decay mixed in with fresh pretzels and cotton candy.

As we pass the Met going towards Vlad's building, a hint of lemongrass and patchouli travels past my nose. It's an earthy and raw scent, reminding me of Allura. It's getting stronger.

I slow our pace and scan the area. Allura continues to talk, but her arm stiffens ever so slightly around mine.

"Summer Court Guards," Allura whispers.

"Why would they be here?" I whisper back.

"I don't know." Allura trembles. "Summer Solstice isn't for another month and a half."

Three tall male faeries approach us from the direction of Immortal, they must have been waiting for Allura to return in a cab.

I bring both of us to a halt, angling my body in front of Allura's; these assholes will have to go through me if they want to get to her.

"Princess," the green-eyed faerie says in the middle, and all of them stop a few yards away from us, bowing deeply.

They all look similar to Allura, deep bronze skin, a golden glow about them, and unusually bright eyes, their translucent wings tucked tightly at their backs. They're all wearing a sort of uniform; dark forest green vests buttoned to the base of their necks with gold buttons, arms bare, and black fitted pants tucked into black, laced army boots.

"Did my mother send you?" Allura asks.

The faerie in the middle nods once. "The Summer Queen wishes to push forward your return to Faery in light of troubling circumstances that have occurred in this realm."

"What circumstances?" Allura asks.

"A member of the Winter Court's Royal family, Marin, has gone missing," he informs her, "as well as other Fae who have recently come through the Crossing. She believes it is not safe for you any longer, and requests your presence immediately."

I scoff. "Requests or demands?"

His green eyes narrow at me, but returns his gaze to Allura. "We are here to escort you safely through the Crossing."

"No," Allura announces.

They all frown. "You've been summoned home, Princess," the gray-eyed Guard on the right states.

"And I'm rejecting the summons. I'm perfectly safe here."

All three take half a step forward. I push my body into Allura, growling at them. The gray-eyed faerie and his other buddy focus their attention on me as the green-eyed faerie sighs. "I'm sorry to do this to you, Princess."

A bright yellow blast shoots toward us. I step into the attack, the blow hitting me in the chest, knocking both of us to the ground. Allura trapped under me grasps my shoulders and murmurs a flurry of Fae Tongue as the light scorches through my veins like the sun has just been thrown at me and has rendered me immobile.

I hear their steps coming closer to me as the film of light holds me in place. Shit.

Allura spits a few more tense foreign words and the restriction eases on my chest as the film dissipates. I'm on my feet and charging towards the group before my next breath. The green-eyed faerie disappears, but I slam into the other two, taking them to the ground. I plant a fist into the straight nose of the faerie on my left, breaking it and knocking him unconscious.

The gray-eyed faerie on my right grips my arm as he chants and pain explodes beneath the skin as if rose thorns are shredding the muscles in my arm. I take hold of the wrist of his other hand and wrench it back, feeling the joint dislocate. He wails in pain, cradling it against him and scrambling back. He mutters a few words and disappears shortly after, along with his unconscious companion.

I turn to Allura to find her holding her own against the green-eyed faerie in a magic battle. Allura's glittery golden strikes slice through the faerie's yellow blasts. The next blow brings Allura's assailant to his knees, and he disappears soon after.

I jog up to Allura. "Are you alright?"

She has a film of sweat across her forehead, and she's panting heavily. She turns, smiles and nods before her eyes roll back, and her knees buckle.

I catch her before she falls to the ground. I easily hoist her light body over my shoulder, collecting our scattered handbags and march towards Immortal.

18

Vladislav

Immortal

DOM SITS DOWN IN front of my desk, sunglasses wrapped firmly around his head. He seems worse for wear after the night's festivities. He smells like a distillery, so he's probably still drunk.

The front door of Immortal slams open and then closes as Dom and I rush to the bar. Aster places Allura on a sofa, still in last night's clothes, dumping their bags on the floor.

I rush straight over to Allura. "Dom, get water for Lu," I instruct as I do a visual check for injuries. She is a little clammy, but otherwise fine.

I turn to Aster. "What happened?"

"Fae Guards ambushed us just past the Met, coming from this direction. I think they were waiting for her."

Dom returns with the water and a clean hand towel. I dip the edge of the towel into the cool water and then gently press it into Allura's forehead.

"Lu?" Aster's voice is strained as she grasps her hand.

"What happened, exactly?" Dom asks. His emotions surprise me; he's concerned, protective and angry.

"We were on our way back from Midnight. They were talking about a summons," Aster explains, her eyes not leaving Allura.

"Her summons back to Court isn't until the Summer Solstice," I inform.

"Yeah, she said as much to them, but they knew about Marin."

"What do you mean?" Dom demands.

Aster blows out a frustrated breath, pushing her hair off her shoulders. "They knew about the Fae getting snatched at the Crossing so the Summer Queen demanded her return immediately."

Dom steps forward, arms crossed. "Why didn't you call me?"

"I was a little busy beating up fae," Aster bites back.

Dom folds his arms over his chest. "You shouldn't have left Midnight without contacting me."

Aster springs up, getting in Dom's face. "You aren't my *keeper*, Dom. I'm perfectly capable of protecting myself and Allura."

Dom's eyes narrow, copper flashing in his brown irises. "If you were so capable, Allura wouldn't be knocked out right now."

Aster's face is alight with fury. "You'd better watch your tone."

It feels like the temperature in the room drops a few degrees. Static energy buzzes in the air as Dom and Aster stare each other down. Both of their bodies are tense, ready to fight, and growls rumble across the room. Dominic is the first to concede, to my shock, and takes a step back.

He blinks a few times. "Who are you?"

"Just another breeding bitch to you," is all the response Aster gives as she crouches back down to Allura. The tension dissipates instantly in the room.

Dom's emotions swirl in the offense. "I'd never see you like that," he mutters as he storms over to the bar, chugging bourbon straight from the bottle.

Allura's eyes finally flutter open. "No—"

"It's okay, Lu," Aster reassures, brushing a hand over Allura's curls. "We're at Immortal, safe."

Allura sits up slowly, taking over the hold on the towel. She moves it to her neck and sighs. "*Goddess*, that was not how I thought Beltane was going to end."

"Are you okay, Lu?" I ask, placing my hand on her knee, transferring a little trickle of calm energy.

She smiles. "Yes, Xander. Perfectly fine. I just used a lot of energy in that little fray." She eyes Dom at the bar and then faces me again. "That situation must make me spend magic energy quicker than previously."

I smile. "Dominic knows."

Allura sighs. "I guess everyone will know soon enough, anyway." She goes to stand, but her eyes roll back, and she buckles back onto the lounge.

Aster places a hand on Allura's shoulder. "Just rest for a moment."

"Are you sure you're okay?" I ask again.

Allura shakes her a little like she's clearing the exhaustion as she hands me back the towel. "I promise you that I'm fine, stop worrying."

"Aster told us Fae Guards attacked you," I murmur for confirmation.

Allura nods. "Summer Court Guards. My mother found out about Marin and pushed my summons to immediately, and I refused. They tried to trap me with a containment spell, but Aster took the hit." She looks over to Aster. "Are *you* okay?"

Aster smiles. "I'm fine. Not a scratch on me."

"So what happens now that you've rejected the summons?" I ask.

Allura sighs, sitting forward, her head in her hands. "She'll probably send more Guards. Maybe even one of my sisters."

"And what about the pregnancy?"

Laughter bubbles out of Allura. "They'll know soon enough. This whole thing is a mess."

Aster collects their discarded bags and holds out her hand to Allura. "Let's talk more about it later. We both need showers, sleep and then food."

"We'll talk about it over dinner," I offer.

They both nod and leave through the staff door. I turn to Dom, who still has a perplexed expression.

"What's on your mind?"

"She's way too strong just to be a random Bitten female. But I can't work out which Pack she's from; her scent is all screwed up." He runs his hand through his hair. "She has to come from somewhere. Why won't she trust me with that information?"

I've never seen Dom so wound-up over a female. Possession punches through me. What is it about Aster that makes me irrationally violent?

The sun is starting its final descent into twilight when Delia appears at my office door in Immortal. "The girls are up and dinner's almost ready."

"Thanks Delia," I murmur, shutting down my laptop and following her into the elevator.

Soft giggles echo through the house as Delia and I enter the foyer and make our way into the kitchen. Aster and Allura are already set up at the breakfast table with drinks and a cheese board.

Allura is drowning in a pair of Ren's sweatpants and a t-shirt, and Aster is wearing a set of mine. The predator in me rumbles with territorial satisfaction at the fact that she's wrapped in my scent.

I clear my throat, trying to quell the thoughts of other ways I can make that scent a permanent claim as I approach the table. Aster sits up as I slide into the seat next to her, a soft smile relaxing her face. The uneasy feeling I always feel around her burns in my gut.

"Did you both get enough rest?" I ask them.

"I think I need to buy the same mattress you have in your guest room," Allura sighs, "it's so much better than mine at home."

"I was thinking about that," I muse, picking through the cheese and dried fruits, "why don't you move in here for the time being? Until this summons situation gets resolved."

Allura laughs. "I love you, Xander, but no. I love my apartment, my neighbors, and my own space."

"You can't stay there on your own," Aster points out, "it's safer if you were here."

"I'd just end up being a prisoner of this building," Allura sighs, sitting back in her chair, crossing her arms.

"The only one of us that lives in Brooklyn is Viktoria," I say, "but your apartment isn't vampire proof."

"It wouldn't make a difference," Allura adds, "the people after me are day-dwellers."

"I can move in with you," Aster offers, "if you're comfortable with that."

Allura's wings flutter excitedly, faerie dust flaking onto my floor. "*Yes*, I'd love that. You can have Marin's room until she's back."

"I can just stay on your sofa—"

"Nonsense," Allura dismisses, slicing off a hunk of cheese.

"That's settled then," I announce, pouring a glass of white wine from the bottle on the table. "I'll send Dom to help you move tomorrow."

"No need," Aster sips her wine, "Sid has a pick-up truck. She can help me do it."

We have a pleasant dinner of steak and greens as Allura tells Aster all about the neighborhood she is about to move into.

"And Jas and Art like you already, so that's a bonus," Allura says as she collects our plates. "It'll be easier for you and Art to train now that you live next door."

"Train?" I ask Aster.

She smiles behind her wine glass. "Allura didn't tell you her neighbor was a wolf?"

"I know, I own the building." I lean forward. "What is Mr. Benson training you on?"

Aster raises a brow as she finishes her wine, not answering my question.

"Is training code for something else?" I growl.

She laughs, standing from her seat. "We better get ready for tonight, Allura," she announces and walks out of the kitchen without a backward glance.

My head spins as her amber rum and milk scent wraps around me like a taunt. What possible training would Aster need? Are they something more? The thought of anyone else touching her triggers that violent, predatory part of my brain.

Eliminate the threat, claim the prey.

No. I shake my head, stand stiffly and step to the fridge, and pull out a blood bag.

I focus on pulling out a glass, pouring the thick liquid into it, and taking a sip. And then another. Amber rum tickles the back of my throat. Fresh milk. Jade green eyes flash in my mind. I love when they turn gold. It means she's thinking about wicked things.

My mind suddenly switches; my single focus to hunt down my prey. I follow her scent, abandoning my glass. Rum and milk saturates the air as I enter the hall to the guest rooms. I pick up the other notes of honey and leather in her scent; my eyes almost roll back as it envelops me at the last door.

I open the door to find my prey standing by the nightstand, dressed only in black lace panties and a matching bustier. It stops just above her waist, leaving her toned stomach bare.

Her entire body is sun-kissed and perfect. That smooth skin. I'm hard at the thought of sinking my fangs in so many sensitive places, marking it all as mine.

Before Aster has any time to react, I'm inches away from her, sharing breath. I want to crush her body against the wall and devour her whole.

The unease burns in pure delight at the thought of touching her. She takes in deep breaths; her lush, heavy breasts just brush my chest, making me want to taste them even more.

The tiny sane part of my brain is holding me back from fucking Aster right here.

"What are you training for?" My voice is guttural and low.

"Hand combat," she whispers, her breath warming my throat. "Defense."

I fight to keep my hands at my sides with every inhale as my body screams for me to touch her.

"Are you doing any other *training* with him?" I ask before I can stop myself.

"What will you do if I say yes?" She echoes my words from the night before.

I growl. "If anyone touches you again, I will wipe them from existence."

Aster's hand lands on my chest and I almost black out, shuddering hard, her touch scorching against my skin. "You think you have any claim on who gets to touch me?"

I chuckle, lowering my lips to brush her ear. "I can hear your heartbeat." I run a finger down her neck, over the thundering pulse. "What are you thinking about, little wolf?"

"I'm thinking about..." her voice trails off, as I run my nose down her throat, inhaling deeply. She shudders. "I'm thinking about how good it will feel to punch you in the face."

I chuckle, lifting my head and meeting her gold eyes. "Liar." I trace her bottom lip with my thumb. "Are you thinking about me fucking you right here?"

Aster slides her hand up the side of my neck and into my hair, gripping it hard. "You're all talk, Vlad."

I push her up against the wall, the hunger in my gut roars at the contact, my entire body going hard against her softness. It's reckless to taunt my predatory side—he finds sick pleasure in the challenge of the hunt.

Aster's chest rumbles under me, and it sends the hunger in my chest into a frenzy.

"Do you want to play, little wolf?"

She presses herself harder into my erection. "Yes."

The grip on my control is disintegrating by the second. Aster grips in my hair with both hands and buries her tongue in my mouth. Our unanimous growls make the hunger burn bright, searing through my entire body. Something snaps and unwinds in my chest.

She tastes like sunshine and raw, animalistic lust. Air is stolen out of my lungs, and for a moment, I am paralyzed. I never have and will never again reach this feeling of pure ecstasy in my entire existence.

I bury my hand in her feather-soft, long locks, lips pressing further into hers. My mind is fragmented into millions of pieces and reshaping its entire structure. The hunger claws further into my chest, releasing a hold on me that has plagued me my entire immortal life.

Medea's bond is gone.

And my sole purpose in life now is to have this wolf and to never let her go.

Aster breaks the kiss by wrenching my head back with her hands. Gold eyes bore into mine so intensely, I feel as if she's trying to rip out my soul.

She pants. "Mate."

19

Vladislav's Penthouse

"**M**ATE."

The word falls out of my mouth.

That damn unease hums in fiery agreement and then settles at the discovery. A mate bond. With Vlad.

Deep bourbon eyes are on me, as if the mate bond realization has settled in him too.

"Vlad," I say as I reluctantly dislodge my hands out of his thick hair. How I want to stroke it for the rest of my life and feel it caress my skin as he...

I lower my gaze to his chest, away from his hypnotic eyes. "We-we should..." I'm speechless, my heart galloping as I try to pull myself out of his grasp.

He holds on to me harder. "Why are you trying to run?" His voice is so soft it makes me look at him again. His usual amber and cobalt irises search mine.

"I don't... It's physically impossible. This must be a curse."

His head tilts to the side. "Does it feel like a curse to you?"

The mate bond responds to his question by stirring. "No, but this can't, *shouldn't*, happen. It shouldn't be possible. There's something wrong."

The light in his eyes drains away, leaving them cold and emotionless. He takes two steps back, my body shivering at the sudden absence of his warmth. His body is rigid as he straightens his suit jacket. "See you at the club."

"Vlad, don't go. Wait—" He's out of the room before I can take a step away from the wall.

The bond rips into my guts. Vlad thinks I've rejected him, the tether between us fraying from my stupid actions. I slide down the wall, clutching my abdomen. A few tears escape down my cheek as the sharp, knifing pain turns into a deep throb, matching my scattered heart rate.

I stand on weak legs and cross to the wardrobe. Mate bonds don't surface between species. It's supposed to be *physically* impossible. I pull on tight, leather, high-waisted pants and slide into gold and black stilettos, buckling the straps. I didn't think I was to have that kind of bond again after Eros.

My mom told me that mate bonds are a call of two souls destined to be one. Bonding with another both strengthens and balances the magic within the two. She also said bonds are believed to transcend to the Other Side. I pull on a black, cropped, fitted mesh tee and make sure the amulet is secure before wrangling my hair into a high ponytail.

Is this some anomaly? A blip in magic—

Realization slices through me and dash out of the room, knocking rapidly on the next door.

Allura opens the door dressed in her lingerie. "Oh, girl, you look hot!"

I push my way into her room. "Do the barrier thing," I whisper, waving my hands around the door. Allura doesn't question the command as she does as I ask.

"You know that big magical apocalypse thing you were told as a child?" I say as soon as the gold film seals together. "It's not bullshit. It's me. I'm the apocalypse. Sweet fuck, something fucked up in the law of evolution or something because I don't understand how this is happening."

I've been pacing the whole time I'm ranting, so Allura grasps my wrist, stopping me. "What's happening, Nova?"

"Not just me. Vlad, too. It's impossible. I don't understand—"

"Tell me what's going on before you hyperventilate and pass out."

"It started when you guys came to Sanctuary to ask me to help with Marin. I thought it was nerves about leaving Sanctuary, or being away from my Pack. You know my leash was pulled so tight there was a physical line I couldn't cross without getting a beating from my dad. Then I thought maybe my Pack exiled me, so it was the feeling of losing that connection."

"Girl, I love you, but get to the point."

"I'm sorry. My wolf has been really antsy recently, always surfacing when... And when Vlad kissed me—"

"Whoa, wait. He *kissed* you?"

"Yeah."

"So, what, you think being attracted to a vampire will start the apocalypse?"

"No! It's the fact that when I kissed him, a *mate bond* between us surfaced out of nowhere." My voice is so loud I'm sure all of New York would have heard the proclamation if we didn't have the barrier in place.

Allura's mouth drops open, her eyes wide. "Holy Mother of Light."

"Can you fix it, Lu?" As the words come out, the mate bond tightens again, making me double over in pain. I wrap my arms tightly around my middle, the pull constricting around vital organs. I think I may be dying.

"Nova, my love, rejecting a bond is painful. Once magic is altered, it can't be changed back. The tear in the realm. This must be that," Allura mutters more to herself as she paces.

I take a few deep breaths as the pain subsides into a throbbing mess again. "What does that even mean, Lu?"

She stops her pacing and turns to me, eyes serious. "Take off the amulet and give me your hands."

I unwind the leather strap, toss it on the bed and then hold out both hands. Allura grabs them and closes her eyes, chanting in Fae Tongue. Our hands glow softly, the magic warm on my palms. I watch Allura's brows pinch together as she continues to mutter foreign words.

Tingles shoot up my arm and warmth spread through my chest, and Allura gasps, opening her eyes wide.

"Is it..."

Allura nods. "A mate bond. I can feel the threads there."

"This... this is too much. I can't, I can't breathe." I'm hyperventilating. My mind and vision hazy.

Allura leads me to sit on the edge of the bed and pushes me forward, so my head is between my knees. She instructs me to breathe in and out deeply, focusing on lowering my heart rate. When I'm breathing easier, I lift my head and flop back on the bed.

"I don't want to freak you out," Allura says hesitantly as I hear her moving around the room. "But you know the bond will just get stronger, more insistent, the longer you're around Xander."

"I know," I whisper, staring at the ceiling. It was a miracle that Eros and I held out for so long, but most wolves don't come into their full wolf magic until their mid twenties, and so bonds that surface at an early age are usually more manageable.

For a strange, mutated mate bond to surface for me now—this isn't going to be easy.

I lift my head and prop myself up with my elbows. "What if completing the bond actually destroys the world?"

Allura turns back to me from the mirror, replacing the cap of her lipstick. "I doubt it will. It feels like any other bond I've sensed."

I rise from the bed. Allura pulls on a matching sweatsuit over the purple lace lingerie and matching thigh-high stockings as I wrap my amulet back on. We leave the apartment, taking the elevator down to Immortal.

As the doors slide open, a menagerie of half-dressed dancers floats about at the end of the hall. Fae wings of all shapes, sizes, and a medley of colors, give the entire scene a surreal feeling. Scents of the sea's crisp saltiness, freshly cut grass, and an abundance of wildflowers swirl around me.

As Allura and I walk down the hall, my nose picks up the faint trail of peach and cedarwood. I leave Allura in her dressing room to track down Vlad.

I find him by the bar with Carlos and Mydas. They have blood sloshing around in their glasses as they laugh amongst themselves. I think about retreating to Allura's dressing room, but Mydas spots me over Vlad's shoulder.

"Aster, you look ravishing." His comment makes every head turn in the room, except Vlad's.

I walk over to the three males, hopefully looking confident, even though I have the urge to cover myself up.

"I'm being told you had an interesting Beltane," Mydas croons. I sidle up next to Vlad. He still hasn't looked at me; his gaze fixated on his drink swirling around in his glass, obviously still pissed about my dumbass comments.

"Oh, we did," Maddox muses from behind the barr. "Aster has a silver tongue; she got all of us snacks."

Mydas' eyes darken. "Did you find yourself a playmate?"

"I didn't expect to see you so soon, Mydas," I comment, ignoring his inquiry. There's a glint in his eyes that screams at my defenses. I lean into Vlad, just enough to brush my thigh against his, hoping Mydas doesn't notice.

"How did your visit go to Court?" Vlad asks, thankfully returning the touch and pressing a little bit into me; the mate bond hums at the contact.

"It's always business with you, Vlad," Mydas complains. Vlad doesn't answer, making Mydas roll his eyes and return his attention to his drink. "The Advisors and the Elders are keeping the masses placated for now, but if the Queen doesn't show up soon, shit will start to fall apart."

"Did you speak to Irena?" Vlad asks.

"I did," Mydas sighs. "She thinks she's here in the States somewhere, but none of the Nest Masters have reported seeing her yet."

"If you hear anything more, let me know," Vlad says as he stands. He downs his drink in one mouthful, then places his hand on the small of my back. "I'll send out Allura for you," Vlad informs Mydas in a cool tone before angling us toward the staff door. I feel Mydas' eyes on us as we leave.

Vlad doesn't release me until we're in his office and he's closing the office door. He crosses the room, taking his suit jacket off and hanging it in the wardrobe behind his desk and then sits behind his desk and immediately opens his laptop.

"Vlad."

He ignores me, tapping away on his computer.

"I'm sorry for what I said before," I try again. "I'm just freaked out by this whole situation."

He still doesn't respond.

I stomp around his desk, closing his laptop and pushing it away from the edge as I plant myself in between Vlad and his work, perching on the edge of the table and crossing my arms.

His eyes flick up to mine, and they are a deep bourbon. He's *furious*.

"You rejected me," he states through clenched teeth.

"I panicked. I needed to get my head around something that's supposed to be impossible."

"And have you? Gotten your head around it?"

I nod. "Allura confirmed the bond, a magic anomaly. And our fates are set."

Vlad leans forward, placing a hand on either side of me, trapping me between his arms. He stands, his body heat radiating off him as he brings his face inches away from mine, eyes still deep bourbon. "But, do you really want this?"

Do I want this? *Us?* The pause makes Vlad growl. I place my hand on his cheek before he moves away. "Hey, listen. There's things you don't know about my past that gives me pause. Things I'll tell you eventually, but for now, can we take it slow?"

He sighs and closes his eyes, his body relaxing as he sits back into his chair. "I'll try, little wolf, but fuck, that's already difficult."

As I stand from my perch on his desk, Vlad captures my wrist, tugging me closer, positioning me in between his thighs. He's tall enough that I'm barely looking down into his now dazzling amber and blue eyes as he wraps an arm around my waist.

"We'll take it at whatever pace you want, as long as you stay."

I trace his sharp jaw, feeling the couple days of growth he always has, and trail my fingers down his neck. He trembles softly under my touch and closes his eyes. I never expected patience from Vlad.

From all the things I've been told since arriving in New York, the warnings were never to promise the powerful Vladislav anything and not deliver it in a timely manner, because he wasn't a patient man.

Vlad is obviously a master of deception for his reputation to be so wrong.

I lean into him, sinking both hands into his hair and press my lips softly to Vlad's. A knock on the door interrupts us.

"I can come back later," Carlos drawls behind us, his amusement lacing his words.

Vlad turns me and pulls me onto his lap, locking his arm around my waist. "Tell us what you found."

Carlos closes the office door behind him and takes a seat in the chair opposite us, completely unfazed by our position. If anything he looks happy about it. He pulls out his phone and taps a few times before looking back at us. "I got in contact with the dealer. He's some mid-level, strange dude, but he's one of the more prominent Lux dealers in Queens."

"Did you work out his supplier?" I ask. Vlad's thumb swipes back and forth softly, lazily along my waist, and it's very distracting.

"That's where it gets interesting," Carlos continues as he scrolls through his phone. "He said that the supplier is a member of Housden's inner circle." Carlos eyes both of us expectantly.

It takes me a second before my mouth pops open. "*Noble?*"

Carlos nods once. "Bingo."

"Son of a bitch," Vlad grumbles behind me. "Get that piece of shit over here tomorrow."

Carlos smirks. "I'm already on it."

Another knock on the door disrupts us, and Allura pops her head in. "We need you boys on the floor."

Carlos nods and joins her in the hallway, heading toward the bar. Vlad loosens his hold, allowing both of us to stand. I slip around him to the wardrobe and pull out his suit jacket, holding it out. His eyes warm as he slides his arms into the sleeves and turns, buttoning the jacket. I notice he never wears ties, so I smooth down his shoulders and the lapels.

I step closer to him, resting my head on his chest, wrapping an arm around him. His smoky cedar and peach scent caresses my senses as he wraps an arm around me, making more of our bodies touch.

Vlad inhales deeply, sending tingling heat through my body, as I relax into his embrace, allowing his body to envelop mine. Being in his arms should be terrifying, but I feel at peace.

I feel safe for the first time in a long time.

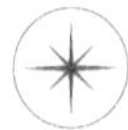

I've put all the unpacked boxes of clothes into the bed of the pick-up, and left Sid to secure them as I bound up to my room to finish packing my backpack. I pull out the only pictures I bought with me: one of Mom and one of Kristjan. I trace the smiling features on my mom's face.

She was once a free-spirited, beautiful soul. But the years spent with my father shattered her spirit. She loved us, her children, fiercely until the day I...

I pull out the aged envelope with my name scribbled over it in my mom's handwriting. I take a shaky breath in as I pull the paper out with trembling hands. It's dated the day before I found her in that barn.

My dearest Nova,

From the moment you first fluttered in me, I loved

you. I knew you were destined for great things the moment you wailed in my arms.

As Kristjan loves to point out, you are truly my youngest and the most precious gift in my life. I love every single part of you, perhaps even a little more than I do for your brothers. And I'm so sad to know I won't be able to see you flourish.

If you have received this letter, then I decided my time on this earth needed to end, and for that, I am genuinely sorry. I'm so sorry to leave you on your own, knowing the terrible life you may have to live.

I should be stronger for you, but I lose another piece of myself as each day goes by. Life shouldn't fracture you into a soulless creature, as it is doing to me, so I need to go.

I want you to remember that your life should be full. Full of color, full of joy, full of love.
You deserve everything, so don't ever settle for anything less. From the way the new Beta Eros looks at you, he might be the one to give you all the love you deserve.

Trust your intuition, my sweet, it will always lead you in the right direction. And trust Kristjan. Your bond was written by the Gods when they blessed me

*he Gods when they blessed me with you both, and
Kristjan is the only one who will always be on
your side.*

*If your life falters, and you believe you will follow
my path, don't hesitate to run. I have entrusted an
important item to Patricia if the time ever comes
when you need it.*

*And my darling, I really hope you never need it,
but my fear is that you will. It is perhaps why you
are reading this letter.*

*Remember, my love for you is eternal, whether
I'm here or on the Other Side.
I know you will be heartbroken and angry at me,
and that's okay.
But don't forget to heal, baby. You don't need to
suffer for an eternity.*

*Live the life you're meant to,
Mom.*

Tears roll down my neck, the air sucked out of my lungs. I
want to scream, and I want to run, but the sorrow will follow
me like a heavy shadow anywhere I go.

I fold up the note gently, placing it back into the envelope.
I lift it to my trembling lips. My soul is bare and aching as I put
the letter with the photos into my backpack.

I swipe my hands over my cheeks and take a slow breath before hoisting my bag over my shoulder and head downstairs.

Art and Jas help me unload the boxes and pile them in Marin's now empty room. Allura packed Marin's things and placed them in the basement storage which the boys have access to. Art and I train hard for the afternoon until we're both drenched in sweat and out of breath.

"You're stronger than last time," Art pants, wiping his face with one of the towels Jas left out for us.

"I feel stronger," I admit, picking up a water bottle. "Must be all your training."

Art smirks. "Please, I don't need the ego boost."

We part ways, both in need of food and a nap. I climb the stairs, enter my new room and fish out fresh clothes before closing myself in the bathroom. I savor the hot spray as exhaustion hits me suddenly like a freight train. I wash away the grime, massage out the knots in my shoulders, and make an effort to scrub my hair.

As I step out of the shower, pain tightens through my abdomen and throbs in my hips. I groan; I forgot about the new moon.

I change into comfy clothes, padding down the hallway to Allura's room. I knock softly, listening for her grumbles, but hear sharp heaving echoing from her ensuite. I open the door, walking over to the poor faerie curled over the toilet, emptying her stomach into the bowl.

"That bad, huh?"

She looks up after she stops hurling and flushes. Her face is sweaty, tears stain her cheeks, and her eyes are red-rimmed but still impossibly blue.

"It's the worst." Her eyes narrow slightly. "You look paler than usual."

"It's a new moon today."

"Oh, a cycle. How delightful for you." Wolves share the same frequency of cycles as humans, monthly, whereas faeries I've been told are every four months. I wonder if vampires have cycles?

I wave a hand towards the toilet. "I bet you wish you weren't pregnant right now."

She groans, turning back to the toilet, resting her head on the edge. "I don't think I'll be moving for a while."

"I'll get you some water and some snacks to settle your stomach."

As I exit her room, descending the stairs, I message Vlad.

> Allura and I are out for tonight.

A text comes through almost immediately.

VLAD

> Is everything okay?

> It's a new moon, and Lu's violently ill.

I'm at the fridge by the time Vlad's message chimes on my phone.

VLAD

> Oh yes, I understand. Is Lu okay?

I laugh, gathering up the bottle of cold water, grapes, and crackers on the counter.

The only time either of us move from the sofa the next day is to get snacks, and in Allura's case, dash to a bathroom to puke. We sleep periodically curled up under our copious amounts of blankets on the sofa, not even bothering to go to our beds.

A sliver of moon hangs in the sky, doing nothing to illuminate the night when my phone buzzes from the coffee table. I lean over, scooping it up.

ART

I hear his chuckle from the front door.

ART

20

Vladislav's Penthouse

MY PHONE STARTS BUZZING on my desk. The caller is a private number.

"Hello?"

"Hi, my love," she purrs. Ice runs through my veins.

"Medea," I spit.

"How did you do it, Consort?" she croons, making me cringe.

"I'm no longer your Consort," I state.

"Answer me!" she screams into my ear. "How did you do it?"

"I don't know what you're referring to."

"The bond," she growls. "How did you break it?"

Laughter almost bursts out of me. "I'm sure you'll work it out."

Medea laughs, her voice honeyed. "Oh, baby. Don't worry, I'll be there soon." The line cuts off.

Carlos appears at the door of my office. "It's happening again, isn't it?"

I sigh, running a hand through my hair. "Between the unnecessary Trials, and erratic behavior, she's succumbing to madness."

Carlos is silent as we leave the office and enter the living area. He takes a seat at one end of the sofa. "Noble is still pissed at you for what you did to him the last time he was here."

I frown, sitting opposite him. "So he won't meet with us?"

"Well, he might."

"How—" the front door clicks open followed by laughter. The bond hums, as Allura, Ren and Aster walk into the room. Aster's eyes shine as we lock eyes. I've missed her more than I care to admit out loud. I stand from my seat, forcing myself not to cross the room and wrap myself around her and never let go.

Allura skips over, planting a kiss on my cheek before doing the same to Carlos, who is also now standing, and then settles into the sofa.

You're staring a little intensely, Ren muses into my head. My eyes flick to him and I grumble a slew of Russian swear words into his head as he drapes an arm around Aster's shoulder and pulls her toward us. Vik, Dom and Maddox also arrive, all taking up residence on the sofa together as I stand in front of them all.

"Carlos was just about to update me about the Noble situation."

"Well, he said he'd meet up with me, as long as I bought Aster as well."

"When?" Aster immediately asks.

"Tonight. He agreed to meet us at Eternal."

I don't like this idea at all, and there's no fucking chance that I'm allowing both of them to go alone, but I already know that if I try any heroics that I would be berated.

"I guess it's a hunting night," Ren sighs, standing from the sofa.

Vik looks at Dom with a heated gaze, the wolf returning the look. "Dom and I are out," Vik announces as she stands. "We'll see you tomorrow."

They leave the apartment as Allura pulls Aster and Maddox toward the guest rooms, telling us that they'll be ready in an hour. Carlos has disappeared as well, probably going down to Ren's apartment ten floors down to rummage through his wardrobe.

I found Medea. Ren announces in my head. His eyes lock with mine. *She's in Los Angeles visiting an old friend of ours.*

Ortiz? I ask, and Ren nods. *She called me just before everyone got here.* I think about the phone call so he can see it in my head.

He frowns. *Your bond to Medea is broken?*

Shit. I forgot about that. *I'm bonded to someone else.*

Ren chuckles out loud. *Who's the poor vampire who's got you to deal with for eternity?*

I clear my throat. *Aster.*

"Excuse me?" Ren chokes out loud. Disbelief and shock pulse off him.

"I don't quite understand it myself."

"Are you sure?" he asks.

I nod once. "Allura claims it's the result of a magic anomaly."

"Result of the pregnancy?" My surprise must flash in my eyes, causing Ren to smile. "She can't keep much from me when Marin incessantly thought about it when we were all together." Sadness curls briefly around him before dissolving back into subdued shock, and curiosity.

"We'll ask her about it later. I need to change."

Ren nods and leaves without a word, and I retreat to my room. I change from my current suit into a navy one with a black shirt, select a gleaming platinum watch and return to the living area.

Aster is in her spot, peering out of the window. She looks stunning in the tight, light gray dress. The sleeves are long, and it's a modest knee length, but the sharp dip of the back is sinful.

Her hair is braided in a thick, shiny rope hanging between her exposed shoulder blades all the way to the curve of her back. I try my hardest not to think about wrapping it around my fist as I step closer, joining her by the window.

"You look delectable," I comment, gazing out into the city.

I notice her smile in the reflection of the glass. "Wearing tape is weird."

"Tape?" I ask, turning to her, her heels making her lips that much closer to mine.

She takes a step closer as she takes my hand, placing it on her hip. My fingers flex as the bond sizzles in satisfaction at the contact. Her eyes burn into mine as she moves my hand along her hip and over the curve of her ass. The fabric is soft, and there's no seams underneath.

"Only tape," she confirms, leaving my hand where it is and taking my other hand, brushing it over her breast, allowing me to feel the tape she's referring to underneath. She moves my hand down her side and circles it around to place it on her ass.

A growl rumbles my chest and I pull her closer, pressing her body into mine, my hard cock between us. "You make it impossible to take things slow."

"This bond has a mind of its own," she murmurs as she curls both arms around my neck. "I've missed you."

The said bond swells at the admission. "I missed you too."

Aster stretches up and presses her lips onto mine softly, almost hesitant. My tongue darts out, running across the seam of her lips and she opens them. She moans as our tongues dance and teeth graze soft flesh. Her heart races as she presses further into me, raking her hands through my hair. She bites down on my lower lip and lust sears through my veins, the feral, primal part of me careening to the surface.

I pull away, breathing hard. "Teeth to yourself, little wolf, unless you want to be claimed right here."

Vibrant gold eyes sparkle as Aster breathes heavily. "I wouldn't even be mad about that."

I growl, reluctantly taking a step back from her scorching heat. "I never thought I'd ever say this, but you were right about taking things slow. I want you to be sure about me."

"Oh." Aster breathes as she blinks, her eyes returning to jade green. Something flashes through her eyes. Hurt, maybe?

Before I can say anything, Maddox and Allura enter the living area arm in arm. Maddox is sporting ripped black skinny jeans, a fitted white t-shirt and blue eyeshadow that extends over his temples. Allura is dressed in a fitted emerald green dress that is long-sleeved and has thin silver chains holding together a slit up to her left hip. They join us by the windows, Allura handing over the leather jacket in her arms to Aster.

"Let's walk. Central Park is calling me." Maddox asks, his emotions burning with anticipation. Ren and Maddox find it amusing to stir up the wolves who reside in the park, as well as prey on unsuspecting couples enjoying the park at night.

We meet Carlos and Ren in the lobby and then head towards Midtown. The crisp air barely rustles the trees, but the slight breeze brings the city's scents and its population around me. I concentrate on the city's steel and moss aroma rather than the warmer scents of the humans walking past.

Ren and Maddox disappear into the park almost immediately, and Carlos and Allura stroll arm in arm ahead of me. Aster hangs a little further back from them, scanning the area.

"Are you okay?" I ask. She jumps, not realizing I've caught up to her.

She gives me a weak smile. "Yeah, it's just that I can sense the wolves nearby, and it's making me edgy."

"I didn't know wolves could sense each other."

Aster's heart flutters. "Ah yeah, some of us can."

She's still hiding things from me, and it's aggravating, but now isn't the time to demand answers. I take her hand and wrap her arm around mine. She stiffens slightly, and then takes a shaky breath and leans closer to me. Our mate bond hums in contentment at the gesture, but it wants more.

"This bond is insatiable," I comment, drawing her heated body closer to me.

Aster smirks. "I know. I swear it wants me to eat you."

"It's a date."

Aster smacks me on the forearm, and we both laugh. Little does she know that the urge to sink my fangs into her, mark her, is, at times, concerning. We walk in comfortable silence for a few minutes as Aster looks around, this time taking in the city and not scanning for danger.

"I thought you drank only from blood bags?" she asks.

"We all do most of the time," I explain, waving toward Carlos. "But our bodies start to reject it after a while, so we have to go for a vein before we go into a state we call Blood Lust."

"Blood Lust," Aster muses, "that doesn't sound great."

"Vampires walk a fine line between being a murderous machine and somewhat normal. For made vampires, it takes a lot of self-control to keep from spiraling to that dark place. Most of us learn control and still feed on humans, but for some, it's much more difficult."

"Have you ever experienced Blood Lust?" Aster asks in a soft voice.

"I have." Memories flash, darkening my vision. "But all made vampires go through Blood Lust right after their change. Mine was quite severe, whereas Renard's was merely a blip in time."

"What does it feel like?"

"The human part of your brain shuts down, and you become a rabid animal, willing to do absolutely anything for blood. Everyone is food; man, woman or child."

A shudder vibrates Aster's body. "It must have been horrible."

"When you're in that state, you feel nothing. The aftermath is the worst part."

The guilt from my years in Blood Lust suddenly surfaces and my heart aches. I did so many horrible things, and took so many lives. Aster is silent, her hand stroking my forearm slow and soothing.

She doesn't have my dark gift, but she can sway my emotions with just a touch. The storm of guilt settles in my heart, coated by the warmth of our bond.

My bond with Medea never felt this... light. It was created by deception and a false love, so it was intense, and rotten. But with

Aster, it's soft and easy, and genuine. I don't realize how much she settles my soul until she isn't near me, even before the bond between us surfaced.

Aster is solace in the chaos, and as selfish as it is, I don't think I will ever let her go.

"Can I ask you a risky question?" Aster whispers.

"You can ask me anything."

"Are there different kinds of vampires?"

I smile. "There are three."

"I knew it," Aster beams. "There are different degrees of saturation and complexity in your scents. You, Mydas, and Ren all have potent, dimensional scents. Everyone else's scents are still strong but more simplistic."

"Mydas, Ren and I are all Lilim-made. We were made by blood transfusion from a Pure Blood. Pure Bloods, true to the title, are the purest form of vampire. Born, not created."

"And the others?"

"Maddox, Carlos, and Viktoria are all Adam-made vampires. A toxin all species of vampires have in their bite made them."

"How do you feed on someone and not turn them if your bite is toxic?"

I smirk, inquisitive little thing. "After a feed, we use some of our blood to heal the wound which counteracts the toxin."

"But wouldn't that also turn a human?" she asks.

I shake my head. "Oh no. There's a lot of blood involved in that process. Besides, only Pure Bloods can create vampires in that way. A few drops of vampire blood can actually heal just about anything. Even in werewolves."

Aster laughs. "How many times have you had to heal Dom from his antics?"

I smile. "I haven't so far in the time we've known each other, his wolf healing has been enough."

"He's definitely got a thick head for a Bitten," Aster muses.

"I've been told there's a couple of types of wolves as well?"

Aster stiffens for a brief moment before relaxing again. "Yes, there's two types. First Bloods and Bitten. First Bloods are descendants of the three original werewolves, and Bitten are made from a wolf's bite on a full moon. First Bloods can change into a full wolf every full moon, but Bitten can only do it if they're with a First Blood Pack. Most of the time, they just get all aggressive and full of attitude at the full moon."

I nod, filing away this new information. "And I'm told female First Bloods are rare?"

"Extremely," Aster agrees. "Female wolves you will come across are most likely Bitten, and even they are rare. The change is brutal to a human body; only a few decide to go through the change, and even less actually survive it."

I'm about to ask her if she remembers her change but we're a block away from Eternal, the long, snaking line up ahead. Carlos and Allura slow, as we bypass the disgruntled party goers in the line and approach the red ropes at the door.

I nod slightly at the bouncer. "Hey Gabriel, how is it tonight?"

The hulking vampire smiles. "It's good, boss, packed with all flavors tonight. Your bro and Maddox are already inside, so if you don't want sloppy seconds, you might want to get in there." His light hazelnut eyes roam over Aster with an approving grin. "But it looks like you've already gotten the prime piece of the whole evening."

"Hey," Aster snaps at Gabriel, forcing his eyes up to her face. "I *am* a prime piece of ass but if you refer to me that way ever again, those pretty eyes will become my new favorite pair of earrings."

Such violence, such sincerity; I'm wickedly hard. Gabriel's eyes widen and his jaw slackens. Allura giggles, hooking her arm into Aster's free one, tugging her out of my grip and passing through the now open ropes.

Gabriel's watches the two women walk into the dark doorway. Awe and predatory lust roll off the vampire. "I think I'm in love," he mumbles.

Carlos chuckles, clapping Gabriel on the shoulder. "She's taken, *hermano*."

"Is Mr. Noble here yet?" I ask, ignoring the possessive bond demanding me to tear Gabriel apart for staring at my mate.

Gabriel clears his throat, his eyes darting to his clipboard. "No, sir."

"If he asks, only Carlos and Aster are here." I walk past Gabriel into the club without a second glance, his fear-spiked emotions an answer in itself.

We enter a dark hallway where Allura and Aster are standing at the end in front of the cloak desk. "Gabriel is going to try to marry you now," Allura chuckles.

"Even if I weren't taken," Aster muses, shrugging off her leather jacket, "he's not my type. I get strong player vibes."

"You're not wrong," Carlos answers as we step up to the desk, also taking our jackets off. "He's fucked almost every female member of my Nest. Even some of the men."

"How was he?" Allura challenges.

Carlos chuckles. "He's not my type either."

I roll the sleeves of my shirt as Allura and Carlos' bickering becomes a low hum. A rapid heartbeat distracts me, and the spike of amber rum and milk in the hallway.

My eyes go to Aster—she's breathing a little too hard, her eyes fixated on watching me roll my sleeves. They linger on my left arm, probably noticing the bottom of my tattoo.

Carlos and Allura disappear past the heavy door in front of us, the colored lights and heavy music flooding in briefly before plunging us back into darkness.

Another wave of her heady scent wraps around me; she's aroused. I step forward, wrapping my arm around her waist, crushing her to me. "What are you thinking about, *petit louve?*"

She melts further into me, her eyes now a liquid gold. "I'm thinking about that wicked tongue doing things hotter than speaking foreign languages."

I growl. "I want nothing more than to take you to my office, lay you down on my desk and taste you until you're screaming my name, but Noble will scent me all over you."

She groans, pushing herself further into my erection. "Stupid Noble."

I sigh my agreement, stepping back and lacing our fingers together as I lead her through the steel door into the wall of sound. The music is heavy with bass, the tempo thumping through my body; it's so loud that even with vampiric hearing, I'll find it hard to hear through the mess of noise.

A sunken dance floor dominates vast space, with lights of all different colors bouncing and swirling around the floor, creating a surreal atmosphere. A large, circular platform in the center of the dance floor holds the DJ bopping away with his headphones on and a plethora of girls dancing provocatively on the edges.

The packed crowd on the dance floor gyrate close to one another, and to our right, a large group of people team around the bar waiting for drinks. Clusters of lively people, drinking and laughing, pack the tables on the dance floor's outskirts. To our left, even the VIP area is busy; each booth seems to be booked.

Aster and I snake our way through the crowd towards the VIP area, where a bouncer simply nods and lifts the rope for us to enter. We climb the dozen steps up to the private bar, before passing all the booths that overlook the main dance floor to a large black booth at the end, where Carlos is on his phone in front of a bottle of champagne and three glasses. He looks up as Aster takes a seat next to him.

His nose twitches, and he smirks. "What did you two get up to?"

Aster shoves his shoulder, making him laugh. He wraps an arm around her shoulders, pulling her closer to him, and I take a step forward, growling.

My reaction makes Carlos laugh harder. "Relax, boss man, I'm masking your scent that's all over her."

Before I do anything stupid, I take one last look at Aster's beautiful face and leave the VIP area. I slip into the crowd, weaving my way to the dim area next to the bar. Maddox, Allura and Ren have a table tucked in a corner, and I slide onto the remaining empty barstool.

Maddox and Ren's emotions are swirling with satisfaction and the thrill of the hunt, their eyes darting through the crowd and occasionally murmuring to each other. Allura's eyes are on me, her emotions twisting with concern and understanding.

"We can see her from here," Allura says to me, pointing forward. I follow her direction and see an unobstructed view of Aster and Carlos, both with a glass in hand and laughing.

A dark shape distracts me as Noble struts across the VIP section, towards the booth.

21

Nova

Eternal, Midtown Manhattan

I CAN SEE VLAD'S delicious body across the club, tucked into a dark corner table by the bar with Maddox, Ren and Allura. I could pick him out of any crowd even without the bond. His presence draws the attention of quite a few people around him, their hungry eyes roaming over him.

If anyone approaches him, I will leap over this railing and hurt them.

A growl vibrates in my chest and Carlos chuckles next to me. "You're as bad as the other."

"We're mate bonded," I huff before I realize what I've just said. I look up to Carlos' shocked expression.

"That's... interesting."

"Blame Allura," I mutter, taking another sip of my drink.

Carlos shakes with silent laughter. "Even if Allura didn't break magic a little bit, you two were bound to end up with each other."

I frown, looking back into his brown eyes. "Why do you say that?"

"You two move with each other like you're one, an effortless give and take of energy. Plus, both of you are loyal to the bone, way too protective of the people you care about and stubborn as hell."

Before I can even process anything he just said, his eyes flick up to something behind me and he stiffens slightly. "Noble is here."

I clear my throat and sit straighter, taking a healthy mouthful of the champagne in my glass. Noble's rotund, vile presence looms at the edge of our booth. His eyes slide down my body, focusing on my exposed legs, and he licks his lips. His candied lemon scent curls around me and I try not to gag as I give him a clipped smile.

"Noble," Carlos croons, sweeping his arm toward the booth. "Please sit. Thanks for coming."

"When I heard you two were wanting to get out from under Vladislav's thumb," he says as he sits down, thankfully next to Carlos, "I couldn't resist."

I just nod and smile, having no idea what lies Carlos spun to get Noble to sit down with us.

Carlos hooks an arm around my shoulder again, his sugared almond scent masking Noble's putrid one. "When this one came into the picture, I knew she was the one and it was time to get out."

"From Vladislav's reaction," Noble muses, tapping a finger on his thin lips, "I thought he may have laid claim on her."

"Wrong vampire," I say, placing my free hand on Carlos' thigh. "Vladislav is just a stickler for his rules."

Noble answering smile turns my stomach. "Good," he purrs, "I know Carlos doesn't mind sharing."

If we didn't need information from this creep, I'd inflict a lot of violence on him, but I restrain myself.

Carlos chuckles. "Before we make any decisions, we need to know your business benefits us."

Noble moves his attention to Carlos, and he dips his chin. "What would you like to know?"

"How does it work?" I ask before Carlos can.

Noble leans forward pouring himself a champagne. "I'd supply the product, and you'll deal it out of Vladislav's clubs, and Sanctuary." He takes a sip of his drink, making a satisfied sound before his eyes return to Carlos. "Your cut will be substantial."

Carlos picks up the champagne bottle. "Are your suppliers reliable? The *sources* are becoming suspicious already, and we don't want to risk the wrath of their higher authorities." The 'sources' I'm assuming being the Fae.

Noble chuckles. "Trust me, my boy, this is easier than you think. The chain of distribution and sourcing is solid," Noble assures.

"I don't know, Carlos," I murmur softly, leaning into him. "I don't like the idea of going into this blind."

"What do you mean, *cariña?*" Carlos croons.

"I trust Noble," I send him a smile, before returning my attention to Carlos, "but what if his boss isn't trustworthy and rats us all out?"

"He wouldn't," Noble interjects. "He has too much riding on this operation to succeed."

Carlos picks up on Noble's tone. "Why are you, or your associate, so eager for us to do this for you?"

Noble's grin is devoid of any humor. "Because once you've both secured clientele in Manhattan, we will take down Vladislav, Beau, and that silly human Sidelle."

White hot rage pulses through my body. I grip Carlos' thigh a little tighter to hide the trembling in my hand, and stop myself from launching at Noble. I will tear his throat out before he can hurt my people.

"That's a bit ambitious for Housden, is it not?" Carlos questions. Could it be him?

"Not when he has friends in high places," Noble admits. What the fuck?

Carlos deposits his half empty glass on the table and sits back, seemingly at ease, contemplating Noble's words while I'm keeping a blank face plastered over the fury burning me on the inside. Carlos eventually sighs. "We'll have to think about it."

Noble nods once and stands, discarding his glass onto the table. "Housden is eager for a way into this territory, so don't make me wait too long to give him the good news."

Carlos nods, then turns his face towards mine and nuzzles my neck. "We'll let you know, Noble," he murmurs against my skin. Noble leers at my body one more time before disappearing. My body instantly starts to tremble, desperate to go after him.

"Hold on a little longer," Carlos whispers against my skin. "He has an entourage at the bar. Gabriel will let me know when they're all gone."

I relax my face, turning my face, resting my forehead against Carlos'. "I'm going to tear these fuckers to pieces," I whisper, closing my eyes.

"I'll be right next to you," Carlos lifts his head when we feel his phone vibrate in his pocket pressing into my thigh. I open my eyes, and turn to the main dance floor. Vlad and the rest of our crew are gone from their table.

"Gabriel says it's clear," Carlos breathes, removing his arm from my shoulders and slumping forward, his elbows resting on his thighs.

I stand up immediately and pace to the railing, taking heaving breaths and fiddle with the amulet on my wrist, trying to calm my racing heart as I watch the lights dance and bounce over the swaying bodies of the crowd. The bond stirs violently, tugging, as an arm slips around my waist, pulling me into a warm body smelling of peaches and smoke.

"They threatened my home, and I'm going to kill all of them," I declare to Vlad.

"What do you mean?" he asks, turning me towards him. Shock widens his eyes, as he takes in my murderous expression, my eyes probably fiery gold.

"The next in the chain is Housden," Carlos announces from behind us.

Vlad goes still, his face whipping to Carlos. "Come again?"

Vlad and I join the rest of the crew on the plush black seats of the booth as Carlos relays all the information we just learned from Noble. Ren lets off a string of expletives in three different languages as Maddox shakes his head disbelievingly. Allura's shocked face is frozen and a tear slides down her face.

"Housden kidnapped Marin then?" Ren asks, his voice gravelly.

"I don't think so," Carlos says, his finger tapping his lip. "But he may have been the person who pointed the person in her direction."

"Shall we ask him directly?" Vlad asks in a calm tone. Everyone's attention burns into him. His lips lift into a sardonic smile. "I got a call from Bartese just before about a slew of Trials that took place last night in his territory, so he's demanding a meeting to discuss matters."

Carlos chuckles. "Housden will definitely want to be a part of that particular meeting."

These men, so devious yet so effective. A satisfied smile settles on my face.

"Enough business," Maddox whines, flagging down a waiter. "Let's party!"

22

Vladislav

Eternal

CARLOS AND REN LINE up another round of colorful shots on the table, while Maddox chats to a human female who hangs on his every word. Allura sips on a bottle of water laughing with Aster by the railing, overlooking the partiers below.

"Let's go *chica*," Carlos bellows, summoning Aster, "you can't get out of this one."

She groans, swaying slightly as she approaches the table. "I've been in every round! Think of my poor liver."

Ren scoffs. "You have supernatural healing, stop complaining and start drinking."

As the three of them start frantically tipping back shots, I slip out of the VIP area and onto the main floor. I take a moment to scan the crowd myself. Ignoring the plethora of women attempting to entice me into their arms tonight, I walk through the crowd slowly, trying to untangle the different notes in the air until I catch a bright mandarin scent.

The tartness gets caught in the back of my throat, and my fangs ache. I follow the citrus trail through the crowd back to the dark area of the club we were in before.

A young woman sits at a bar table, cradling some sort of blue cocktail close, watching a group of women giggle and dance at the edge of the dance floor. The group tries to coax her to them, but she shakes her head, pointing at the pile of bags and drinks on the table.

Her scent wafts over to me, making me salivate. As I near her, the predatory part of my brain pushes to take control, but I hold it back. I don't want to kill the poor girl.

Her eyes grow a little wider, and her cheeks pink as I approach. I flash her a smile and introduce myself, and she becomes flustered as she takes my outstretched hand. My dark gift seeps into her skin as soon as our hands connect, and I push feelings of compliance and calm. I feel awful as I lean down and sink my fangs into her neck. Her blood flows into my mouth from the wounds, tasting of her altered emotions, the alcohol she's consumed, and the same tangy mandarin of her scent.

I take what I require, using a fang to pierce my thumb, seal the four small wounds, and then use my gift to make it feel to her as if she had been daydreaming.

As I walk past the bar, I instruct a bartender with the gift of compulsion to visit the girl and erase her memory of me, just to be sure it doesn't come back to bite me later. I make my way back through the crowd but stop as I spot Allura, Maddox, and Aster on the dance floor.

Maddox dances with a new human, a male this time, with his tongue down his throat.

Allura and Aster sway together with the resounding beat. The males around them ogle at the sight, both human and supernatural. Allura naturally has the sensual magic that all faeries do, but I'm completely transfixed by Aster.

She has her eyes closed and her head back, her facial expression blissful. She rolls her hips in a carnal rhythm, her hands roam over her body, and a sheen of sweat makes her skin glow under the lights.

I make my way to her as if in a trance; her scent curls under my nose. It's a heady mix of leather, amber rum and milk, now tainted with peppery tequila. My predatory side pushes forward again, but I use every shred of control I have to make it to the outskirts of the makeshift circle around them and not claim Aster in the middle of this dance floor.

Aster opens her eyes straight at me as if she sensed my arrival. The mate bond burns with a fiery delight as her gaze rolls over my body, and she saunters closer to me.

She sways those tantalizing hips slowly as she stands a breath away from me, taunting me with her lack of touch. I growl low, but her returning breathy laugh shows she heard it.

I stay where I am, no matter how much my body is screaming for me to take her into my arms. Aster finally runs her hands up my chest, over my shoulders, and around the back of my neck. I place my hands on her hips, pulling her closer to me, needing to feel more of her.

She inhales as her face leans closer to mine. Her entire body goes rigid. Wrath burns through her expression, and her eyes turn a rich gold.

"You fed on someone?" She takes in another deep inhale, gripping my neck. "A *woman*?"

I nod, not knowing what to say.

She grips a handful of hair painfully, tilting my head down so I'm forced to stare right into her fury-fired gold eyes.

"If you so much as *look* at another female again, I will rip you to shreds." Her voice is guttural and possessive.

I pull her closer, pushing my throbbing hard-on into her stomach. "I didn't think you'd be this possessive, *ma petit louve*?"

She growls and crushes her lips to mine. The sweet, zesty lime, and acidic peppery tequila mixed in with the taste of Aster nearly sends me over the edge. My fangs drop suddenly, and they prick her bottom lip. I jolt back, trying to assess the damage, but she grips my hair tighter, crushing her bleeding lip to mine.

Her blood explodes across my tongue, frying every brain cell I have. The predator in me roars in my head as I pull her closer to me.

She tastes of her rich amber rum scent. Of secrets and unfulfilled fantasies. She tastes of *life*.

We separate from each other and realize many people are staring. Not the humans, but the supernaturals. Fuck. I wrap an arm around Aster's waist and the other around Allura and direct them back to our booth. Both collapse onto the soft leather seats as I look over to Ren and Carlos, their faces alight with humor.

"Well, you've definitely stirred up the gossip chains, Vlad," Carlos comments.

"With that display, I'm going to be hearing it from everyone," Ren complains as he pours a tray of champagne. Maddox arrives shortly after us, with a pleased expression warming his face.

We all take a glass of champagne, and Allura picks up the glass with the apple juice.

"To creating a scene," I toast, the group repeats my words and we drink.

As I dress for tonight's meeting, an unease settles over me. We now know Housden is one of the major suppliers of Lux in the city, but the question still remains – who's running the Blood Pit for the supply and where is Marin? She's still alive since we haven't recovered her body. If we don't get to her in time, this city will feel my wrath.

I slide on my charcoal gray suit jacket over my navy shirt and head over to my watch drawer to select a watch. As I'm admiring the collection, a soft knock sounds from my bedroom door.

"Come in," I call, pulling out one of many platinum watches and fastening it to my wrist.

"Your room is a bachelor's dream," Aster comments at the entrance to the wardrobe, admiring the neat rows of shirts and suits.

"It's fine," I counter, taking in Aster's devious outfit. The black dress is tight, hugging every curve, and the sleeves off the shoulder are elbow length, but that silver twinkling zipper running down the whole front is making my hands twitch.

"Just tape this time?" I ask, my eyes tracing the curves over her breasts above the neckline.

"Shall we find out?" Aster asks, voice soft, her free hand going to the zipper. I suddenly realize her other hand is filled with two pairs of heels.

I stride forward, stopping inches away, my eyes catching her heated gaze. My hand lands low on her stomach, my finger finding the zipper trail. I trace the tracks up toward her chest, her eyes melting into gold, her breathing labored.

I reach the zipper tongue and tug it slowly, revealing what's underneath. My eyes dip down and I groan; she's wearing a red lacy strapless bra.

"Christ, woman," I breathe, slipping my hand into her dress, clutching her side, tracing my thumb over the flesh spilling over the cups.

"Which shoes shall I wear?" she asks, her voice breathy, as she holds up the hand full of shoes.

I continue to stroke her heated skin, enticing a hitch in her breath with each pass, as I study the choices.

"These," I muse, plucking the red-bottom heels from her hand. My hand on her waist slides down her body as I sink to my knees, unzipping the dress as I go, exposing more flesh until it falls open to reveal matching red panties.

Her arousal coats the air, and my mind starts to go hazy. My eyes bore into hers as my hand skims down her bare thigh, circling to her calf and lifting her foot. She's unbalanced, making her pitch forward and use my shoulders to balance herself, bringing her lace clad body closer to my face.

I slide the heel on and place her foot back to the ground, before starting the same path with the other leg and sliding the other heel on, then grab her hips as I stand and lift her legs around my waist.

Her hands move from clutching my shoulders, to wrapping around my neck as she crushes her lips to mine. Our teeth clash, and our tongues dance in the rough kiss as I step over and push Aster's body against the closed door to my bathroom.

Her thighs clutch tighter around my waist as she drags me impossibly closer, pressing my straining cock harder into her core. I clutch her loose hair close to her scalp, pulling myself away from her lips, breathing heavy as I stare into her gold eyes.

"Aster," I growl.

"I need you," she pants.

"We can't," I whisper, "our guests don't need the distraction of gossip."

"Let them," she growls.

I chuckle. "So defiant, little wolf."

"Fuck me, Vlad," Aster pants, her eyes liquid gold.

I groan, resting my forehead on hers, wrestling with the bond in my chest burning for me to do as she has asked. "If I do, you'll have a mate bite and then fucked into next week."

She whimpers. "*Please.*"

Hearing her beg almost sends me feral. I force down the raging bond as I lift my head, hooking a finger under her chin and bringing her lips to mine for a subdued kiss. "We have to find Marin."

We untangle from each other and Aster slips into my bathroom, zipping her dress up and gathering up her wild curls into a high ponytail as I straighten up my suit. I sidle up next to her, smoothing down my own hair as she checks her make-up for any mishaps.

The gold glitter still sparkles on her eyelids, and the rich blood-red stain on her pouty lips is remarkably unchanged. She's a succubus in the flesh, ready to consume every heart in the universe.

"What exactly are Nests?" Aster asks, stepping back from the sink, adjusting the neckline of her dress.

"Vampires group in Nests, similar to Packs. Nests help with regulating younger vampires, so they don't go around accidentally turning masses of people or killing sprees."

"I presume young vampires are as cocky as young wolves."

"You have no idea." More like utterly incapable of resisting their thirst if they aren't part of a Nest.

"Are you a Nest Master?"

I laugh. "Oh, no. And I'm no longer part of a Nest either."

"No longer?"

"That is a story for another day. As Beau has mentioned, I'm a Rogue vampire. Not part of Court or a Nest."

Aster wraps her hands around my bicep as we leave the bathroom, heading toward the foyer. "Tell me more about this Court."

"Vampires have a Queen who oversees everything. She has a Court, which comprises her strongest and most loyal vampires. Throughout the world, there are Nests; the strongest vampires are always Nest Master. Then there are Rogues like me, usually too strong to be in a Nest without being Master. Some decide to start Nests, and some like me are out here minding our own business."

"I'm assuming even Rogues are under the Queen's rule, right?"

"Unfortunately." My hatred for Medea simmers. The thought of her being anywhere near Aster sends a fresh wave of animosity through me.

"Are you okay, Vlad? You've vamped-out a little." I look down at Aster's concerned gaze and focus on my breathing.

"I'm okay," I reassure, stepping forward, opening the front door for her.

"You have a rough history with the Queen, huh?" she asks as she waits for me to close the door.

I nod in answer, lacing her fingers through mine as we head for the elevator.

"So, who's part of what Nest?"

"Ren is a Rogue like me. Vik and Maddox are part of the Manhattan Nest, under Beau, and Carlos as you know is part of the Housden's Nest in Queens."

"Are they all coming here because you're neutral ground, or your connection to the Queen?" Aster asks as we step into the elevator.

"I no longer have a connection to the Queen," I correct, pressing the basement level. "But they think I still have sway over her."

Aster nods, eyes fixed on watching the numbers count down. "None of them like werewolves much, do they?"

"No, not particularly."

She smiles, turning her jade green eyes to me. "I know the drill. Don't go punching people."

I return her smile. "That would be beneficial to our plans."

As the doors slide open to the hallway of Immortal, Aster and I step out together. A flurry of excited energy filters over to me as we walk down the hall where dancers dart in and out of dressing rooms in various stages of undress.

One of the male dancers spots us and bounds over, grasping Aster's hand and tugging at her. She pecks me on the lips before trailing after the dancer into a dressing room.

Is anyone here yet? I ask Ren telepathically as I slip into my office.

Mydas is at the bar wanting to speak to you before everyone arrives.

Send him to my office, I say as I sit behind my desk. A few moments later, Mydas strides in with a soft smile on his face.

"I honestly don't know how you're around so many beautiful creatures all the time, and not constantly hard," he comments as he takes a seat opposite me.

I refrain from rolling my eyes. "You get desensitized pretty quickly." I pull out my phone and scan my emails. "What was it that you wanted to discuss?"

"They appointed a new Advisor at Court," Mydas announces, his lust haze dissipating to anticipation.

"Without the Queen's presence?" I ask.

"The Elders and the remaining two Advisors made the decision in her absence." His emotions spike with a hint of smugness.

"They appointed you?" I assume.

The smugness blazes around him, before settling into pride as he nods. "I'm honored to serve our species as your new Advisor."

I force the smile onto my face, even though I have the urge to toss him out of my club immediately. "Congratulations, brother."

Mydas is not to be told any further information about anything, spread the word.

What's happened? Ren asks immediately.

He's been appointed Advisor, he's not to be trusted. He may be our vampire brother, but anyone associated that directly with the Queen always has ulterior motives.

I half-listen to Mydas blathering on about having to inform Bartese about his move from his Nest to the Court for a few minutes before Carlos knocks on the door, advising us that guests are arriving.

The bar lights are brighter than usual, and the music is soft. Mydas heads directly for the bar with Carlos where Aster helps Maddox polish glassware.

If Mydas even attempts anything with my mate, I don't give a fuck who's here, he's going to lose a hand. Aster's face lights up as I reach the bar. She picks up a tray of glassware, depositing it on the other side of the bar.

"I'm surprised Viktoria allowed you to step behind the bar so soon."

She laughs. "She needs someone to do the grunt work. I've been instructed I'm not allowed to touch any types of liquid." She struts down the length of the bar and into the stock room.

Mydas turns to me, about to say something really stupid but his face falters on mine.

"She's off-limits," I state.

Mydas pouts, turning back to Maddox, who slides him a drink. Carlos steps away from Mydas' side, melting into his post by the VIP entrance as laughter filters down from the entrance. I cross over to the entrance as Bartese and his second in command stroll in.

"Bartese," I greet with a respectful nod and lead him to a sofa. Shortly after his arrival, Mr. Ashcroft of Chicago and his second appear. Ashcroft is the *only* Nest Master in the city of Chicago. How he runs so many vampires, I'm not sure.

Next to arrive is someone I have not seen in a long time. "Greyson Ortiz, it's been lifetimes."

The tall, black-haired vampire takes my outstretched hand. "Vlad, how long *has* it been? Over two centuries?"

I smile. "And what a quiet two centuries it's been."

Greyson shakes his head, chuckling. He was the previous Queen's ex-Consort; we met at Court when we both darkened their hallways. His Nest in Los Angeles isn't big, but he's got some strong vampires under his guidance.

Behind Greyson, Beau descends the stairs, conversing with a male vampire taller than both of us with golden hair and ice-blue eyes.

Greyson steps back enough for the other vampire to extend his hand. "Vlad, this is my second, Nate."

I shake Nate's hand. The contact sends waves of power through me like all oxygen has been stolen from my body. He's got the power of an Ancient. His aura is confident, but *just* confident, which is odd; usually, a person feels multiple things at once. He must be able to limit my gift, which is a rare ability.

"Nate, welcome to Immortal."

"Thank you, Mr. Vladislav; I have heard good things about the place." His low baritone voice is laced with the same power as his touch. How he is Greyson's second and not Master is wholly lost on me.

I turn to Beau. "I didn't know you were coming this evening."

Beau smirks. "I couldn't resist a bitching circle."

The three new arrivals follow me to the rest of the vampires; Greyson and Nate take seats on an empty sofa as Beau trails over to the bar. The last to arrive is Housden, followed by Noble. Housden's emotions are wary, but still pretentious, whereas Noble's emotions range from hostile to straight up arrogant.

"Mr. Housden," I say politely, holding out my hand.

Surprisingly, he accepts the hand shake. "Vladislav."

I pull my hand back and glare at Noble. I ignore him and gesture towards the group, indicating to them to take a seat. I walk over to the bar, passing Maddox with a tray of drinks as I step up beside Aster.

Her eyes are wide as she assesses the room. She's breathing slowly, panic flickering in her eyes. I reach to touch her but remember that I can't use my gift to take the edge off. She steps closer to me, brushing her hand on the back of mine.

I lean down to her, my lip just brushing her ear. "The blonde vampire, Nate, can you tell how old he is?" I whisper so softly I'll be surprised if Aster can hear me.

She shudders and pulls back slightly to look into my eyes. "I'd have to get closer, but from here, I'd say very, very old."

I nod once, brushing my knuckles against hers before turning back toward the vampires. I hear Ren close the doors above and appear at the bottom of the stairs. He meets me at the front of the stage, facing all the men.

"I thought we might get business over with so we can relax for the rest of the evening?"

Most of them nod or voice their agreement. Beau remains at the bar as Mydas joins me in front of the stage.

"I hear a promotion has been decided," Housden muses, eyes on Mydas.

Mydas bows his head. "The Queen has graciously offered me the position of Advisor, which I have accepted."

Murmurs of congratulations course around the group, but I see Greyson rolling his eyes. I keep my face neutral as I try not to laugh.

"There are other matters we're here for," Ashcroft says, pulling the attention of the room. "We've all had unexpected visits from our Queen."

"They aren't *visits*, Ashcroft," Bartese interjects, "she's showing up, holding Trials and slaughtering our people."

"What justification is being given for these Trials?" I ask the room.

"She took out a dozen of my Nest members from ridiculous things like looking her in the eye or false accusations of treason," Ashcroft answers.

"She took out a Lilim-made from my Nest because she believed he was trying to seduce her," Bartese adds. Beau saunters over with a drink in his hand, sprawling over an armchair.

"Has she executed any of yours?" I ask Beau.

He chortles. "Medea knows better than to interfere in my territory."

"Why would you be immune to her judicial outcomes?" Bartese asks, sitting back in his chair.

Beau examines his nails before flicking bored eyes to me, dismissing Bartese completely. Anger rolls off Bartese, his body ready to strike against Beau, but his second puts a hand on his arm, quieting the Nest Master.

I keep my face neutral as I turn my attention to Greyson. "Has she held Trials in your territory?"

A swift shake of his head. "She stayed with us a few days but didn't perform any Trials. She was more obsessed with reminiscing about the past, insisting certain events happened when they didn't. Her thoughts were scattered."

Unknown to most, Medea's vampiric gift was the gift of hyperthymesia, precise memory, so for her memories to be fractured is a serious problem.

We're in deep shit. Ren comments into my mind.

I know. Her madness has escalated far too quickly.

All vampire Queens eventually dissolve into madness with no known cause. Extensive research and experimentations have gone into the subject by vampires from the start of time, but there are no definitive conclusions. Some say it's the purity of demon blood that eats away at their brains. Some say it's a curse from God. Whatever it is, it doesn't happen this quickly. It usually takes centuries before any signs occur, let alone for the madness to progress.

"You're bonded to her Vlad. Surely you can reason with her," Bartese states.

My eyes automatically flick up to Aster. I can't use my gift on her, but I can *see* the rage blazing in her liquid gold eyes fixated on the back of Bartese's head. Possessive looks good on her.

I clear my throat, focusing on Bartese. "I'm no longer bonded to Medea."

The room goes quiet. As Medea's former mate and Consort, I should be bound to her for life. The only way to break an established mate bond is by death.

"How is that possible?" Nate is the one to ask. His eyes burn with intensity and focus solely on me. How do I explain to a possible Ancient that I'm now mate-bound to a wolf? Beau's sand eyes catch mine, and his whole face lights up in understanding.

I go with a half-truth, returning my gaze back to Nate. "I honestly don't know. The bond severed last week."

"Has she taken another Consort?" Ashcroft asks Mydas.

"She has not," he confirms.

Multiple conversations erupt throughout the room. I signal for Aster and Vik to come through with more drinks as a distraction.

23

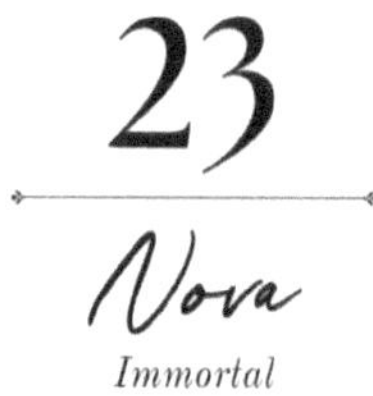

Nova

Immortal

MADDOX PLACES DRINKS ON Vik's tray, motioning for her to go towards Housden and Ashcroft on the right, then points out the drinks on my tray and which one goes to whom. I nod to the instruction and walk over.

A wall of vampire stench floods my system; this many vampires in one room makes it hard to distinguish each person's individual scent. The only one I can determine is Nate's. And it's a strange combination.

Usually, vampires smell dark, seductive, and overly sweet, whereas faeries smell light and floral or like the ocean, and wolves smell rich, of the earth and sun.

But Nate has a combination of all categories. His scent is a combination of toasted cardamom and crisp green apples mixed with burned pine and a hint of lavender. It reminds me of apple pie on a winter's evening around a blazing bonfire; it's intimate and warm.

I place drinks down for Bartese and his second on the table between them, not disturbing their conversation. I walk around to Ortiz and Nate, placing their drinks down the same as the other two, but Ortiz's head whips to me. "*Werewolf.*"

I straighten swiftly and take a step back. Everyone's eyes are now on me. Odin, help me.

Ashcroft turns to Vlad. "You have a werewolf here while we're discussing this? Are you trying to get us all executed?"

Vlad's eyes narrow as he stands a little taller. "She's a Lone Wolf. Her loyalties are to me."

"Don't patronize us, Vladislav. Female wolves are property to their males," Bartese comments with a dismissive wave of his hand.

"I killed the last man who thought I was property," I retort without thinking.

Beau shakes with laughter as Bartese looks at me as if he's offended to even hear my voice. I clutch my tray harder and inhale slow and deep as fury pulsates through my body. If only I could rip off Bartese's arms and use them to beat him senseless.

Vlad crosses his arms over his chest, his eyes on Bartese darken ever so slightly. "Make another vulgar comment about my employee, Bartese, and consider your invitation to this establishment revoked."

The mate bond warms as I turn on my heel to leave.

"Aster, love, sit with me," Beau purrs, eyes shining.

I lift my eyes to Vlad, and he barely inclines his head. I saunter over to Beau, depositing my tray on the empty table next to him, perching myself on the rolled arm of his chair. All eyes lock on us as Beau slips an arm around me, pulling me firmly onto his lap, resting his cool arm along my thigh.

"Please, continue," he gestures to the group.

"What games are you playing, Beaufort?" I murmur quietly.

He rests his chin on my shoulder. "Play along, love, if you want to survive this evening." His voice is barely a breath.

Bartese's face screws up in disgust. "You *sully* yourself with this animal?"

I launch off Beau toward him growling, letting my wolf temper slip. Beau's arm snaps around my waist, chuckling hard. "Patience, love. We'll play with Bartese later," he purrs as he strokes his fingers down my arm slowly.

I smirk, snuggling myself back into Beau as Bartese's eyes darken.

"Perhaps you can still reason with Medea, Vladislav," Ashcroft offers, returning the attention back to Vlad.

"It won't do much; her madness is accelerating faster than expected," Vlad responds.

"Surely you can re-establish the mate bond with the Queen and settle some of her eccentricities?" Bartese asks. I *really* don't fucking like this guy.

Ren scoffs behind Vlad. "Their bond is severed, you can't fix that. Use your head."

"Watch your tongue, Renard, before I cut it out of your head." Bartese is seriously going to get himself beaten by someone if he doesn't rein in his arrogance.

Ren steps forward, but Vlad's hand strikes out, holding him back at the chest.

"Renard is right," Vlad surmises.

"Then what do you think we should do?" Ashcroft asks the room.

"We *could* kill her," Ortiz responds. He's been reserved this whole time. The response sends the others into a collective argument about treason, so they squash the idea.

"We could partition the Court to retire her," Ashcroft says, stroking his stubbled chin with his thumb and index finger.

The others agree, making plans to gather evidence for Medea's removal from the throne.

Vlad crosses his arms, his eyes darting in Carlos' direction before sweeping across the group. "We do have another matter to discuss before we can enjoy the rest of our evening."

Carlos joins Vlad, Ren and Mydas by the stage, his smile relaxed, but his brown eyes start going molten in wicked delight.

"Oh shit," I breathe.

"What do you know, love," Beau murmurs into my ear.

"It's a good thing I'm in your lap, because you're going to be *pissed*," I whisper back.

"As many of you know," Vlad starts, "the Lux problem has increased over the years."

Before Vlad can continue Carlos disappears, so does Noble, and then in less than a breath, Noble is slammed through the glass table beside his discarded chair.

"What the fuck is going on?" Housden bellows, leaping from his chair. Ren appears next to him, locking his arms around Housden, anchoring him in place.

"Lux has become a particular annoyance in New York City," Vlad continues, his arms unfolding and going into his suit pants pockets, "and it's come to my attention that these two are responsible for the distribution and sale of it."

"You disrespect a Nest Master with these vicious *lies*," Housden hisses, struggling in Renard's arms.

Vlad only smiles, turning his attention to Ortiz. The black-haired vampire chuckles and stands from his sofa. "Vlad, you cheeky bastard, how did you know I wanted to wreak havoc today?"

"Don't you always?" Vlad comments and Ortiz crosses the space and stands a foot away from Housden. He just stares at him, but Housden stops struggling and his face goes blank.

"He's all yours," Ortiz purrs.

Vlad turns to Mydas. "Advisor Mydas, would you like to start this inquisition as representative of the Court?"

Mydas straightens and nods, striding over and standing just behind Ortiz. I wish I wore pants tonight so I wasn't restricted in movement if this shit gets ugly.

"Who is responsible for the Lux distribution in your territory?" Mydas asks Housden.

Housden's eyes are glazed over as he continues to stare at Ortiz. "Noble runs the logistics."

"And who's his supplier?" Vlad asks.

"I am," Housden drawls.

"What the fuck?" Ashcroft breathes.

"He's fighting pretty hard against me," Ortiz grunts, stepping closer to Housden.

"How are you getting your supply?" Vlad asks.

"W-wine crates," Housden stammers.

"Wine," Vlad muses, beginning to pace, his face hard. "Who is—"

"Why are you doing this?" Mydas demands, cutting off Vlad.

"To... to take over Manhattan's territory," Housden answers.

Growling vibrates my back, and I clutch Beau's arms around me hard. "Easy, Beaufort," I mumble.

"Why?" Beau asks, his voice calm, but he's buzzing with death.

"I want all of it," Housden breathes, "all five boroughs."

Bartese jumps up, stalking over to Housden but is held back by Mydas. "You mean to say you were to try to take my territory too?"

"Y-yes," Housden is now trembling and breathing hard, his face screwed up in agony.

"Where are the Fae you kidnapped?" Renard hisses into his ear.

"I d-don't know."

"Liar," Vlad accuses. "Who's supplying you with the Lux?"

"H-he has a Pit," Housden is straining against whatever Ortiz is doing to get him to talk. "It's... there's more... It's in—"

Bartese breaks from Mydas' hold and rushes Housden. Ortiz and Mydas dart back as Bartese's fist punches through Housden's chest, blood spurting all over him as he wrenches out his heart. Renard drops his body, stepping back as Housden decays rapidly on the concrete floor.

"No one takes what's mine," Bartese growls as he throws the shriveled organ onto the floor.

Vlad rakes a hand through his hair, he looks frustrated. Bartese, the dumb bastard, just lost our way to Marin. I don't realize I'm growling until Beau strokes my arm softly.

"Short tempered fool," Beau breathes into my ear. "He could have at least waited until we knew the source."

"Whoever the source is has Marin," I bite through clenched teeth, "and he just killed our lead."

Mydas turns his attention to Noble who's still in Carlos' choke hold in a pile of glass. "As the Court's representative present, I sentence you to death. You and Housden broke the law of all species, forbidding the sale and distribution of Lux."

"No," Noble croaks, eyes wide. A feral smile spreads across Carlos' face as Mydas nods toward him. Carlos gives Noble the same treatment as Housden, he sinks his fist into his chest and rips out his heart, discarding the organ next to Noble's decaying body.

"Well," Ashcroft says as he stands, "this meeting was a lot more eventful than expected."

"It was," Vlad says. "Carlos will lead you all to the private alcoves while we clean this up."

As Renard and Mydas have a hushed conversation about disposal of the bodies, Carlos leads the rest of the men across the bar and past the indigo curtains by the bar. Vlad walks past Beau and jerks his chin towards the bar, indicating us to follow.

"Shall we?" Beau murmurs, rising from his seat, handing me the tray as we follow Vlad who disappears into the storeroom.

He's seated at the head of the table by the lockers when we enter and close the door behind us.

Beau's beaming face flicks between Vlad and I as he takes a seat on Vlad's left. "I never thought I'd see the day when I'd be this delighted and confused all at once."

"Now that you know," Vlad says as he taps on his phone screen as I sink into the chair on his right, "I'd appreciate that you don't paw Aster from now on."

I snort, sitting back and crossing my arms. "He can cop a feel all he wants, it's never going to happen."

Vlad raises a brow, eyeing me briefly before returning his attention back to his phone.

Beau chuckles. "Maybe you and Vlad will get bored after a century or two and decide to share."

"Doubt it," I mutter, examining my nails. A century or *two*. Am I going to be around for that long?

Footsteps sound at the entrance of the room, distracting me from those thoughts. Nate and Ortiz stroll in. Ortiz claims the seat next to me and Nate takes the seat next to Beau.

Ortiz angles his body towards me, and takes a swig of his drink. "I'm Greyson; this is Nate. And who may you be?"

"Aster," I offer with a smile.

He inclines his head in return. The room is saturated with vampire stench. Nate and Beau's scents war against each other, and it's hard for me to filter through to determine Greyson's. Finally, I pick up a tendril that reminds me of freshly baked cherry pie.

My eyes flick to Nate. He's looking over at me with appraising eyes. Where Viktoria's eyes are more gray-blue, Nate's icy blue is the color of glaciers.

His eyes meet mine. "You're not like other werewolves."

"And you're not like other vampires," I add. His eyes flick to my wrist as I play aimlessly with the amulet and they narrow slightly.

The storage door opens and closes quickly as Allura flutters over in a white silk robe with Ren on her tail. She plants a soft kiss on my cheek, then Vlad, and surprisingly Nate, before sitting in Renard's lap as he occupies the last chair on the other end.

"It's so good to see you, honey," she beams at Nate, grasping his hand across the table.

His face warms with a smile, and he cups her hand with his free one. "It's been too long."

Allura releases Nate's hand and looks over to Vlad. "I didn't expect that meeting to end with two dead bodies."

Vlad slides his phone into his jacket pocket and crosses his arms over his chest. "Bartese lost our lead to Marin. And I thought the Queen's escalation was being exaggerated, but from what you've seen Ortiz, she's disintegrating a lot faster than the last."

"It's only happened recently," Greyson muses, "my daughter, the Obscira, says she was mostly normal when she left Court."

Surprise flashes in Vlad, Ren and Beau's faces.

"*Daughter?*" Vlad asks. "To Ravia?"

Greyson nods. I flick my gaze to Nate, and he's... tense. He doesn't like talking about her. Does he not like her? Or the opposite? I'm thinking it's the latter.

Beau snickers. "The Obscira is your daughter? That little temptress owes me a motorbike."

Greyson chuckles. "I'll tell her." He focuses his attention on Vlad. "How *did* you break your bond to Medea?"

Vlad doesn't respond but looks over to Allura the question in his eyes.

Allura hesitates, but Vlad inclines his head. She glances at me briefly before focusing on Nate. "I'm pregnant."

Nate's eyes grow wide, and his face warms. "I thought there was something different about you."

"It's a halfling. Summer and Winter." I watch the light drain from Nate's face as Allura continues. "It caused a rip between this realm and the Other Side and there were... changes."

Allura's eyes travel along the table. "Think of the Other Side as a well of magical power, and it needs conduits to filter that magic into the realms. These conduits are the leaders of the species, usually the strongest and most 'tapped in' to their Other Side power. They need to be the right fit or else because when magic is unbalanced, it disturbs the whole ecosystem and can be catastrophic to the conduit." Allura sighs. "I think that's been happening to vampires for millenia." She looks back at me. "And I think you two being mate-bound accelerated Medea's deterioration."

Both men look between Vlad and me for several seconds.

"A vampire, mate-bonded to a *werewolf*. How?" Greyson asks.

"Unbridled Other Side magic has endless possibilities," Allura answers. "Why did it develop a cross-species mate bond between these two specific supernaturals? No one knows. Did it change more? Highly likely, but we won't know what else it affected until it presents itself."

The room is quiet for a few moments. I turn to Vlad, meeting amber eyes with a small smile. Beau sits back in his chair, watching me with his usual grin on his face. Nate is assessing me again, but his stare is not as intense as it was before, it's more understanding than anything else.

Greyson, however, is purely dumbfounded, which makes me smile. "It's super weird, I know."

Greyson blinks at me and laughs. "I'm sorry, but I've been around for a long time, and this has never happened." As hard as it is to filter out Nate and Beau's scent, I realize Greyson is older than I thought.

"Are you older than Nate?" I ask, perplexed.

Greyson's eyes flick to Nate for a moment before returning to me. "By several hundred years. I was turned amid the Second Crusade, and Nate, at the height of the Renaissance. How do you know that?"

"It's all in the scent. As vampires age, their scent gets stronger." I don't mention the fact that Nate's scent is almost as heady as Beau's.

The door to the storeroom opens and Carlos slips in. He's in an entirely new outfit with a grin on his face. "The bodies are gone and the place is back in order."

"Up to your old spy tricks I see?" Greyson asks with a smile.

Carlos shrugs, leaning against the wall behind Ren and Allura. "They took a friend of mine so I'll do what's necessary."

"That bottle of wine you stole the other week," Ren says, "that must have been Lux."

"Go to Housden's estate and destroy every crate," Beau instructs, his eyes hard, his amusement gone.

Carlos nods, pushing off the wall. "I'll try and find another link to the source as well." He leaves the storeroom. Pleasantries are exchanged around the table; Greyson and Nate promising Allura to report any strange occurrences on the West Coast. Vlad walks them out, followed by Allura, leaving me, Beau, and Ren at the table.

"You keep me on my toes, love," Beau says as he stands, reaches for my hand and places a kiss on my knuckles before strolling out of the room.

I stand and begin to follow, but Ren grabs my wrist as I walk past, rising from his seat, looming over me. His eyes are intense, swirling emeralds.

"I'd do *anything* to protect my little brother, so, if you hurt him, you won't see another sunrise." He releases me, picks up his drink, and strides towards the exit.

Vlad calls an early night and Ren takes Allura and I back to her apartment. I shower and change into sweats before passing out as soon as my head hits the pillow.

I have a rare dreamless night, but still wake up at dawn. As I check my phone, I see a new message.

UNKNOWN

> It's Kris. Dad's traveling to Daygrsson territory to see High Alpha Serafiem, and he's taking a hunting party. So if you're in the area, you better move on. Also, rumor is that the three Lárusson heirs have a bet between each other to who can catch you first, so they also have hunting parties.

> Wherever you are, stay safe. Pat, Teddy, and I miss you. This phone will be cut tomorrow.

So it's not just one son, but *all* of the Lárusson heirs after me. Great. I send a short reply.

> Hey. Thanks for the heads up. I'll watch my back. Miss you all.

Another message pops up from Sid, informing me that Allura's doctor's appointment is this morning. I groan, rolling out of bed, crossing the hall and knocking on her door. She doesn't answer so I open the door and slip into the room, walking up to her huddled form.

I jostle her softly. "Lu, wake up."

She groans. "No."

I snort. "Yes. Come on. We need to be ready in an hour."

She grumbles something I don't understand and then snuggles further into her blankets. I try to shake Allura awake again, but she rolls to the other side of the bed. I blow out a frustrated breath. I guess I'm pulling her out.

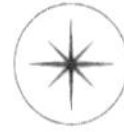

Allura comes out of the doctor's office quite literally glowing. The humans won't be able to see it, but the woman is leaving faerie dust *everywhere.* She hands me half a forest of paperwork, including ultrasound pictures and floats back to the reception desk to discuss her next appointment.

I take a photo of the ultrasound and send it to Vlad. *Congratulations, Uncle Vlad.*

I snicker to myself as Sid bids farewell to the doctor and the nurse as we leave the office.

"So, High Alpha Lárus came to see me yesterday," Sid says as we climb into the pick-up.

My heart skips a beat. "I heard his sons have a wager."

Sid nods, eyes on the road. "He said one of his hunters came across a Pack-less female working at my bar. I told him you have been here since February." Which is a month before I arrived.

"I'm sure he wanted proof."

Sid scoffs. "Babygirl, if Sidelle says it happened, then it happened. But I showed him security footage from a day in February anyway, and he's satisfied." Her devious eyes flick over to mine for a second and then back to the road.

"Thank you. I have about three life debts to you now."

"No, you don't, Nova. As I've told you, my calling in life was to heal the misused and lead them to their happier lives. And I will do it until I can't anymore."

Allura, whose adoring eyes haven't left the ultrasound pictures the whole car ride, finally looks up, eyes weary. "I never wish you to leave us, Sid. New York, heck, the *world* wouldn't be the same with you or Sanctuary."

Sid places a soft touch on Allura's knee before returning her hand to the wheel. "Good thing that I don't plan on leaving any time soon."

24

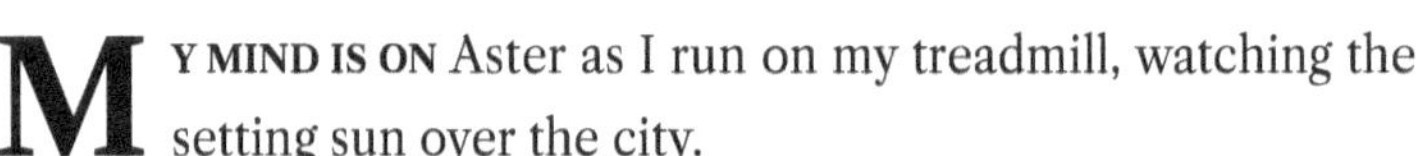

Vladislav's Penthouse

MY MIND IS ON Aster as I run on my treadmill, watching the setting sun over the city.

Ever since the bond snapped into place, my protective instincts are a little overbearing, even in my eyes. I've resisted the urge to call or text her today to check-in, knowing full well that she is safe with Allura and Sid, but now that the sun is going down, maybe I should go over to their apartment and double-check?

No, you don't, stalker. Play it cool.

I roll my eyes. *Stop snooping in my head, Ren, and finish those reports.*

I hear his laughter in my mind. *How about you stop projecting your thoughts so fucking loudly, and I might get some work done?*

I stop the treadmill and climb off, pulling the towel off the handle as I leave the gym for a shower. As I walk past my office, I toss the towel right at Ren's face.

"That's disgusting!" he hollers as I continue down the hallway.

That's what you get for being a nosy asshole.

I take a quick shower, dressing in black slacks and a white shirt. As I'm picking up my phone from my nightstand, Ren appears in the doorway, hands in his pocket, amusement coating him. "Did the cold shower help?"

"Surely you have better things to do than annoy me," I muse, checking my phone for any missed messages.

Ren laughs. "I've caught up with reports, *boss*, so I have free time to annoy my little brother about his new girl."

I roll my eyes, pocketing the phone. "Have you heard from Carlos today?"

"Nope, he's probably still at the Housden estate."

"Go see if he's found anything."

It's Ren's turn to roll his eyes, but his amusement still swirls around him. "You got it."

I'm in my home office immersed in financials when I hear the front door open and close. The sound of heels clipping against the hardwood floor echoes through the house, coming closer.

"I'm in the office," I say, not taking my eyes off the laptop in front of me. The heels are closer now, and then the sound stops. Rich amber rum and milk snakes under my nose, and the bond pulls hard.

I look up to a vision of ecstasy. Aster peruses the bookshelves by the door, her glorious oak hair sways in a thick braid between her shoulders, a few curly tendrils escaping near her ears. Her long-sleeved white shirt is slightly sheer and snug over her toned back and arms. The high-waisted skirt that tucks in the shirt is a spectacular shade of emerald green and cups her ass to perfection, stopping just below her knee.

Aster turns, and I bite down the groan threatening to disturb the quiet space. The skirt has a slit so high up her right leg that it shows the lace tops of her sheer stockings. The shirt is unbuttoned to show off her glorious chest.

"Aster."

"Vlad." She saunters over in those glossy black pumps and perches on my desk beside me. The position exposes more of her thigh. How I would love to run my teeth over the edge of the lace

"What are you working on?" Her voice comes out husky.

I trail a finger from her knee, slowly following the stocking upward. "Financials. Very boring."

"Mhmm," she mumbles.

Her heartbeat picks up, her chest rising and falling slow and deliberate. My finger inches higher and higher, reaching the lacy top. I splay out my hand, grasping her muscled thigh, gazing up at her.

"How was your afternoon?" My hand moves higher, rotating towards her inner thigh, lifting the skirt a little.

She clears her throat, sitting a little straighter, but not removing my hand. Her eyes simmer a rich gold. "Oh, you know, the usual. Nap, training, food."

"In that order?"

She lets out a shaky breath. "Sure."

A laugh rumbles in my chest, and I move my hand again. Aster tries to control her breathing, but those delicious breasts are rising and falling quite fast now. Her arousal taints the air, making me hard, grating on my self-control.

I stand and lean in, moving my hand forward to cup her core. I growl in her ear; the lace is already soaked. "You're driving me insane."

She crushes her mouth to mine and grinds into my hand, her arms wrapping around my neck. My other arm circles her waist, pulling her closer as her tongue snakes into my mouth, demanding a taste. I press the heel of my palm harder against her clit, my fingers playing with the edges of her panties.

She groans into my mouth as her hand tangles tightly into my hair while the other roams down my body until she's palming my hard cock. Now I groan, kissing her harder.

She pulls her mouth away, breathing hard, eyes intense gold. "Touch me, Xander."

I push aside the fabric, and sink one finger deep into her slick core. Her eyes roll closed, her back arches.

My fangs drop. "*Fuck*, Aster," I growl and scrape the tips of my fangs along her neck muscle.

"Gods, I might die if you don't *move*," she mumbles, trying to move her hips.

I lock my arm tighter around her waist, and she whimpers. Her hand squeezes my cock through my pants, making it jump. She might be the death of *me*.

I give in to her request, gliding my finger lazily in and out of her, making her groan and pull my face back to hers for a devastating kiss. I can taste the want, the *need*. She runs her tongue over my left fangs, and I almost blow. I sink another finger into her, pumping faster, harder, stroking upward, my thumb circling her clit.

"*Fuck*," she pleas into my mouth, her hips falling in time with my hand, her muscles quivering around my fingers.

"Let go."

Aster shatters around me, clenching hard on my fingers, her entire body violently shuddering. She grips my shoulders, almost piercing the fabric of my shirt as she rides her orgasm. Her grip loosens and she drapes her arms limply around my neck, forehead on my shoulder. "You ruined my new panties."

I laugh, sitting back down on my desk chair, taking her with me. "You asked me to."

She lifts her eyes to mine, back to their piercing jade green. "I did. Let me return the favor."

Her hands drop to my belt and undoes it, then unbottons my pants. My phone chimes with a message on the desk but we both ignore it as she pulls the zipper open and tugs out my shirt. Her soft fingers slide along the edge of my boxers as the phone rings.

I growl, lean forward, and answer the phone. "This better be fucking important."

"You need to get downstairs, now."

Aster's hands freeze at the urgency in Viktoria's voice. "What happened?"

"*Now*, Vlad." The line drops.

Aster slips from my lap, and I pass her my phone as I readjust my clothing.

"I'm going to use your bathroom real quick," she says as she tucks my phone into her bra and straightens her skirt.

I nod, taking her hand and leading her to my room, we don't need our activities to distract from whatever disaster is happening downstairs. As we enter the walk-in wardrobe, Aster slips into the bathroom and I change into a fresh suit.

I hear the faucet turn on as I slide into the marble bathroom wearing an emerald suit and light blue shirt. Aster appraises me in the mirror as I use the second basin to wash my hands. My eyes wander over her face, her body, the moments we just shared making my blood heat.

Aster smirks, turning off her faucet. "Don't get any ideas, we have places to be."

A growl vibrates in the back of my throat as I pick up a hand towel, drying my hands. She does the same, then readjusts her top again, and smooths down the escaped tendrils of her hair. I grasp her hand and tug her into my arms, one hand grabbing her ass and the other grabbing her braid, tilting her head back.

"I'm not finished with you yet."

"Same," she purrs, sliding her hands into my hair and pulling my mouth to hers.

The kiss is sweet, chaste even, but the undercurrent of urgent lust is there. I could have her for an eternity, and it won't be enough to satiate my thirst for her. I press her body into mine more, needing to feel more of her, my hands exploring her ass.

She pulls back. "Let's go before we end up fucking on this counter."

"Later," I growl as I peck her once more and take half a step back.

She smooths down the lapels of my jacket, then takes my hand, and we exit the bathroom.

As we get down to Immortal, Aster tries to pull her hand out of mine, but I squeeze tighter. They all know anyway, it's not like I can hide things well from my people. As soon as I push the bar door open, I know something's wrong. The smell. It's stale blood, and reeks of sugared almonds.

Emotions slam into me. Allura is behind the bar distressed. Vik is pissed, standing at the entrance of the bar with Maddox who's heartbroken. Ren, who's pacing near the door, is on another level. He's a tornado of rage, and unhinged devastation. And he's also covered in blood.

His bright emerald eyes hone in on me and he charges toward us. I pull Aster behind me as Ren and I collide. He screams obscenities incoherently in three different languages, ripping at my suit, his eyes wild and furious.

Vik and Maddox are next to us in the next second, wrenching my brother off me.

Heat at my back distracts me, and I catch Aster before she tries to get around me and approach Ren.

"I need to smell his shirt; calm him down," she asks behind me.

Taking a deep breath, I place my hand on Ren's chest. I focus on calm, serene places and feelings, plunging them into Ren's body. The tornado of rage tries to resist the change, but it gets swallowed up quickly, and Ren's face goes blank, his shoulders dropping.

Aster steps around me, approaching Ren carefully like you would a wounded animal. She dips her head toward his chest and inhales.

"What happened?" I ask.

"Carlos," Ren whispers, his eyes back to cobalt blue and watery. "He's gone."

Carlos. No.

"Who would do this?" Maddox asks, his voice broken.

"We got too close to finding Marin," Vik bites, "and they fucking took him from us."

Aster stumbles back, knocking into me. "Fuck."

"Aster?" I brush my hand down her arm and she flinches away from me.

She steps closer to Ren again, almost pressing her face into his bloodied chest and takes a deep inhale. She chokes, turning fast on her heel, her glittering golden eyes boring into me.

"He's dead," she growls.

"Who?"

"Frankincense and fucking blueberries. *Mydas* did this," she spits.

"What?" Vik demands.

Maddox releases the near catatonic Ren, shaking his head, and disappears. Mydas is his Sire. Vik also releases Ren and storms over to the bar, where Allura is sobbing with her face buried in her hands.

"Are you sure?" I ask.

Aster's hand presses into Ren's chest, over his heart as she steps closer. He closes his eyes, one of his hands over hers.

"I found Carlos in the wine cellar below the Housden estate," he mumbles in barely a whisper. "It looked like he had destroyed most of the Lux before he was..."

Aster curls her free arm around his arm, pressing herself to his side. "Let's go get you cleaned up."

25

Nova

Immortal

I LEAD REN TO Vlad's office, guiding him to stand by the desk as I fish out a shirt from Vlad's stash of clothes in the wardrobe.

I help him to undo the ruined shirt and wet a clean part with water from a bottle on the desk and wipe off dried blood from Renard's neck and face. He pulls on the new shirt, his face still blank and his eyes glazed over.

My heart breaks for him to lose someone he thought of as a brother. Especially since the person who took him is also considered a brother. Once he's buttoned the shirt, I hug him. He returns the gesture, his chin resting on top of my head.

"What the fuck am I supposed to do now?" he whispers, his voice husky.

"For now, you grieve. You can worry about the rest later."

"I'm going to hunt Mydas until I rip his heart out."

I pull back, looking up into Renard's hard eyes. "I'll help."

Renard clicks his tongue as he steps back. "He's *mine*. There's no fucking way I'm letting my brother's girl go after a murderer."

His brother's girl? "If Mydas took out Carlos, then he's the leak in Immortal. He's the one who took Marin."

Realization widens Renard's eyes. "Shit."

"Don't do anything stupid," I say, stepping into his path to the exit. "She's not dead yet, we need to keep it that way."

"We need to track him from the Housden estate." Renard tries to step around me, but I mirror his steps.

"A wolf will track him better." I pull my phone out of the waist of my skirt, sending a message to Art to come to Immortal. "I have someone."

Renard blows out a breath and nods, raking a hand through his hair before turning to the desk, and taking a seat, pulling up Vlad's laptop.

I leave him to it, returning back to the bar. Vlad is nowhere to be seen, but I follow his scent toward the storage room. He's alone sitting at the table as I step in and close the door.

He looks up as I approach, but the look on his face makes me halt. This is the ruthless Vladislav they talk about. There are two empty blood packs on the table next to his ruined suit jacket, and the burning salty smell tells me it's frat blood.

His nostrils flare and his muscles bulk, his eyes going a fiery bourbon brown. He rises from his seat, predatory energy seeps down the walls.

Am I fast enough to run?

It's a really stupid decision with him in this state; he'd probably find it amusing, like playing with his food.

His cedar, smoke and peach scent hits me, and my eyes almost roll back as the bond rages to life. Gods, I need to get out of here.

My survival instincts overwhelm me and I take a step back—big mistake. Vlad tracks the movement with a wicked smile twisting those beautiful lips. My traitorous heartbeat gives me away as I turn to escape, but he's faster than I thought. He's suddenly in front of me, wrapping my waist with a bruise-worthy hold and pulling me close.

"Where do you think you're going, little wolf?" His voice... he doesn't even sound like himself.

"Nowhere." I offer him a smile. Maybe if I play along, he'll let me go.

A laugh rumbles his chest, sending waves of pleasure through my entire body.

Honestly, this mate bond needs to realize he might *actually* eat me.

Vlad leans down to my neck, breathing deep as he runs his fangs over my carotid artery. My heartbeat spikes, and I loosen a shaky breath. He crushes his lips to mine, the mate bond burning deep in my gut, radiating heat through my veins.

I taste his scent—cedar, peach, and that hint of tobacco—and the acidic frat blood on his tongue. He presses me against the wall as he pours rage, sex, anguish, and longing into our kiss.

I'll never be able to let him go. He tastes like home.

My tongue darts out and skims his right fangs. He rips his mouth away from me, his eyes blazing as they lock on mine. "Do you want to play, little wolf?"

"I always want to play with you, Xander," I pant.

He smirks, his eyes dropping to my neck. "Do you want me to mark you, claim you right here?"

My wolf decides to join the party, my mind whirling with her demands as I growl. "Too many words, not enough action."

A growl vibrates through Vlad as the world blurs for a split second, and then my ass lands on the table. He sinks to his knees and pulls me to perch on the edge, hiking up my skirt to my hips and hooking my knees on his shoulders.

I start trembling as his tongue slides down my thigh, his fangs grazing my sensitive skin, the bond burning in my chest. Vlad lifts his head, a feral glint in his bourbon eyes.

"Do you taste as good as you smell?"

"Find out."

Vlad tears my panties at my hips this time, pulling the fabric away, his eyes fixed between my legs. Those large hands wrap over the tops of my thighs in a bruising grip as his tongue slides through my wet folds, and I almost black out.

My hips jerk up as Vlad's tongue circles my clit, my hands sinking into his hair, gripping hard.

He growls, the vibrations careening me closer to orgasm as he laves every inch of me. I can barely breathe, can barely think about anything but his tongue as carnal need drowns all rational thought from my existence.

Vlad slides a hand down and sinks two fingers into me and I clap a hand over my mouth, smothering the groan.

His fingers fuck me hard and fast, his tongue rolling over my clit in tight circles; the overwhelming stimulation rips the orgasm out of me so fast I choke on my own cries.

My thighs lock around him so hard I'm surprised if he's even breathing. My body aches and trembles as I come down from my high, my breathing calming.

I dislodge my hand from Vlad's hair as he stands, his face completely feral. His hand strikes out and grabs my neck, dragging me into a sitting position, his mouth crashing into mine. I can taste my arousal and *him* as he claims my mouth.

Tongues dance and teeth knock as Vlad kisses me with a ferocity I can't quite comprehend.

He pulls back, his hand still wrapped around my neck, his breathing labored. "*Mine.*"

I hook my hands into his waistband and tug myself closer to him, pressing my core into his erection, wrapping my legs around his hips. As I'm about to claim the man in front of me, when I hear familiar voices in the bar.

"Vampires only, *wolf*," Viktoria growls.

"Down girl," Art drawls, "I'm here to see Aster."

"Shit," I breathe, trying to get off the table, but Vlad is immobile.

His hand around my neck tightens slightly. "Why is *Carter* here?"

I grab his wrist and squeeze, trying to remove his hand as I meet his hard, bourbon eyes. "I called him to track Mydas."

Vlad blinks a few times, like he's trying to clear the fog in his head, and he finally lets go of my neck. "Sorry, *chérie,* I lost myself for a moment."

I release his wrist and slip off the table, rearranging and smoothing down my skirt. We both shuffle out of the storeroom to find Maddox holding Viktoria in place as she tries to charge toward an amused Art.

Art's large, towering body in jeans and a t-shirt is such a rugged contrast to the refinement around him. He takes a couple steps toward Vlad and I before he halts, his nostrils flare. Fuck.

Viktoria takes in a lungful of air and turns toward us. "You're fucking *kidding* me, right?"

Vlad sighs next to me. "Vik—"

"One of your closest friends was just ripped to pieces by one of your vampire kin, and you're fucking a wolf in the storeroom?"

"Vik," Maddox says softly, still holding her in place.

"You don't think I care about that?" Vlad asks, stepping forward. My hand strikes out, landing on his chest. I really hope I don't have to break up a vampire brawl. "Someone I trusted and thought of as family has betrayed us, my anger and disappointment is indescribable."

"Doesn't stop you from getting your dick wet," Vik spits. Her eyes turn to me; they're liquid silver as disgust burns in them. "You don't belong here."

Vlad slips my hold and steps toward Vik with a growl but I manage to grab the back of his shirt and stop him from doing something he'd regret.

"We don't have time for this," I say. "We have a vampire and a faerie to track."

Vik finally shakes off Maddox's hold and jumps over the bar top. "Don't pretend like you give a shit."

"Viktoria," Vlad rumbles, halting her at the staff door. "Breathe a word of this to Dom and there will be consequences."

Her shoulders go rigid, and she's silent for a moment. "Yes, *Sire*," she spits and then pushes through the door. Sire? Did Vlad turn Viktoria?

"I'll go with her," Maddox murmurs softly and disappears.

I release Vlad's shirt and he turns, raking a hand through his hair. I pull his phone from my bra where I stashed it earlier. "This thing goes off every minute. I'm surprised you haven't tossed it out a window."

He smiles, the notion not reaching his eyes as he scrolls through the missed messages. "Dom will meet Vik and Maddox at Mydas' apartment and track him from there."

Ren enters the bar with Allura close behind him and his ruined shirt in his hand. He merely looks over to us, his nostrils flaring slightly, before thrusting the ruined shirt into Art's hands and walks out. Allura watches him with concern, but then turns back to Art and stretches up to place a kiss on his cheek.

"Can you go to the scene, see if you can track Mydas from there?" I ask, and Art nods.

"I'll be in my office," Vlad announces and then disappears, Allura following him.

What a fucking mess.

"You keep *interesting* company," Art murmurs as he sniffs the shirt in his hands.

"Shut up and go track."

We all spend the night on autopilot, entertaining customers and making money. My heart hurts every time I look over to Carlos' spot and he isn't there, and then I'm awash with rage that he was taken from us.

Vlad called in Gabriel from Eternal to take up Ren's post at the door for the night, and Ren has spent the night in Vlad's office. I run the bar with Allura since Viktoria and Maddox haven't come back.

Dom and Art both had no luck in tracking Mydas to a specific location, the trail always ending at a street, probably because he got into a car. We close up in the early hours.

"I should stay with Ren tonight," Allura says as we sit by the clean bar with Vlad.

I nod. "Go. I'm going to crash at Sanctuary tonight."

"You'll stay in the Penthouse," Vlad announces.

I smile at the possessive tone, looking up into those beautiful amber and cobalt eyes. "I need to see the old lady, plus, the jog there will be good."

Vlad frowns. "Stay."

I brush my fingers down his forearm. "I can't. Not today."

"Let me drive you at least."

I shake my head. "It's almost dawn, go home."

He sighs and we all stand. I changed into workout gear that I stashed in Allura's dressing room earlier before heading out of the back alley entrance and setting a decent pace towards Sanctuary.

When I get there, I'm breathing heavily but not at all tired – training with Art is paying off. Sid's soft vetiver scent greets me as I enter the foyer and settles me slightly; this place feels like coming home.

Sid's office door suddenly bursts open and she rushes out, her eyes immediately blazing into me.

"Marin," she chokes, her phone clutched tightly to her chest, her caramel brown eyes wide with shock.

"What?"

"She just called me. I have an address."

I sprint up the stairs towards my old room, rip open the dresser and pull out the spare clothes I left behind for emergencies, and the belt holster hanging on the back of the door. I change into thick jeans, tucking my t-shirt into the waist and feed the holster into the belt loops, securing it tight and clipping the thigh buckles into place.

Shrugging on a leather jacket and pocketing my phone, I leave the room, checking the knot in my amulet's leather cord as I continue down the hall, opening the door at the end.

The previous hotel room was converted into a storage room years ago, storing Sid's collection of human weapons, fae magic weapons, and other things I don't particularly want to know about.

I rummage through the rows, pulling out a few throwing blades, slipping them into their pockets on one of my thigh holsters. I pull out two Glocks, holstering them in their position on the belt at the base of my spine. I pull out a multitude of magazines and a few hunting knives, filling the other spots on the belt, and then move on to the fae magic.

The rows of vials glow iridescent, otherworldly colors. Many are various shades of yellows, greens, blues, and browns from the Summer and Winter Courts. Some vials on the top shelves look like white mist floating in clear liquid, or a captured blindingly white star, probably from some other court.

I don't even glance at the bottom shelf, housing additional vials with darker liquids, the whole thing locked up tight. I was told never to touch those vials.

I pull out two chartreuse vials, two ocean blue ones, and two golden vials. The gold ones are teleportation spells, allowing me to get out of a situation fast. I strap the vials into their holders on my remaining thigh, then leave the storage room.

I pull my phone out, reading the address Sid already sent to me as I jog down the stairs.

"Did you find everything?" Sid asks as I pocket the phone, zipping it closed.

"Call Allura, make sure she's here when I return with Marin. And Dom."

Sid nods. "Bring them home."

The rundown building in Hell's Kitchen reeks of death. The horrors that have occurred here contaminate the air around the building. I let out a slow breath, willing my heaving gut to calm. I'm standing in an alley across the road from my destination, hidden in darkness.

I close my eyes, concentrating on the scents around me. I filter through the stench of rotting food, old blood, urine, and terror to single out the vampires: ripe blueberries, Mydas, and another scent of toffee snakes around me. I spit the taste on my tongue onto the ground. Gods, it's awful.

I try again to find... there. A tendril of fresh winter snow. Marin.

I dash across the street, my muscles hardening, eyesight focusing, adjusting to watery gray dawn light. I pull out a blade, approaching the door and open it. The vampire on the other side has no time to react as I slice through his neck from behind, his decaying body dropping instantly.

I prowl down a hall, scanning the rooms I pass. No other vampires in sight. At the end, I come upon a stairwell. I sniff, finding the winter snow and blueberry scents leading down.

I take the stairs two at a time silently; the scents getting more potent. I travel three flights down to the bottom level, and a singular door looms. Damn, no other entrance point. I put my ear close to the door, no voices, or footsteps; hopefully, it's another hall.

I turn the handle with care, pushing the door open slowly. Thankfully, a hallway. Only one light bulb flickers in the space, but again, there's only one door at the end. Fuck. I race down, tasting Marin and Mydas' scents in the air, stopping at the door.

I put my ear to the door again. A whispered, angry voice travels through.

"That was way too fucking close," Mydas growls, pacing footsteps the only other sound in the room. "But they'll work out it's me eventually, he has bloodhounds."

"Bloodhounds?" another voice asks amused. The voice is smooth, cultured, completely unbothered.

"Vladislav has taken in a stray bitch," Mydas responds. My hand twitches on my blade.

The other voice chuckles. "Maybe he'll breed his two pets and have a whole litter of mutts."

Mydas scoffs. "I'm afraid he isn't that smart. And of all people, Beau seems to be entranced with the girl."

The other voice clicks his tongue. "As long as it isn't the Consort, you know our Queen won't be very happy if he's unfaithful."

The rest of their conversation fades away as a heavy door slams shut. So there is another entrance point; it must be from another side of the building. I take a measured breath, calming my heart. Get Marin, and get the fuck out of here, we can deal with Mydas and the mystery voice later.

I pull out a green vial with my free hand, the blade still in the other, as I kick down the door.

It rips off its hinges, and I toss the vial into the room. Or Pit. The large room has no windows and no lights apart from a few bare light bulbs swinging from the high ceiling. Paint peels off the walls, and there's blood caked everywhere.

Vampires, so *many* vampires, whiter than death itself, drape over large black cushions lining the edges of the room. Some feed on humans and others have their heads back, eyes closed, with ecstasy across their faces.

In the middle of the room, three women are chained to the floor — all faeries. The vial hits the floor near them, and a burst of green light blinds the room. Hisses and shrieks fill the space as vines burst through the floor, piercing the hearts of vampires nearby. I throw a blade into the eye of the vamp trying to rush me from the left, palming another one and pulling out a Glock.

I work my way into the Pit towards the left, taking down the vamps on the outer edge quickly, but I know they're just fodder. The genuine threats are the ones closer to the center of the Pit. The vines disappear, and I throw the other green vial into a cluster of disoriented vampires on the opposite side of the space. The vines take care of them as I continue my way around.

I throw the last knife of my thigh collection, and I've used half my mags; there's a lot more vampires than I thought. My ears are ringing from the pops of the Glock, so I savor the rest of my bullets, switching to hand combat and my hunting knives. Two male vamps run towards me, fangs exposed, dirty sharp nails out.

Dodging the one on the right, I sink my blade into the eye socket of the other one. His blood spurts out onto my arm and my face as he goes down shrieking.

I try not to swallow the foul liquid as I narrowly miss a swipe from the remaining one. My fist connect with his jaw, stunning him, then I plunge my blade into his ribcage.

I start a deadly dance with my knife and fists. Hit, stab, kick, stab. Fatigue starts to set in and I stumble. A female vamp clocks me in the jaw, sending stars into my vision, pain exploding in my head.

Turning back to her, I grab a chunk of her blood-matted hair to expose her neck, and shove my blade into her jugular. Her cool blood slips between my fingers. I leave the knife in her neck, pulling out another one.

I turn in time to get punched in the gut, winding me, making me lose my new blade. A knee connects with my mouth and nose, splitting my lip and blood spurting out of my nose. I fight the dizziness, rolling out of the way of the foot coming down to crush my ribs.

I face my enemy, his face is feral, both sets of fangs long and thick, his eyes burning a wildfire red. He launches at me, claws first, but I step away, landing a hard elbow into his back, the move sending him to the floor.

His roars are silenced by three bullets to his head. I turn my Glock toward another vamp rushing towards me, emptying the mag into his chest. The room goes eerily quiet, my ears aching from the gunshots; the only sounds are muffled gurgling blood and whimpering humans.

I holster my gun, rushing to the fae chained up.

All three shiver in their scraps of clothes. They're all covered in violent, oozing fang wounds, knife scars, and claw marks. Two human girls who are still somehow alive after that whole mess crawl over to us. I pour the liquid of one of the blue vials onto their wrist cuffs, the iron freezing and crumbling away.

"Which one of you is Marin?"

The faerie with dull blue hair clears her throat. "I am." Her voice is hoarse, like she's been screaming for hours.

"I'm a friend of Allura and Sid's. We've been looking for you."

"Thank the Light," her voice trembles as she pulls one human towards her, hugging her close. One of the other faeries pulls in the other female, and the third faerie drags herself closer to the group.

A tendril of toffee tickles my nose, and a low, sinister laugh comes from behind me. Blueberries and frankincense follow the toffee. Fuck.

I turn to see Mydas standing with a tall, well-dressed vampire, both standing by a heavy steel door. The toffee vampire's skin is so pale, it's basically translucent, and his hair is white as snow. His eyes are black with a red molten center; he looks like the actual Devil.

"Marin, you little vixen, why did you spoil all our fun?" the toffee vamp croons. My hearing is still slightly distorted, but his voice still grates on my nerves.

I'm spent, bleeding, and pain radiates through my entire body, but these motherfuckers are going to die today.

Mydas tilts his head, his eyes glittering with amusement. "Aster, darling, I didn't think they'd send you."

I'm out of bullets, I have two blades left and three vials. Without taking my eyes off the vampires in front of me, I pull out a golden vial, passing it behind me. "Get out of here."

"What about you?" Marin asks, a little alarmed.

"Mydas and I are going to have some playtime." I stand up straighter, my body protesting, as I step towards the vile creatures.

I hear Marin mutter something about holding hands, and then warm light bursts out behind me. It makes toffee vamp hiss and covers his eyes. I use the advantage to strike.

I ram him into the concrete wall next to the door, Mydas jumps out of the way. It cracks, and dust rains all around us. I straighten and swivel to Mydas, launching myself at him knife first. He steps out of my way, slamming an elbow into my ribs, smashing me into the steel door.

I grunt at the force but jump back, out of reach of both vampires.

I feel the air rush towards me as I strike out my arm, blocking a blow from Mydas but the toffee vamp sinks his claws into my hip. Skin and muscle tear as I roar and throw both vampires off me. They fly in opposite directions as pain almost drags me into unconsciousness.

I toss a blade toward Mydas, the weapon sinking deep into his chest before I turn to the toffee vamp, stumbling toward him as I grasp my last blue vial. I toss it at him; the glass bursts on his chest, the blue liquid crawling over his torso, freezing him in place.

He tries to claw at it, panic setting into his eyes.

I palm my last blade and the golden vial. As I charge towards my target, I pull the cork off the top with my teeth and drink the whole vial.

I think of a safe place as I collide with the vamp; we both fall into a rushing golden tunnel as the magic sucks us into its portal.

26

Vladislav's Penthouse

T HE MORNING SUN GLITTERS off the windows of the buildings surrounding Central Park.

How I hate the sun right now.

Ren stormed up here two hours ago when Allura rushed out with Dom to go to Sanctuary. Marin called her. She's alive. But my reckless mate went after her, and I'm losing my mind.

"Come have a drink," Beau calls from the dining area.

He was in my apartment when I arrived back at dawn, having heard the news of Carlos' demise. I stalk over to the dining table where Beau and Ren sit opposite each other, both with a drink in hand.

Beau stands from his seat and holds out a tumbler of vodka. "She'll be fine."

I reach for the glass, but a swirl of violent golden light appears and catches my eye in the living area. My chest burns as I step into the space, and two figures fall out of a swirling beam.

312

Hugo connects with the floor, trying to claw what looks like ice from his chest. Aster lands knife-first into his chest, sinking the thick blade directly into his heart. Hugo's eyes bulge, mouth gaping, and then he's lifeless. He decays, going gray, and shriveling up.

Aster scrambles backward, heaving in big gulps of air, clutching at her wrist for the stone she always wears. She releases a relieved breath before fumbling with the pocket of her ruined jacket, pulling out her phone.

She taps frantically, bringing the phone to her ear. "Did they make it?"

A barrage of shouts rambles through the other end of the line.

"*Sid*, did they make it?" Aster shouts into the phone.

I hear a *yes*, and then a garble of more frantic shouting. "I promise Lu, I'm fine, I'm," she finally looks around. "I'm at Vlad's apartment. Help the girls; I'll be back soon."

She hangs up the phone, tossing it away from her, running her hands over her face. She's filthy, covered in blood and gray dust, her leather jacket torn at one shoulder, her jeans have tears everywhere, exposing raw, jagged wounds smeared with blood. The bond roars in my gut, demanding blood from everyone who just laid hands on her.

She removes her split knuckled hands from her face, and I'm kneeling in front of her instantly. She flinches, fist flying towards me but I catch it in my hand, enticing a growl from her.

She takes a second to register my face. "Oh, Xander, sorry."

My name rolling off her tongue settles some of the worry in my soul. "No need for apologies." I hold out my other hand. "May I?"

She nods. I release her fist, taking hold of her chin gently, and she shudders. I inspect her face; the split lip is well on its way to healing. Her left eye and cheek are bruising, but her nose is still leaking blood, air whistling as she breathes out. "Your nose is broken; I can reset it if you like."

She nods gruffly, squeezing her eyes shut and locking her jaw. I don't warn her as I wrench her nose back into its normal position; she only gasps at the movement, gripping my thighs. I turn her head from one side to the other and move my hands down her shoulders and arms, using a feather-light touch.

Her breathing is calmer when her eyes flutter open, the jade green irises rimmed red.

"No bites that I can see," I confirm, enticing the ghost of a smile on her face, but she doesn't say anything. I grip both her elbows and lift her up as I stand, Aster groaning as she becomes upright.

She leans her forehead into my chest and takes a slow breath before lifting her head and stepping out of my reach, looking behind me. "You're going to need a cleanup crew in Hell's Kitchen."

Beau chuckles behind me. "I can see you've been busy."

Aster smirks, and then her eyes roll back. Beau moves swiftly to catch her as she passes out, scooping her up in his arms. I notice the pool of blood left from where she was sitting. Blood drips from her back. "Lay her out on the dining table, on her side."

Beau carries her to the table where Renard has cleared it of glassware. He carefully lays Aster down, her back facing us.

"Fuck," Beau hisses.

The right side of Aster's back is a disaster. Her jacket is shredded, and so is the t-shirt underneath. Four gouges, claw marks, are etched deep in her back, slashing from her spine and across her right hip. Thankfully, Hugo most likely, didn't sever her spine or any vital organs.

Ren carefully turns Aster, so she's lying flat-faced and Beau rolls up his sleeve, his fangs lengthening. I grip his forearm and growl.

"Don't try me right now," I warn.

Beau bows his head and takes a step back, hands up in defense. I turn my attention back to Aster, opening a vein in my wrist with my fangs, and hold the gushing wound over her back. My blood drips into the gouges, the bleeding finally stopping and the exposed muscles slowly stitch together.

Ren rolls her back to her side, her front facing us, as we take a seat at the dining table.

"It's never boring around here, is it, Vlad?" Beau comments, setting our drinks in front of us and taking a seat next to me. He softly brushes escaped tendrils of Aster's hair off her slack face.

I've never seen him so fascinated by someone before. Possession stirs violently in my gut and I growl my warning at him. The urge to scoop Aster away from Beau is so devastatingly strong that I'm using every ounce of concentration to plant myself on the spot.

I would fight one of the oldest vampires in existence for Aster.

Ren scoops up his drink and rounds the table, inspecting Aster's wounds again. "I can't believe she took out Hugo."

Why the fuck did she go on her own and almost get herself killed? Anger at her stupidity bubbles, the bond a furnace in my gut.

A whisper of agony rolls down my spine, and then it disappears. Those emotions...*felt* different. They didn't read the same as other people. I shake it off; the stress of this whole thing is probably fucking with my gift.

Beau takes a sip of his drink, amusement playing on his face. "I'm actually impressed."

"Good." Aster croaks. My shoulders drop; I've never been so relieved to hear someone's voice before in my life. She tilts her head down, making eye contact with me. "Can I get off the table now?"

I look over at Ren, and he shakes his head.

"Not yet, *chérie*. You're still closing up."

She lets out a breath. "Can someone get my phone? Sid will come in here guns blazing if I don't call her back."

Beau chuckles, standing. "I would expect nothing else from Sidelle."

He disappears and reappears in a matter of seconds, handing Aster her phone. She places it on the table, poking at it, dialing Sid, putting it on speaker.

"What the *fuck*, Aster?" Sidelle answers with a sneer.

"Sidelle," Beau purrs, amusement blazing around him.

"Listen, you little shit," Sid spits. "I don't have time to play your games. Where is she?"

Aster can't hold in her laughter, but the movement makes her groan, breathless, as her face screws up in pain. I grip her calf, sending a wash of soothing energy. Her body goes slack, face smoothing out.

It worked. What the fuck?

"I'm-m, I'm here, Sid," she slurs into the phone.

"What. Happened?" Sid bites out.

"Well," Beau answers, "our lovely Aster looks like she went into a Nest and cleared it out."

"Aster?"

She mumbles, her eyelids heavy. "Mhmm. S-so many."

"Did you get the leader?"

Beau chuckles. "Oh, she did. Hugo is decaying on Vlad's floor as we speak."

"Hugo the Brute?" Sid asks.

Beau sits back in his chair, arms folded over his chest. "Yes."

"You allowed that *animal* into your territory?"

Beau's eyes narrow at the phone. "Our Queen exonerated his exile, I didn't have a choice."

Sid laughs, the sound cold. "I expected more from you, Beau. You should have been on his ass, watching his every fucking move."

Anger ghosts through Beau, his eyes hardening. "Careful, Sidelle."

She clicks her tongue dismissively. "Get your shit together."

"Mydasss," Aster hisses, "he was there. I... knife in his chest."

"We'll sort it out," Sidelle confirms. "Vladislav?"

"Yes, Sid?"

"Look after my babygirl." The line cuts off.

27

I FEEL LIKE I'M wrapped in soft satin. It's cooling, relaxing, serene. From somewhere far away, I can hear male voices.

"Sidelle has some balls." The voice is deep, a little gruff, and amused—Renard.

"She'll get herself into a tough situation if she doesn't consider her words," Beau responds.

"You're a fool to even consider threatening Sidelle."

That voice. That voice caresses my ears as clear as a summer's day. The pitch is low, deep, refined. It's the voice of deadly promises, warmth, comfort, pleasure, and a thousand other possibilities.

I follow the thread leading to that voice, pulling me out of the quiet reverie of my satin dream towards Xander.

I peel open a heavy lid, but only one; the left one is completely swollen shut. A dark, blurry figure comes into view. I blink my non-injured eye, clearing my vision. Beau sits back in his chair, arms folded over a blood-streaked shirt, glowering at someone to his right.

"You're cute when you pout."

He turns to me, his mouth lifting on one side, those beautiful sand eyes shining. "Welcome back to the land of the living."

"You mean the undead?"

Beau laughs. "Touché." He stands, his hands out, his bergamot and blackcurrant scents tickling my nose.

At least I can still smell, thanks to Xander. I grab both of Beau's hands, allowing him to pull me up. My entire body screeches in protest, and I groan. The world turns violently as I come up to a sitting position on the table, swinging my heavy legs off the concrete surface, dangling them over the edge.

"How old are you, anyway?"

Beau chuckles. He still hasn't released my hands. His skin is cool and smooth, like marble. "It's rude to ask one's age, *especially* a vampire."

I lean in, taking a lungful of his scent. "I say, well over a thousand years."

Beau's smile deepens. "You just keep surprising me, love."

He lets go, taking half a step back. Gripping the edge of the table, I slide off carefully. My body is wrecked, but I manage to place both feet on the floor and stand without falling over or passing out. My back is tight. The skin pulls oddly, and the muscles feel like they have stitched together wrong.

I look up into Beau's face with my good eye. "You still haven't answered my question."

"Relentless thing." He walks over to the buffet, picking up the bottle of vodka, refilling his glass. "I was born in the back of the gladiator pits."

Okay, I didn't think he was *that* old. Surprise hits my gut, but it doesn't feel like my surprise, then disappears. Xander watches Beau intently in my periphery. When did my brain suddenly decide it was *Xander*?

"Were you a gladiator yourself?" I ask Beau, distracting myself from the garbled mix of emotions my tired brain can't analyze right now.

Something crosses his face as he nods, taking a swig of his drink, then looks to Xander. "Does she ask *you* these titillating questions?"

Xander smiles. Xander. My brain refuses to acknowledge him as anything else now. Stupid bond.

"She told me her mouth gets her in trouble."

Beau's eyes sparkle, flicking to my mouth.

I cross my arms over my chest. "Not going to happen. I have vamps to burn and injuries to heal."

"I'll be more than happy to take care of Hugo," Ren says behind me.

"How many vampires did you eliminate?" Beau asks, leaning against the buffet.

"I don't know the exact number, but a few."

Beau has a hard, calculating look on his face. I unfold my arms and spread my feet apart slightly. I won't last long in a fight with this many injuries, but I'll take at least one of those pretty eyes with me if he tries.

A predatory smile crawls across his face. "Still willing to fight me, love." He pushes off the bar, discarding his drink behind him. "I thank you for your service; many people will be glad you disposed of Hugo."

"Who exactly is Hugo?"

"Hugo the Brute," Xander interjects, "is the true definition of a monster."

"He was exiled," Beau adds, "but lunacy impeded that order."

"He was a fucking asshole," Ren barks, coming around the table to sit next to me. "He should have been eliminated decades ago."

I keep the thousand questions I have to myself. I don't need to make an enemy of Beau by accusing him of incompetence. My phone buzzes on the table by Ren. He passes it over, *Sid* flashing on the screen. "Hey, Sid."

"Don't just *'hey'* me, Aster," she chastises into my ear. "How bad is it?"

I sigh. "One eye swollen shut, all the cuts healed, no broken bones this time, and my back, I don't even want to know."

"You should have gotten out of there with the faeries."

"And let Mydas and Hugo go free?" I bark a laugh. "You forget who you're talking to, Sid."

She sighs. "The doctor is here, so Dom and Allura are on their way to you."

I hang up as Ren disappears in the direction of Hugo. I perch back on the table, shuffle closer to Xander, resting my head on his shoulder, twining my fingers through his.

Beau's phone buzzes in his pocket. He pulls it out and sighs, bringing it to his ear. "Queen Medea, what a pleasure."

Xander freezes next to me. I grip his hand tighter.

A sensual, feminine laugh comes through the phone. "Beau, darling, it's been an age."

"Indeed, it has. How may I assist you this fine afternoon?"

"I wanted to know if you have seen Hugo recently?"

Beau laughs, the sound both dripping with promise and warning. "I have, just moments ago, in fact. He's looking a little gray."

Silence on the other side of the phone. "What authority did you have to execute him?" Her voice is full of poison, making me cringe.

Beau's eyes narrow onto my face. "Apart from the fact that he was in my territory without my knowledge, he was also hosting a Lux Pit."

"You murdered a member of *my* Court for a minor indiscretion?"

Beau's power flares, hitting me like a hurricane of scent, and his eyes burn sunset orange. I flinch, and Xander wraps an arm around me, keeping me, or maybe himself, steady.

"*Minor* indiscretion?" Beau booms. "Do you forget your own laws about Lux, my dear Queen?"

"Don't mock me, Nest Master."

"Don't send your pathetic pets into my territory, Medea. I'll send you Hugo's ashes for your throne room." He hangs up, pocketing the phone. The sunset fire in his eyes simmers down, as does his power. "Apologies for the outburst."

"She gets under your skin too, huh?"

Beau chuckles, twisting to pick up his drink. "Most of the Queens have gotten under my skin in the last two millennia. None of them know how to respect their elders." He tips back his entire drink.

"What are vampire Kings like?"

Xander scoffs; his arm lingers around me. "There has never been one. Our ruler must be a Pure Blood and there hasn't been a male Pure Blood born since the beginning of our species."

"Is it rare for a male to be born?"

Beau chuckles. "It's not only extremely rare, but Pure Bloods also don't allow them to be born."

The sound of the front door bursting open halts my tirade of questions as quick footsteps rush in. Allura's tear-streaked face comes into view as she pushes through Beau and Xander, throwing her arms around my neck tight. I groan at the contact. Dom rushes in after her, also looking overly panicked. Allura's body trembles with her sobbing.

She pulls back, her blue eyes bloodshot. "I hate you right now."

My lip quirks up. "Good to see you, too."

She holds me at arm's length, assessing my face, eyes traveling down to my toes. She turns me around, and she gasps.

"*Dios mio*," Dom gapes behind me.

"That bad, huh?"

"I can make it better than it is," Allura assures, "but there will still be scars."

I turn back around. "Why is it this bad in the first place?"

"You must have gotten vampire toxin into your system at some point," Xander explains as Allura props me back on the table, chanting in Fae Tongue.

Her small hand glows a vibrant yellow as it covers my injured eye, and pleasant heat sinks into my skin, like the sun beaming down on a summer's day. She stops chanting as she lowers her hand and I can see out of both eyes, the pain and swelling in my face gone.

"Your back won't be as pleasant." She turns to Xander and points to the chair next to her. "You sit here and everyone else out."

Dom steps up to me, and traces my jaw before walking out without another word. I press a gentle hand into Xander's slightly trembling forearm; he looks like he's about to fight him.

Beau leans against the buffet. "I'd like to stay."

Allura lifts a glowing hand. "Out."

Beau's eyes narrow on Allura, but eventually pushes off the buffet and disappears around the corner. We hear them all leave the apartment as Xander sits as instructed, Allura turning back to me. "Lay on your side, head in front of Xander. I won't be able to stop once I start."

I sink onto my side, looking into Xander's beautiful face. A whisper of concern curls in me, then disappears. Allura rounds the table as she begins her chanting again. The entire room lightens in a warm glow. Warmth, like summer wind, starts in my back, but it's getting hotter.

Xander keeps his eyes on me as searing heat now crawls up my back. I grip the end of the table, biting down the groans—sweat beads on my forehead and neck, my breathing labored.

The gouges feel like they're being ripped open again, and a yelp slips out.

"I'll just live with the scarring," I state as I try to lift myself off the table.

Xander grips my shoulders hard, keeping me in place. The heat is now sizzling through my veins. Liquid, maybe blood, oozes down my back. I don't want to do this anymore.

"Xander."

The cobalt in Xander's left eye engulfs the amber, and both irises dazzle. That satin feeling slips over my mind again and my eyelids droop closed; the pain disappears from my body. Allura's chanting sounds so far away, but Xander's even breathing is like a whisper in my ear.

I think this is what it feels like when he uses his gift. How he is doing it, I have no idea as I'm still wearing my amulet but I revel in this soft satin dream for what seems like a long time, Xander's hand warm against my skin, no pain at all in my body.

"Aster?" His voice pulls me back to his dining room. Allura's chanting has stopped. I open my eyes, cobalt and amber eyes swimming in my vision. Xander smiles. "How are you feeling?"

He releases his hold on me, letting me push myself upright, doing it with ease. "I feel better than I should at this point." I twist at the waist, the tightness in my back and hip gone.

"The damage isn't as deep in your muscles anymore; it's more a surface scar now," Allura huffs as she collapses in the chair next to Xander. "I need a nap."

I laugh, slipping off the table. "So do I. And a long, long shower."

Hugo's body is gone, and most of the mess I left in Xander's apartment has disappeared as Dom takes us home in the fading light of the afternoon.

Allura curls up on the sofa and passes out as soon as she's horizontal. I drag myself upstairs to have a shower, washing every inch of myself multiple times.

I inspect my back in the mirror. There are four pink, jagged scars that run from the side of my spine, circling across my hip and teetering off at the start of my thigh. I don't even want to know what they looked like before Allura worked her magic.

I change into sleep shorts and a cropped t-shirt, taking off my amulet for the first I've been here—it's like a heavy weight lifting off my soul. Nagging aches seem to disappear instantly, and yellowing bruises are gone.

The amulet may hide my identity, but it also suppresses my wolf. My eyesight now seems sharper, my nose more keen. I leave the amulet and descend down the stairs, intending to join Allura for a well-deserved nap on the sofa when the back door clicks open. I find Art putting a big pastry box down on the counter as I reach the kitchen.

"Sorry, Jas wanted me to—' Art stops, choking on his words. His nostrils flare and then he averts his gaze immediately to the floor and crosses his arm over his broad chest, his fist meeting his shoulder.

"I-I didn't realize you were an Alpha," he stammers, not lifting his bowed head.

"I'm not." I approach the counter opposite him, my hands starting to tremble slightly. I breathe evenly, trying to curb the panic threatening to consume my body.

"With all due respect, that's a lie."

"Stop bowing, it's weirding me out."

"Yes, Alpha," he responds, straightening up but keeping his eyes on the floor.

I dash upstairs, take my amulet from the bathroom counter, and then quickly return to the kitchen. The tension is immediately different when I enter. Allura is awake now, busy making drinks. Art looks up at me, confusion written into every feature of his chiseled face. "What is going on?"

"Nothing," I say with a shrug.

"Aster," Art rumbles.

"You haven't told Lárusson about me, have you?"

He scoffs. "Why would I give that asshole any indication that there's a Lone female in his territory for him to claim as property?"

I let out a breath. Thank Odin for that. A steaming cup of black tea, a small jug of creamer, as well as plates for the pastries, appear between us as Allura appears next to me. We all sit in silence as I rip a croissant in half, contemplating what to do. The logical thing would be to kill Art, but he definitely doesn't deserve that. I could go on the run again, but where? Or—

"Are you the female Jónasson is hunting?" Art asks, his attention on stirring sugar into his coffee.

I clear my throat. "Yes. I'm High Alpha Jónasson's daughter. My name is Nova."

Art's head whips to mine. "His *daughter*?"

I nod in response. I let him mull over my words.

He brings the cup to his mouth and takes a careful sip. "Do you have any idea what the reward is for your capture?"

"Knowing my father, probably the honor of breeding me until I die."

Art's eyes swirl with bright copper. "It is. They also threw in an obscene amount of money and a High Beta position."

Allura gasps in horror beside me. I'm really not surprised.

He loosens a breath. "Why didn't you tell me, Ast—Nova?"

"Because you're a wolf. The entire species is hunting me; I don't trust anyone."

His eyes narrow. "Fuck the rest of them; this is *me*. You can *always* trust me."

Tears prick my eyes. "That's hard for me to do. I-I'm sorry."

His eyes soften. "I get it."

Pain flashes across his eyes before he looks away from me. With what happened to Genevieve, yeah, he would understand. He helps himself to a few pastries. "Being First Blood born makes sense why you're also an Alpha."

"I'm *not* an Alpha."

He cringes a little at my tone as he chuckles. "Even with whatever trick you used to suppress that energy, I felt your command loud and clear."

I blow out a frustrated breath, shoving half a croissant into my mouth. When wolves come into their magic at twenty-three, some are gifted with an extra kick that develops into Alphas or Betas. I didn't feel any different this birthday, I was too busy running for my life.

First Bloods are mostly part of the High Alpha's Pack, so the only people who *may* present the potential for Alpha energy are the firstborn sons of High Alphas, typically their successors.

So for Art to claim I have Alpha energy is ridiculous because I'm the last born of my father's children.

Allura flutters around the kitchen, pulling out cereal and a bowl. "Can females not be Alphas?"

"They can," Art answers for me. "There's just never been a recorded case of a female wolf having Alpha energy. But Nova here has it rolling off her in waves."

"I shouldn't," I muse, lifting my wrist. "This amulet is Fae magic. It should block everything."

"It's working for the scent," Art confirms, holding his drink to his lips, "but your Alpha authority is peeking through, and it will probably get worse closer to the full moon."

Allura's brow creases as she breezes over to the wall of books, muttering to herself about a spell, cereal discarded.

I turn back to Art. "Claiming I'm an Alpha is delusional."

He chuckles, taking a mouthful of coffee. "I'll prove it to you." He turns his body to me. "Tell me how many wolves are in this street."

I frown. "How is this—"

He holds his hand up. "Indulge me."

I blow out a breath and close my eyes, concentrating on the street. Wolves have a general sense of each other when they're near and a general sense of territory lines, usually by smell. "In our street, it's just us." I can feel both our energies buzzing like an internal thread connected to the earth.

"Okay, how about the suburb?"

I take a deep breath, concentrating on that energy connecting me to the earth, but the connection feels fuzzy. "I can't feel much."

"Take the amulet off and try again," Art instructs.

I unwind the cord, placing it on the counter. Art grunts as I close my eyes again.

The threads to earth buzz and spark in the back of my mind. I follow the threads, pulling me elsewhere, branching out further and further, like tree roots, some lines thicker than others. "There... there's fifteen? No, wait, seventeen, not including us. One pack. A Bitten Pack. The Alpha lives by Fort Greene Park, the Beta lives near him."

Art chuckles. "Alphas are the only wolves able to do that." My eyes open to his amused, satisfied face, his eyes averting straight away. "It's a way to communicate with their own Pack and also a way to size up rival Packs."

"How did I not know any of this?"

"They keep it between Alphas and Betas. Betas can do the same thing to an extent, but it takes a lot of effort. We can only focus on one thread, compared to an Alpha who can feel the entire network. Usually, we only use the technique when we're on a hunt." He flinches at his own words.

Allura rushes back in with a heavy-looking ancient book, plopping it down on the counter. She's a little winded but picks up her cereal, looking at us. "What did I miss?"

I shake my head, returning my attention back to Art. I understand how much he hates wolf hierarchy and their stupid, backward views; it ripped his mate away from him and any sliver of light from his life.

"How about you become my Beta?"

Allura drops her spoon in her cereal bowl, choking a little on her mouthful of food. Art's mouth drops open in disbelief. "You want one of the Bitten to be the Beta to you?"

I smile. "I have trust issues, big ones. But I do trust you, Art, even though I haven't been very forthcoming." I grasp his warm hand on the counter. "You have never lied to me, and that's a big thing for me. You're already an anchor to reality in the disaster that is my existence, a-and I know being a Beta is a literal life sentence—"

"I'll do it."

I blink. "What?"

He squeezes my hand, then stands from his stool, sinking to one knee, and crosses his arm over his chest again. He bows his head, "Nova Jónasdóttir, as the Bitten, I, Carter Benson, renounce my ties to the Lárusson Pack and offer my loyalty and allegiance to you as my Alpha. I accept the honor of being your Beta and offer my service and protection to you and the Pack until my dying day."

"I know I'm the one who offered, but are you sure?"

Art lifts his face to mine; I can *feel* the effort he's using to hold my gaze. "I'm already ostracized by most Alphas around here. You know I can't accept a role where I must enforce rules I abhor. I should thank you. You saved me from some serious shit I was about to get myself into if you didn't stumble in when you did, looking all helpless. So yes, stupid, I accept your offer."

"Excuse me," Allura announces, "while I throw up." She rushes out of the room.

I laugh. Art is still kneeling, expecting my answer. "According to you, I'm not at all helpless." I pull him from his shoulders. "Please sit; there's one more thing you need to know."

"What else could there possibly be?" Art asks, returning to his stool. He picks up his abandoned croissant and takes a bite out of it. I hope he doesn't choke.

"I'm mate-bound."

Art is even more confused. "Okay?"

"To a vampire."

Art stops chewing. "Come again?"

I offer a knowing smile.

He blinks a few times and then continues to chew on his food, eyes glazed over. When he swallows, he focuses back on me. "To a *vampire*?"

"Yes."

His eyes widen slightly. "*Vladislav?*"

I nod.

"How?"

"Magic."

Art finishes his food and downs his drink. "I'm not going to ask questions I know I won't understand the answers to." He stands, brushing the crumbs off his chest. "Let's do this, no take-backs."

My shoulders relax, the buzzing of anxiety in my head slows. I step around the counter and fish out a small knife from the dishwasher.

Art's breath hitches behind me. "What happened?"

"I took out a Lux Pit today," I say, turning around, pulling down my t-shirt. "We found Marin."

"Shit, why didn't you call me?" Art hisses, running his hands through his hair.

"I didn't have time."

He crosses his arm over his chest. "Well, after this blood bond, it's my duty to be by your side, so don't be pulling that shit again."

I laugh, rolling my eyes as I hover the knife over my palm, ready to make the first cut.

"I, Nova Jónasdóttir, accept you, Carter Benson, as Beta of, ah... we need a Pack name."

"Perhaps a middle name?"

"I, Nova Jónasdóttir, accept you, Carter Benson, as Beta of the Zephyrus Pack. As Alpha, I shall endeavor to lead with integrity and strength to ensure our protection, continued prosperity, and peace for generations to come."

I slice the center of my palm, then the inside of my forearm below the elbow crease, handing the knife to Art. He does the same. We press our palms into the cuts on our forearms, grasping in a warrior's embrace.

My eyes fall closed as the blood in our veins sing to life, and our wolves' energies merge. We both shudder as the connection is complete, and our wounds heal. When I open my eyes to Art's, I expect them to be gold, but his eyes are glowing a deep sapphire blue with a small ring of gold around his pupils.

"Your eyes aren't gold anymore," Allura whispers from the doorway, looking at me.

I blink slowly a few times, the surge of the bond subsiding. Art does the same, his eyes returning to their dazzling hazel. "Not just an Alpha then," he muses.

"What do you mean?"

He chuckles. "You're a *High* Alpha. We just created a new First Blood Pack."

My mouth falls open, no sound coming out—Art's face beams in victory.

A First Blood Pack. With me, as it's High Alpha.

Odin, help us.

"I have no fucking clue how this next full moon is going to go."

Art barks a laugh. "Challenge accepted."

"Before we worry about that," Allura says, scooping up her big book and my amulet. "We need to fix this."

"It's broken?" I ask.

"Not exactly," she explains, as we follow her out of the back door and toward Art and Jas' back door. "When you fought the Pit there was a lot of blood sprayed around, and it unbound some of the spell."

Their place is the same as ours, but a mirror image. Their stairs and front door sit to the left of their apartment, and where we have one large light gray sofa taking up the entire living area, and the boys have gone with a three-piece sofa set in navy. Shelves still dominate the wall opposite the sofas, but the contents are mostly video games, books, and collectible model cars.

We find Jas at the dining table in front of a mountain of books and papers. He looks up curious, pushing his glasses on his nose. Sometimes I forget how handsome he is with unblemished dark tan skin, hooded eyes of deep, soulful brown, and straight hair black as onyx, always in a neat, brushed back style.

"We need some of your supplies," Allura says as she pecks Jas on the cheek.

"A spell, fun," he beams, standing and stretching. "Let's go upstairs. You can fill me in."

Art goes to his fridge, pulling out two bottles of water and passing me one as I peek at Jas' collection of papers. He looks like he's working on mapping werewolf Alpha Packs, particularly the Jónasson Pack.

"You know our Pack bond makes you High Beta if your theory stands?" I muse.

Art chokes on the water he was drinking as Allura and Jas appear in the kitchen again, both their arms full of jars.

"So, *Nova*," Jas draws out my name.

"Uh oh," Art chuckles, recovering from his coughing fit.

"I need to pick your brain," Jas challenges, with a glint in his eye.

"I knew this was coming," I huff. "Later."

He nods, motioning for all of us to follow us into the shared garden.

Allura shucks off her oversized cardigan, and kicks off her shoes, then finds a spot in the middle of the grass and sits cross-legged. She places a wooden bowl in front of her along with two amber vials and her book next to the bowl.

Jas places a jar of dried flowers next to the vials, which he unscrews the lids ready for use, and then pours salt from a large jar around Allura, creating a closed ring.

The amulet is placed into the bowl and Allura pulls a clump of dirt from the ground, covering the amulet entirely. She flips her book open, scans the page, and takes a deep breath. With one hand still buried in the grass, Allura begins to chant in Fae Tongue with her eyes closed and her head tilted to the sky.

"She'll need a few drops of your blood," Jas whispers, eyes focused on Allura.

"How am I not surprised?" I murmur as Allura's hands start to glow in a golden light.

My spine tingles, my wolf bristling but curious at the sensations pulsing from Allura. I've never felt it since I'm always wearing the amulet.

I turn my attention to Art standing next to me with his arms crossed, eyes watchful but curious. His energy filters toward me—I get a sense that he's concerned, curious, heartbroken, but also somewhat at peace. Like things are slotting into place for him.

I turn back to Allura who adds the dried flowers, elderflowers by the scent, into the bowl which catch fire as soon as they hit the dirt. She continues to chant, her whole body glowing in her golden light as she picks up one dropper of juniper berry oil, and pours the oil over the small fire, dousing it.

Black plumes of smoke curl up as she takes the second dropper of rosemary oil and squeezes half of it over the blackened mound, the oil hissing as it makes contact.

Jas pulls out a pocketknife and takes my hand. He lowers it to just over the bowl, then gives my palm a swift scrape of the blade. I wince as I close my hand, allowing the blood to drip onto the black pile below.

After the third drop, Jas hands me a hand towel, and does the same to Allura, slicing a thin line in her palm and guiding her hand to drip blood onto the pile. White plumes of smoke rise each time the blood lands. She then places her hand back into the earth and closes her eyes.

She's quiet for a few moments as her skin dims. When she's back to her usual bronze tone, she opens her eyes with a smile on her face and pulls her hands from the earth, fishing out the amulet from the bowl.

"You *literally* set it on fire. How is it not destroyed?" I ask.

She laughs as she wraps it around my wrist. "The dirt protected it from being damaged."

Jas turns to Art. "Did it work?"

I turn my head. Disbelief is written all over Art's face. "Yeah, you smell and feel Beta again. Fuck, magic is wild."

28

Immortal

A **FEELING OF RELIEF** echoes through everyone as we finish for the night. It's been particularly busy, and everyone's worn down by the heartbreak over Carlos. I kept checking on Aster for any signs of discomfort from her injury, but she hasn't winced once, even in sky-high heels.

As Vik and Maddox leave, my phone rings.

"Beau."

"Vladislav," he greets. His voice is a little too formal, his usual amusement gone. This isn't good.

"What is it?" I ask as Aster sidles up to me at the bar; I switch the phone to speaker.

"He's not dead," Beau growls.

"Who?"

"Mydas," Beau practically spits his name. "We didn't find him at the Pit, and he's nowhere in the state, I checked."

Fury pumps through my veins but I lock it down. Of course the cockroach isn't fucking dead, that would be too easy.

A growl slips from Aster. "Motherfucker."

Her eyes glow with her fury, but not gold. They glow a brilliant sapphire blue with a golden ring around her pupil. That's new.

"He's probably groveling at Medea's feet," I tell Beau.

"He'd be smart not to come back," Beau responds and hangs up.

Aster turns to leave but I grab her wrist. "Your eyes aren't gold anymore."

"Yeah, that's a long story."

"Where are you going?" I ask as she tries to tug free from my hold.

"Going to hunt that bastard down," she grumbles.

I tug her toward me, her chest meeting mine, the bond pleased with the contact. "Beau will have people on it."

The crease between her brows deepens. "A wolf will track him better."

"Maybe on a hunt, but he'll cover his tracks now. Beau will go through the vampire gossip chain to find him. He has spies everywhere."

Aster blows out a breath, her eyes finally melting back to beautiful jade green.

I trace her cheek and jaw, releasing her wrist. "Tell me that long story over dinner tonight?"

She smiles, leaning into my touch. "Who's going to watch Allura?"

"Ren can take her to his place for the evening. She likes it there."

She arches an eyebrow.

I chuckle. "It's purely platonic between them, I promise." I lean in, tilting her head, exposing her throat. "Unlike us."

I run my tongue up the muscle of her neck, toward her ear and nip her lobe. She gasps, her hands landing on my chest, the bond burning with satisfaction.

Footsteps sound in the back hallway and I hear Dom and Ren conversing. Aster steps back, clearing her throat, her face flushed, and perches on a bar stool.

Dom walks in with Ren by his side and their emotions wash over me. Ren is still in deep grief over Carlos, like everyone else, I'm surprised he's even here tonight.

Dom's emotion, however, makes me want to tackle the man to the ground. His grief is overshadowed as he takes in Aster—lust and the want to claim her pours out of him in waves. I unbutton my jacket and step towards the two men, hiding my trembling hands in my pants pockets.

"Dom, you never come in on your nights off."

He smiles. "I know. But assholes think I'm your secretary, so here I am."

I motion for Dom and Ren to take a seat on a sofa as Aster comes over with a bottle of scotch and three tumblers.

"Message from your wolf leaders, I presume?" I ask as Aster pours the drinks and then perches on the arm of the chair I'm sitting in.

Dom doesn't hide his appraisal of Aster's white satin dress she chose tonight, his eyes lingering on her exposed thigh crossed over the other, adorned in glittering diamond chains. I want to show him that he will *never* have a claim on her, but I resist the urge.

Dom nods, taking a swing of his scotch. "They assigned me a bounty. The female from the Jónasson pack."

"Did you need to take leave for this hunt?" I ask, not drawing attention to the fact that Aster's shoulders have stiffened slightly. My gifts don't work on her again.

Dom sits forward. "I do. We've tracked her to New York, but I've lost the trail."

"You could have advised me in a message."

Dom clears his throat. "I know. But the High Alpha is aware of your 'habit' of collecting strays, and he wanted me to ask if you could inform us if you come across any."

My eyes flick to Aster then back to Dom, raising a questioning brow.

He sits back, a small smile on his face. "He already knows of Aster. He spoke to Sidelle."

The fact that a High Alpha is aware of her presence unsettles me. "I'm glad that's cleared up."

Dom's eyes light, flicking back to Aster. "You know, he's considering initiating you into the Pack."

Rage flashes through my body. She's *mine.* I force myself to remain in my chair and not rip Dom's throat out as Aster scoffs. "No thanks, I'm good as I am."

Dom barks a laugh. "I told Izar as much, but he is very curious to meet you."

I stand up slowly, barely containing the fury boiling beneath my skin. I stick out my hand. "We'll organize that another time. Good luck on your hunt, Dominic."

He stands as well and accepts the handshake. "I'll let you know when I'm ready to come back."

He turns to leave, Ren following him out. We both listen to their footsteps before Aster tugs on my arm, turning me to face her. "You look like you're about to combust."

I wrap an arm around her abruptly, crushing her to my body and our foreheads coming together. "I don't like the way they think of you as some sort of property to be traded."

Aster's hands caress the sides of my face, and she closes her eyes. "That's how wolves work: females are the most valuable asset to own, even though we aren't treated very well."

"Anyone who tries to take you from me will have their hearts fed to them," I growl.

Aster chuckles, my anger dissipating. "Let's go have dinner." She collects the glassware and bottle, returning them back to the bar and picks up her jacket. "I still don't believe you about Allura and Renard being platonic."

"It's true," I argue, hooking her arm into mine as we walk towards the elevator. "They're flirtatious, sure, but he's never tried to sleep with her, which *is* shocking for Ren. He's protective of her and she cares for him, but they would never cross that boundary."

Aster leans forward and presses the elevator button, body brushing past mine, sending electricity shooting through the touch. I take in a shallow breath, trying not to pin her against the wall.

Aster seems to have the same reaction, going stiff next to me, trying not to move. "It must be nice to see someone caring for Ren," she breathes.

The elevator door slides open, and we step inside. "It is. He seems at ease when she's around. Not so angry all the time."

Aster is silent next to me, eyes watching the levels of the elevator tick higher until they hit the Penthouse. We step out into the hallway and towards the apartment's front doors, Aster stepping back as I type in the code for the front door.

I smirk. "You are allowed to know the code."

"I didn't want to assume. This is your home, your haven."

The door unlocks, and I hold it open for Aster. "This is yours now too, open to you always."

I'm surprised to see tears shine in her eyes before she drops her head, walking inside. Delia's humming floats over from the kitchen, so we both make our way there.

Delia is going back and forth from the stove and a chopping board on the island bench. She's set out two places on the glass table with a bottle of champagne waiting.

I offer Aster a chair, but she hesitates. "Can I borrow some clothes? I'm desperate to get out of these ones."

I chuckle. "Let's go get comfortable before we eat."

Aster changes into one of my t-shirts, and a pair of boxer briefs, twisting her long mane into a high bun and moving to my bathroom to wash her face. I change into sweatpants and a black t-shirt and then we both make our way to the kitchen, where Delia has set up two spots at the breakfast table.

I pull out Aster's chair, then sit on my own and pour two glasses of champagne as Delia approaches with two plates. She places the larger steak and roasted vegetables in front of Aster, and the much smaller one in front of me, with a bag of blood next to it.

I raise my champagne flute, and Aster takes hers. "To the future, whatever that may hold."

"To the future," Aster repeats as we clink glasses.

We fall into a pleasant conversation as we dine. She's easy to talk to and has a wicked sense of humor. When we both finish our meals, Delia appears again to wash up.

"Should we move this party to the living area?" I ask.

Aster nods, standing up to stretch. She checks her phone, her brows creasing.

"Problem?" I ask.

"It's a week until the next full moon," she muses more to herself.

I place a hand on her hip, lowering my lips to her for a swift kiss. "Go get comfortable; I'll bring over dessert."

She nods and wanders off as I collect the plate of chocolate-dipped strawberries from the fridge. I pop open a fresh bottle of champagne and gather up two fresh glasses.

Aster is sprawled out along the sofa; her long hair, now unbound, splays out, the ends just brushing the floor. One of her bare legs hooks over the back of the sofa, and one lays along the seat. Her eyes are closed, her brows slightly pinched.

I place the bottle, plate, and glasses down softly on the table, lift her outstretched leg and take a seat, laying her leg across my lap. Her eyes flutter open, and a smile warms her face.

"What were you thinking about?" I ask.

"The next full moon."

"Mm," I muse as I lean over and pour out the champagne.

Aster fiddles with her bracelet, looking up at the ceiling, worry clouding her eyes. "I have no idea how this whole thing is going to turn out."

I offer her a full glass. "Whichever way it goes, I have faith you'll find the answers you need."

She looks at me, propping herself up on an elbow and accepting the glass. She takes a sip, her eyes ablaze with challenge. Good Lord. "Tell more about this ex of yours."

I roll my eyes, my mood souring slightly. "Why would you even want to think about her?"

"Because she seems to be a thorn in your side, which means she's now a thorn in mine, and I want to know who we're up against. It feels like there's something about to go down. And soon."

She has a point. Medea is spiraling, and it's better to be prepared than ambushed. I sigh, settling further into the sofa. "Fine."

She leans over, picking out a strawberry from the pile, and returns to the same position; one elbow propped up, champagne in her hand, and a mouth full of strawberry. Her eyes pierce through me, demanding all my secrets.

"Renard and I were born in the south of France in 1716 to a beautiful woman named Cèleste, and her estranged, or dead, husband. That we aren't sure of."

"You're *twins?*"

"Yes."

"But he looks older than you."

"Well, he was born first, so in theory, I am his younger brother by minutes. But he was made a vampire later in his human life."

She takes another strawberry. "How old were you when you turned?"

"Twenty-seven. Ren was thirty-eight."

She nods, nibbling on her strawberry, mulling over the new information. Even the way she eats is distracting. I fight the urge to explore her body with my hands, taking a sip of champagne instead.

"Our childhood was typical of someone from that era, Ren married his wife when we were twenty, and I went to work in the stables at the palace in Versailles."

Aster chokes on a laugh. "*You?* Manual labor?"

I smirk into my glass. "I know. Hard to imagine, but true. The stables are where I met Medea. She walked her horse over because he was lame. I was entranced immediately." I finish my drink, placing the glass on the table.

Aster clicks her fingers. "Tell me she was a Lord's mistress or something?"

I smirk. "The King's mistress, naturally. Mistresses had power in those days. And Medea gets off on power."

Aster lifts her leg off the back of the sofa and sits up. She abandons her glass on the table, places her head in my lap, and drapes my arm over her waist. My other hand automatically starts playing with her long, soft tresses.

"She strung you along for seven *years* before turning you?" she asks.

"Turning someone all starts with the mental aspect. You can't turn someone if they aren't willing, their body rejects the change, and they die. Seduction of an eternal life plays a vital part. That's why most vampires you meet have an alluring nature. Then there's the bloodletting and feeding of blood; it's too technical for my liking."

"Do you remember your turn?"

"Like it was yesterday. It was messy and intense. My heart suddenly started stuttering in the gardens that day. I got to the stables before the pain and convulsions began. It felt like acid was burning through my body. I didn't exactly die, but it was so common those days that the other stable hands just dumped my body in one of the palace's many dungeon rooms."

I have been staring out of the window, so I look down. Aster's expression is a mixture of shock and straight-out disgust. She blinks; her mouth opens a few times as if to say something, but then closes it again.

"When I woke, the urge to find my Sire, Medea, was so intense I almost went into the sunlight," I continue. "If you create a vampire, you have to exchange either blood or a bite one last time to complete the sire bond, depending on how they were created. Sire bonds are powerful, but not as powerful as an incomplete one. After she completed the bond with me, she made me wait in the dungeon, when all I wanted to do was rip someone's throat out."

Aster scoffs, leaning over for another strawberry and sip of champagne. "Don't you always want to rip someone's throat out?"

I smirk. "These days, it's because people piss me off. Back then, it was Blood Lust. As I mentioned before, mine was severe. I always needed to feed. Medea and I had to keep moving so we didn't get discovered. I used to rip through villages in one night. And I didn't give a shit who I killed; men, women, children, all were just food to me."

Aster turns to her side, her head still in my lap.

"You seem very restless tonight," I comment.

She lets out a breath. "That insatiable feeling you talk about? That's how I feel right now. I haven't had a Pack to run with for almost two months, and it's wreaking havoc. Wolves usually go for runs in the days leading up to the full moon to expel pent-up energy."

"I'm sure Carter would join you on a run."

Aster sits up and brings her knees to her chest, snatching up her champagne flute and taking a mouthful. My body instantly craves her warmth back.

She seems nervous or panicked.

"Is there some wolf law I don't know about that prevents it?" I ask.

She looks over at me, a seductive smile on her lips and shakes her head, obviously trying to distract me from the stress she's hiding. "How long did the Blood Lust last?"

I give in to her redirection. "Forty years. A blink of an eye for a vampire, but definitely longer than most. Once it subsided, I regained my passion for other things in life. Women mostly, and food. My taste buds are exceptionally more precise now than they were as a human."

"When did you decide it was a good idea to marry Medea?"

"Around forty-five years into my vampirism. She was everything to me for a very long time. As she moved up the ranks in the Vampire Court, she used me for whatever she needed; muscle, sex, distraction."

Aster rolls her eyes, then moves to cozy up to me again. I reach for the bottle, pour more champagne into her flute, and then sit back and tuck her into my arm and she leans her head back. "Why did Medea turn Ren as well?"

Anger bubbles in my heart. "She wanted both Vladislav brothers for herself, so she seduced him away from his wife and four children."

"To leave four kids fatherless is so fucking cold."

That's just a sliver of her destruction. I tip my head in agreement. "He tried to resist her, but her pull is magnetic. Ren's biggest regret is leaving his family behind. He worshiped the ground his wife walked on, and the love for his children was palpable. He hated me for a century for leading the devil to his doorstep."

Aster gets off the sofa and stretches. She walks around the coffee table to the space in front of the television. She sinks onto the floor, crossing her legs and leaning back on her hands.

"You just can't seem to sit still tonight, can you?"

She nods in response. As she's about to say something else, I move towards her, pinning her under me. I feel her chest rise and fall faster, and her heartbeat spikes.

"Can I offer something to relieve some of this tension?"

A growl vibrates through her chest into mine as I lower my mouth to hers. I'm flipped suddenly onto my back, and Aster uses her body to pin me to the floor. Her raw strength still amazes me. Vampires are fluid and stealthy with their actions, whereas wolves are all brawn and barely any thought. It's fascinating. I try to bring my arms up, but she pushes them back, further pressing her body into me.

I raise my head so our mouths almost touch. "Why won't you let go?"

She closes her eyes, touching her forehead on mine. "Because you don't even know who I am."

"Tell me, *chérie*."

She sits up, straddling my hips, the panic in her eyes returning. "You're not going to like what you hear."

Vladislav's Penthouse

I LET OUT A shaky breath as Xander sits up and wraps both arms around me, keeping me in his lap. My heart gallops as I meet his eyes. How do I approach all of this?

"Why were you so nervous about Dom going on a hunt?" Xander asks softly.

Fuck it. I clear my throat. "Because I'm the one he's hunting."

Xander raises a brow in question, but doesn't speak.

"My real name... It's Nova. I'm the daughter of High Alpha Jónasson, a First Blood female. The only one born in the last two generations."

Xander traces swirling patterns on my back, still saying nothing. He's known since I started here that I was hiding my history from him, and the fact that he isn't demanding the information is refreshing. My heart swells.

"There are not many wolves who know I exist. My mom insisted I be kept secret. My father, like my grandfather, rules our Pack with an iron fist, so he saw me as an excellent negotiation pawn for future dealings."

My heart aches, and I try not to tremble. "He left me alone until my first shift at thirteen. It just went rapidly downhill. I'd seen how he treated my mom, and it was brutal. Females turned him into an animal. I don't know if it was the fact that we were an easier target, but he unleashed most of his violence on my mom, with me coming a close second.

"He always avoided visible marks. I was a prized possession after all, but it didn't stop me from almost ending up in a human hospital a few times." I will my turning stomach to hold.

Xander goes very still under me. I look up to see fury burning in his expression, his eyes a rich bourbon, his jaw tense. I drop my eyes to his chest. "I was sixteen when Eros roamed into our territory."

Tears sting my eyes, and I swallow the bile threatening to escape. I slide my hands over Xander's shoulders, soaking up some of his strength. "He was a Bitten Alpha from the Daygrsson Pack, wanting to find if he was more suitable to another High Alpha, as it wasn't working out for him back home.

"He found me in a field one day sobbing with a black eye. He bundled me up, took me back to the Pack Den and beat my father until he was unconscious.

"My father promoted Eros to High Beta immediately when he woke up. Eros only accepted the position on the condition that my father was to never lay his hand on a woman again."

"Is it rare for a Bitten wolf to be a High Beta?" Xander asks.

I nod. "High Betas are usually the sons of the High Alpha. But Eros had so much power for a Bitten Alpha my father wanted to be in command of that power. He did treat the Pack better, but by that point, it was too late."

My lip trembles. "My mother hung herself shortly after Eros arrived. It devastated all of us, even Eros, after only knowing her for a short time."

Xander wipes the tear from my cheek with his thumb, planting a soft kiss on the corner of my lip. I smile, pushing myself out of the warm confines of his arms, and sit cross-legged in front of him, picking up the abandoned drink behind me.

I take a healthy mouthful, enjoying the fizzy distraction on my tongue. "A mate bond snapped into place for Eros and I when I turned eighteen. We were inseparable. At last year's Beltane, I was finally ready to complete the bond, so we decided to do it then, as the Daygrsson Pack was coming for the first time since Eros had become High Beta.

"By this point, only the other two High Alphas and some of their sons knew I existed. Viggo, High Alpha Daygr's only son, had this delusional hatred for Eros for indiscretions that were blown way out of proportion or simply non-existent when he was with their Pack.

"He hated the fact that he had a high-ranking position and had a mate bond to me. Especially because he thought my father would sell me to High Alpha Daygr as Viggo's mate."

I blow out a breath and drain the rest of my drink. "Viggo challenged Eros to a duel for the right to own me. Pack law for *all* wolves, First Blood and Bitten alike, states that when a duel is announced, both High Alphas must agree to it, *especially* with High Betas and heirs involved.

"But Viggo just attacked, and he was losing, before he pulled out a hunting knife soaked in wolfsbane and murdered Eros."

I clear my throat, blinking away the tears stinging my eyes. "I was so blind with agony and fury that I don't remember a lot of what happened next. But another Pack law states I had the right to retaliate for the unjust murder of Eros, but they denied me the demand for a duel because Viggo was the only heir to the Daygrsson line and I'm a First Blood female."

"Not anymore," Xander spits out.

I bark a laugh. "Well, yeah. My father retreated to his old self after Eros' death. His violence was out of control. I finally ended up in a hospital on Winter Solstice with a broken jaw, and both my hips fractured."

Xander's entire body vibrates with anger. A slight tremor rattles his glass as he picks it up and tips back the entire thing.

"On my birthday back in March, on Ostara," I continue, "he sold me off to Viggo. After my father tried to strangle me with his bare hands the same day, I decided I was done. So, I killed Viggo the same way he killed Eros, with my festering desire for vengeance and a knife soaked in wolfsbane to the chest."

Saying the words out loud is like a weight being hoisted off my soul. I feel like I can breathe easily again. I don't know what I'm expecting from Xander; maybe for him to call Dom immediately or break our mate bond.

He has a blank expression, the aggression from before gone. I take his moment of contemplation to admire him.

His face is cut angles of perfection. His sharp jawline is always sporting a few day's growth, but he keeps it neat. The high and sharp cheeks would give him a fae-type look if it weren't for those beautiful almond-shaped eyes. I envy his dark, long lashes framing his amber and blue irises.

And that mouth; soft and luscious, with a perfect, soft cupid's bow. The few occasions he's smiled, I know behind those kissable lips he has perfect teeth with a double set of fangs. The only not-so-perfect thing about his face is his nose.

"Have you broken your nose before?" I ask. His nose has a slight bend to the left, only noticeable if you're this close to his face.

His eyes refocus on mine, the question jostling him out of his reverie. "I did when I was human. Ren punched me in the face over something I don't recall. My mother put it back in place enough to ensure I could breathe."

He stands from the floor, offering me a hand. He hoists me up, an arm snaking around my waist. "I know it's hard for you to trust anyone, but I want to be your solace. No more secrets between us. You're mine now, and no one will ever hurt you like that again. If your family comes after you, they'll have to go through me."

The mate bond and my heart swell in symphony. For the first time in my life, I believe that there is the possibility of freedom. And Xander might be the person to grant it. The bond hums in agreement.

Before I can fall too deep into the fantasy, reality creeps in. "What about Dom?"

Xander entwines his fingers with mine, leading me towards his bedroom. "He's been loyal to me for a long time; we'll talk to him."

"How did he come into your employment?"

Xander releases me as he goes towards his nightstand, switching on a light.

I drift over to the spectacular view. The lights sparkle throughout the city, some going on, some going off, and some flashing. The sky has a drop of color in it; the sun will rise soon. Central Park below is dark, but I can make out the trees dancing in the breeze.

My eyesight is becoming sharper the closer it is to the full moon, and my other senses as well. This entire room encapsulates Xander's scent, and it's stirring up the bond. I can see myself never wanting to leave this room.

My ears pick up movement behind me, and I watch Xander in the reflection of the windows walking up, wrapping an arm around my waist, and pulling me against him. It still shocks me; his touch is warm and not cold like other vampires.

He plants a kiss into my hair. "Dom was twenty-one when he was exiled from the Lárusson pack," he says, leaning his face against the side of my head and looks out to the city. "He has never told me why, I met him at Sanctuary one night shortly after his expulsion. He had just moved to New York, trying to mind his own business, when a whole Lárusson Beta Pack confronted him. To uphold Sidelle's Sanctuary status, I assisted him in ridding the bar of the miscreants and offered him a job. I needed a day-dweller's help in running the operation."

"If they exiled him, why is he working for them now?"

"I'm not too sure. In the twenty-five years I've known him, he kept his distance. I don't know what's changed."

Exhaustion sweeps over me suddenly, my body demanding me to sleep. "These pre full moon energy swings get me every time." I stifle a yawn.

Xander turns me around, leaning his head forward. "Let's get you in bed, Nova."

"It's weird to hear you say my actual name," I whisper.

"Nova," he rumbles, rolling my name over his tongue like he's tasting it, making me shiver.

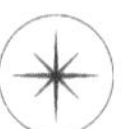

I wake up boiling hot. I try to lift my arm to throw the blankets off, but it's trapped.

I open my eyes to Xander's beautiful, serene sleeping face. He refused to let me sleep anywhere but his bed last night, and we weren't even touching when I passed out, but now he's wrapped one arm over me, trapping my arms in between us, my hands flat against his naked chest. His other arm has snaked its way under my pillow, and our legs tangled together.

I've never been so comfortable in my life, but so gods damned *hot*.

I run one hand up, feeling the smooth skin of his neck, and stroke his silky black hair. He stirs, tightening his arm around me.

"Good morning," he mumbles without opening his eyes. His gravelly voice sends tingles through my entire body.

"You mean good afternoon."

"You're on vampire clock; it's morning." He cracks his eyes open, and I almost groan. His eyes are shining their stunning blue laced amber. "You have the most amazing eyes," I say before I can stop myself.

He smiles. "So do you, *chérie*."

My cheeks heat. "If you keep it up with the French, we won't leave this bed for the rest of the year."

Vlad blinks a few times. "I didn't even realize I was doing it."

"Was Medea the last person you spoke French to?"

Vlad sighs. "She ruined the language for me. Most people don't even know I speak it."

I lace both hands into his hair, bringing his lips to mine. "Don't let her steal parts of you any longer. Let's both start fresh."

Vlad rolls onto his back, taking me with him. "*Oui, ma belle.*"

I groan, crushing my lips to his, gripping his hair tighter. Our tongues dance as I feel him getting harder underneath me. I move my lips to his jaw, then his neck, kissing, sucking, and nipping. His breathing is controlled as I graze my teeth along his collarbone, working my way down his broad chest with my tongue.

I shuffle lower, tasting his golden-beige skin until I reach his sweatpants. I palm his cock through his pants, making him groan. I tug the pants, releasing him. This time I groan—sweet, merciful gods.

I trail my fingers lightly up the long shaft, delighting in Xander's hips jerking up. I follow the path of my fingers with my tongue.

"*Fuck*, Nova," Xander moans, sending a jolt of pleasure through my entire body.

As I reach the tip, I swirl my tongue around its thickness, tasting the saltiness, before closing my mouth around the smooth skin. Xander's gasp turns into a growl as I push more of his cock into my mouth, devastatingly slow. He hits the back of my throat halfway down, so I grasp the base, working my mouth back up again slowly with hard suction.

I repeat the maneuver repeatedly, working my mouth, my tongue, and my hand up and down his cock, increasing in speed. Xander growls push me on, frying more of my self-control. The bond tears through me, wanting, *demanding* to be completed. I increase the speed again; my efforts more frenzied. Xander's hips flex upward in sync with my movements, filling my mouth more.

My eyes flick up to his; his eyes are molten bourbon; his fangs have dropped. The eye contact drives him over the edge as he slams my head down, coming into my mouth. I swallow quickly. I give his cock one last slow, hard suck as I release him from my mouth.

He pulls me up towards him, rolling us over, lips bruising mine. He presses me into the bed as I wrap all my limbs around him, wanting him closer. Wanting him inside me. I want to fuck Xander for the rest of eternity. I gasp as he releases me from the blinding kiss.

"You're a little devil," he pants.

I giggle. "You love it."

He traps an earlobe in his teeth. "I do."

The mix of teeth and his hot breath playing on my skin makes me tremble. His fangs scrape my neck as he kisses me and I groan. Heat throbs in my core, my stomach clenching at the thought of Xander marking me with his teeth. My nipples are painfully hard at the thought of him sinking fangs into my breasts.

"We need to stop before I become your breakfast," I mumble.

Xander chuckles against my neck, making me tremble again. "You don't seem too opposed to the idea." He rubs my nipple through the t-shirt with his thumb.

"I'm not, but I, uh, I can't. Things. I have things. And people." I'm a babbling mess as he continues to kiss, lick, and nip my neck, his hand cupping my breast firmly. His mouth returns to mine, and both of his hands find their way into my hair.

I don't even bother trying to hold back as I let it all out in this kiss. I want him. I *need* him.

Xander and I eventually cease our make-out session and get out of bed. As we're just sitting down for breakfast, we hear laughter in the foyer. Allura and Ren enter the kitchen, both their faces beaming. Allura's wings flutter, refracting light from the early afternoon sun as she skips over, planting a kiss on my cheek.

"Good morning," she says in a sing-song tone, also planting a kiss on Xander's cheek and taking a seat at the table next to him, dumping her bag on the floor.

"Someone's in a good mood," I comment to Allura, but eyeing Ren in the kitchen. He seems in a weirdly good mood, too. What did they get up to?

Ren retrieves a bowl and fishes out cereal from the pantry, Allura's favorite type. He pours it into the bowl, collecting milk, a banana, and a bag of blood from the fridge. "I see you know *exactly* how Lu likes her cereal, Ren. Did you get that from snooping in her mind?"

His eyes flick up to mine as he is cutting the banana into the bowl, smirking. "Allura is another little minx who won't let me into her head, so I worked it out the old-fashioned way; observation."

"Don't you find the quiet-minded ones a lot more intriguing than all the others?"

"God, no. It's annoying as hell."

Allura giggles behind me. "He likes that he can't read mine. He *hates* that he can't read yours."

I scoff. "Trust me, there's nothing interesting in there."

Ren walks over to the table with the cereal, the blood, and a tall glass as he takes the seat next to me, eyes narrowing. "I'd like to be the judge of that."

"Maybe soon."

My answer surprises him. He'll hear my thoughts if I ever take this amulet off, and I hope someday I can. Being with Xander, him knowing my past, I want to be all of me. He makes me feel safe, safe enough to not want to hide from the world anymore.

Allura snatches the bowl out of Ren's still hands. "I want to go baby clothes shopping today."

My face gives away my dislike for that idea as Xander and Ren laugh. "I'm not opposed to babies; I'm opposed to shopping."

Allura pouts, crossing her arms over her chest. "How about you take Jas while Art and I go for a run?"

Allura's whole face lights up, and her wings vibrate, faerie dust flaking onto the floor. Ren leans forward, eyes narrowing on Allura. "Who is *Jas*?"

I laugh. "Oh, Ren, are you *jealous*?"

He leans back and scoffs. "No."

"He's definitely jealous; I can hear it in his head." Xander muses.

Ren barks a string of nasty words in Russian to Xander, making him laugh. Seeing Xander happy makes my heart sing. Could he be any more beautiful?

Allura stands and sits down on Ren's lap. "You'll always be my number one, Ren. Jasper is our human neighbor, and I'm fairly certain he'd flirt with *you* more than he'd flirt with me."

"Good," he says as he wraps his arms around her, pulling her closer. Allura glows as she snuggles in further. Good gods, could they get a room?

I clear my throat. "Okay, before I barf, I'm going to go change real quick, and we'll go."

I pull off Xander's t-shirt as I enter the guest room, leaving me only in borrowed boxer-briefs as I rummage through the clothes I have stashed here. I manage to find a pair of jeans, but no casual tops. As I try to find a suitable bra, footsteps echo in the hallway and the door opens. Heat at my bare back stirs the bond.

Xander trails his fingertips down my spine, across my ribcage, and under my breast. Tingles explode across my skin, my stomach clenches, my nipples pebble. His lips land softly on my shoulder while his hand cups my heated breast, his forefinger and thumb rolling my nipple.

"You still haven't told me about the new eye color," Xander murmurs into the crook of my neck.

"Oh," I breathe, swaying slightly at the avalanche of sensations through me. "I... Art and I..."

Xander growls, his arm going around me, his fingers pinching my nipple, making me gasp at the shocks of pleasure shooting through my veins. "You and Art did *what* exactly?"

I laugh breathlessly. "So possessive."

"Nova."

"We, well no, it was me. I started a new Pack."

His grip loosens, and I'm slightly disappointed. "What do you mean?"

I turn in his arms, peering up to his heated gaze. "He found out who I am, and I panicked a little, so I suggested we become Pack."

"That's smart," Xander muses, "it makes him loyal to you. But how did you *start* a new Pack? Don't you have to be an Alpha?"

I shrug. "Yeah. Art said I was, and when we blood bonded, we may have created a new First Blood Pack."

His eyes narrow in contemplation. "If it's true, then that's huge."

"I know."

Xander leans down and brushes his lips over mine lightly. "You better get ready."

"Probably." I press myself into him, feeling his erection hard against my stomach.

"Tell Carter," he growls in my ear as his fingers trailing over my waist, cupping my ass, "if you get hurt in any way, that he will lose an important organ."

I huff a laugh. "I will."

Xander's mouth is on my neck again, kissing and sucking at the over-sensitive flesh. His hand slips around my hip, into my boxer briefs, his fingers circling over my clit, then two sink into me. My legs quiver; the run can wait, I need Xander to fuck me right now.

Suddenly his hands disappear and a swirl of cool air encases me. I stumble forward, catching myself, as I turn to Xander backing out of the room, sucking his fingers into his mouth. A wicked grin curves his face as he pulls them out. "Enjoy your run."

I storm up the stairs, banging on Jas and Art's door. Xander and his wicked hands. Fuck. Art better be ready to *run*. Allura floats up the stairs, humming to herself. Humming. Gods, it's annoying.

Jas opens the door, face beaming, "Hey there, friends."

"Where's Art?"

"He'll be down in a minute. Come in, have a seat."

Allura pushes past me, kissing Jasper on the cheek. "Ignore grumpy-pants over here. She's wound-up *real* tight."

Jas understands her connotation, laughing as he hooks an arm into Allura's, leading her to a sofa. Art barrels down the stairs in workout gear.

As soon as he sees my face, he falters. "Damn, Alpha, who did you wrong today?"

"You mean, who didn't *do* her today," Allura calls from the sofa.

I roll my eyes. "Let's go."

Art shouts his goodbyes over his shoulder as he closes the front door behind him and we set off.

By the time we got back, we were both soaked in sweat, breathless, and ravenous. Jas and Allura cooked up a feast and we demolished it before Allura and I left to nap before work. My nap was too short, as well as the blistering hot shower I had right after it.

I decided to wear a tight, deep burgundy dress tonight with a thigh slit up the left leg, the neckline is modest, just showing my collarbones, and the sleeves are to my wrists. It hugs every curve, comes in at my waist, and the color accentuates my skin tone and hair. Xander will be on his knees by the end of the night.

I slip into sky-high gold pumps, pin half my hair up, allowing the rest to fall down my back, and ask Allura to apply a sharp winged liner to my eyes.

"You look like a siren, waiting to lure victims to their deaths," she comments as she applies gloss to my blush lips.

I smile, assessing her handiwork in the mirror. "That's what I was going for."

Art almost falls over when he meets us out the front, waiting to give us a lift to Immortal. His cheeks flame, and his eyes refuse to leave the floor.

I wrap myself in a jacket to save him. "I'm covered up now."

Art flushes harder, offering me a hand to assist me down the stairs. As we climb into the car and shoot off into the night, my phone buzzes in my pocket.

XANDER

Can't wait to have my hands on you again.

Who said you still had touching privileges? I sure as hell didn't.

XANDER

Do you really want to deny yourself that pleasure?

Oh babe, I think it's you who's going to be regretting your stunt today.

XANDER

Oh, really? We shall see, chérie.

Lust snakes up my body, setting my heart racing. I put the phone away, not really paying attention to Allura and Art's conversation as I crack open the car window.

Trickles of wolf energy ebb and flow toward me as we cross the bridge into Manhattan. My hand lands on the stone around my wrist. Gods bless magic for giving me a reprieve. The amount of energy I'd be overwhelmed with would be devastating. I've only ever known Jónasson Pack energy through the pre full moon phases, but having so many Beta Packs in one place is intense. No wonder there isn't an Alpha Pack set up in New York City.

"Art, where's the nearest First Blood Pack to here?" I turn to look at him.

"One of Lárusson's sons has his Pack in Atlantic City," he says, keeping his eyes on the road. "The two Packs in New York City itself are both Bitten Packs."

"Two and a half hours away. That's good."

His eyes flick to mine, then back to the road. "Why do you ask?"

"To know how much of a head start I have when shit hits the fan."

"Don't you dare think about leaving, Nova." The hardness in Allura's tone makes me turn to her in the back seat. Her eyes are aflame with rage.

"I might not have a choice, Lu. We both have bounties on our heads."

"Where you go, I go," she states.

"Same here," Art muses.

My heart pangs. "You both can't do that. I expect both of you to watch each other when the hunting parties catch up to me."

"You mean *if*," Art counters.

"No, I mean *when*. I murdered the only heir to the Daygrsson line, probably starting a war between two First Blood Packs. They won't stop until I'm captured." I don't mention that I'm sure they will rape, breed, and beat me until I'm no longer of use to them and then most likely kill me.

"Fuck the Daygrsson Pack," Art says as he pulls into the private alley behind Immortal. "That son of a bitch deserved everything he got. High Alpha Serafiem can make more devil spawn if he wants to; he's old, but he's not that old."

He parks by the back door and turns his entire body to me, gripping my hands, his eyes an angry sapphire blue. "Listen to me, Nova, and listen to me closely. You're a fucking *High Alpha*. When you decide to take that amulet off, you'll realize you can take on all three First Blood Packs with your eyes closed. Plus, you have a *vampire* as a mate, who's well-respected in vamp circles. You don't need to fear anyone, ever again." His eyes soften, his thumb swiping the tear escaping down my cheek.

Sniffles sound in the back seat as Allura leans forward, placing her hand on ours. "You aren't a pawn in your father's political games anymore. You have us in your corner we would die for you."

"I don't think it's necessary to die for me."

Art's eyes narrow. "I would give my life to see you finally free."

I don't know how my heart hasn't torn itself to shreds. "How was I lucky enough to come across a bunch of losers with death wishes?"

We all laugh, dissipating the intense emotions lingering in the car. I check my make-up in the vanity mirror before hopping out, shortly followed by Art and Allura.

Art walks us to the door. "By the way, if you're planning on murdering Vlad with that dress, it will *definitely* work."

30

Vladislav

Immortal

I FILL MY GLASS with whiskey at the bar as the staff door opens—amber rum and milk swirl around me, and my body instantly stirs. I turn, and I bite down a groan.

Aster, no, *Nova*, saunters over, her hair swaying in sync.

That dress; Good Lord. The color of blood, her toned thigh, which is bare, cuts through the high slit. The neckline sits just on her shoulders, showcasing her perfect neck and collarbones. My tongue aches to trace her exposed skin. She brushes past me, going directly to the back room, saying hello to Vik and Maddox as she disappears.

I scoop up my glass and follow her, closing the door behind me. She's putting her jacket into her locker at the end. "Good evening, Nova."

She turns, a pleasant smile on her seductress lips. "Good evening, Mr. Vladislav."

Oh, really? We're playing that game. "You look exquisite tonight."

Her smile deepens, her head turning to the mirror on her locker door. "Thank you, Mr. Vladislav."

I take a few lazy steps towards her as she applies gloss to her lips. "Did you know that red is my favorite color?"

"I had no idea. It's a fantastic color, but I prefer gray myself." She closes the locker and turns, her attention on her phone.

I drift over to her, like a damn moth to a wicked flame, placing a hand on either side of her head, inhaling her intoxicating scent. Her head tilts up to mine, our lips moments away from devouring each other. Her eyes burn in challenge. "Did you need something, Mr. Vladislav?"

"I want to bend you over that table."

Nova smirks, taking my drink and brings it to her lips. I watch her throat bob as she swallows the golden liquid, a growl rumbling deep in my chest. She slips under my arm and places my now empty glass on the table, then turns back and slams my back into the lockers, crushing her delectable body into mine. The bond roars in victory at the contact.

My cock is hard as stone against her as she traps my earlobe in her teeth. I run a hand up her bare thigh, sliding it up and under the split in her dress.

"*Merde*," I bite out as I press my hand against her *naked* core, my fingers sliding through her wet folds. No panties. With a dress slit this high? She better not be planning on—

Nova pulls back, a wicked grin on her face. Fuck no. I step forward, ready to take her up to the Penthouse, away from the possibility of someone touching her, but she turns on her gold heels and saunters away.

Ren is standing by Nova at the bar as I exit the storeroom. He's standing *too* close. They both look over at me and Ren chuckles. "I knew she'd be a troublemaker."

All I can see and feel is the patrons desire to touch Nova, and it's putting me on edge. She's perfected the way she moves around the club to avoid touches, but I have to swallow a growl every time she bends over to serve a drink.

I want to punish or pleasure her right now. Probably both.

As she's about to clear empty glasses, a regular patron, Mr. Collins, grips her forearm and pulls. She falls chest first directly into his lap, splayed out like a misbehaving child, waiting to be spanked. And he does just that, landing a hard palm across her ass.

Fury floods my system, and I take a step toward them, but a guttural growl escapes Nova, making me pause. A snapping sound echoes over the music as Collins yelps and Nova drags him up from his seat by his bent wrist. His companion stands swiftly next to him, but she captures him by the throat before he can touch her.

Ren appears next to Nova, pulling the companion to the exit as she twists Collins' wrist again. "This is your last night here."

He chuckles through a painful moan. "You have no authority to make those decisions, little bitch."

"She does," I muse as I approach them, reining in my rage.

"Pay your tab before you leave, or I will break more bones," Nova commands, shoving Collins back and making him hit the floor with a thump.

I crouch down beside Collins slowly, a predatory smile spreading over my face. "Be grateful for her generosity, because if you *look* at her again, we will take the pleasure of ripping you to pieces."

Terror fills Collins' face as he scrambles towards the bar, throws an obscene amount of cash toward Vik and disappears. Nova adjusts the hem of her dress, picks up her discarded tray and returns to the bar. The awe, fear and respect pulsing from the patrons in the club makes pride bloom in my chest.

They all know exactly who they're fucking with now.

Vik and Maddox go home, leaving Nova perched on a stool browsing her phone as she waits for Allura to change. I pull the phone from her hands, place it on the bar and grip her jaw, pushing in between her legs, pressing my body into hers.

"No panties, little wolf?" My voice is low, dangerous.

She smirks as she wraps her legs around my hips. "This is a strip club, is it not?"

I growl, my grip on her jaw tightening slightly. "No one gets to see you naked. Do you understand me?"

Nova trembles, her eyes darkening to sapphire blue. She jerks forward, crushing her lips to mine, and the last of my control frays. Her greedy little mouth consumes me like she's also barely controlling herself.

A growl rumbles in her chest as I loosen my grip on her jaw, my hand sliding up her thigh, and I sink two fingers into her wet heat. "You're always so ready for me, little wolf."

"Fuck," she mumbles as her head drops back. She whimpers as my fangs graze her neck and my fingers work in and out of her slowly, her hips bucking as I circle my finger over her clit. I want to see her come over and over until she begs me to stop.

"You have no idea how much pleasure I get from making you come," I whisper into her ear, biting her earlobe.

Her phone buzzes on the bar beside us, making a throaty laugh escape her.

"You're going to have to wait for that pleasure," Nova purrs as she untangles herself from me and stands, pulling my hand away. Her eyes burn into mine as she brings my fingers into her mouth, sucking hard, her tongue swirling the tips, tasting herself.

I wrap my arm around her waist, trapping her in against me. "Don't you *dare* tell me you're leaving."

She pushes at my chest, and I reluctantly let her go. "Has anyone ever told you that patience is a virtue?"

I trace her cheek and bury my hand in her hair. "Fuck patience."

She snorts and shakes her head, smoothing down the lapel of my jacket, but I see something like hesitation play over her flushed face. I understand it—she's from a world that would take advantage of her, but no more. This will all be her choice in the end. I need to give her that freedom.

She plants a sweet kiss on my lips. "Art is waiting out back."

"I will wait for you. Always."

Her jaw slackens, and her eyes fill with tears, but they don't fall. She cups my jaw, running her thumb along my bottom lip. "Thank you."

I turn my face and plant a kiss onto her palm before turning and collecting her jacket. We walk down the hall, stopping at the back door and summoning the elevator at the same time.

"I gotta do some wolfie things during the day, but I'll see you tonight," she promises as she puts on her jacket.

"Stay safe, *chérie.*"

31

Nova

Allura & Nova's Apartment

"I'VE NEVER BEEN THIS tired in my life," I say as I drop onto a bar stool in Allura's kitchen.

Allura chuckles as she fills the kettle. "You're fighting a mate bond. It's understandable."

I groan, my head pulsing. "I know, but I just can't seem to do it."

"I'm sure if you tell Xander, he'll be more than happy to—"

"Shh," I slur, "for someone who seems so nice, you have a filthy mind."

Her tinkling laughter floats through the room as I close my eyes to the stabbing headache behind my eyes. Xander and I are walking a dangerous rope. Can I actually let someone in like that again? I'm a broken, fragile being with a ring of steel around my heart. I've had to be with my history, but can I truly let those chains go?

Mint and licorice steam curls under my nose and I open my eyes to a steaming cup of herbal tea in front of me.

"After all this time knowing him, Lu, do you think he's good?" I ask, scooping up the mug.

"For a vampire his age, he's very accepting of all species. Most of them that old are elitists to the core." Allura steps around the island with her own tea and tugs my arm, leading us over to the sofa.

I collapse into it, careful not to spill my drink. "But is he *good?*"

"Yes."

"How is this my life now?"

"That's the nature of magic. It's intense, raw, and damn powerful."

I stare at the wall ahead of me. Like the apartment next door, the wall is entirely bookshelves, except for a wall-mounted flatscreen. A plethora of books of all sizes and ages fill the wall with some shelves crammed to capacity. A few of the shelves are free of books but display an assortment of stunning, raw cut crystals and candles, adding to the abundance of color.

"I think I really like magic," I admit in barely a whisper.

Allura giggles. "Me too. Now, drink your tea and go to bed. You look like you're about to pass out."

I do just that, scalding my tongue in my haste, then drag myself up the stairs. I manage to peel out of my clothes and dress in a tank top and sleep shorts before putting my hair in a bun and crawling under the heavy duvet.

My sleep is suspiciously peaceful for it being three days before the full moon, and I wake up at around midday. A message on my phone tells me that Allura is next door hanging out with Jas. Xander hasn't messaged yet; he's probably still asleep.

I change into workout gear, and head down to the kitchen, eating cereal while making toast.

Pain bursts through my abdomen, making me drop the bowl on the counter. What the fuck? I crumple to the floor and screw my eyes shut. My wolf roars in my ears, demanding to be free. Claws are trying to rip out of me.

I hear the back door slam open as if I'm underwater. Heavy footsteps rush toward me and then blazing hot arms scoop me up, carrying me until I'm placed gently onto a soft surface. I think it's the sofa. My phone rings incessantly somewhere in the kitchen.

The pain, the clawing has turned into searing acid everywhere. I'm liquefying from the inside out. My head swims, and my stomach rebels; I roll to my side, heaving off the side of the sofa. The contents of my stomach are like shards of glass ripping up my esophagus.

The phone is *still* ringing.

"Answer my fucking phone."

Heavy footsteps rush to the noise.

"Vladislav." It's Art. He's coming back towards me.

"I can feel her; what the fuck is going on?" Xander is roaring on the other end of the phone.

Another wave of nausea assaults me. I puke my guts up again. Tears flow down my face freely, and my nose runs.

"I felt it next door; a massive surge of Alpha energy ripped through the place. It sent me to my knees."

"It feels like she's dying, Carter!"

"Give me the phone. Put this on her forehead." Allura is here now. A cool, damp cloth is laid across my head, easing the pain in my skull.

"She's okay," Allura states.

"Fucking bullshit!"

"Control yourself, Xander. She can probably feel your panic through the bond, which will make it worse."

Some of the pressure in my head is subsiding; I feel less panicked. Maybe that *was* Xander through the bond. Maybe also a bit of me. I manage enough strength to fumble for the cloth and pull it down to my neck. I can feel Art hovering above my head, probably watching me.

"What is it, Lu?"

"She's High Alpha to an entirely new First Blood Pack. It's new magic. I think she's going through what the original High Alphas went through for their first turn. From what Jas and I have found, it started three days before the full moon."

Allura and Xander's voices fade out as I drift off.

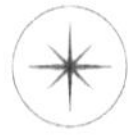

I remember reading about our original ancestors' first turn. The legend says after the mighty wolf, Fenrir, was tied to a rock with the Gleipnir, a magical chain, he tore another god's hand off with his teeth.

As punishment, they placed a sword in Fenrir's mouth to keep him from biting someone ever again, and left him imprisoned for all of eternity.

Three Viking humans, Jónas, Daygr, and Lárus, came across the giant wolf. They taunted the beast, making him salivate. They tried to remove the sword, but it cut all three of them, exposing them to the potent toxin in Fenrir's saliva.

All three went through delirium, pain, and fever for three nights, until they suddenly recovered. Every sense was heightened, their metabolisms increased. As the full moon approached, their height and muscle mass changed.

On the night of the full moon, they met in the woods; each pair of eyes were glowing silver, copper, or gold. They all fell to the ground when the full moon was at its peak, their bodies tearing apart and coming back together as massive white wolves. They bit many men and women the first turn; some became the Bitten, but most didn't survive.

I come back to consciousness curled up on my side under a blanket, with my head in someone's lap. A tendril of peach and smoked cedarwood drifts past me.

"How are you here?" My voice is hoarse, like I've been screaming for hours. Was I?

Xander's hand rubs slowly over my shoulder and down my arm. "The sunset was about three hours ago; I came over as soon as the stars allowed me."

Damn, I was out for ages. I peel one eye open, and the world is blurry. I try the other eye and then blink a few times. The coffee table comes into view; a large bottle of chilled water and a steaming teapot with a mug next to it on the glass surface.

"I really expected the entire lounge room to be covered in vomit."

I feel Xander chuckling under me. "The first thing Carter did after he scooped you off the floor was to get a bucket."

I pull myself upright. The entire room spins violently—pain throbs in every single part of my body. I groan, leaning forward and holding my head in my hands. Xander runs his hand down my back soothingly. The pain in my body eases.

"Thank the Gods for your gift," I mumble.

"It comes in handy sometimes."

I freeze. Wait. His gift is working. My hand lands on either wrist and then my neck. "Where's my amulet?"

"It's in the kitchen. Allura took it off so your body could release a surge of Alpha energy."

"Did she tell you what it is?" I ask. I haven't had the chance to explain it to him.

"Yes," he says as he leans forward, picking up a teapot, pouring red liquid into the mug. It smells tart and fruity. "Lu says you need to drink this entire pot and promised you'd feel better."

I oblige, picking up the cup and sipping on the tea. It tingles on the tongue, soothing warmth spreading through my body. I sit back, cradling my tea, bringing my knees up to my chest. Xander's arm lays across the top of the sofa behind me, and he goes back to reading a book.

His emotions pummel through the bond; his need to protect me is almost overwhelming, and he's fretting over my wellbeing.

I rub his thigh reassuringly. "I'm fine, Xander."

He looks up from his book, blinking. "I'm sorry?"

"I said I'm fine."

He looks at me, confused.

"I can feel your concern for me."

He puts the book down. "So, you can feel it too? Through the bond?"

I nod. "I think I felt it once after the Hugo fiasco."

"Allura said that your blood undid some of the spell, and that's why I was also able to use my gift on that day."

"Fae magic makes no sense to me," I muse, sipping more tea.

Xander runs a finger down my arm, drawing my attention. His face flickers with terror, the emotion mirroring through the bond. "Your pain tore me from a deep sleep so violently it made my stomach heave. I could hear your screaming in my head. I almost walked into the sun because you weren't answering your phone."

I rest my head against his shoulder, not sure what to say. Xander's arm drapes over me, encasing me in his warmth. I continue to sip on the tea, and he resumes his book. I listen to his breathing, his slow, rhythmic heartbeat. A *heartbeat*. I didn't think vampires had them.

I finish the tea, the magic doing its trick. I feel normal. Actually, better than usual. I feel like I can breathe easier. I feel stronger, my senses keener.

"Feels like you're feeling better." A sly smile creeps over Xander's lips, his eyes not coming off the page.

"Don't get used to this connection. I have to put the amulet back on, eventually."

His face lifts to mine. "I'll take full advantage of it until you do."

I place the mug back on the table, swinging my legs into Xander's lap and propping myself up on the sofa pillows next to me. "Shouldn't you be at Immortal right now?"

He puts the book down, his arm draping over my thighs. "Ren can handle it on his own."

"Who's looking after Allura?"

Xander smirks. "Carter."

My mouth drops. "In no way is Ren okay with that."

"He didn't have a choice, really. Allura said you couldn't be moved. Carter refused to leave Allura for your peace of mind, and Ren knew I wouldn't let you stay here alone."

My heart warms. Protectiveness and concern creep across the bond again. "Hey." I place my hand over his. "You don't need to worry about me so much."

He chuckles softly, entwining our fingers. "I will always worry about you."

My heart constricts—stupid heart. Someone like him shouldn't be worrying about a delinquent. I'm a liability, and not...

"You are worthy of feeling safe, Nova." Xander's eyes flash in anger. His grip tightens on mine. "Don't even think about running. I *will* find you and drag you straight back here."

My heart stutters. Good gods. Heat sears in his eyes, mixed with anger. I can feel his need for me through the bond, the wanting to protect me, and the sliver of reconciliation I give to him. I'm determined to make that sliver whole.

"You belong here," he continues, voice dropping an octave, "with me. For eternity."

Gods, I want this man.

I clear my throat, sitting straighter, bringing my knees to my chest, my mind hazy.

"Nova," Xander pulls my chin towards him, bourbon eyes locked on mine.

The bond tightens, forging new connections, rooting itself deeper in my being. I feel more. Xander's determination, his loyalty, his possessiveness. Something more. It's electric, setting my entire body on fire.

"Okay," I say breathlessly. "I'm here. I'm not going anywhere. So, please stop looking at me like that, or we will end up destroying this sofa."

My stomach clenches hard at the low, rumbling laugh. He's not helping this situation at all. I lean over and scoop up the water bottle, relishing the cool liquid entering my heated body. Xander picks up his discarded book and resumes his reading. Hunger rumbles my stomach, so I clamber off the sofa.

A swift stinging swat lands on my ass, sending heat to my core and making me gasp. I turn. "Hands to yourself, Xander."

He grips my thigh, traveling upwards slowly. "Oh, really?"

Another jolt of blaring heat. I push his hand off, taking steps back towards the kitchen. "I'm definitely not sure about that, but I'm hungry."

Xander puts his book down, and with the grace of a big cat, he rises from the sofa. Oh boy.

"Hungry for what exactly?" His voice is low again, a growl accompanying it. He takes a step forward.

"For... yes. For food. Definitely food. Probably food?" I continue to back up.

Xander matches my steps with a wicked spark in his eyes; he's playing with *his* food.

Odin, help me.

My heart races as he stalks forward, slowly. My back hits the island bench, Xander's eyes narrowing on my hands, catching the edge. He's in front of me suddenly, lifting me onto the island.

I shove my hands in his hair, capturing his bottom lip with my teeth. A growl rips through him as he tears open the back of my t-shirt. I shred through the front of his shirt.

My body is hot, too hot. My heart is racing too fast. I push on Xander's chest, struggling to stand up, my lungs heaving. "Ah, fuck, here we go again."

Pain short circuits my nerve endings; my blood feels as if it's on fire. I would be on the floor if Xander wasn't holding me upright.

I'm panting, sweat breaking out across my whole body. "F-Fever. Water. Cold."

Xander understands my mumbling and scoops me up in his arms. I close my eyes tight, fighting the pain. We ascend the stairs, a door opens, and I'm deposited onto cool tiles. Water runs and hands peel off my clothes, my body feeling like lead. I hear more rustling, and then I'm being picked up again.

The brisk, cool water hitting my overheated skin is heaven. I breathe easier. I lean forward onto a bare chest. "Stupid moon."

Xander chuckles under me. "I've got you, *chérie*." His arm is firm around my waist as he tilts my head back, allowing the water to flow through my hair, cooling my scalp.

My eyes flutter open, catching those beautiful amber and blue irises. He smiles, and my heart stirs. I want to stare at him for a lifetime. Perhaps longer. The pain subsides, leaving aching muscles behind. The fever breaks, and now I'm shivering from the cold. I turn in Xander's arm, changing the temperature of the water.

We're both *very* naked right now.

"If I had any energy left right now, this would be a much hotter shower."

Xander chuckles, the sound vibrating through my back. "Pass me something to wash your hair."

I hand him the bottle of shampoo. His fingers massaging my scalp are heavenly. I insist on washing his hair in return, relishing in the groans of satisfaction as my fingers work slow, firm circles on his scalp. We both wash off hastily, my energy fading quick. I need to lie down.

Xander wraps me in a towel, slinging another one over his hips, collecting his clothes from the floor. My eyes catch the tattoo on his arm.

Whisps of black ink wrap around his entire upper left arm, finishing on his forearm just below the creases of his elbow. Some tendrils are more solid than others, some barely a shadow, all of them weaving and snaking around each other, not touching but fitting together like a sleeve of smoke. It almost looks like it moves.

My tongue tingles at the thought of tracing all of them. How am I this amped up but so ready for a two-day nap? It doesn't help that he's there, hair wet, water trickling down his impeccable body. I want to follow its path with my tongue.

"Stop staring at me like that, Nova, or we will finish what we started in the kitchen."

32

Vladislav

Allura & Nova's Apartment

Pink stains Nova's cheeks as she averts her eyes. God, she's beautiful.

She tentatively leaves the bathroom, leading me to her bedroom. She rummages through her closet as I towel myself dry, slipping back into my sweatpants. She looks absolutely spent; I can feel the exhaustion in our bond as she manages to dress in sleep shorts and a tank top.

We slide into the bed, Nova resting her head in the crook of my arm, and entwining her legs with mine, flinging an arm across my body, and hugging me closer. I play with the damp strands of her hair, inhaling her milk and rum scent.

The bond stirs with contentment from all aspects and eases some of the tension in my bones. Nova's aura without the amulet is fascinating. She feels things more profoundly than I thought and with more complexity.

The lingering trauma from her Pack dampens any positive emotions, and it makes violent fury simmer deep in my blood.

I want to hurt every person who has ever hurt Nova—preferably physically. To think about harming any part of her would be like ripping my own heart out. Nova traces swirling shapes on my bare chest with her fingers, tempering the fire within. She has the same power over my emotions as I do with other people.

"Xander?" she whispers.

"Hmm?"

"I want to ask you something that might sour the mood, but I'm itching to know."

Inquisitive little thing. "Ask me anything you want, *cherie*."

"What... made you leave Medea?"

"There are so many reasons." I knew the question was coming, eventually. Few vampires understand why I left her.

Nova must feel my hesitation because she lifts her head, eyes and emotions full of worry. "We can drop it. I won't ask again."

"I want to tell you." I trace her jaw.

She plants a soft kiss over my heart, then puts her ear against it, waiting.

"Ren's turn was the start of the end," I start. Nova squeezes her arm around me firmer; I resume playing with her hair. "Medea is cold and heartless, but she's far more than that. She wants to control everything, wants everyone around her to adore her, *worship* her, but she's empty. Venomous."

I sigh. "The mate bond trapped me; I couldn't bear the thought of staying, but I also couldn't fathom leaving. But by the time Medea had become Advisor to the Queen and I had met Viktoria, I was begging Medea to release me from it."

Nova turns her head, resting her chin on a hand over my heart. "Medea must have been *pissed*."

"Furious. She threatened to kill Viktoria, and I threatened to walk into the daylight. That gave her pause, only because her reputation at Court would have been tainted if her mate decided to see the Other Side prematurely."

Nova's brow furrow. "You were her power-play for the throne."

I nod. "It's rare for Pure Bloods to produce offspring, so Vampire Queens are mostly handed down to whoever is deemed to be the strongest and most promising courtier. But for a Queen to have a devoted Consort, with the potential to produce an heir?"

"Massive power move," Nova surmises.

"Exactly. So, Medea needed me more than I needed her, and she knew it, so she had an insurance policy in place." I take a deep breath. "Shortly after she turned Renard, she had turned my mother."

Nova's mouth drops open, and a small, strangled noise catches in her throat.

I clear my throat. "We're told never to seek out your old life for obvious reasons, but Medea was militant about it. What she was hiding is that she had Cèleste caged in a dungeon in the very palace we were residing in at the time."

Nova's heart aches through the bond, along with mine.

"When Medea finally allowed me to see her," I continue, "I was horrified. Medea had never completed the Sire bond with Cèleste, so she was a rabid animal. All skin and bone and her mind was completely lost to Blood Lust."

A tear slides down Nova's cheek. I look up at the ceiling, my own tears threatening to ravage my body. "I contacted Ren for the first time in centuries and told him of our mother. He was ready to annihilate Medea, but it would have meant him being gone too, so we did the only thing we could. I renounced Medea as my mate after Ren and I released Cèleste from her eternity of misery."

The stench of her burning flesh after we had ripped her heart out still haunts me to this day. She was meant to live out her days with her grandchildren, not stuck in a dungeon in insurmountable pain forever.

I haven't realized Nova moved until she's kissing away the tear that escaped down the side of my face. She's lying on top of me, holding me tight, as if she can keep the pieces of my fragmented heart together. Nova's the only person on Earth that truly knows how this event affects me; she can feel it through the bond, and she knows from her own mother's demise because of another soulless tyrant.

I curl my arms around her then roll to the side, so we are lying face to face.

"Thank you for telling me," Nova whispers.

"My soul is yours, little wolf," I murmur as I rest my forehead on hers, inhaling deeply, and drift off into a dreamless sleep.

I wake up to an empty bed and jolt up in a panic. Nova's gone. I turn and my phone, which I left upstairs last night, on the side table. I scoop it up.

Hi, sleeping beauty. I'm fine. I felt excellent when I woke, so Art and I have gone on a run. I'll be back late this afternoon. I've closed all the shutters downstairs, so it should be light-tight. Allura's next door. Blood in the fridge. See you later, xo.

I breathe easy, shooting a quick message back.

I miss you. Enjoy your run.

I wander out of Nova's room tentatively, but the place is shut tight, as she said. I find the blood in the kitchen fridge and grab a glass before settling down on the sofa, catching up on the other messages on my phone.

Immortal survived, but if you let Carter near this place again, we'll have fucking problems. He's too flirtatious with the girls. And Allura adores him.

I laugh at the irony of that particular statement coming from Renard.

I'm going to stay in the building tonight in case anything arises. Hope your girl is good, and you've broken some furniture.

Another one pops up as I finish reading the last.

She's back in New York. Took out some of Moretti's Nest, and he's seeing red. He's demanding to see you tonight.

Fuck. Moretti is Staten Island's Nest Master, and we have never seen eye to eye. So, if he wants to meet, then it must be bad.

I message Renard back.

> What exactly is 'some' of his Nest?

RENARD

> Wiped out about a third of it, plus his second. I didn't get details, just a 'request' for a meeting.

> Tell Moretti to come to Immortal at midnight.

I down the rest of the blood, knowing I'll need the boost for that meeting. Maybe Nova's friend Jasper has some hacking expertise to track Medea's exact location?

The front door bursts open so forcefully I'm surprised it doesn't come off its hinges. Violent, searing sun rays flood the room; my entire right arm and shoulder are exposed directly. The flesh and muscle instantly start burning and disintegrating before I throw myself into the corner of the room, back into the shadows.

Nova rushes into the room; her terror rips through the bond. What the—?

Shockingly, Dom barrels in after her with an unconscious and profusely bleeding Carter draped over his shoulder.

"Put him down on the sofa." She darts out of the door and slams her palm on the other door. Allura and Jasper scurry in, and Nova slams the door shut behind them.

"What happened?" Jasper demands.

Nova pants, her heart racing. Her clothes are ripped, and she's muddy. Her feelings are frazzled; the same feelings of terror and panic pulse through her when she remembers the horrors of her Pack.

Who the *fuck* touched her?

33

Nova

Allura & Nova's Apartment

"A BITTEN PACK CORNERED us on our run. Tried to... tried. And then Art stepped in. But there were too many of them. Too, too many."

I'm hyperventilating, swaying on my feet. Hands grip my upper arms. Warm. Cedarwood and peach. Xander. Safe. I loosen a shaky breath.

It all happened so fast. We stopped for a brief break, and my phone buzzed. *I miss you.* Art was teasing me about the dumb smile on my face. I scented the Pack too late. They surrounded us.

Art told me not to expose myself, to pretend to be what the amulet passes me off as. They demanded he hand over the 'unclaimed bitch', and insisted they'd look after me. Said I looked like good breeding stock.

"One of them had a knife. And another had the jar of wolfsbane steeped in alcohol. Why are wolves carrying wolfsbane as a weapon!" I shout to no one in particular.

I choke on a sob, Xander's arm around me is the only thing keeping me from collapsing on the floor. "They threw it at him after they cut him up. He's only injured because of me. Please, Lu. You need to help him!"

Art's blood saturates the air. Metal, salt, and rot. Wolfsbane. It makes my eyes water. Allura's hands are glowing, hovering over Art's body as she chants in Fae Tongue. Her jasmine and orange scent intensifies in the room, mingling with the smell of charred flesh.

I turn. "Fuck, Xander!"

His right arm hangs limp beside him, the flesh charred and bloody. The muscles are wrecked, eaten away, the bone exposed. The damage travels over his shoulder.

Tears are now falling freely. What is *happening* today?

"I'll be healed in a couple of hours. Focus on Carter."

"Aster," Allura's voice resigned.

No, no, no, no.

I turn back to her. Tears shine in her eyes. "There's nothing we can do. There's too much wolfsbane in his system."

"No. *No!* He isn't dying." I whirl back to Xander. "Give him your blood. You said it could heal anything."

"I said *almost* anything. But I can't; I'm mending an injury. I barely have enough to heal myself."

"How do you heal faster?"

His eyes darken. "I feed."

I pull off my tattered shirt, leaving me in just a sports bra and shorts, holding out my arms. "Which vein gets you the most blood the fastest?"

"I'm not going to—"

"Which one, Xander!" I'm frantic. Art needs to be healed and needs to be healed *now.*

"I'd have to drain someone, Aster." His eyes are almost black, his voice hard.

"I'm not taking no for an answer." We lock eyes. The bond flares with both our emotions, even past the amulet. My frantic despair. His fear. He's terrified he'll kill me. I soften a fraction. "*Please*, Xander. Please save him."

His eyes falter. "I'll try."

He grasps my neck with his uninjured hand, tilting my head to the right, exposing more flesh. His fangs drop, and he sinks them into my neck.

The pain is intense. Erotic. His grip tightens on my neck. I feel a pulling sensation, my mind going hazy, my eyes flutter closed as pleasure bursts through my veins.

I'm euphoric. It's beyond physical. I feel a deep sense of serenity in my soul. My mouth pops open, a small gasp stuck in my lungs.

And then it's all gone. The world rushes back. I open my eyes as Xander pierces his thumb with a fang, rubbing it on the wounds on my neck.

His arm is back to normal. He rushes over to Art on the sofa, his breathing barely existent now, as I collapse on the floor. Xander punctures his own wrist with his fangs and then shoves the wounds into Art's mouth. Dom helps me off the floor and over to Art's side.

He looks dead.

No. No, he can't be gone. He's barely lived, and I need him. I place a hand over his, squeezing tight.

Come back to us, damn it.

Art's injuries finally stitch together, the color returning to his ashen skin. Xander stops feeding him, his own wound closing as soon as it leaves Art's mouth. Art breathes heavily, his eyes flickering open. He looks up at me, a shadow of relief on his face before he rolls to his side, puking up black liquid all over the floor.

"It's the wolfsbane," Allura explains as she rushes to the kitchen. I hear her emptying her own stomach into the sink.

"At least she was polite enough to puke in a sink," Art slurs, wiping his mouth with the back of his hand and flopping back down onto the sofa.

Despite myself, I laugh. As does Jas. Allura returns with a bucket of cleaning supplies and cleans up, with Jas assisting.

A warm hand squeezes my shoulder as honeycomb and teakwood scent swirls around me.

"Are you okay, Aster?" Dom asks, turning me towards him.

I nod stiffly; he tilts my head to the side to examine my neck, and I step out of his reach and cover my neck with my hand. Confusion flashes through his eyes before he turns to Xander near the front door, looking at his phone.

"What are you doing here?" Dom asks, his eyes taking in Xander's casual attire.

"I'm here by request of Allura," Xander says while still typing on his phone. It's not exactly a lie.

Dom turns and narrows his eyes suspiciously at Allura behind me.

"How did you end up in this situation?" Xander asks, drawing Dom's attention before he can ask more questions.

"I got a report from the local Pack yesterday that they scented a new female wolf in their territory, so High Alpha Lárus wanted me to check it out. I didn't realize Aster had shacked up with Carter."

I can feel Xander holding back on correcting him. "I'm surprised you got involved," he says instead.

"I usually wouldn't, but..." Dom's eyes flick to me before he fishes his own phone out.

Rage boils under Xander's skin; he's barely keeping it together.

Fatigue threatens to drag me into unconsciousness as I slide down onto the floor. A wave of pain crawls over my skin. Oh fuck, not again.

Dom squats down in front of me, his hands reaching out, but I bat them away. "I'm fine. I just need a nap."

"You're shivering, Aster," Dom counters as he scoops me off the floor and hugs me to his chest. I want to be put down, but the strength in my body has left me. The edges of my mind are crumbling, so I close my eyes, holding back the building energy in my body while Dom is here.

"Bring her upstairs," I hear Allura instruct from somewhere behind me. "She's weak from the blood loss."

Each step Dom takes up the stairs sends shooting pain through my whole body. My insides feel like they're melting. My skin is too tight. I think I'm actually dying.

Dom finally puts me down on the bed and brushes the tendrils of hair from my face.

"If you're sticking around for a bit, Dom, Ren could really use some assistance at Immortal. Moretti is making an appearance tonight," Xander says in a calm tone, but I can feel the territorial possession radiating across our bond.

Dom breathes slowly, his breath warming my cheek. "I'll be around for the next couple of days, so I'll head over."

As soon as I hear the front door click closed downstairs, I roll off the bed, hitting the floor with a thud. I try to rip at the amulet on my wrist, but I can't grip it. Needles of pain spread every inch of skin like fur is trying to erupt through. I'm hot, and I'm freezing. I'm sobbing.

I need it to stop. I don't want to do this anymore.

"What do you need, *chérie?*"

That voice. Low, deep, refined. *Mine.*

"Xander," I whimper, reaching out trying to find him. My hand connects with a solid, warm arm and I hold on for dear life as I curl up as tight as I can, the pain now attacking my bones. They're stretching, reshaping, and breaking. There's too much build-up.

A light touch brushes against my wrist and my amulet lifts away and the energy in my body pops. Pain ripples from my core to the tips of my toes, my fingers, and the top of my head. I can breathe again. My throat is burning from the screams.

All the energy in my body is spent as I'm splayed out on the floor, trying to breathe easier. I can barely hear the conversation happening above me.

"This is the last wave," Allura says.

"If this is what it's like now, what the fuck is the full moon going to be like?" Xander's angry. Angry that he can't help me. He's panicked; he doesn't want to lose me.

My heart constricts. I should tell him, I should... My head is fried. Shit, Art. I roll onto my hands and knees. The floor comes into focus as I try to drag myself toward the door, but my wasted body crumbles to the floor.

I need to go check on Art.

Allura's feet come into view, and she sinks to her haunches. "You need to sleep it off, Nova."

I whimper. "Why?"

That's all I can manage. I want to demand why this is happening. Why me?

"Fucking magic," I slur as the darkness swallows me up.

I wake up alone in bed. I'm in a t-shirt—Xander's shirt. *And* his sweatpants. His scent surrounds me. Am I at the Penthouse?

I try to open my eyes, but they're heavy, refusing to lift. I use my nose, scenting around me. Xander's smoked peach and cedarwood scent is all over me, but the room smells of jasmine and faintly of fresh snow. I must be at the townhouse.

I'm finally able to open my eyes. My room comes into view. Why am I so sore? The run with Art must have...

The day's events slam into me. The run. Xander's arm. Art. The pain. Fuck, *Art*.

I spring out of bed, sprinting down the stairs. The apartment is dark, the only light coming from the almost full moon through the window and the flatscreen.

Three heads turn from the sofa. Jas has a book in his lap, with his feet on the coffee table. Allura is curled up against Art, who's got a handful of popcorn ready to shove into his already full mouth.

"What time is it?" I'm dazed. How many days was I out? Where's Xander?

"It's after ten. You were out for a while," Allura answers as she picks some popcorn out of Art's bowl, returning her attention back to the flatscreen.

"Xander went to Immortal," Jas answers my silent question, eyes going back to his book.

"Has anyone seen my phone?" Did I lose it on the run?

"Kitchen, charging," Art says as he chews on more popcorn.

I clamber through the apartment to find it by the toaster.

XANDER

Message me when you wake.

I smile at the screen.

Did you leave here naked? I'm dressed in the clothes you had on before I passed out.

XANDER

I had to get his scent off you. The only scent you should wear is mine, little wolf.

So you did leave naked?

I pull out ingredients for a sandwich while I wait for Xander's reply.

XANDER

Maddox dropped off a suit for me. Your smart mouth is back, so you must be feeling better.

I snort.

I feel fine now. It looks like we're having a Pack sleepover. I hope your meeting doesn't go too long. Moretti seems like a dick.

I finish making a sandwich while I wait for a response.

XANDER

Can confirm, Moretti is definitely a dick. He'll probably keep me until dawn. Tell Art to keep his hands to himself. We'll have problems if I scent anyone but me all over you tomorrow.

Jealousy looks good on you, Mr. Vladislav. I wish you were here to show me in person.

XANDER

Enjoy your night, baby. I'll be dreaming of you.

34

Vladislav

Vladislav's Penthouse

MORETTI DID, IN FACT, keep me until the sun threatened the horizon.

He driveled on about how Medea must be put out of her misery and how out of sorts he is about having to make new Adam-made vampires to revive his Nest. Then there was the rant about how his now-deceased second, was the only loyal soldier he had, and it was going to be impossible to replace him.

By the end of it all, I wanted to rip my hair out.

And now I can't sleep. Maybe because the dreams of her being torn apart keep wrenching me out of sleep, or perhaps it's her blood still simmering in my veins.

I had never taken the blood of a supernatural before; on the streets, fae blood is sold as a forbidden elixir, and vampires wouldn't dare try to feed on werewolves without risking their lives.

Nova's blood felt like walking in the sun. It was electric and powerful. Is all werewolf blood like this, or is it just *her* blood? My body fully healed in a matter of moments, and I've never felt this satisfied after a feed ever in my immortal existence.

She tasted like a vintage amber rum and sunshine, reminding me of late summer days laying in a field of wheat.

The thought of never seeing her lounging on a beach in the sunlight aches a little in my heart. But if I had never turned, I would have long passed by now, condemned to die and never meet Nova.

That thought hurts me even more.

I roll over in the bed, burying my head in the other pillow. More of her scent needs to be in this penthouse. More of *her* needs to be here. The faint tendril of rum and milk tickles my nose as I drift off.

Something stirs me from my sleep—footsteps approaching my room. I open my eyes, adjusting to the pink dusk sky. Nova opens the door and the energy in the room changes. The bond roars to life.

Mine.

The word, and feeling, screams from both ends of the bond as we lock eyes. I'm out of the bed and burying my fingers in her hair, devouring her lips before my next breath.

She wraps her arms in a vice grip around my neck, pushing me back towards the bed. We collapse onto the soft surface, Nova straddling me, breathing hard.

"*Mine.*" Her voice is hoarse, eyes a wild sapphire blue with sparks of gold, her pupils dilated.

She pulls off her shirt, revealing the red satin bra. Jesus Christ. I grip her hips, bucking to the side, flipping us over. She kicks off her sneakers as I tug her leggings off in one motion. Matching red satin panties.

"Fuck, you're beautiful."

Her laugh is throaty. "Pants off, immediately."

My turn to laugh. "Did anyone ever tell you that patience is a virtue, little wolf?"

She growls. "*Fuck.* Patience."

I sink to my knees, pulling her toward the edge of the bed and take those damn red panties off, then I bury my face in the soft brown curls. I swirl my tongue over her clit, reveling in her choked growls.

"*Please,*" she pleads. Fuck. I'm undone by the sound. The taste. The wolf. Everything.

I worship her with my tongue, sucking hard on her clit. She's panting and fisting her hands in the sheets, her legs locking around my head. I sink two fingers into her, and her hips jerk as she hisses. "Fucking hell, Xander."

Every time she says my name, my mind short circuits. It rolls off her tongue like it's like a prayer, a curse, and a promise.

I growl, my mouth locked on her clit as I stroke up with my fingers, increasing the pace. Her back arches off the bed; she's delirious, saying nonsensical, filthy things. I feel her clutching at my fingers, spasming, close to climax.

"Come for me, Nova," I growl and lock on her clit once more.

She implodes, screaming my name, legs clamping down.

Seeing Nova in this way, wild, undone, and sated, makes the bond preen in my chest. *Mine.*

Her body finally relaxes, allowing me to pull out. She pulls me up towards her, planting her lips on mine, tasting herself, moaning. A part of my brain snaps, the predator erupting through. My fangs drop, my whole body going hard.

Nova wraps her legs around my waist and pulls away, eyes narrow. "Why are your pants still *on*?"

She uses her wolf agility to flip me onto the bed and buries her face at my neck, inhaling deeply. Her tongue runs a hot path up the muscle and I shudder, my hips jerking up. What delicious torture.

"I want to taste every inch of you," she growls, nipping my earlobe.

"Is my neck where you really want to start, little wolf?"

Nova sits up, her hands sliding up my chest, her eyes following the movement. "Where *would* you like me to—"

She grips my shoulder, angling it towards me, and her eyes blaze. "What the *fuck* is this?"

"What—"

Nova's fingers dig into my shoulder painfully, her eyes boring into mine. "Is this *her* mark?"

"Nova—"

She growls, her hand moving from my shoulder to my neck, crushing my windpipe. "You're *mine*. Do you understand me?"

I'm about to offer her my whole existence when the crack of a door being kicked open sounds in the apartment. I sit up; Nova and I look at each other, perplexed. Her face turns to stone, eyes burning, nose flaring.

The stench of poisonous apples hits me as Nova growls. "Who is that?"

"Medea," I choke. Nova's eyes burn with rage and she tries to leap off me. I grab both wrists. "Deep breath."

Nova nods in response, wrath vibrating her entire body as she puts her clothes back on. I'm back with a t-shirt on in a second as I lead us out of the bedroom into the living area.

The clicking of heels gets closer; evil incarnate appears from the foyer.

At first glance, Medea is stunning. Skin a flawless alabaster, hair a sunlit ash-blonde falling in impeccably styled layers to her waist. Her face is an artist's dream, with small features that are symmetrical in every way. Her lips are full, lush, and rosy. Enticing. Her large eyes are striking, a blue so light and crystal clear that they are almost translucent.

She's the same height as Nova in heels, and her body is lithe; the tight burgundy dress she's wearing hugs her soft curves. Her movements are fluid, feline, mesmerizing.

The more I look at her, the more I see the rot.

Her long, pointed nails remind me of bird talons. Some people might find her seductive expression alluring, but all I see is the smugness clouding her eyes, the calculating, soulless bitch hidden under the beauty.

Her body is too slim; she's lost weight in the last few centuries, and her skin is paler, her veins a touch too blue. I want to wrap my bare hands around her long neck or tear her dead heart out from under her small chest.

I *despise* her.

I feel Nova's surprise; I don't think she expected Medea to look so 'nice'. Threads of mutual hatred for the snake in front of us lace through the bond.

Medea crinkles her nose, eyes roving over Nova, assessing her. "Who's our new pet, Alexander?" Her voice is smooth, promising, tempting. It makes me want to shove ice picks in my ears.

"One that bites," Nova states, arms crossing over her chest.

Medea laughs, the sound inviting, making me want to throw up. "Oh, she's a feisty one, Alex. I think we shall indeed keep her."

"There is no *'we'*, Medea."

Praise to whichever faerie gave Nova the amulet that's currently wrapped around her wrist. Medea can't scent or detect the bond. Her eyes flash with irritation, stepping closer to me.

"Oh Alexander, don't be so dramatic. We don't have time for this nonsense. We have to go." *Alexander;* I hate my full name on her lips.

"Go where?"

"Home. To Court."

I scoff. "No."

Anger twists her face as she flashes in front of me, claws crushing my throat, digging into my flesh, almost breaking the skin. "You are my *mate* and Consort, and I am your Queen. Your leave of absence is over."

I grab her wrist firmly, pulling her hand off my neck, her claws leaving gashes that heal instantly. I release her wrist, taking a few steps back. The bond bubbles with possession; Nova is barely holding herself together.

"We aren't mates anymore, Medea." I keep my voice cold.

She clicks her tongue, rolling her eyes. "Come on, Alex. Are you still holding onto that silly disagreement?"

"My *mother* wasn't a disagreement. You stole a life. Multiple, in fact. And for what?"

She pouts, eyes softening. "For you, baby," she purrs, hand caressing my chest over my heart.

Nova appears between us, shoving Medea away from me, a growl piercing the room. "Don't touch him."

Her fangs drop, and she hisses. Medea charges Nova, knocking her to the ground, her teeth snapping and aiming for Nova's neck. I take a step to pull the demon off her, but Nova grabs a handful of Medea's hair, pulling her down and twisting, so Medea's face slams into the floor.

Nova jumps up, keeping a low fighting stance, taking a few steps backward, eyes fixed on her opponent. Medea recovers quickly, launching herself at Nova. Nova blocks with her left arm.

One of Medea's talons catches her amulet's leather strap, slicing through it and the stone drops to the floor.

The air pops, the energy shifting. Medea's face stills, eyes wide, flicking between Nova and me.

Her nose flares, face hardening. Her eyes usually darken to a storm gray when she vamps-out, but now they are pure black. Medea releases a guttural, violent roar, launching again at Nova, claws shredding Nova's outstretched right forearm.

Nova throws a hefty punch into Medea's thigh, the bone snapping. It halts the clawing enough for Nova to slam her shoulder into Medea's gut, running her into the wall behind her, destroying it.

Nova rolls back, scooping up the amulet, any trace of the bond disappearing, just as Dom and Ren rush in from the foyer. Nova pants, uninjured hand trembling slightly, but clutching the amulet hard.

Her arm is healing, but her blood stains the floor. Again.

"I'm going to end you, mutt!" Medea's voice is alien, rasping, venomous. She's ferocious as she thrashes in Ren and Dom's grip.

I catch Nova's waist as she tries to launch at Medea again. "Just fucking try me, you pathetic leech."

Ren and Dom manage to wrestle her out of the apartment.

35

Nova

Vladislav's Penthouse

ALL **I** CAN SEE is red.

The red of blood streaked across the timber floors. The red of *her* dress.

"Fuck!" I tear out of Xander's arm, storming through to his bathroom.

I catch myself in the mirror. More red. Blood coats my arm. The slashes from her claws are now red marks, fading as the seconds tick by. My shirt is tattered, red bra peeking through underneath. My hand clutching the amulet has turned red.

Her lips. Her *marks* on Xander.

My fist lashes out, shattering the mirror. Red. My knuckles split, oozing more blood. Pain radiates from my hand down to my elbow.

My wolf surfaces, eyes blazing sapphire in the fractured reflection. We're going to rip that bitch to shreds. Right now.

I return to the living area, scenting the air. Rotten apples saturate the whole place, feeding my wolf. *Hunt.*

Before I can follow the horrid scent, both my wrists are trapped behind my back, and Xander is gripping my jaw, forcing me to look into his bourbon brown eyes.

"No fucking way." The bond. He felt what I was about to do. Fuck. I struggle against his grip.

"She needs to die," my voice is not my own, but my wolf. "She tried to take what's *mine.*"

"And if you go after her, she'll try to take what's mine." His deep, menacing voice shoots scorching pleasure through my body.

I lean forward, slamming my lips to Xander's, devouring him. He releases my arms, keeping his grip on my jaw tight. I wrap my legs around his waist, locking my arms around his neck as he pushes me up against the cool glass of the window.

He pulls back, pinning me with his hips, his stare deadly. "Are you good?"

I nod, my body finally relaxing. I take a deep breath, inhaling Xander's peach and smoky cedarwood scent.

My emotions always roller coaster the day before a full moon, but this shit is next level. As soon as *her* hand landed on Xander's chest over his heart, all I could think about was removing it violently.

Medea has no right touching him, not even *breathing* on him. If she looks at him again, I'm going to gouge her eyes out.

Possession runs riot on my senses as I shudder, fighting the need to cause Medea a brutal death. Xander holds me firm, waiting for me to calm, so I don't run out into the night and hunt the bitch down.

I bring my clenched fist between us, uncurling my fingers around the stone amulet. "Lu is going to be pissed this almost got destroyed."

"Let's see if I have anything that will suffice." Xander grasps my other hand, leading me into his dressing room. He pulls out the slim second drawer of his watch display; an extensive array of cufflinks lay displayed in their pristine beauty.

"Pretty," I muse, drifting over to the drawer, my fingers twitching, desperate to touch.

Xander smirks as he pulls out a long velvet box from the back, placing it on top of the glass. He opens it, and it reveals a neat selection of chains and picks out a long, delicate gold chain, holding out his hand for the amulet.

I drop it into his hand. "I wouldn't think that was your style."

He smiles as he feeds the chain into the amulet loop. "It isn't. The chain belonged to my mother."

"Gods, don't give it to me. I'll end up breaking or losing it."

Xander steps forward, wrapping the chain around my neck, clipping it into place. The amulet sits midway down my sternum, long enough to hide in clothing. "My mother would have wanted me to give it to someone worthy." He tucks an escaped lock of hair from my bun behind my ear, tilting my chin up. "And you, *ma chérie*, are worthy."

My heart aches—his faith in me is almost overwhelming. He slips to the back of the closet, pulling out a t-shirt and boxer briefs. He places them in my hands, kissing me on the cheek. "Make yourself at home. Delia will make you something to eat when she arrives."

"You don't want me at work?"

Xander's eyes darken as possession snakes through the bond, sending heat through my body. "If anyone touches you, or looks at you in the wrong way, I will start a war."

"I shall leave you to change." My voice is breathless as I retreat to the bathroom, fighting the urge to jump Xander.

I shower, taking my time under the exquisite water pressure to scrub off the blood and violence from earlier, purposely putting that devil woman out of my mind. As I'm wrapping myself in a towel, Xander enters the bathroom dressed in black slacks and a crisp white shirt.

Glass crunches under his leather shoes. He chuckles at the disarray of his vanity. "What am I going to do with you?"

Heat flames my cheeks. "I'm sorry."

He turns to me and tilts my chin up, forcing me to look at him. "No need to apologize; she brings the worst out of people."

"I hate her," I confess in a whisper.

Xander nods, eyes swirling with bourbon. "So do I, love, so do I." He plants a swift kiss on my lips, wrapping his arms around me. "How is my hair?"

I laugh. "Perfect as always." I run my hands through the silky strands, brushing them away from his face. "Do you *really* need to go?"

Xander sighs. "Unfortunately, I do. Bartese is coming in tonight."

"I want to punch him in the mouth."

Xander's chest rumbles with laughter, his arms squeezing a little tighter. "He's an uptight asshole just like the rest of them."

"And you aren't?"

A sly smile lifts Xander's mouth. I yelp as he hauls me over his shoulder, exiting the bathroom and depositing me on his bed. He hovers over me, each hand on either side of my head, his lower body pinning me to the mattress. "I'm definitely not uptight."

"So, you're just an asshole?"

He smirks. "Only sometimes."

I hook my hands around his neck, bringing his lips closer. "I don't think you're as much of an asshole as you claim to be."

"Hey, don't mess with my reputation." I laugh as his lips meet mine, his arms wrapping around me, hands in my damp hair.

I pull back slightly, my nose brushing his. "If you don't want my scent all over you, you better go."

"I'm sure Bartese would love that," Xander grumbles and then crawls off the bed, pulling me into a seated position. He disappears into the closet for a moment and returns with my borrowed items and his suit jacket. He places my clothes next to me, then leans over to steal another kiss. "Be good for Delia."

"I'm a delight to Delia, thank you very much."

Xander rolls his eyes. "Be gentle; she's already going to freak out about the giant hole in the wall."

"I'll keep her distracted."

He stands, sliding on his jacket as he walks towards his bedroom door. "More than likely, I'll be home just before sunrise, so don't wait up."

"I hope Bartese doesn't give you too much grief."

Xander laughs, turning back towards me. "I hope so, too. I'll see you later." He lingers in the doorway, the bond bubbling with longing.

My heart stammers. "Bye."

A smile plays on Xander's face as he disappears into the hallway, his footsteps receding. I flop back on the bed, gripping the towel around me.

This whole situation is happening so fast. Wounds that shredded me are slowly stitching together. The constant uncertainty of my life is lifting. My future seems bright again, full of color.

And the other things... Is the bond being a manipulative bastard? Or is this real?

It's deep into the night, and my brain won't shut off. Curled up in Xander's bed without him feels odd. I roll over, scooping up my phone from the nightstand and message him.

How's work?

XANDER

Why are you still up, chérie?

I've adjusted to vampire time, and it's weird not having you next to me.

XANDER

Hopefully, I won't be long, but who knows, Bartese is exceptionally difficult tonight.

I put the phone back on the nightstand, turning, and burying my face in Xander's pillow, inhaling deep. I concentrate on his smoke and peach scent, the delicious combination lulling me into a doze.

I'm not entirely unconscious when the bed dips next to me, and a chuckle tickles my ear.

"I require my pillow, *chérie*." Xander tries to tug the soft cloud under my head.

"It's mine now," I mumble, gripping it tighter.

He chuckles again, his warm hand brushing down my body, leaving trails of tingles on my skin. "Care to trade for a vampire pillow?"

"Okay," I mumble, lifting my head, releasing the soft fabric. The pillow disappears and replaced with the crook of Xander's arm. His body wraps around mine, encasing me in delicious warmth.

"What time is it?" I mumble into his neck, savoring his scent. This Xander pillow is way better.

"The sun is just about to rise," Xander murmurs into my hair.

"Stupid Bartese."

My body wakes me up reluctantly. I'm still tangled around Xander, practically laying on top of him. I try to roll off, but Xander pulls me in tighter, still deep in slumber.

I peel open an eye. The sun peeks through a crack in the closed curtains, and I can hear Delia humming in the kitchen. It must be around lunchtime. My stomach growls on cue. I somehow manage to slip out of Xander's arms without disturbing him, collect my phone and pad out of the room.

The brightness of the living room makes me squint as I hear the front door open and laughter filter through. Allura, Art, and Jas enter from the foyer, their eyes immediately on the destroyed wall next to them.

"What on earth happened here?" Art demands.

"Medea happened."

"Medea was *here* last night?" Allura balks.

I stretch. "Yep. Showed up wanting her mate back."

Jas crouches down by the hole, hand tentatively tracing the jagged edges of the plaster. Allura's eyes narrow on my amulet around my neck. "She knows, doesn't she?"

I nod. "She went batshit. That's when I sent her through the wall. Dom and Ren got here just after dragging her out."

"Do *they* know too?" Art asks, eyes focused, his arms crossing.

I shake my head. "I had the amulet in my hand before they got here."

Everyone in the room seems to let go of a collective breath. It's still strange to have people that worry about me this way. Apart from Kris and Junior, my other brothers only cared enough that I didn't die, so my father would keep his attention on me and not them.

"Let's go harass Delia for food. I'm starving," I announce, distracting myself from wandering further into that dark corner of my mind.

36

Vladislav

THE BOND STIRS IN my chest as I enter the kitchen. "Good morning, everyone."

Jasper, Carter and Allura sit around the breakfast table with Nova as Delia sets down plates of food. I plant a soft kiss in Nova's hair and saunter over to the coffee pot and fill a mug, then return to the seat next to her.

I can hear her racing heart, and shallows breaths, her need to complete our bond rumbles down our connection. I push the challenge back to her and she clutches her coffee cup a little harder.

"I don't think we've officially met," Jasper proclaims across the table, holding out a hand. "I'm Jasper, Carter's roommate."

I accept the handshake. "The historian, yes?" He nods, his eyes shining.

We all settle into a comfortable conversation as Nova pushes her plate closer to me, letting me pick at her food while she eats a bowl of soup. I pull her feet into my lap, my arm resting on her shins, my fingers tracing circles on her calves. I've never felt this at ease before, and it's heartwarming.

After assisting Delia in clearing up the table, Jas returns with a heavy leather-bound book and a few pens, taking the seat on the other side of Nova, his eyes boring into her.

Carter chuckles. "It's Jas Inquisition time for you, Nova."

She groans, sitting a little straighter, setting down her coffee. "Show me what you have."

Jasper pushes the book in front of Nova. He has the Jónasson family tree going back generations. Nova points to a name at the top of the page. "You're only missing two High Alpha's here," she informs and gives the name to Jasper, who scribes like mad on the page.

She points to the bottom of the page. "And for the current generation, Junior, here, mate bonded with Patricia two years ago. And they just had a son, Theodore, a couple weeks ago." She rattles off the names of three other brothers and their birthdays. "Then it's Kristjan, my twin, and *then* me."

Jasper looks up. "You and Kristjan are twins?"

Nova nods. "Yes. But my dickhead twin was born six minutes before me and has to make the distinction that *I'm* the youngest." I smile at the similarities of our brothers.

"And who's next in line?" Jasper asks, in scholar mode, scribing away.

"Stefan. That's if he mates with anyone. Then it would be Junior."

Jasper smirks as he finishes his writing, looking like he's just discovered the world's greatest secrets, and then turns to a clean page in the large book. He looks back at Nova. "What's your Pack called again?"

"Don't record our little troupe. We're basically a Beta Pack."

Carter scoffs. "Take that amulet off and say that again. You're a High Alpha. There's no doubt about that." He looks to Jasper. "We're the Zephyrus Pack."

Jasper writes it at the top of the page. "Zephyrus Pack. First High Alpha Nova, previous Jónasson First Blood. High Beta, Carter Benson, previous Lárusson Bitten. Nova mated to—"

"We aren't a mated pair yet." Nova's eyes catch mine, her cheeks pink.

"We will be soon enough," I announce without any shame. I turn my attention to Jasper, who's smirking.

Nova pulls her legs out of my lap, sitting straighter. "So, tonight."

Carter nods, leaning his elbows on the table. "How do you want to play it out, Alpha?"

"I honestly don't know what's going to happen, but I think we should get out of the city. Sid's basement won't hold the two of us even with strong Fae wards."

"I agree," Carter remarks.

"We'll need lots of space," Nova muses, her brows pinching in concentration. "And no wolves in the area."

"There's a state park about forty-five minutes out of the city heading north," Allura offers.

"When will you be leaving?" I ask.

"Soon," Nova offers with a small smile. "I'm assuming we're going to need to do some hiking."

"Plus," Jasper adds, "we'll have to prepare for the containment barrier."

"A safety precaution," Allura states as I'm about to ask what Jasper meant. "It's to contain their change to avoid detection from any other wolves who may be in the area."

I nod. We all finish our lunch; Carter, Jasper, and Allura leave to visit an apothecary for spell supplies close to Immortal. Nova and I help Delia pack all the leftover food into containers before she dismisses us from the kitchen. I lace my fingers with Nova's, pulling her to my room.

As we enter I release her hand, my body going still behind Nova. She doesn't dare turn around. I close the door, stepping deliciously close to Nova, heat radiating off her.

"Take off the amulet." My voice is gravelly and deeper than usual.

She shudders as she lifts the chain over her head with shaky hands and tosses it to the bed. The room's energy is thunderous, buzzing against my skin. The bond roars to life, lighting up in my chest. Possession, violent and deep, rumbles through the bond from Nova, and I groan.

I push fierce protectiveness and loyalty back at her, and other threads of feelings, ones with softer edges, letting her feel it all.

Nova's scent washes over me. Amber rum. Leather. Milk. It's all around me, thick as I gulp it in. My eyes roll back.

"Fuck," Nova pants.

"I'm going out of my mind," I whisper, my breath on her neck.

"You and me both," she murmurs, another shudder rolling through her.

My fingers trace a scorching path down the side of Nova's body to the edge of her t-shirt. I pull it off, leaving her in nothing but boxer briefs. She steps back into my chest, my arms snaking around her waist as I bury my nose in her hair and inhale deeply.

I can feel two emotions warring within Nova. One side wants to complete the bond right now and let down her walls, and be free. The other side of her is in a panic freefall.

"*Chérie*, take this, us, at your own pace," I murmur softly, "we have eternity."

"It's irrational to think about what others would say."

"About us?"

"About me mostly," she confesses.

I turn her in my arms, tilting her chin up to me, catching the fear in her jade green eyes. "No one is going to look at you any differently."

She smirks. "They will; I have a vampire as a mate."

I return a small smile. "True, but that's not what I meant."

"I know," she huffs, "but I just... they'll expect me to mourn Eros longer."

"You will mourn him your whole life in one way or the other. Don't let anyone else in existence dictate any part of your life."

She raises a brow. "What about you?"

I chuckle. "*Especially* me. I'm a possessive bastard, but I don't want to *own* you. I just want to be with you."

She wraps her arms around my torso tight, resting her cheek on my chest, over my heart, her entire body relaxing. Her emotions of doubt swirl, like she doesn't deserve any semblance of peace.

"Stop doubting yourself, *chérie*."

"Easier said than done," she mumbles into my chest.

The front door opens in the foyer, the laughter of her friends echoing through the apartment. She squeezes me a little tighter.

"I wish I could be there with you," I say into her hair.

Nova pulls back. "It's for the best. The energy is going to be intense; I can feel it simmering under my skin."

I trace her jaw, sinking my hand into her hair, my mouth brushing hers. "I'll be waiting for you, so come back to me."

Nova smiles. "I will."

Nova

State Park out of New York City

○

T HE SKY IS TURNING inky black, and the fire we're gathered around crackles and pops.

Allura and Jas huddle together under a thick blanket, with mugs of steaming tea in their hands, compiling a list of baby names. Sid is immersed in a beaten-up book nearby, also cocooned in a thick blanket with a headlamp wrapped around her head.

Art and I sit around the fire, consuming the food Delia packed for us. Both of us have been ravenous the whole day. Typically, a wolf's metabolism chews through food stores on a full moon day, but this is next-level hunger. I haven't stopped eating since I left Xander's, and I'm still hungry.

"Where is all of this food even going?" I comment as I shove more soup-soaked bread into my mouth.

"Honestly," Art murmurs around a sandwich. "I don't know."

We demolished all the food over the next hour, both of us finally somewhat satisfied. Allura is now dozing against Jas as he transcribes into one of his many notebooks from another book.

Sid looks at her watch. "We're almost there. Let's get set up."

I stand and stretch, feeling the wolf energy slithering under my skin. Even after a final run and training session with Art, the hike to this spot deep into the state park, and still having my amulet on, I feel like I could run for days.

Art follows suit, standing, stretching, and removes his clothes. I remove mine as well, not wanting to shred through them as my entire body is breaking apart.

We both get down to our underwear, neither of us at all bothered by the brisk air. Allura and Jas are now over with Sid in the clearing near our camp, pouring salt and other things onto the ground, creating a massive ring in the dirt.

I turn to Art, catching his hazel eyes. "Are you ready?"

"Are you?"

"Not at all."

He places a hand on my shoulder. "We've got you. I've got you."

"This energy feels volatile. There's not enough of us. What if it kills us?"

Art scoffs, crossing his arms over his chest. "I'm offended you think that you're that weak."

"I might be."

He laughs. "Hardly. Take off the amulet." My hand lands on the warm stone sitting on my sternum, hesitating. Art chuckles, pulling the chain over my head and tossing it on top of my discarded clothes.

A tsunami of power washes over both of us and we shudder. My wolf rears up against my skin, pushing to come out and play. I'm breathless, my hands gripping my thighs as I try to fight back the wolf under my skin. Sweat forms down my spine and over my chest.

I breathe in and then out. Repeat it. The wolf settles a fraction, allowing me to straighten, all my muscles trembling.

Art is still buzzing, his eyes a brilliant sapphire and gold. The gold ring is no longer just a solid ring around his pupil; it flecks off, scattered through the sapphire to the edges of his iris, winking and sparkling like... "stars."

"Yours too," Art confirms.

"Let's do this."

Art's eyes hit the dirt, and he trembles. "Yes, Alpha."

The Alpha energy seeps out of me; it's in my bones. My awareness of Art as a Pack member sinks in further. My wolf pushes dominance, but not aggressively like most Alpha energies. She wants to belong. She needs a Pack who's loyal but not afraid of her. As do I. Our energies, intentions, and focus all sync, and I let it roll over me, closing my eyes briefly.

The absence of city noise is unsettling. Even after coming from a life in farmlands, I didn't realize I'd grown to love the sounds of a bustling city—the sounds of my home.

With the moon inching higher into the sky, I open my eyes to Art watching me. His eyes drop as soon as ours meet. No matter how right the Alpha energy feels, I'm never going to get used to the position.

The thought that wolves may actually respect me now is, sadly, a startling concept.

We both walk down to the circle, walking through a small opening in the salt and into the center. Jas closes off the ring with more salt and pours a concoction of oils across the patch, then places a massive cluster of clear quartz over the spot. Three other clusters sit along the salt line, one at each cardinal direction Allura explained to me on the hike. The air stills and warms, pressing into me slightly.

"I can feel it," Art murmurs as he approaches the salt ring. He holds out his hand tentatively. The air at the barrier shimmers, refracting gold light like Allura's magic.

I turn to the faerie over on the other side of the circle. She's got her arms wrapped around a spellbook with a satisfied smile on her face.

I catch Sid's eyes next to her, and they're worried. "We'll be fine, Sid."

"Don't be going all crazy on me now."

I laugh. "I'll try."

Sid straightens; her eyes hard but watery. "Come back to us whole."

I swallow and nod, tears at her command stinging my eyes. I think I was always meant to find these people and make them my own.

Art returns to the center, and we both take a seat on the ground a few feet from each other. He won't turn until I do, so for now we close our eyes and calm our minds as Sid taught us to.

I listen to the forest's song; the night birds, cicadas, rushing water, and rustling trees. I listen to all the heartbeats around me; Art's strong beat, Sid's soft rhythm, Jas's smooth pace, and Allura's fluttering. Wait. Not just Allura.

I smile. Those fast flutters of her babe's heart echo through my head as I move onto another sense, smell. Rosemary, raspberries, and vetiver settle into my bones. A whisper of brine mixed with Allura's orange and jasmine makes my smile deepen. The earthy tones of white birch, moss, stagnant water, and the warmth of a deer swirl around me.

My wolf lurches. *Hunt.*

Here we go.

Heat starts in my chest and radiates out through my veins, seizing my muscles. Sweat coats my entire body. Hot. I'm too hot.

The spasms start in my arm and leg muscles; stretching, tearing, locking up. I turn onto my hands and knees, panting. I groan as pain pulses through all the joints in my hands. Bones break and realign. My hands reform into claws and then paws; my wrists dislocate and reconfigure. My elbows pop next, and then my knees and my ankles; claws wrench out of my feet.

The wind burns my skin as pores open, and hair pushes out like needles.

I take a breath before the worst part starts. I scream as my ribs expand and my hips and pelvis completely shatter. Fabric tears from my body. I fall to the side as my organs realign, and pain ravages my face: everything breaks, reforms, stretches, snaps, and burns. I pass out momentarily.

The pain stops, and I'm really warm. My mind is heavy as I take in a deep breath. It feels different; this isn't my body. I open my eyes. Everything is bright but muted in color. I can see every detail of the rock ahead of me. The veins of the leaves. Every petal on that flower. Is it blue? Or is it white?

I smell sunshine. But there's no sunshine. A heartbeat catches my attention; strong, juicy, far away. Fur. Hooves. *Hunt.*

I roll onto my paws and howl into the sky. The sound is guttural and piercing. The earth beneath me shakes. Power blasts around me, vibrating the air.

Another howl joins in melody. Its timber is a lot deeper, weaving into mine, and the earth shudders again. *Danger?*

My howl cuts off, my head whipping over to the stranger with a snarl. The other wolf is enormous. He's much taller than me and bulkier. But his fur... His fur is pitch black, and his ears are tipped with gold hairs. I meet his glowing sapphire and gold eyes and puff out my chest, growling again. He snarls back, holding his ground, but not asserting his power.

He's familiar. I sniff. Earth, oak, rosemary. Rosemary. *Pack.* Art. It's Art. And I'm Nova.

I stop growling. His energy rumbles through the earth. He's intact; I can feel his amusement, his respect for my position. Beta. He's my Beta, and I'm Alpha. I pounce and tackle him to the ground. We both roll a few times before both jumping back onto our feet. And then we launch again, playing, nipping, and chasing. *Pack.*

The sound of wind chimes in a soft breeze distracts me. No. Not wind chimes. A laugh. I turn my head to the source of the sound. A small female stands in the distance with something in her arms. She has brilliant wings, glowing with golden light. They look like they're made of fractured glass and fireflies. Her eyes glow unearthly blue and shimmer with unshed tears. She's crying, but she's smiling.

Her sweet orange, jasmine, and brine scent registers in my head: Allura. I bound toward her; it's Allura. And I'm Nova.

Alarm sparks in her eyes as I race toward her and then collide with an invisible wall. I yelp as I stumble, shaking my head. I forgot about the barrier. Allura holds out her hand flat against the border, and I press my head into her hand. *Pack, but not wolf.*

My heart swells. Yes, she is Pack. She laughs again, and I can feel the imprint of her hand through the magic veil. Art bounds up next to me, learning from my mistake, and stops just before the barrier. Allura steps over to him and does the same, holding out her hand, and Art presses his nose into her, making her laugh more.

Two humans approach. A man, with wire-frames and dark hair, smelling of raspberries: Jas. And I'm Nova. He bows his head, eyes turned down as he holds out his hand tentatively on the barrier. Permission to join the Pack. I push my nose into his hand. *Pack, but not wolf.* He steps over to Art to repeat the same.

The female human steps up. Her hair glows silver under the moon's white light, and her eyes shine a caramel brown. Her smile is serene; those eyes are watery.

She drops to her knees at the barrier, both hands on the invisible wall. Her vetiver scent curls around me. Sidelle. And I'm Nova. I yelp, running my body hard against the barrier and her hands over and over. Sid laughs and sobs, pushing at the barrier. *Savior. Pack, but not wolf.*

Sid widens her arms so her hand stretches out towards Art, and he pushes into her hand. Sid collects herself and stands, wiping off her knees.

"They'll play and fight for a while." Her voice is rich, soft, serene. Her voice is a sanctuary to madness.

Art yips, tackling me to the ground. I buck him off, scramble to my feet, and face him. We circle each other, growling in challenge, and then launch.

We fight, play, and run around the entire perimeter of the barrier for a couple hours, testing our strengths and forging our Pack hierarchy. My body is quick and exceptionally strong. Power rolls throughout the space and in my blood. I can feel the Pack bond with everyone, but I don't have mental communication with our non-wolf members.

The moon has started its descent, which means Art and I can change back whenever we want. I can feel that we're both completely spent, ready to sleep for the next week, so we do one last run around the barrier. Allura and Jas walk back from the fire with our clothes in their hands.

They deposit the material at the edge of the circle as we come up to a stop, panting. Scents of cedarwood and peach slice through the barrier and flood my senses. *Mate.*

My body shudders, and I howl. *Mate.* I need to find him. *Mate.* Why isn't he here? My howl turns into a growl, and I slash out a claw at the barrier. I need to get out and find him. *Mate.*

I bolt to the other side of the barrier, slamming into it. Why won't it break? I dash back over to where my clothes are and paw at the ground. I need to get a better scent so I can find him. *Hunt.*

I howl again; it's fractured and loud—the earth trembles. I need out. A sharp nip stings my flank, and I toss my head towards the wolf responsible with a vicious snarl. Art growls, lowering to the ground, ready for a fight.

Pack. I stop snarling and straighten. I let out another howl. This one is short, but it echoes through the ring, rumbling through my body and Art's, calling upon our wolf energies to let us go.

Both of us collapse onto the ground with whines as everything breaks and reforms again. It takes a lot less time to turn back, and soon enough, Art and I are sweaty, panting messes on the dirt in our human forms.

I open my eyes to Art's exhausted face. "You bit me on the ass."

He huffs out a laugh. "You were losing your shit over a scrap of fabric with some scent on it."

I laugh, too. "My bad."

After Art and I pull some clothes on and stumble up to the camp, I pass out as soon as I hit the softness of blankets. I dream of amber and sunshine, peach groves, starlight, and the sea.

I wake just after dawn; the camp is quiet, the fire a small pile of red coals in front of me. Art is curled around Allura across from me, with Jas on their left and Sid to their right.

I sneak out of the camp quietly, following the sound of rushing water nearby. I come across a small grotto behind a few large birch trees.

The water is clear enough to see the smooth rocks in its depth, and a sheet of falling water comes off the edge of the cliff nearby, with two little streams carved on either side of the pool, water running off further into the forest.

I strip off my clothes, wading into the crisp, deep pool, finding a rock to sit on with my back to the waterfall. I tuck my knees to my chest, wrapping my arms around them and resting my cheek on my knees, closing my eyes, letting the hard spray ease tension in my back and shoulders.

All the muscles in my body are stiff, and every single bone in my body aches, but this is the first change that my mind isn't scrambled somewhere between beast and reality. If anything, my mind and my wolf's feel merged, like we've become one and the same.

The crunching of leaves snaps my attention to where I entered the water. Art rounds a tree, eyes landing on the waterfall, and then me under it, smirking. "Morning, Alpha."

"You know I'm naked, right?"

He laughs, discarding his clothes next to mine and entering the water with a hiss. He picks his way over to a rock beside me and perches on it, pushing his back into the waterfall.

"Was this the first time you'd turned into a full wolf?" I ask.

"No, I've done it once before, but last night was a lot more intense."

"Same. But also..."

"You feel a lot sharper than yesterday? I do as well."

"Your coat was black, with gold-tipped ears, which I didn't expect. First Bloods turn into white wolves."

Art tips his hair back into the spray, chuckling. His head turns to me, hazel eyes blazing. "Nova, your coat was so black that it looked like it swallowed up the light."

"What the fuck?"

"That's because you're Lumeis," Allura calls from the edge of the water. Jas is standing beside her, removing clothes, Allura also following suit.

"Is it not weird that we're all naked?"

Jas chuckles as he makes his way over through the clear depths with Allura. "I grew up with wolves, Allura is a stripper by trade, and we all saw you two buck naked last night."

I laugh. "Valid point."

Art's eyes turn from amused to horrified. "No one mention this to Vladislav."

Allura bursts out in that wind chime laugh as she sinks onto a rock in front of me. "I'm *absolutely* going to tell him."

Art groans. "Odin, help me. I'm going to be murdered."

I huff a laugh. "You'll be fine." I turn my attention to Allura. "What exactly is a Lumeis?"

Allura lights up, literally, her wings buzzing and faerie dust flaking from the tips out of the water. "There are legends of objects blessed by the Other Side that have all kinds of power. Usually, it's weapons because living things can't come back. But you guys are *definitely* Lumeis."

Jas laughs. "You're not making sense, sweetie."

Allura giggles. "Sorry, getting ahead of myself. In Faery, the crossing to the Other Side is called Vimornium, it means the Gateway of Endings and Beginnings in common tongue. The Fae of Old used to push weapons into the gate and pull them out, forging them with Other Side magic to destroy the worst monsters. They called them Lumeis, or Star Born, weapons. None of them exist anymore, all destroyed in our Great War.

"Anyway, Fae have tried to do the same to animals and supernaturals, but anything living that passes through that gate can't come back, and any living thing that touches or consumes the magic without completely passing through turns into stardust. Well, except for the Charo, they're guides for souls when they're passing over."

"How are we Lumeis if we've never seen or touched this crossing?" Art asks, pushing away from the waterfall and floating around the water.

"Because of the tear, right?" I ask.

Allura nods her head enthusiastically. "It must be. Tears like that are the same magic but diluted in a way because it's passing through multiple realms. It's still potent enough to change a lot of things, but not enough to consume life. That's how you're now Lumeis. And Art became the same when you when you exchanged blood because you're now bound."

"Vladislav would be Lumeis as well," Jas says, staring up at the sky.

"He would be," Allura confirms. We both push off our rocks, and head toward the shore. "We don't know what it's changed for him yet. We'll find out, eventually."

Crunching from behind the trees echoes through the grotto as Sid steps out with her arms crossed over her chest. "If all of you are done gallivanting around nude, I would like to get back to my hotel."

It's mid-afternoon by the time we get back to Sanctuary.

Allura and I go up to my old room to see Marin who has been staying there while she recovers from her ordeal. She's in good spirits and tells me to stay at the apartment as long as I want, as she's quite comfortable at Sanctuary for now.

We leave Sid complaining to the new front desk attendant about the books being wrong and climb into Art's truck to drive back to Brooklyn.

Jas and Art talk about sports of all things while Allura and I sprawl out in the backseat.

I turn from the window to Allura. The fluttering heartbeat of her babe makes my heart warm. "I can hear them now."

Her translucent wings brush against my arm like a warm caress as they beat excitedly, her eyes swimming with emotion.

I smile. "Their scent is just coming through too."

Tears fall as she rubs both hands over her flat stomach. "I can't wait to meet them," she whispers.

"Do faeries have the same gestation as humans?"

Allura sighs. "Unfortunately no. Faeries are pregnant for eleven months. Our kind jokes that the extra time is for wing growth."

My eyes widen. "Oh gods, you have to birth a child with *wings.*"

Allura laughs, patting my thigh. "Wings aren't solid until about a year old, they're almost fused to a baby's back at birth. I'll be fine."

Eleven months, which means we have around eight months left. Jas launches into a conversation about nurseries, as my gaze returns back to watching the city slide past out the window.

The amulet dulling my Alpha senses now grates on my nerves. I unclasp the necklace and put it into my bag next to me. A ripple of energy wraps around everyone in the car and then settles. My wolf brushes against my senses, alerting me of her presence but not fighting to be free.

The wolf energies ebbing and flowing outside the car are a whirlwind of sensations. I can feel that I'm on Lárusson territory and feel their Bitten population roaming the streets and parks.

I'm surprised not to feel the urge to leave the region, though. Usually, if wolves are in another territory, unauthorized or otherwise, there's a feeling of wrongness about the land, an urge to leave and go back to their own territory.

"I think it's a Lumeis thing," Art murmurs from the driver's seat.

"We don't have territory."

"Lone Wolves feel the borders too."

"True." I turn from the window to look at Art. "Do you think they can sense us?"

He catches my eye in the rearview mirror before looking back at the road. "When I was around the others before last night, they couldn't tell the difference. Now, I'm not sure."

"Please don't put yourself at any unnecessary risk if they can tell."

He nods. "Yes, Alpha."

I bark a laugh as I loop the amulet back over my head. "I will never get used to that."

We pull up at our townhouses and start unloading the car. Allura and Jas take care of the magical objects while Art and I get the personal bags, dropping them on our shared landing.

"Everyone grab their shit so I can go back to bed," Art instructs.

"My messenger bag is in the front seat," Jas murmurs as he bounces down the stairs towards the car.

Driftwood, sandalwood, and wheat scents drift on the wind. Bitten wolves. And close.

I leap off the landing towards Jas, but I'm too late; he gets tackled to the ground by a hulking male Bitten wolf. Two more appear in front of Jas, and I growl, drawing their attention.

The wolf to my right with ruddy brown skin barks a laugh. "You think you got some sway over us. I don't think so, sweetheart."

His blue-eyed buddy to my left joins in the laughter. "Where's your master, *breeder?*"

I can see Jas breathing hard on the ground. Blood tangs in my sinus. He's hurt.

"Take Allura inside," I tell Art as I lift the amulet over my head, tossing it backward, knowing one of them will retrieve it.

One of the apartment doors closes as I release control of my power. It blasts around all of us, the Bitten trio trembling at the impact, terror filling their eyes. I roll my neck and my shoulders, basking in the energy thundering through me. My wolf is ready to pounce.

"I think you should let go of my Pack member before this goes any further." My voice is mine and my wolf's, a growl lacing every word, as does an Alpha's command.

The three fight the command, Blue Eyes falling to his knees, panting. The big wolf on top of Jas scrambles off him, clutching his head as he whines in submission. The other wolf must be the leader of these assholes as I can see the struggle in his eyes, but he remains standing.

"You must be the little bitch High Alpha Jónasson is looking for."

"Do you want to find out?"

He laughs, turning and pulling Jas off the ground. He clamps down on Jas's neck, ripping flesh out and tossing him to my feet.

I see red.

A roar pierces the sky as my entire body combusts. Muscles tear, bones break, fabric disintegrates, and fur covers my body. I launch at the enemies, tearing through them in a matter of seconds.

Body parts, blood, and gore stain the sidewalk and spray up Art's car. Blood clumps in my fur and fills my mouth.

I'm in wolf form, without a full moon.

Vladislav's Penthouse

PAIN AND RAGE SLICES down the bond. As I pull out my phone, it rings.

"What happened?"

Nova's panting. "Where's Dom?"

"Down at Immortal. Where are you?"

"Townhouse. Send him. Jasper got attacked. And I, fuck, I need a day-dwelling cleanup crew."

"I'll send one. Are you okay?"

She takes in a shuddering breath. "No."

"I'll send Dom. I'll be there as soon as I can."

"Okay," she whispers and hangs up.

I send a message to Bartese for a cleanup crew and to Dom; he immediately confirms he's leaving.

I check my watch. Just under two hours until sunset, fuck.

Raking my fingers through my hair, I go to my closet and change into workout gear. I go to my gym and climb onto the treadmill, starting up a hard run. I concentrate on the rhythm of my footsteps, the view of the buildings out my window.

My phone chimes forty minutes in, with Bartese confirming the cleanup, so I forward the text to Nova and hit my run harder. Sweat beads on my head; my breathing is steady but a little faster. The phone rings an hour later, and I stop the treadmill.

"Yes?" I pant into the phone.

"This is an actual shit-show," Dom comments.

"What's going on?"

"A Rogue Pack was breezing through when they scented Aster. They went to take out Jasper, bit him, and then Carter slaughtered them. I'm surprised no humans witnessed any of this; there are limbs everywhere."

I doubt it was Carter from Nova's reaction. "How's Jasper?"

"Still alive."

"But?" I coax.

"He's in transition. Allura used her magic to knock him out for now. At least the poor bastard can get some rest before the other shit happens."

"Is cleanup there?"

"Yeah."

"I'll be there in an hour."

I park my car in front of the townhouse and pull out the duffel bag I bought with me. Everything is eerily quiet as I approach Carter's apartment door, knocking softly. The shape of wings darkens the door's frosted window as Allura pulls the door open.

The usual glow in her bronze skin is gone, even in her wings. Her aura is swimming in distress and panic. I step into the apartment and wrap my free arm around her, using my gift to ease her emotions.

"Thank you," she mumbles into my chest, then steps back toward the living room. She perches next to Carter on a coffee table in front of a large navy sofa, peering at what I'm assuming is Jasper. Dom is pacing behind an armchair on his phone to the left, near the kitchen.

"Where's Aster?" I ask the room.

Carter's eyes leave the sofa to meet mine, pointing up, then returns to his vigil over Jasper.

"She won't see anyone," Dom says, still pacing, now off his phone.

"I bought her some clothes; I'll see if I can coax her out."

Dom nods and watches me climb the narrow staircase. I follow a thread of amber rum past three doors in the hall to the door at the end. I slip into the room quickly and quietly. It's a decent-sized bedroom, with a large bed, a dresser, and a door that's cracked open to reveal a shower.

The room reeks of Carter, and blood, and Nova. The bed is still made, but I know she's here. A soft whimper whispers through the room, and my eyes flick to the window.

On an armchair facing the window overlooking the gardens below, Nova grips her knees to her chest as she rocks slightly, her amulet chain sparkling in the moonlight around her wrist.

She's naked and covered in dried blood with a thin blanket draped around her.

"Aster?" I say softly, using her other name knowing Dom is probably listening from downstairs. I approach slowly, not wanting to startle her.

Her head turns to me, eyes a blazing jade green, even in the dark. Tears stream down her face, cutting clean rivets through the dried blood on the bottom half of her face and neck.

She launches off the chair, throwing herself against my chest, wrapping herself around me. Sobs rake her body, and her tears soak my shirt. I run my hands down her hair and back.

She calms eventually, sniffing and wiping at her nose and cheeks as she pulls away. My shirt is smudged with blood. "Fuck, I'm sorry."

I tilt her chin up, watery green eyes on mine. "What happened?"

She clears her throat, pulling me to the bathroom and turning on the shower.

I discard my clothes, both of us stepping into the hot spray. The water at our feet turns a ruddy brown as Nova washes off the blood from her face, chest, and arms. She scrubs at her nails as I wash her hair, ensuring every strand is free of blood. Once she's clean, she leans into my chest, her shoulders relaxing. I turn so my back is in the spray, reveling in the feel of Nova being back in my arms.

Last night was brutal, our bond ravaged through me in the middle of Immortal, and it was almost impossible to ignore it. She was calling to me through it, begging me to find her.

"I killed them," Nova says into my chest, keeping her voice low.

"They hurt your friend."

She lifts her head, looking straight at me. "I turned and killed them."

I blink. "You turned?"

She nods. "I don't even know how I turned so fast. One second I was me, the next I was tearing them up with my wolf teeth."

"Can Carter turn at will too?"

"He turned when he heard my howl. We were losing Jas, but Allura used magic to slow the bleeding. I managed to turn back and gave Jas the choice to go or be turned. He said he wasn't finished with this life, so I gave him my blood."

"Wouldn't the bite have turned him, anyway?"

"He had lost too much blood for the bite to change him. I didn't know if it would work, giving him my blood, but I felt it, the change locked into place, and he started healing. Allura helped speed it up and even removed most of the damage as she did for my back."

"How long is the process?" I ask.

"Three days, but with our new status, I have no idea."

"New status?"

She tells me about Lumeis, Vimornium, and her new wolf form.

Allura and Nova are curled up in blankets on the floor next to Jasper. Nova is dressed now in the clothes I brought with me and one of Carter's sweaters; we also used his soaps to cover any traces of my scent around Dom.

Nova wants to wait to tell Dom, she doesn't trust him yet, which is fair enough. The bond in me however does not like smelling another male on its mate.

Carter has taken the armchair closest to his head and Dom in the other one opposite him, both watching a recorded basketball game, and I brought work with me, working from their dining table.

My eyes roam over to Nova again. She's napping with her head resting beside Jasper's while Allura reads a huge, ancient book in her lap.

Emotions rumble around me. Carter has gone past the panic and anxiety threshold into the numb stage. Allura is still stressed, but subdued as my gift continues to work its soothing magic.

Nova's emotions are dormant as she sleeps, as are Jasper's. Dom's emotions are an interesting mix of concern, anger, but mostly jealousy. A seething, oily coat of jealousy; it's an odd sensation to feel from him. His eyes flick to Nova for the briefest second before returning to the game, and lust flares, before being smothered by hurt and anger.

It clicks: Nova in Carter's clothes and that comment he made the other day. He thinks she's with Carter. He doesn't know how wrong he is.

Carter and Allura make the place light-tight, Carter offering me the spare room upstairs. Dom left as dawn peeked, saying he'll check in with Ren later today.

"*Chérie*, come upstairs and rest properly; I know you need it."

She shakes her head, settling further against the couch by Jasper's head. "I want to be here when he wakes up."

Carter collapses into his armchair. "I'll watch him, Alpha; I'll call you the moment he wakes."

She shakes her head again.

Carter and I exchange a look. I can feel the exhaustion lacing all her emotions. I bend down and scoop her up, blanket and all, making her yelp.

"Put me down," she commands.

"The fact you can't even push out of my arms is answer enough. Carter will alert us when Jasper stirs."

She sighs but stops struggling, allowing me to carry her upstairs. I place her in our borrowed bed, stripping down and climbing in next to her. We both end up tangled together as we pass out.

The flood of pain, panic, and confusion jolts me out of sleep. My eyes are immediately on Nova, but she's fast asleep on my chest. I hear whispered voices and then a groan.

"Nova, wake up. I think Jasper is conscious," I croon as I jostle her.

Her arms tighten around me briefly before she lifts her head to mine, blinking. She looks confused before realization hits her and she tries to launch out of bed.

I tense my hold around her. "He's okay, love."

She loosens a breath, dropping her back to my chest. "Gods, I'm tired."

"I can imagine."

We both get out of bed and change, making our way down to the living area. Allura sets a tray of food and coffee in front of Jasper, who has his head in his hands. Carter watches him with a creased expression from his armchair; I don't think he's moved all day. I check my phone, it's late afternoon.

Another heartbeat distracts me in the kitchen. "Delia?"

She steps into the living room with another heaping tray of food, settling it on the coffee table. "I thought everyone would need food."

Nova pulls away from me and wraps her arms around Delia. It startles the woman, but she returns the gesture, patting Nova on the back softly. Nova pulls Allura into a crushing hug, then Carter, and then turns to Jasper, dropping to her knees, tears in her eyes.

"I'm so sorry," her voice breaks.

I can't see Jasper's face, but he lays a hand on her cheek. "Thank you."

Nova blinks. "For what?"

"What do you mean, 'for what'? You saved my life."

"I doomed you to an existence you shouldn't have."

Jasper chuckles softly. "You keep forgetting I was literally raised by wolves. And my best friend and roommate is also a werewolf. I was already in this world, babe."

"But—"

"But nothing. What's done is done; I'm confident this was my fate all along."

Nova's shoulders relax as she leans her forehead into Jasper's thigh and he wraps an arm around her shoulders.

I draw closer to the group, sitting in the other armchair. There's scarring along Jasper's neck, light pink contrasting on his golden skin. His hair is all over the place, but he looks good, different.

"You aren't wearing your glasses," I comment.

Jasper turns to me. "I don't need them anymore." His nose twitches, and he grimaces. "You smell like an entire orchard of burning peaches."

The room erupts in laughter; the tension breaking. Nova stands from the floor, stepping over Jasper and Allura and settling into my lap. "This peach is all mine, so don't get any ideas."

Jasper laughs, pulling the entire tray of food Allura brought over into his lap. "Yes, Alpha."

We all eat as Carter and Nova educate Jasper on being a wolf.

"When am I going to turn for the first time?" he asks Nova.

She sighs, leaning over to put her plate down before settling back against my chest. "Honestly, I don't know."

Carter stands and starts collecting plates. "The first full moon is usually a Bitten's 'transition.' But they rarely turn into a wolf unless they are with First Bloods. Being Lumeis, who knows. Do you feel a wolf?"

Jasper nods. "Crawling under my skin, restless."

"Maybe we should go to Sid's tonight?" Allura offers. "Use the basement?"

Nova turns to me, forehead creased. "What do you think?"

I blink. She's asking for my opinion. "I'm not very versed in wolf matters."

Nova smiles. "Honestly, this is out of my ballpark, too."

I turn to Jasper. "Do you feel you need to turn?"

He nods, raking his fingers through his hair. His movements are smoother, more tactile.

"I think you should go with your instinct. If you think you need to turn, the safest place in the city to do it would be Sidelle's."

Nova leans down and gives me a swift kiss before turning to the group. "I'll call and let her know we'll be there just after sunset."

We arrive at an unusually somber Sanctuary. Sidelle must have informed everyone that the bar was closed for the night in case things go differently than planned. The silver-haired human greets us at the front desk, leading us to a hall on the left, and a heavy metal door.

She turns to the group. "No one apart from Nova and Jasper can pass the stairs."

We all nod before she opens the door, pulling it with some effort. The space is dimly lit by small sconces on the walls leading down. We descend into the warm, narrow space two at a time, with Nova and Jasper leading.

Nova takes her amulet off and hands it to Allura before she and Jasper cross the threshold into the large room, leaving the rest of us at the base of the stairs. I can feel the pulsing of the spell in front of me, images of rain in the forest flashing in my head.

"Who created this spell?" I ask, my hand twitching at my side, the urge to run my hand over it strong.

Allura steps up next to me, lifting a glowing hand to the ward. "Is that...Celestial magic?"

"Yes," Sid confirms.

"It feels familiar," Allura muses to herself.

Allura drops her hand and my gaze returns to Nova and Jasper. They sit on the floor in the middle of the room with their eyes closed, both in their underwear, breathing deep. After a few moments, Nova opens her eyes, turning her head to mine. Her eyes glow her wolf's, a deep sapphire with gold flecks.

Her nostrils flare, and then she tilts her head back. I think she's howling, but no sound passes through the barrier. The ground beneath us trembles for a few seconds as both of them fall to their sides, shuddering and panting, and behind me, Carter growls.

My eyes don't leave Nova; her arms contort, snapping the wrong way. Her wrists, elbows, and knees pop and dislocate, now wolf legs. She gets on all fours as her torso expands, stretching, and her skin covers in black fur. Her face reforms, muzzle replacing her small straight nose and sharp jaw.

The wolf in front of me pants with her head down. Nova's fur looks as if it's made from the shadows themselves, black that absorbs the light.

"Remarkable," Sid whispers. "She was white as pure as snow the last time she turned here."

"Jasper seems to be okay," Carter comments.

My eyes drag away from Nova to Jasper. He's also a black wolf, but his coat reflects the lights in the room. He has gold tipping his ears, and his eyes are the same gold-flecked sapphire. Those eyes dart around the room, taking in his surroundings, and when they land on Nova, he lowers them immediately, bowing his head.

She turns her attention to him, taking in his stance, and then rubs her muzzle against his ear then steps back. Jasper lifts his head apprehensively before Nova launches herself at him.

I jolt forward before remembering the barrier, and it zaps me.

Carter chuckles. "Don't worry, Vlad, they're just building a Pack bond. They'll play for a while."

I watch the two wolves pounce, and nip, and chase, making a smile creep onto my face. "Incredible," I whisper.

Nova's head whips to me as if she heard me. No, she *definitely* heard me.

She bounds over to the barrier, standing in front of me. Her eyes blaze, searching my face. I hold out my hand, careful not to touch the barrier. Her attention focuses on the hand, and she lurches into the barrier. It zaps her, making her stumble back, shaking her head.

Carter chuckles. "You two seriously need to complete your bond."

Allura giggles. "I agree. Get a room already."

I smirk, dropping my hand; I also concur with their assessment.

Jasper bounds up to Nova, concern in his eyes. She shakes her head again and then tilts it back, a silent howl. The ground trembles again, and the wolves fall. The change back is swift, fur disappearing, bones realigning. The barrier disintegrates as soon as Nova and Jasper are in their usual form, sweating and panting.

I cross the threshold straight to Nova, bending down onto my haunches, unsure if I should touch her. Her scent is thick in the room; my eyes roll back and close as it coats my senses. The bond floods my system, our emotions crashing together in an indiscernible wave around me.

I open my eyes to see Nova push herself into a sitting position on shaky arms, snagging the t-shirt placed next to her and pulling it on. Her eyes greet mine, and they flash between sapphire and jade, an exhausted smile softening her features.

"Beautiful," I murmur as I trace her jaw lightly.

Her smile deepens as I take her hands, pulling her up to her feet. Allura sticks out leggings, and Nova accepts them, her eyes not leaving mine, and pulls them on. She launches herself onto me, wrapping her legs around my waist, her arms around my neck as I catch her and crashing her lips into mine.

"Take me home," she murmurs between kisses.

"We won't make it to Brooklyn."

She pulls back, jade eyes blazing. "Not Brooklyn. The Penthouse."

Something in me bursts. Home. She's home.

I take a few steps with Nova still wrapped around me when her phone shrills through the space.

Her eyes don't leave mine. "Ignore it; let's get out of here."

As I reach the stairs, a few messages chime.

"Gods," Nova groans, climbing off me, accepting the phone from an amused Allura, reading the screen. "What the fuck?"

"What is it, *chérie*?"

Her phone rings again; this time, she answers it. "Kristjan?" Her brother?

"Nova, we're coming."

"What?" she stammers, her eyes locked on mine.

"The whole Pack. Dad knows you're in New York, and we're leaving right now."

"How?"

"Get out of there, Nova. We'll be there tomorrow night. Go."

39

Nova

Sanctuary Hotel

IT'S HAPPENING. TRULY HAPPENING.

Just as I... as I found my people. My home.

I stare at the blank phone in my hand. Tears sting my eyes. "I have to go."

Xander's eyes narrow. "What?"

Art steps forward.

I clear my throat, stumbling back towards the stairs. "I have to get out of here."

"What's happening?" Xander asks. The bond rumbles in panic.

"Nova," Art pleads, "you don't have to leave."

I can't look at him, any of them, not when I have to go. I stare hard at the floor, taking another step back. "My father and the Pack are coming. I have to go."

"No," Xander declares, stepping forward. I take another step back.

"I'm sorry I've been such a burden to all of you; I'll be out of New York by tonight." I turn to the stairs.

A scorching hold on my wrist wrenches me back. I break my fall by slamming my palm into a granite-hard chest; cedarwood and peach swirling around me. I choke on a sob.

Both of his hands cup my face as he tilts my head up, forcing me to look into his eyes. His beautiful eyes. They swirl bourbon and amber with whispers of blue.

"I will never let you go," his voice is filled with so many things. "Do you hear me? You don't get to run away from this. From *us*. Do you understand that?"

Tears slide down my face. "Xander, please, just let me go," my voice is barely a whisper.

"No."

"Don't put yourself in the middle of a war that I started. I'm not worth it."

Dark bourbon consumes his irises, anger piercing down the bond. "Not *worth* it?" he spits. "God, how many times do I need to remind you that you are? I will do nothing else in my life but set you free. And if that means forfeiting my own life for yours, then I will fucking do it. You mean everything. *Everything.*"

He pulls me into a bruising kiss, and all the air leaves my lungs. I paw at his back, making sure *this* is real. That *he* is real.

He pulls back, anger still thundering around us, but another feeling piercing through our bond: family—a family without ulterior motives. I look around Xander at the others. My heart tears apart. Art catches my eye, and he nods. My Beta is ready to go down with no hesitations.

He balls up his fist, crossing his arm over his chest, bowing swiftly. "Pack, until the end."

Jas does the same; his expression is just as hard as Art's.

Allura leaps forward, pulling me from Xander and crushing herself around me. She says nothing, but I feel it. Pack. Family. She pulls away, stepping to Art's side, who wraps his arm around her.

Sid comes into view. "Decide where you want to be, babygirl." Her eyes flick to Xander and back to me, then she walks out of the basement.

"We'll go get supplies from the townhouse," Art announces as he pulls Allura with him, Jas trailing after them.

I turn my attention back to Xander. He's still intensely angry, but it's under control. "The Penthouse?"

I nod, slipping my hand into his and the amulet over my head as he calls Dom to meet us at Sanctuary. Xander gathers my duffel bag, and we exit the basement. As Dom's sports car purrs into the driveway, I let go of Vlad's hand and get into Dom's car.

The drive to Xander's building isn't long, but the silent tension presses in on me. I practically jump out of the car when Dom stops in the alley behind the building. I fumble with my keys, getting the door open, jogging down the stairs, and bashing on the elevator button. I tap my foot as I wait for the damn thing to make its way down as Xander appears next to me.

He says nothing, but I can feel the storm about to erupt down the bond. We step into the elevator, the doors sliding closed silently as I hit the top floor's button. We shoot up, rising higher and higher, the tension palpable. I feel caged. Trapped.

"Fuck," I whisper as the doors slide open, and I storm out of the confines, down the hall.

Before I get to the door, Xander appears in front of it, and I stop short of slamming into him. His eyes burn as he takes a step forward, making me retreat. He takes another, and I try to sidestep him, but Xander's fast, stepping in my way, knocking me back towards the wall. I scramble, my heart in my throat, pressing my back into the cool surface as he looms over me, close but not touching.

"Why are you trying to run away?" The exact words he said to me when the mate bond surfaced.

My heart constricts. "I have to."

His eyes narrow. "No, you don't."

"They'll follow me and leave you all alone."

"What type of life will you have if you're always running?"

I swallow. "No life at all, that's the point."

Xander blinks, and I use the distraction to slide away and towards the door, entering the access code and stepping into... home.

I catch a sob before it escapes, taking every detail in. I feel Xander behind me; the door closing with a click. "If you're leaving, why are you here?"

"I need to see it one last time."

Xander is in front of me, both hands buried in my hair. I'm expecting anger or hurt in his eyes, but they are alight with determination, searching mine desperately. "If you want to leave, fine, go. But don't leave unless I'm the future you're coming back to."

"What?"

He steps forward, pressing me into the door, forehead resting on mine. "I'll let you go," he whispers, "if that's what you think you need. Go, escape across the realms, but you'll be coming home to me. I'll wait for you."

"Why? Why would you wait?"

He lifts his head, his eyes going near black. "Because bond or not, *this* was inevitable. We are one and the same. We do anything for our people, give too much, feel too much. We work hard, love hard, fight hard, and probably fuck harder."

I shudder, my eyelids drooping closed as his words sink into my skin. Were we destined to find each other even without the bond? One and the same, he said.

Two souls, tortured and scarred, expected to wilt but determined to break the system, create a new one.

I open my eyes to my future: my amber and blue destiny.

The bond sings between us as I wrap my arms around his neck, pouring everything into a branding kiss. Tears fall freely as our tongues war, desperate and consuming. My hands grip his silky locks as Xander slides his hands down my body, lifting me by the thighs and wrapping my legs around him.

The air rushes past me as I cling to Xander, and then he's pressing me into his bedsheets. I pull away from his mouth, panting, looking into his now bourbon eyes. "I see you. All of you."

His eyes shudder. "You're all I'll ever see."

I tear open his shirt, buttons flying. The rest of his clothes and mine disappear, leaving both of us panting and naked. I sit up, lifting my hair and tilting my head down. Xander unclasps the amulet, placing it on the nightstand.

The bond unleashes in an inferno of unfulfilled desire; it's a desperate, broken connection to each other, and white-hot, demanding *love*.

My breath hitches as I pull Xander down, rolling us, so I'm straddling him. My mouth returns to his, needing to taste him, feel him. His hands run down my back, feeling every inch of skin going lower, settling on my hips.

I grind against the length of him, coating him in my wetness. A groan rumbles through his chest and into my mouth, his hand holding my hips down, grinding me harder against him.

I lift my hips slightly, snaking a hand down between us, gripping his cock, guiding the tip to my entrance. I sink slowly, so slowly, onto his thick tip. Just an inch. My breath hitches, the stretch burning, biting. I ease down another inch, getting accustomed to the burning, becoming addicted to the stretch.

Xander is impossibly still, his hands still gripping my hips hard but not moving, letting me set the pace. I sink another inch, pushing myself up from his chest. I feel his breathing, controlled and deep. But his heartbeat, it's actually *racing*. Strong and erratic.

I lock eyes with Xander. They're hooded, blazing amber and blue, focused on mine. I sink down to the hilt, my eyes rolling back and my spine arching.

"*Fuck*," I moan.

"Easy, *chérie*," Xander grinds out of a locked jaw, making me clench around him.

I whimper. I'm full, so *fucking* full that I might break. I lift my hips slowly, almost the whole length, before easing back down, sending shock waves through my entire system as his cock drags along nerve endings I didn't even know existed.

I repeat the motion, the burn disappearing, as I ride Xander slowly. My hips relax, the movements smoother, taking him deeper, easier, finding a rhythm.

The next lift, Xander moves, meeting me with a hard thrust as I come back down, ripping a growl, or a sob, out of me.

He sits up, our bodies pressed together, his arms wrapping around me. Our gazes lock. "Did I hurt you, *mon amour*?"

I shake my head, panting. "Do it again."

His gaze turns feral as he twists, pressing me into the mattress. He pulls out to the tip and then slams back into me. I choke on a whimper, and he does it again, forcing the air out of my lungs.

"Ah, fuck, *Xander*," I whimper, wrapping my legs around his waist as he thrusts again, hard, rough, branding.

He lets go, unleashing an unrelenting rhythm, sending me into a delirium. I meet his thrusts, needing him deeper, harder, everywhere.

His mouth lands on my aching nipples, torturing one at a time. His hand grips my hair, his other one replacing his mouth on my breast, as he shoves his tongue into my mouth. I claw at his back, drawing blood, making him growl and slam into me harder, our hip bones crashing into each other.

He stills, completely sheathed, his mouth pulling away from me. His pupils are wide, almost all the color gone, and he breathes hard.

"You're *mine*, Nova," he growls with the next thrust.

I grip his hair tight. "And you're mine."

He responds with another powerful thrust. And again, and again. His fangs drop.

I turn my head. "Do it."

His eyes trace the lines of my neck and shoulder as he stills. His eyes flick to mine. "This means eternity."

"Yes," I whisper, "eternity."

Xander leans down, kissing me tenderly, his lips trailing kisses from my mouth, across my jaw to that tender spot just below my ear. I shiver, pressing my thighs around him, my hands grip his shoulders. They harden and shift under my touch as I feel the tips of one pair of fangs dragging up the column of my neck.

I clench hard around his cock, getting impossibly wetter. This time Xander shudders, his tongue now tracing the trail his fang made. His hand slips between us. He rears his head back barely an inch before plunging his fangs in my neck, as his thumb finds my clit, circling hard.

I erupt in a scream, clamping down on Xander's cock, the orgasm ripping through me. Xander moves again, as he marks me as his inside and out, thrusting frantically, consuming me, breaking me.

Xander lifts his head from my neck, his mouth smeared with blood as he crushes his mouth to mine. I taste the saltiness of my blood and his fire. My jaw aches as I pull back, a hand pulling Xander's hair, exposing his neck. My wolf canines push through, and I sink them into the flesh of his shoulder, marking him as *mine*.

He roars as his blood spilling into my mouth. Salt, peaches, smoke. His thumb continues the torturous circles over my clit, making my back arch and my bite detach, sending me over the edge again as he buries himself, coming apart with me.

The bond between us forges and mends old and new wounds, the scattered pieces of my heart reshaping into something new, something not entirely mine. I feel Xander there, in the spaces that were once hollow, once broken. Pieces of me settle into him, the tethers of our bond creating something that will only be broken by death.

Xander drops his head to my shoulder, both of us panting. My body feels weightless, but my soul whole and settled. I trail light fingers over the ridges of Xander's back muscles, basking in the shudders it produces. He pulls out of my body slowly, my muscles aching in wicked tenderness. Xander rolls onto his back, pulling me on top of him, wrapping his arms around me.

I rest my head on his chest, my fingers finding the lines of his tattoos. "They are beautiful."

The lines are sharp, arching and flowing across his skin, the whisps weaving together but never touching. Xander lifts his arms, allowing me to continue exploring, tracing a particularly long, dark tendril under his arm and back around toward his elbow.

"It tells the story of my life," Xander mumbles, "each tendril is a year of my existence; the deeper the color, the more lives I took that year."

I lift my head. "Why did you decide to detail that onto your skin?"

"As a reminder of who I was and who I don't want to be any longer."

I look back at the tattoo. A symphony of shadows telling the song of destruction, a lullaby of sorrow, a life once lived. "How did you get it tattooed with supernatural healing?"

Xander's lips lift into a lazy grin. "Liquid silver in the ink. The exposure isn't enough to poison me, but it leaves the ink."

"That's the same method we use, but with wolfsbane." I lift my elbow, showing him the tattoo on my arm.

"Kris and I got this for our twenty-first birthday."

Vlad traces over the moons with a soft touch. "What's the saying, 'beauty is pain'?"

"No wonder I hurt every time I look at you."

He chuckles. "Would you like me to kiss it better?"

I lean up, my lips brushing his. "Maybe I want you to make it hurt more?"

His eyes darken. "Is that a challenge?"

"It might be."

"You don't want to bring that side out of me, Nova."

My tongue darts out, running along his bottom lip. "Give me everything."

A scorching hold grips my throat, and the air blasts around me as I'm slammed into the wall. Xander's body pushes into me, his eyes dark bourbon staring into mine. His grip tightens around my neck, my breath catching, his hard erection jumping against my stomach. My muscles roll, clenching hard, and I'm wet, quivering.

I arch my back, my nipples rubbing on Xander's chest. He hooks my knee over his forearm, lifting me, and sinking into me in one move, a groan vibrating low in his throat.

My eyes roll back as I wrap my legs around his waist, choking on a moan. His hand around my throat doesn't falter as he fucks me slow, hard, and deep. The world dims, stars dancing in my vision as the lack of oxygen makes me lightheaded—Xander's thrusts quicken.

My body is heavy, an orgasm on the precipice taunting me with oblivion.

Xander's hand slides from my hip, his thumb finding my clit, and I fall over into ecstasy. The hand on my throat disappears, and I scream my orgasm, the oxygen returning to my body igniting an inferno, my entire body alight. Xander slams into me once, twice, before roaring his own release, his arms wrapping around me, taking both of us to the floor, still buried deep in me.

We get off the floor after the world pieces itself together, both getting into the shower. The steamy hard pressure does wonders on my tender body, as well as the sweeping touches from Xander. After we're both clean, we change into clean clothes and force ourselves to the kitchen.

I fight the need to beg to be fucked across the kitchen island as I open the fridge door, looking for anything to distract me. Xander's arms snake around me, pressing his erection into my ass.

"Don't tempt me," he purrs into my ear.

My body vibrates from the exertion of keeping my body still. Odin, help me.

The front door opens, and multiple footsteps approach.

"Thank the Gods," Art chuckles as he enters with Allura and Jas. I shut the fridge, turning towards my Pack, Xander keeping his hold around me.

Jas's face screws up. "You two reek of sex."

Xander's chest shakes with laughter, and I shrug. Allura rolls her eyes, floating over to the breakfast table with two duffel bags, the other two following her.

"Smells like you finally got laid, Xander," Ren's voice comes from the foyer. He rounds the corner, humor blazing in his eyes.

He takes in our embrace, and then his face slackens, eyes locked on mine.

"I can hear you."

I frown. "What?"

His eyes turn emerald green as he taps his temple. "I can *hear* you."

My hand drifts to my neck; I'm not wearing the amulet. Ren stalks forward, focused on me, his muscles bulking in size.

Xander pushes me behind him, sizing up his brother. "Renard."

Ren pauses and blinks, his eyes going to Xander. He sucks in a breath. "Sorry, I got stuck. All her thoughts overwhelmed me." Ren's usual cobalt eyes return to me, his face softening. "I'm sorry."

I frown again. "For what?"

"I caught thoughts about your past. You deserved better."

I step around Xander, placing a hand on Ren's heart, his slow heartbeat barely detectable. *You also deserved better too.*

His eyes shutter as he covers my hand with his, dropping his head. He releases a second later, a devious smile lighting up his face. "Eternity is going to be much more interesting now."

40

Vladislav's Penthouse

○

WE'VE BEEN ARGUING ABOUT the best way to deal with the Jónasson Pack's impending arrival.

The only thing we agree on is that we're all staying in the building for the advantage of being in the skies and strength in numbers.

"We should tell Dom," Ren argues, "maybe he can talk the Lárusson Pack into helping us."

Art pushes out of his chair, pacing in front of the window. "We can't trust Dom."

"That's a brother you're talking about," Ren warns.

"He's a Lone Wolf; he only thinks about himself," Art counters, sitting back in his chair. "And High Alpha Izar is worse. He'd be brokering a deal with Jónasson for Nova faster than any of them."

"We're going to be ambushed," Ren breathes, running his hands through his hair.

Everyone is quiet, letting that sink in. Emotions of frustration and concern filter through the group, but there's a thread of resignation coming from Nova. She fishes out her phone and dials a number. It rings twice before I hear someone answer.

"Daughter," the voice croons.

Everyone's attention focuses on Nova. "Central Park."

"Excuse me?"

"Find me in Central Park at sunset tomorrow." She hangs up.

The emotions in the room turn into a torrent of outrage ready to burst, but Nova raises her hand. "Controlled bait. Now we know where they'll be, and we can make a plan."

Our bond sizzles with Nova's Alpha command, and both Carter and Jasper try to fight it. They're protective bastards.

Good.

Nova stands from the table and takes a small paring knife from the magnetic strip it's stuck to on the wall.

"Jas," she calls, rolling up the sleeves of her sweater.

He stalks over, his aura sour, but mostly confused. "Yes?"

"Roll up your sleeve."

"Why?"

"Just do it," she growls. He does it immediately. Nova meets his eyes, and her eyes switch to sapphire and gold. "As High Alpha of the Zephyrus Pack, I offer you the position of High Beta."

His eyes widen, and Allura gasps from the table.

"The position is for a lifetime," she continues, "and could potentially mean your death. But I trust you with my life, and like Art, like all our Pack members, I will never take you for granted. We will change it, all of it, and we'll leave this world a better place."

Jas drops to one knee, arm over his chest, head bowed. "It's an honor." His voice comes out rushed, his emotions swirling with a multitude of things. "I, Jasper Yoshida, as Lumeis, offer my loyalty and allegiance to you as my High Alpha. I accept the position of High Beta and offer my services to you and the pack until my dying day."

"I, Nova Jónasdóttir, accept you, Jasper, as High Beta of the Zephyrus Pack. As High Alpha, I shall endeavor to lead with integrity and strength to ensure our protection, continued prosperity, and peace for generations to come."

Jasper stands, and they both slice their forearms and palms, then grasp in a warrior's embrace. I can feel their wolf energies through my bond to Nova, which is an odd sensation. I almost feel energized.

Jasper lifts his head and scoops Nova up into his arms, twirling her around, letting tears fall freely as they both laugh.

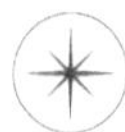

Everyone retreats to the guest bedrooms, Ren going to his apartment downstairs with Allura. Nova pulls me back to our room and immediately fishes one of my t-shirts from my closet. The bond warms at the fact that she wants to wear my clothes over her own.

She turns to me, eyes and aura concerned as she slides off her pants. "Are you okay with this plan?"

I nod. "It's a sound plan." My anger slips through the bond.

Nova rubs over her heart. "I can feel that."

I wrap my arms around her, eyes narrowed. "I just found you, and your own family is trying to take you away from me."

"This is the best chance we have at getting them to let me go."

"You don't need to get their permission; you're already free."

She traces my jaw with a light touch. "I'll never be free of them unless my father acknowledges that I'm no longer his property."

I sigh, resting his forehead against hers. "I hate this."

"Me too."

"Can't I just tear him to pieces and be done with it?"

Nova laughs softly. "It's the easy way out for that asshole. Listening to him accept me as his equal will be much, much more satisfying."

"He should pay for his indiscretions with his entire weight in flesh," I growl.

"So bloodthirsty," she chuckles as she catches my bottom lip with her teeth.

I wake alone. Panic washes over me and I bolt upright, tugging on our bond, looking around the empty room. The room's door is open, did she leave? Nova's amused response douses my worries and settles me instantly. She's safe, somewhere in the penthouse.

I check my phone; it's the middle of the day. Purposefully heavy steps sound down the hall, and I hear the door of either my office or the gym open.

Ren's deep chuckle filters toward me. "You know you won't tan in here."

"I know," Nova says as I climb out of bed and find my sweats. "You're here early."

"I could hear you screaming in my head."

Surprise bubbles down the bond. "What?" she asks.

I hear steps and then Ren sighs. "The magic in that stone you wear is powerful because you have a really loud head. Second to Xander, only because we're blood. Most of the time, I just hear words from people, and sometimes, I see images. Yesterday, I got a cacophony of things from you."

"That would have been fun for you," Nova muses.

"You were thinking about boning my brother, like *a lot.*"

I hear a thump and a short chuckle from Ren before it goes quiet again. "You were also thinking about the bond, and your asshole father, and..." He trails off and then he clears his throat. "I saw it, scorching into my synapses, the barn. Your...mother." He must have seen Nova's mother's demise through her memories. I can feel the whispers of Ren's devastation even from a few rooms away.

It's quiet from the two as I collect my phone and Nova's, slip on a shirt and quietly leave the room.

"I'm assuming by now Xander has told you about our past," Ren muses. "So seeing that image and knowing you were so young... it will haunt me."

"I'm sorry you had to see that," Nova says softly.

"I'm sorry we weren't there to get you out earlier."

It's quiet again as I approach the door.

"You're family now," Ren proclaims, "so I'll always have your back."

I step into the doorway to find Nova and Ren sitting on the floor by the window, both watching the sky, Nova resting her head on Ren's bicep. Now with the bond completed, I don't have the urge to murder him for being this close to her.

Comfortable? I ask Ren in his head.

His head turns to me and he smiles. *You should get help for the stalking tendencies.*

I roll my eyes as I enter the room. *Remind me that I owe Maddox money for our little wager. He said you'd flirt with Nova the first night.*

Asshole, Ren pushes into my head as I sink onto the floor next to Nova.

"What took you so long?" she says, not moving from her position.

"Ren has seen me naked enough for several lifetimes, so I thought I'd put pants on."

Nova lifts her head and turns her heated gaze at me, lust swirling in our bond. "I haven't seen you naked enough."

"Disgusting," Ren groans as stands. "Please clean up when you're done."

41

Central Park, Manhattan

A FTER A VERY NAKED afternoon with Xander, I cross the road, and venture into Central Park as the sun sets.

I haven't stepped foot in it since arriving in New York, but I could always feel the strong Bitten presence stalking the park. But tonight, the energy is quieter than usual, like they had the sense that shit is about to go down.

I doubt my father has notified High Alpha Izar that he's in his territory. He wouldn't want to acknowledge his failings at not knowing his wayward daughter was living under Lárusson's nose this whole time.

I stop in a wide clearing, knowing we'd be shielded from human eyes being this far into the park. It doesn't take long for my family's scents to swirl around me: amber rum, cherrywood, and freshly cut grass.

My father stalks across the clearing, followed by all my brothers. My heart pangs in my chest. I miss my brothers, deeply miss them.

But despite feeling the loss of them in my life, anger bubbles in me as my eyes sweep across the faces of the men who were supposed to protect me.

Why didn't they protect me?

The Pack gets closer, and my eyes land on Kristjan. I school my face to look blank, but my heart is leaping from my chest. I want to sob and throw my arms around him. My wolf, who's mostly suppressed under the magic of the amulet, whimpers in the abyss; he's the piece missing from my new home. Movement behind him snatches my attention—the scent of hydrangeas.

My head whips to my father's stupid, smirking face with a scowl. "You brought Patricia as well? Really, Dad?"

He doesn't deign me with an answer.

My eyes flick back to my sister-in-law, who's half-hidden behind Kris and Junior. Her eyes are soft, shining with happy tears. "Hi," she mouths.

How I desperately want to fall into her arms as well and tell her about everything. But if she's here, then...

"You brought a *baby* here as well?" I boom, seeing the tiny bundle strapped across Pat's torso. I turn my fury toward my father.

His eyes darken, gold flashing through them as he stops about a yard away from me. "As High Alpha, I can summon whoever I want to a meeting."

"What the fuck is wrong with you?"

His eyes flicker gold again. "Watch your tone. You're already a betrayer to your blood. Don't make me add more to your punishment when we get home."

I scoff. "I am home."

"You are *my* daughter, and a member of *my* Pack; you're returning with me at once."

I cross my arms over my chest. "You stopped being my father the day you put your hands on me."

"I have every right to punish you as I see fit."

"You have no right to treat *anyone* like your personal punching bag."

He waves a dismissive hand toward me. "Stop wasting your breath." He turns to his left, looking into the clearing. "Step forward and claim your prize, wolf."

Teakwood and honeycomb scents hit me then as Dominic walks into the clearing, stopping at my father's side.

Fury rages through me, and I let it show. *Dominic.* The fucking traitorous bastard.

His brown eyes search mine, confused. "Don't you want your Pack back?"

My wolf rears up, pushing against her magic stronghold, begging me to let her tear his throat out. "No, I don't."

"Because of the way they treated you last time?" He steps toward me slowly, carefully, like he's approaching a wounded animal. "It'll be different this time. You'll have me at your side."

"I want to be free."

"You can have the best of both. Pack and freedom."

I take an involuntary step back, Dom tracking the movement. "You think *exactly* like them, Dom. How am I supposed to believe anything you say?"

Another two steps. I'm almost within reach. "I told you already. I'd never see you like that. You can be you. With me."

"I don't want you."

Dom's face falls.

My father's laugh booms behind him. "Nova, you forget that you have no choice. The hunt I issued states that the person who found you has the right to mate you. And Dominic will become a High Beta among your brothers as promised."

I narrow my eyes onto Dom, shoving at his chest. "You sold me out for a *position?*"

His eyes flash copper as he catches my wrists. "I didn't sell you out; I saved you."

I try to get out of his grip, but he squeezes tighter, pulling me closer to him. "You don't even know these wolves, Dom. You especially don't know him. You just sold your soul to a madman."

"Why are you fighting the inevitable?" he whispers, his scent swirling around me, making me want to gag.

"You betrayed me, and you betrayed Vlad, for what? An Alpha who'll use you like fodder? Did you not hear about what happened to Eros?"

"Viggo had every right to do what he did."

Old fury ignites as I shove Dom with a force that sends him on his ass. "No wonder your other Pack doesn't want you."

Dom scrambles to his feet, copper eyes blazing. Before he can take a step forward, growls erupt through my brothers as they scent the air.

"Another Pack," Stefan grumbles.

I take a few quick steps back as Art and Jas appear behind me. Art drapes an arm over my shoulders while Jas smirks at my previous Pack with his arms crossed over his chest.

"Hey, assholes," Art drawls, pulling me closer to him.

Dom growls. "Get your hands off her, Art."

He laughs. "Why?"

"She's *mine*."

He laughs harder. "I don't think so."

Dom stupidly launches forward, which results in Art landing a powerful punch to his face, sending Dom scrambling again.

My father steps forward, his Alpha energy pulsing out of him. "Let go of the girl, pup, and stay out of First Blood business."

Both Art and Jas erupt into laughter, and I smirk. My father's eyes blaze liquid gold as he straightens. "As a High Alpha, I command you to release my property."

Rage slams through me as I pull away from Art. He still snickers behind me. "How very wrong you are, dude."

"Your blatant disrespect just signed your death warrant."

"You'd have to approve that with my Alpha," Art argues.

"High Alpha Izar will agree with me."

Jas chuckles. "This guy is an idiot."

Dad turns his attention to Jas. "You're now dead too."

My turn to laugh. "Too bad you won't have a chance to act on those threats."

"You know nothing of it," he seethes, "you're nothing but a body to warm Dominic's bed and bear his children. He can fuck, beat, or kill you as he pleases. Know your place."

Suddenly, two of my brothers are behind me. They grab Art, who fights their grip and snarls curses. One of them knocked out poor Jas.

An arm wraps around my waist, pulling me back into a hot body.

"There's no point fighting this, Nova," Dom growls into my ear. His teeth are too close to my neck, luckily my mate mark is on the other side. My heartbeat goes into overdrive as he pulls me towards my father, his nose on the flesh just below my ear, inhaling deeply.

Fuck. I push at his arm; I need out. Trapped. No. I can't be. I kick my legs out, but Dom's arms are steel around me. He growls again, teeth scraping my flesh. I force my elbows behind me like I did to Art in training; the move doing the trick as Dom's arm loosens, allowing me to push forward.

I turn, and white light blinds me as pain explodes through my cheek, radiating through my jaw.

"Oh shit," Art breathes behind me. "I would run if I were you, Dom."

I look up with teary eyes, cradling my face, to see Dom flying backward, landing at my father's feet. I turn to where Xander is adjusting his cufflinks. He pops one hand in his suit pants pocket, with a lazy smile across his mouth but death in his eyes.

He holds his free hand out towards me, eyes on the Pack, not even caring about what's going on behind him. I slip my hand into his, allowing him to pull me up.

"This is wolf business; I suggest you leave," my father warns.

"I had every intention of staying out of it, but I don't condone violence against women in my city."

"Stay out of this, Vlad," Dom spits, now upright next to my father.

"You made it my business when you put hands on Nova."

My father seethes. "Who the fuck do you think you are?"

Xander smirks. "I want to say your worst nightmare, but she now takes that title." Xander holds out his hand out to me again.

I grasp the amulet, pulling the chain over my head, dropping it in his hand. My wolf stretches out, rising up to the surface, and Alpha energy pours out of me.

All eyes burn into me, shock shared through the whole Pack. My brothers are all confused, except Kris. He has wild amusement marring his entire face as he cackles. Pat has a slight smile on her face beside him, and so does Junior. Dom's mouth gapes open, and my father's eyes are gold pools of fury.

"You are so fucked, Dad," Kris comments, still laughing.

His head whips to Kris. "Shut your mouth, *runt.*"

Kris laughs harder, strolling away from our family towards me.

"What is the meaning of this?" Dad booms, eyes glaring at Kris.

Kris sighs as he comes up to stand beside me. "*Fuck you*, is the meaning of this."

"As your father and High Alpha, I command you to—"

"I renounce my ties to the Jónasson Pack and offer my loyalty and allegiance to Nova as my High Alpha," Kris announces.

"*High* Alpha?" Stefan spits, stepping in front of our father.

"Impossible," Dad seethes.

I snort. "Are you going blind with your old age?"

He puffs up, calculating the threat. "I'm the High Alpha of Jónasson Pack; what black magic have you poisoned yourself with?"

I fold my arms over my chest. "I'm no longer part of the Jónasson Pack."

He crosses his arms. "And which High Alpha do you serve now?"

"Is your hearing going too? I *am* a High Alpha."

"Are you taking Lux? Are you a delusional junkie whore now?"

Junior sidles up to our father. "You shouldn't insult a High Alpha like that, Father." I don't let my surprise cross my face at Junior's acknowledgment of my new status. My heart warms.

Dad's eyes burn into Junior, making him flinch. "You should watch your tone, boy."

"Just because you don't want to admit it to yourself, Nova is a High Alpha."

"You've gone soft since you've had a child, son. Females can't be High Alphas, and Nova is my property until the day she stops breathing."

I turn to my other brothers holding the rest of my Pack. "Release my High Beta and return to your Pack."

The Alpha energy pours out of me as all three wolves balk, releasing Art, retreating to my father as Art rouses Jas.

I turn back to Dom, stepping up to my father's side but then stills, head whipping to Xander, and then me. His nose flares and his eyes burn copper. "No."

Xander laughs that menacing, deep, sensual chuckle. "Oh, yes," he purrs.

Our merged scents must carry across to the rest of them because they all stare at Xander. He sighs beside me, wrapping an arm around my waist. "Now that we've distinguished that Nova is no longer part of your Pack or under your instruction, it's best you leave our city before things escalate."

Our city. Gods, I love him.

Fury pulses off my father, his breathing labored, eyes on the arm around me.

Junior grips his forearm. "Let's go. You can call a High Alpha meeting and discuss it amongst the four of you."

My father turns, punching Junior through the ribs; the sound of his hand crushing his heart in his chest echoes in my head. Blood sprays. Junior's face slackens as his lifeless body drops to the ground.

I erupt, a roar ripping through my vocal cords as I turn immediately, charging for my father.

Junior. His own son. My brother.

Horror coats my father's face as he takes in my wolf. I slam him to the ground. He shields his neck and head from my teeth with his arms as I shred them to the bone. He killed Junior for what?

Stefan tries to charge me, but another black blur tackles him, Jas, and pins him to the ground, growling a warning in his face.

My father gets his knees up and kicks me off him, just enough to scramble backward as two bodies step between us. I snarl but don't attack my brothers; they don't deserve to die for his crimes.

Art's giant wolf body steps in front of me, snapping at my brothers, watching them as I pad over to Junior.

A broken howl rips through my vocal cords into the night sky, trembling the earth. Howls join me from Art, *all* my brothers, and Pat. Her cry tears a piece of me apart as she collapses beside her mate's body.

She clutches Teddy and rocks back and forth, cries turning into screams and sobs, as I change back to my usual form. Kris sinks onto the ground next to Pat, shaking his head as he looks at Junior.

"He will pay for this," I promise Pat hoarsely.

A warm jacket drapes over my shoulders, Xander's scent cleansing my nose of the stench of blood. I push my arms through the sleeves, buttoning the front and standing, facing the rest of my family. Jas jumps off Stefan, and backs up with Art so they are flanking me, remaining in wolf form.

"Get. *Out.*" I push my Alpha power through each word.

All my brothers flinch. Stefan rises from the ground, stepping forward as he clears his throat, eyes not lifting. "We'll take our fallen and go."

"No!" Pat bellows. Her head whips to Stefan. "We are no longer part of your Pack. We're staying here with Nova."

"Patricia—" Stefan starts.

My father roars behind my three remaining brothers as they pull him back, retreating, leaving Dom lingering.

Dom's eyes blaze copper at Xander. "How?"

I can feel the stillness in our bond—the quiet. Xander's beyond furious. "You betrayed me."

"You don't know what it's like."

"What it's like to what, Dominic?"

"To be a wolf without a Pack," Dom growls.

Xander steps forward. "I know *exactly* what it's like. That's why I took you in, Dominic."

"It's not the same, Alexander," Dom booms. "I thought it might change with Nova, another wolf, maybe... but you took her as well."

He knew about the bond. He must have sensed it when Medea ripped off my amulet in the apartment.

Confusion ripples in the bond, and then realization. "Is this about Anika?"

Dom's face hardens in wrath. "You took her from me."

"You drove her away. I simply got her out."

"We were happy," Dom seethes.

"You would have killed her."

"I never would have hurt her!"

"That's enough, Dominic. What's done is done."

Silver flashes, barreling towards me, and pain explodes through my abdomen. "You won't win this time," Dom states.

I look down at the thick hunting blade stuck in my gut. It has shattered my bottom rib, and I think a piece of it has sliced my lung—the next breath, cold floods my veins: wolfsbane.

My knees buckle, and I hear a roar in my head, in my ears, in the bond.

I look up with hazy eyes as Xander charges Dom, who's trying to flee, but he's way too slow. Xander's head strikes Dom's neck as the world fades out of focus, and I fall into nothing.

ative
42

Central Park

I TEAR OUT DOM'S throat, his blood covering me.

He betrayed me. Dominic. The one fucking male I thought would never run back to the wolves who rejected him.

I turn back to Nova, who's passed out on the ground. Her emotions are dormant, and my heart scatters. No. She can't be *gone*. I'm next to her, rolling her to her back. Her breath is shallow, but she's still breathing.

Kristjan kneels on the other side of Nova. He grasps the hilt of the knife; his skin sizzles as he wrenches the knife out. Carter sinks to his knees next to me as black liquid oozes out of the wound, and Nova's breathing stops.

"No!" Kristjan bellows, putting his ear to Nova's chest. He starts sobbing. Devastating loss pours out of him, his aura flickering in and out.

Panic seizes my heart.

No.

I'm about to rip my wrist open and force feed her my blood, but she suddenly gasps for air, rolling over and puking up black liquid.

I loosen my breath as Kris rubs circles on Nova's shoulder and I pull out my phone, messaging Ren to come to the park.

I lift my head to Nova's twin. His tear-streaked face has the same features as her—the small cheekbones, and large jade green eyes—but he takes a lot from his father, like his square jaw and sharp mouth.

He catches me staring and smirks, extending a hand. "I'm Kris, Nova's brother."

I accept the warm embrace. "Vlad, Nova's mate."

"I know," he says, his eyes returning to his sister.

She groans, laying flat again wheezing. "Fucking asshole," she croaks. She lifts her hand, cupping her brother's relieved face.

"Hey, sis," he whispers.

She sobs, launching herself into his arms. They laugh and cry, clinging to each other. Kris pulls her back, searching for more injuries. "How are you not dead?"

"It's a long story." She cradles her brother's damaged hands and then turns to me, her face stained with blood, dirt, and tears. "*Mon coeur.*"

She smiles, then takes in the blood-drenched appearance, eyes hardening. "What a *bastard*."

"He's dead now," I say as I open a wound on my wrist with my teeth. Nova extends Kris' hand and I tip my wrist over them, letting my blood drip into his wounds; within seconds they are healed as if he never touched the wolfsbane.

Kris' eyes blow wide. "What the *fuck?*"

Nova smirks, patting his face. "Later."

She turns back to me and wraps her arms around my neck, crashing her lips into mine. I pour all of me into the kiss, wanting her to know my devotion to her. I pull away reluctantly, giving her a once over, settling it in my mind that she's here, still here, in one piece.

"*Je t'aime.*"

She smiles. "I love you too."

She gives me a swift kiss before turning to her sister-in-law. Jasper is kneeling next to her, not touching or saying anything.

Nova and Kris crawl over to the other side of the body of their fallen brother. She lifts her head to Nova, her aura completely broken. "Why?"

Nova's lip trembles. "I don't know."

The female wolf shakes, leaning her head into Jasper's shoulder as she sobs.

I'm here. Renard announces into my head.

I'll need you to carry Nova's brother's body and transport it to the townhouse. Ren steps out from behind me, approaching slowly, purposefully loud to Nova's sister-in-law's side, sinking to his haunches.

"I'm Renard," he murmurs softly, offering her a small smile.

She sniffles, hugging her child closer, lifting her head to Ren. "Patricia."

"I would like to ask you permission to move the body of your mate."

"To where?"

"To your new home," Nova announces, drawing Patricia's attention. "There's a garden where we can prepare him for proper passage."

Patricia's eyes go back to Ren, and she nods once. Jasper wraps an arm around her, pulling her up and steps back as Renard repositions and hoists Nova's brother into his arms.

Nova, Kris, and Patricia climb into my car, followed by Carter, Ren, and Jasper in Carter's truck, transporting the fallen. Kris sits up front, watching the city zip past. The two females sit in the back hold hands across the back seat but stay silent.

Fussing noises echo in the car from the babe.

"He's probably too hot," Patricia mumbles behind me as rustling eats the silence. My gaze flicks to Nova in the rearview mirror, and her eyes are soft, peering to her left.

"He's even more beautiful in person."

"Do you want to hold him?"

"I'm covered in blood, Pat."

"Here," a sheet of white flashes in the mirror as I flick my eyes to the road. "Cover yourself with his blanket."

I hear more rustling and then a gasp. My eyes return to the mirror, and my heart almost bursts out of my chest. Nova cradles her nephew to her chest, peering into his face, new tears falling down her face. She's so fucking beautiful.

She catches my eye in the mirror, and her eyes glow.

We arrive at the townhouse in record time and climb out of the car, Nova still cuddling the babe. Carter introduces himself to Patricia before escorting her up the stairs towards Nova and

Allura's apartment. Kris and Jasper enter the other apartment, leaving the door open as Renard carries in Nova's brother's body.

I wrap my arm around Nova's waist, peering down at the curious boy in her arms. He smells of new life and hydrangeas, like his mother. I brush his soft curls on his head.

"Isn't he amazing?" Nova coos.

"A cherub."

"Is it terrible that I want to eat him?"

I chuckle as we ascend the stairs, entering Carter and Jasper's apartment, where a feast has been laid out over the entire surface of the dining table.

Delia appears from the kitchen and darts straight over to us. "And who might this be?"

"This is my nephew Theodore, or Teddy." Nova pulls her eyes from Teddy and looks around the apartment. "Where's Allura?"

"She's at the Penthouse sleeping off another bout of bad nausea. She sent me when Ren told her about your brother." Delia holds out her hands. "Pass him over to *yia-yia*. You go get cleaned up and then have something to eat."

After a hot shower, fresh clothes, courtesy of Carter, Nova and I head back downstairs. Patricia showered and changed in the apartment next door, borrowing some of Nova's clothes, and the rest of the men freshened up.

We all eat, talk, and drink. Everyone gets to hold Teddy, the babe soothing some of the sadness amongst the group.

Shortly after eating, Kris and Pat perform the blood-bonding with Nova, pledging themselves to the Zephyrus Pack. Patricia even insists on initiating Teddy, pricking his heel with a pin, Nova doing the same with her thumb and pressing the wounds together.

Patricia passes a sleeping Teddy to Delia as she goes outside with Kris, Jasper and Renard. Carter explains to Delia and I that fallen wolves are washed and wrapped in white as part of their funeral traditions, and then they are burned on a pyre the following night, passing on to the Other Side.

Nova remains curled up against me, sipping on tea and watching Teddy sleep in Delia's arms. Her aura buzzes with sorrow, but mostly she's numb. Jasper and Ren enter from outside, their emotions solemn as they drape over seats. Carter frowns at the back door, then slips out into the yard.

"Who's Anika?" Nova asks no one in particular.

"Anika?" Delia asks, looking at me.

I nod.

Delia shakes her head, closing her eyes briefly before looking at Nova. "Anika is my late sister."

"Your sister?"

Delia nods. "Remember when I said Vlad saved my life? My sister and I both ended up in a Blood Pit when we were young and stupid."

"Holy hell," Ren mumbles, leaning forward, resting his elbows on his thighs. He's never heard this story.

"We were there for about three months," Delia continues. "The vampires would shoot us up with so many things, trying to chase a high they couldn't get. They tried everything, but the best high they got was shooting us up with Lux."

"This was before they kidnapped faeries?" Nova asks.

"This was about thirty years ago," I answer. "Vampires weren't as addicted to it as they are now."

Jasper rises from the couch, scooping up Teddy from Delia and taking him into the kitchen as Patricia comes in from the backyard, followed by Carter and Kris. She wishes everyone goodnight as Carter escorts her to the other apartment.

We turn our attention back to Delia, who accepts a cup of tea from Jasper. "Vlad rescued us from the Pit, but we were heavily addicted to Lux by that point. It took us years to recover, but we did eventually. I got married, had babies, and settle into normal life. But Anika struggled for longer."

"I found her living on the streets," I add, "trying to sell herself for Lux, so I made her come back and work for me."

"Where she met Dom?" Nova asks.

Delia nods. "She got her act together, finally started living."

"So, what happened?"

"Dom wanted more," Delia explains. "He wanted to turn her, start a family, but she was still healing, needed more time. Dominic was stuck, his baser instincts for a Pack overwhelmed him, so it drove a wedge between them."

Nova turns to me. "Did they have a mate bond?"

"Yes," I answer. Her eyes swim with emotion, pressing closer to my side.

I wrap my arms around her shoulders, needing more of her warmth. "She went back to the Lux, and didn't come back."

Nova places a hand on my thigh. "You found her?"

I nod stiffly. "I told Dom she left him; I didn't want him to know that he drove her to her demise."

"Fuck," Renard whispers, rubbing his hands over his face.

Everyone dispersed shortly after our chat, the sun chasing the night-dwellers home. Nova and I enter the elevator, and she presses the button for the top floor.

"Remember when you gave me that bank card? I worked out what the 'A' stands for, but what does the 'L' stand for in your name?"

I laugh. My inquisitive little mate. "It stands for Lucien."

Nova's eyes sparkle. "Fitting," she mumbles, pulling me in a blinding kiss.

My phone buzzes in my pocket. I ignore it, savoring the taste of Nova, the feel of her hair through my fingers. The elevator doors slide open, and I grip Nova's hand, pulling her into the hall. My phone rings again. I groan, pulling it out of my back pocket. 'Allura' flashes on my phone screen.

"Lu, we're in—"

"Hi, lover," that silky, wretched voice purrs.

"Medea."

Nova's eyes boil in a sapphire fire. She darts to the front door, bashing in the code. I rush after her into the apartment. "Where's Allura?"

"Well," she drawls, "I went to your apartment to destroy that silly bitch that thinks she can take what's mine, when I found this beautiful little butterfly."

Nova and I almost collide in the foyer, Nova shaking her head. Allura isn't here. The taste of rotten apples lingers in the air.

"What did you do, Medea?"

She clicks her tongue. "You think I would hurt such a precious creature? Give me some credit, Alex."

"*Medea.*"

"Don't use that tone with me!" she shrieks.

I say nothing, waiting for her reply.

"For now, I'm going to keep her, but maybe after she births the new butterfly, I'll pin up her pretty wings in my throne room and keep her spawn as my pet."

The line goes dead.

Acknowledgements

If you're on this page, I salute you.

First, to the readers: Thank you. Thank you for going on a journey inside my brain. I live here every day, which is probably concerning, but it's a safe place in my mind that I cherish and wanted to bring out into the world to be someone else's safe place.

To my best friend—Em: Always and forever. My number one fan, my sounding board, my soulmate. You are one of the major reasons this book exists. Thank you for always believing in me and pushing me to do what I love to do. Thank you for encouraging me to actually publish this little slice of my heart and threatening to publish it anyway if I set the manuscript on fire and deleted it all.

Thank you for all the middle of the night calls about actual dumb shit, and the late-night runs for coffee and crazy theories sessions we've had. You always let me rant like a lunatic.

To the Hive—Car, Murs, Tay and Sarah: We met online, and I felt like a piece of myself was found. You share in my struggles and celebrate the victories. The universe put us together, and I'm thankful every day. Thank you for reading not-so perfect pieces of this book, and still seeing the vision. You're all amazing beyond words.

To the Heathens & Seventh Circle: How did I do this before I met you all? Thank you for accepting me for me and thank *you* for being you. I love every one of you.

To those who believe they aren't worthy or aren't enough. You are always worthy of love and respect. Don't let those who live a closed life stop you from being the beautiful, free spirit you are. Find the sliver of light in the dark.

You are who you are supposed to be. You are enough. Always.

Remember: Words have power, wield them wisely.

Also By Cassandra B. Andreucci

OTHER SIDE SERIES

Betrayer of Blood

Wrath of Darkness

VICIOUS GAMES SERIES

Dark Siren

Broken Songbird

WANT MORE?

ENTER THE WORLD OF CHAOS
SCAN THE QR CODE BELOW

www.ingramcontent.com/pod-product-compliance
Lightning Source LLC
Chambersburg PA
CBHW050102120726
47904CB00004B/1181